Also by Margaret Graham

After the Storm
(previously published as Only the Wind is Free)
Annie's Promise
Somewhere Over England
(previously published as A Fragment of Time)

Easterleigh Hall

Margaret Graham has been writing for thirty years. Her first novel was published in 1986 and since then she has written a further thirteen novels, and is now working on her fourteenth. As a bestselling author her novels have been published in the UK, Europe and the USA.

Margaret has written two plays, co-researched a television documentary – which grew out of *Canopy of Silence* – and has written numerous short stories and features. She is a writing tutor and speaker and has written regularly for Writers' Forum. She founded and administered the Yeovil Literary Prize to raise funds for the creative arts of the Yeovil area and it continues to thrive under the stewardship of one of her ex-students. Margaret now lives near High Wycombe and has launched Words for the Wounded which raises funds for the rehabilitation of wounded troops by donations and writing prizes.

She has 'him indoors', four children and three grand-children who think OAP stands for Old Ancient Person. They have yet to understand the politics of pocket money. Margaret is a member of the Rock Choir, the WI and a Chair of her local U3A. She does Pilates and Tai Chi and travels as often as she can.

For more information about Margaret Graham visit her website at www.margaret-graham.com

Margaret GRAHAM

Easterleigh Hall

arrow books

Published by Arrow Books 2014

2 4 6 8 10 9 7 5 3 1

First published in Great Britain in 2014 by Arrow Books

Arrow Books
Random House, 20 Vauxhall Bridge Road,
London SW1V 2SA

www.randomhouse.co.uk

Addresses for companies within The Random House Group Limited can be found at:
www.randomhouse.co.uk/offices.htm

The Random House Group Limited Reg. No. 954009

A CIP catalogue record for this book
is available from the British Library

ISBN 9780099586838

The Random House Group Limited supports the Forest Stewardship Council®
(FSC®), the leading international forest-certification organisation. Our books
carrying the FSC label are printed on FSC®-certified paper. FSC is the only forest-
certification scheme supported by the leading environmental organisations,
including Greenpeace. Our paper procurement policy can be found at
www.randomhouse.co.uk/environment

Typeset in 11.5/14.5pt Palatino by Palimpsest Book Production Limited,
Falkirk, Stirlingshire

Printed and bound in Great Britain by CPI Group (UK) Ltd, Croydon, CR0 4YY

For the 'grands', Mabel, Josie and Megan

Chapter One

Easton Colliery Village, Durham Coalfields, Saturday 3rd April 1909

'D'you want it down your back or all over your big head?' Evie Forbes asked, grinning as she dragged the heavy pan of hot water to the edge of the kitchen range.

'Now, now, I was just asking if it was ready yet, lass.' Jack could hardly talk for laughing, set her off again as she refolded the cloths she had wrapped around the handles to protect against the heat. 'You scrub your brother's back, pet,' her mam had said, 'while I do guard duty. It'll seem less suspicious.'

Her mam would be on the front doorstep of their terraced miner's cottage, her shawl wrapped tight against the early April breeze. She would be pretending to watch for young Timmie as he clattered home in his boots from his surface shift at Auld Maud, Easton's pit. In reality she was waiting to intercept Evie's employer, young Miss Manton, who was likely to come barging in upsetting the apple cart with the news mother and daughter were waiting for. She'd said nearer three forty-five, but timing wasn't her strong point.

Evie snatched a look around the room. Her father was already in his Saturday evening clothes, sitting in the armchair to the left of the range, reading one of the out-of-date *Times* newspapers he collected free from the Reading Room every Saturday. Jack was standing calf-deep in the tin bath, waiting – for her. The two men seemed to suspect nothing.

'Ready, is it?' Jack called. Evie gripped the handles. 'Just right for boiling lobsters so you'll be good and pink, but screaming's optional. And you just think on, lad, as to what lass'll want to be seen with a pink miner on a Saturday night.'

She eased the pan over the edge of the range, feeling the weight of it in her shoulders, arms and back. The steam not only hurt her eyes but it messed her hair, stripping it of curl. She'd look like the woman with snakes in her hair at the Easton and Hawton Miners' Gala later this evening, but there was no time to sort it out now with Jack insisting, 'Hurry it up, Evie. I've places to go, people to see.' He was grinning, his teeth white in his blackened face. The tin bath was only a couple of steps from the range but it was far enough.

'Don't you hurry, Evie lass,' Da called. 'Take your time and be careful.' He sounded quieter than usual, even more weary.

'I will, Da,' she said as she staggered under the

weight but then Jack reached out and took the bath from her as though it was as light as a feather, his pitman's hands impervious to the heat. 'Here, give it to me, our Evie.'

He tipped it into water already slecky from her father's bath. Around his waist was a gathering of sacking hiding his crown jewels. 'Aye, well,' her mother always said, nodding towards his modesty, 'we must be thankful for small mercies.' Jack always replied that there was nothing small about his mercies and then he'd be slapped with the rag which could, if one was an optimist, be called a flannel.

Aye, these things were what she loved – the family, the continuity, the fun. Could she bear to leave them if it came to it? Would Miss Manton come? What news would she bring about the interview for Assistant Cook that Evie had attended at Easterleigh Hall?

Jack returned the pan to her before whipping the flannel off the clothes horse that was propped alongside the bath. He was such a bonny lad and he was more than her brother, he was her marra – her close friend, in other words – and she loved him more even than she ached for Simon Preston, and she knew that what she'd done could alter their relationship. But she wouldn't think of that, couldn't think of it.

'So, are you meeting young Si?' Jack teased, settling down into the bath.

'No, don't be daft. I hardly know him.' Her voice was crisp. She busied herself taking the pan to the scullery, hoping that she'd see Simon but it would depend on whether Lord Brampton, his high and mightiness, was letting his servants out of their cage. Hang on, lass, she urged herself, because it might just be that she'd be in that same cage next week if she'd passed the interview. She shook her head. No, she mustn't even imagine that, in case it didn't happen.

At the thought she felt almost relieved, for if she didn't get the position she could stay here with her family and continue to cook for her wonderful employer, Miss Manton, who explained so many things, and took her to the Suffragette meeting every month, and who was so eager for her to improve. She shook her head at that thought. To really improve she *must* become the cook she, her mam and Miss Manton longed for her to be, the cook who could earn enough to help her family as well as carve a future for herself in the hotel world.

She wiped around the pan. It was cold and damp in the small back scullery and Jack was calling, 'Come on, Evie, stop dreaming. I'm in a right hurry. I've things to do before the Gala. I've a life to live, you know.'

She spun on her heel, hurrying back into the warmth, her hands on her hips. 'I haven't, I suppose. I'm just here to scrub your back and clean up you and me da, not to mention Timmie, am I?

That's it, is it? Well, you just wait and see.' She was smiling, keeping her eyes fixed on Jack, ready to dodge.

There, she was too quick for him as he flicked water at her. 'By, lad, you'll have to be quicker than that.'

She heard her father laugh along with them, heard the laugh turn into a hack of a cough and for a moment she and Jack stared at one another, but what was the point of letting the sudden tug take hold? They broke eye contact at the same time. Evie reached for the carbolic soap on the stand. It was still slimy from her father's wash.

Sitting in the bath Jack hung his head, his knees up. The sacking floated in the sleck. She bent, he gave her the flannel and she washed his back. She hated the smell both of the coal and the soap, and though the carbolic shifted the greasy dust the scars remained, the deep dark blue of twilight too deeply engrained to ever fade. It was like the damned pit shadow that never left them, as potent as the glowing stinking slag heaps and winding engines and gear that loomed over the village.

She rubbed more fiercely; be pink, damn you, she thought. Her brother eased his shoulders. 'Hang on, lass, leave me some skin.' She saw she had knocked off some of the button scabs which formed when the miners scraped their backbone on low seam roofs. The blood was a dirty red. Her father hacked again. Blue-ridged scars, black lung, dirty blood. But no, Da hadn't got it yet, though he would unless she could get them out.

She ran the rag gently now. 'Sorry, Jack.' Over the ridged skin, gently round the bleeding sores, fear clutching ever tighter at her heart.

Every single day she wanted them out of the pit, and one day *she* would make it happen. Miss Manton and her friends at the Suffragette meetings said women could do anything they set their minds to, and Evie's first meeting a few months ago had opened up a whole new world.

The water was cooling again and would now have a greater depth of muck. Poor Timmie, but that was the hierarchy of a mining house – father first, eldest next, youngest last. At least Timmie was busy on the surface sorting the shale from the coal, so there was no need to worry about him yet awhile.

Jack was singing, slurping the water over his chest and his legs where the past cuts left their twilight trail. There was a fresh one across his thigh. It looked red, blue-black and angry. Well, they were all damned angry, weren't they? Her da hacked again into what passed for a handkerchief. She snatched a look. It was like a nervous tic, this pitman's look, when anyone coughed. But there was no black phlegm, not yet. 'What's your mam doing on the step?' he asked.

'She's waiting for the bairn.' Jack rubbed his face, removing the coal dust.

'Aye, standing on the step talking to her next door

more like. She knows he'll come in from the back alley as usual.' The two men laughed.

'How're the pigeons, Da and what's in the paper?' Anything to move the conversation on. It did. Her father said, 'You'll read it yourself in a moment but as for the birds, I'm right worried about Alfie.' He droned on, and her shoulders sagged with relief. She slapped Jack on the back. 'You're done.'

Every day her mam insisted the bath came out. It meant heaving in full buckets from the communal back-alley tap when Evie came in from her work, but it saved on the bedding. Her mam was not about to put up with any nonsense such as 'never wash the back or you'll let the strength out'. 'Bugger that,' she'd say, 'and into the bath with you.' Evie grinned at the thought. Her mam also made them read the newspaper before passing it to their neighbours, and agreed wholeheartedly with Miss Manton that education and training were the way up. She wrung out the flannel and draped it on the side of the bath.

'Now you're as clean as a whistle so you can get yourself ready for whatever it is you're up to at the Gala, my lad. Which poor girl will go on the swing boats with you tonight?'

She straightened up, easing her back, more glad than she could ever say that Miss Manton had agreed to train her as a basic cook rather than a housemaid, or she could have ended up on hands and knees brushing up the debris from the rugs and brewing a back that would be the bane of her life. Miss

Manton was a good woman, a true Christian her mother said, but then added that she had to be, putting up with the sermons of that parson brother of hers.

Jack patted himself dry with sacking while she picked up his clothes from the floor. They were stiff enough with coal and dirt to walk to the scullery on their own but she helped them on their way, adding them to her da's pile. It was good to have Gala day to think about. It was this she'd concentrate on, as worrying never boiled a kettle, her mother always said. These sayings would lead everyone in the vicinity to commit group strangulation one day, but today the thought of them made her want to cry. She didn't want to leave. How could she? She stared at the men's clothes, still holding the shape of the bodies that had been within them. She picked up Jack's hobnail boots which she had cleaned and greased earlier and took them to the range. She touched his clean trousers on the clothes horse.

'Your clothes are warm, bonny lad.' She knew her voice shook. No one noticed. She patted the clothes horse, looking around the room to give Jack his privacy as he dressed, studying the pictures of the Northumbrian coast painted by Ben, her da's marra. It was as though they'd been joined at the hip since school, her mam always said. Ben had joined a pitmen painting group that met in a nearby hut. Well, it made a change from leeks, whippets and pigeons. She looked at the oil lamps, and the dresser displaying her mam's best plates which were only used at Christmas, the proggy mat in front of the range. She loved every bit of their home, but it wasn't their home, was it? It was the colliery's, Lord Brampton's in other words.

She listened to the crack, spit and hiss of the fire. They had a free ton of coal every month along with the other miners as part of their wages. It was dirty coal, too full of shale to be marketable, still, beggars couldn't be choosers. She banked the range again, though it was unnecessary. Her father was watching, but it was as if he wasn't seeing. 'Da, are you right grand?'

Her da just returned to his paper, rustling it. She tried again. 'That wind's sharp today, Da. The parson went to Fordington and he said the surf was strong and tumbling.'

Her father said from behind the paper, 'Good, it'll bring up the sea coal. We'll take out the cart tomorrow after dinner. The wholesaler will be there, he's offering good prices so we can put more into the savings. We've got to remember that everything we do is for the savings.' His voice was fierce suddenly, and strange. 'Are you coming with Timmie and me, Jack?'

Da looked over his newspaper at his son, who was singing again as he did up his braces. Da's voice wasn't right yet. Could he know about the job interview? She concentrated on Jack, not on anything else.

'Always do.' Jack reached for his shirt, dragging it on, buttoning it up. 'But right now I'm off to Numpies to get a shave.' He ran his hand over his stubble, and his dark brown eyes seemed to grin all on their own. The young men went to Numpies, the old ones did it themselves. No one shaved during the week.

As Jack put on his boots Evie took the flannel through to the scullery, checking the grandfather clock to the left of the range. It kept good time and was useful for pawning. Three thirty. Please don't come yet, Miss Manton. Make it when the men have gone, Jack to the barber, Da to his pigeon loft at the bottom of the yard. Then, if she had passed her interview she would wait until the men were mellow from the Gala and break it gently that she was to be working for the owner they loathed. It was crossing the line, it was betrayal, but necessary, as it was the only establishment that could give her the training she wanted within easy distance of home, of her family. And why shouldn't Bastard Brampton pay for their escape from his bloody pit?

She opened the back door, shaking the flannel vigorously. She dadded the coal-drenched shirts and hoggers, the short miners' trousers, against the wall again and again, coughing all the while as the dust caught in her throat. There was a blue sky but the wind was sharp. There were nails banged into the wall further to the right where they'd hung their pit jackets, which she dadded as well. Her hands were black. What about their lungs? She would sort out Timmie's clothes when he came home. This might be the last time.

She reran yesterday's interview in time to the beating of the clothes. Miss Manton's former cook Mrs Moore worked at Easterleigh Hall, and she had promised Miss Manton she'd contact her if a position ever came up for Evie as kitchen assistant or even better, assistant cook. During the week the assistant cook was discovered to be pregnant and cast out, back to her family who thankfully had taken her in. Miss Manton had driven Evie in her trap for an interview with Mrs Moore after which she had been passed to the butler, who then led Evie upstairs to Lady Brampton.

Evie had never seen such carpets, such curtains, such opulence. She had never been spoken to with such disdain. For a moment Lady Brampton had diminished her, made her falter in her plans. But only for a moment. She had previously been told by Mrs Moore to back out of the drawing room, for it would offend her Ladyship to do otherwise, and at that point Evie had promised herself that one day, when she had completed what she considered a paid training, she would take great delight in offending her Ladyship good and proper.

Miss Manton was to deliver the result before the Gala. If she had been accepted it would be to start tomorrow in the afternoon, as further references would not need to be pursued in the face of Miss Manton's and Mrs Moore's recommendations.

'What do you think then, Evie? Smart enough for the lasses?' Jack was standing at the entrance to the scullery. Evie stopped dadding and smiled. 'I told you, you're a bonny lad.' She noticed the bag he was carrying and her heart sank. So, he was bare-fist fighting tonight, she should have known. The purse would be good with the Gala and all. She looked at him. 'Be careful,' she whispered. 'I will,' he mouthed. 'There's a five-guinea purse. It's a fortune. The bets are coming in from everywhere. I have to do it.'

She knew what he meant. The whole family were saving to buy one of the three houses owned by the farmer, Mr Froggett, way out at the end of the village. The one they were aiming for was very small and therefore cheaper than the others. Property owner-ship was the only way they could gain power over their own lives and free up Jack to support Jeb, the union rep, without threat of eviction from the colliery cottage. Every penny any of them earned went into the pot after rent and food. This included Jack's bare-fist fights, the sea-coal money, the allotment vegetables, her wages, her mother's proggy rugs, everything. 'Be careful, be quick, be strong,' she whispered.

Her da called, 'What are you two gaggling about? I've got good lugs, you know. Your cap's here on the clothes horse, bonny lad.'

For a moment Jack looked at her. They shook

their heads at the same time. Jack said, 'I was telling her young Preston should be there this evening, let out of the Hall gardens by our all-powerful all-bastard of an owner for a couple of hours. How the lad can bring himself to work there beats me. He said he'd be at the shooting gallery at seven if I want to catch him, or if anyone else does for that matter.' Jack winked at Evie, who blushed, torn between longing to see Simon and fearing Jack's reaction to the result of the interview. 'You need your scarf,' she nagged.

Jack grinned at her and left his bag by the back door before striding to the clothes horse. She followed him, longing to hurry him up. It was almost 3.45.

He picked his scarf from the clothes horse, and his cap. Their da was standing in front of the range now, his paper folded carefully on the armchair. He had backed against the fender, his pipe in his hand, but the tobacco was not properly tamped and was spilling from the bowl.

He usually wasted not a shred. His pose was one he took when they were in trouble and needed a talking-to. Evie shot Jack a look and felt the tension across her back. He'd heard about Easterleigh Hall, then? Or was it the fight? He'd been strange since his arrival home. All she could hear was the ticking of the clock, the cracking of the range fire as it began to burn through the bank.

'What's up, Da?' She knew her voice was too high. She coughed, lowered it. 'Is everything all right?'

Jack had become quite still at her side. It was what he did until he knew which way to jump.

Da's jaw was set, his eyes narrowed. His hand shook. More tobacco spilt. It was this, as well as the look in his eyes, that set the panic rising. It was nothing to do with her, or Jack. It was the same look he'd had when he'd told them six years ago that his job had gone, with the Top End Pit closure, and they had packed up to walk the roads until they reached her mother's sister in hope of a job in the Hawton Pit. There had not been one. For months they had de-thistled farmers' fields, collected sea coal, anything to find enough to eat. They'd all slept in Auntie Pat's outhouse, for that was the only spare space. It was that or the workhouse, but then Da had found work at Auld Maud. She saw her panic reflected in Jack's eyes when he turned to her, then back to his father.

'Da?' Jack asked. 'Is it that you've lost your job? Why didn't you tell us, man? Why did you just sit there reading the paper like nothing was wrong?' He wasn't still now, he was raging, filling the whole of the room as he did when angry. He was pacing, roaring. He threw his scarf and cap to the floor. 'I'll bloody kill the bastards.' The fire must be roaring too because Evie felt impossibly hot. So terribly hot.

It was their father's name on the colliery house. Jack was unmarried, so not eligible for one. They'd be evicted and all the cooking in the world would not stop that. It had come too soon. She wanted to call her mother but Jack's pacing was fencing her in. She was shaking, all over. Just shaking.

'Stop it, stop it.' She was shouting too, at herself. Jack turned, looked at her. 'It's all right, pet. I'm sorry. It's all right.'

She waved him away, ashamed. 'Not you – me. I must stop shaking. I must.' She could hardly speak.

Jack stepped forward, held her. 'We'll be fine. Honest we will, pet. Don't worry. I'll find us somewhere, I'll do double shifts to pay for it. I'm nineteen, a good strong hewer and I can match any at the coalface.' His voice was shaking too now, and he was no longer a strong man but a frightened boy who was seeing their lives and hopes ruined, again.

She let him hold her for a moment but then straightened. 'I can help more, I'm getting . . .'

Her father cut through. 'Listen to me.' He half turned, placed his pipe on the mantelpiece, not looking at them. The oil lamp alongside the tin her mother kept for the rent money was soot-smeared. Evie had forgotten to clean it. She must, now. She must change their luck, do everything right. Yes, she'd clean the lamp. Her father repeated, 'Listen to me. I'm your da, I have a responsibility, so shut the noise. I have changed my job, not lost it. D'you hear? I've changed my job.' It was only then that he faced them.

Jack let her go; they didn't understand. How could he change his job? He was a top hewer. Da hacked as though in confirmation, then looked down at his empty hand. He recaptured his pipe from the mantelpiece, held it, his fingers white from the tightness of his grip.

Jack moved then, homing in on his father, gripping his arm, shaking it so that even more tobacco fell from the bowl on to the rug. He stared hard into his father's eyes. Da said nothing for a moment, no one did and Evie could not understand what was passing between the son and the father.

'I was offered . . .' Her da's voice was rough, as though it hurt to produce the words.

'Just tell us,' Jack said, his face pale, almost as pale as his chest, so recently bared for his bath. Pitmen had pale chests because they never saw the sun. Evie wondered why such stupid thoughts surged to the surface when something was terribly wrong. She watched as her da shook off Jack's grip as though he couldn't bear to be touched, and now he put up his hand. 'It's for the family. I've just taken a job that will help us, that's all.'

He stood as Jack did just before the fight bell rang – braced, on his toes, alert, all of these things. His stance was mirrored by her brother. She was excluded – outside the ring.

'What have you done?' Jack asked, but it was as though he knew, or feared he knew. He was an inch from his father's face now. 'What the hell have you done?' He was roaring again. 'The only job on offer is the Deputy. You wouldn't? No Forbes would go over to Bastard Brampton's side. No, Da. No.'

He flung himself away, kicking with his bare feet at the clothes horse, at the tin bath. He kicked again, and Evie moved, pulling him back, pulling him far from her father. Jack wrenched free. She took hold of his arm again, holding him, glad now her ma was on the front step for she shouldn't see this.

'No, Jack. Let Da speak.' Her voice was controlled, tight. 'Let him speak.' She moved, placing herself between them. She was panting. It was from fear and shock, because in the growing silence Evie knew, from the shame in his eyes, that Bob Forbes had indeed changed sides, for in Brampton's pit the deputies did not join the union, they joined the Brampton Lodge, the management's 'club'. It was the way Brampton ran his pits. He put one against the other, weakened, divided and ruled.

Da spoke again, his grip as tight on his pipe as before. 'It was offered when Fred Scrivens lost his legs. The pay is good, and it's not true management, Jack. I'm your deputy safety overman, and I repeat, the pay is good. If I'm deputy then slowly we'll break Brampton's way of dividing us. I'll start a bridge between the miners and management. Besides, we need all the money we can get as soon as we can get it, because who knows what terms will be offered when the Eight-Hour Act comes in. All I do know is that there'll be trouble, and you know that too.'

Her da stopped. Neither man said a word for at least a minute. Neither of them moved. Evie knew that she would never forget that moment – two statues standing in front of the fire, flanked by Da's chair and her mam's. There was just the ticking of the clock, the crack, spit, hiss of the fire which lit up the clothes horse, the bath, the mat, the sideboard they had found on the beach along with the driftwood and the coal, the dresser.

'Think about it lad, we'll be going from twelve-hour shifts to eight hours next year and are we being consulted about the terms? The union agents are taking it upon themselves to hack a deal. Have you heard what they're talking about? Has anyone? We're being left out and the talk is of a strike because of it. Who knows how long we've got to build up our strike money, and our house money? Who knows how long I've got to try to bridge the gap, if I can. There's work to do.' Da was stabbing his pipe at Jack, whose head was thrust forward as though he could hardly contain himself, though he let his father continue.

'Bastard Brampton is licking his chops because he's going to use this change for his own good. He's an owner and they'll most of them do the same, you know they will. Yes, he'll abide by the act, put on an extra shift but he won't make up the piece rate to compensate for the shorter shift, he'll bloody well cut it, if the past is anything to go by. We'll all suffer. I'll likely get to hear about the changes early. I'll tell you. You and Jeb'll get sorted in advance. I'll try and get the deputies softer towards the men, more careful with their safety checks. We're losing too many men, far too many. I've been thinking about this for a while.'

It was more of a speech than Evie had ever heard from him in her life, and his breath was coming in gasps. Jack stepped forward. Evie dragged him back. Jack shouted, 'D'you think me and the lads don't know all this, so don't try and make yourself out to be a bloody knight on a white charger. Nothing'll change Brampton or his damned management and yes, we'll no doubt strike because I'm not expecting the skies to part and a miracle to happen and where will you be? Well, you won't be with us, you'll be the same as a blackleg, because you've changed sides. You've shamed us, man. You've bloody shamed us.'

Evie turned on Jack. 'Listen to Da, he's using Brampton. Listen to him. He's using the bosses to get what he wants while he can. He's using them to bring improved safety.'

Jack shook his head, gathering up his cap and scarf from the floor, heading for the back door. 'He's betrayed us, that's what he's done. Our own da has betrayed us. He's Brampton's man now, a bloody scab.' The slam of the door was all that was left. Evie and her father looked at one another. He was shaking his head at her. 'You understand. At sixteen, you understand. I'll be out alongside the men when there's a strike, and back to a hewer after that. But Evie, I might leave things better. Ben, me marra, understands. He's paired up with his brother, and the shift is onside too.'

She nodded. 'All we can do is to use those Bramptons, Da. That's all we can do. I'll talk to our Jack at the Gala.'

Her father sank into his armchair, coughing, trying to get his breath. 'Aye, well he'll likely put up a good showing at the fight. He'll be so damned angry he'll pulverise anyone who puts up against him. We should put on a bet.' His laugh was hollow.

'You know he's fighting, although at Christmas you said enough is enough?'

Her father raised his head. 'I know most things that go on in this house and I know also that we're all trying to do the best we can. You do what you want, lass, but don't tell your mam I'm in on it, she likes to think she's got a secret.' His smile was tired, the hand which he held out to her was calloused and embedded with black. She gripped it tightly. 'I'll talk to him, Da,' she repeated.

Her da said, laughing as he coughed, 'He'll take it hard, you and me going over to the dark side.' The laugh didn't reach his eyes.

'I might not get it.'

'But one day you will,' he said.

Chapter Two

It was a ten minute walk to Old Bert's Field, and
Evie heard the steam engine pumping out its music
the moment she stepped from the scullery into the
yard. It was a glorious evening, and the excitement
would have made her smile, if she wasn't already.
She touched her hair. There was little wind and she
felt hopeful about the curls she had rescued by tying
up some strands with bits of rag and hanging over
the range.

She left by the back gate, hurrying down the alley,
pausing as Mrs Grant called to her from the communal
tap. 'You have a good time, our Evie. Make the most
of your last day. Glad you have the job. That Miss
Manton is a good sort and a bloody good boss, for
one who's little more than a bairn herself. By, she
must only be twenty-seven, if she's even that?'

Evie laughed. 'No need for the telegraph round
here.'

'Nay, lass, we all have big lugs in this alleyway.
We'll miss you though, and don't you worry about
your Jack, He'll settle and see how it's right for you,
just like he will about your da.' Her sacking apron
was splashed with water and black from her man's

bath. She was scrawny and thin but as strong as an ox, and had bred six children without trouble, though one had died last year in the pit. The purple beneath her eyes had deepened daily since then.

Evie shook her head. 'I haven't told Jack yet, Mrs Grant. I don't want anyone to say anything until I've seen him.'

'No one will, you mark my words, and this will be the best day, knowing you've got it but haven't started rolling up your sleeves and being put in your place from morning to night.' Then she laughed. 'Take no notice of me. I'm just jealous.'

Evie sped on. Miss Manton had come just ten minutes after Jack had stormed away. Her mother had peered into the kitchen first, and shooed Da out into the yard to check on his pigeons. He had winked at Evie as he went. Miss Manton entered the moment he had gone, her hair escaping from beneath her hat as it always did, holding out her hands to Evie. 'Clever you,' she'd said. 'I need to find a new cook, but it'll have to be someone special to come up to your standard.'

Miss Manton had gripped Evie's hands, her leather gloves soft but cold from the wind. 'You are on the way, dear girl. Now remember what I told you about Mrs Moore. Her hands are so bad that she can't do her job properly. The rheumatism is in her back and legs too and she needs your help in order to keep her job, but she doesn't know she does. Do you understand what I mean?' She'd given Evie no time to reply, rushing on. 'Yes, of course you do and in this way you'll learn more quickly. I'm also afraid that she is drinking to help with the pain. Be aware, be kind. Protect her. Work hard, make something of yourself. Your brother will come to understand.'

She'd spun on her heel. 'Now I must run. I am going to the Gala, for Edward is to bless it. I'll break the news to him that you are no longer in our employ. Trust me, my brother will be downcast, he so adores your forequarter of lamb, not to mention your honey-roast ham.'

Then she stopped, and took an envelope from the pocket of her tweed coat. She turned once more. 'For you, Evie, with my gratitude for your efforts on our behalf, and I hope to see you at the Suffragette meetings on a Sunday, or even a Wednesday afternoon, when you can get away. Get a message to me and I will meet you in the trap at the crossroads near Easterleigh Hall and we can talk French as we journey. You know I feel how important another language is, especially when owning and running a hotel as you intend to do one day. You are a force of nature, my dear, isn't she, Mrs Forbes? She'll end up with the Claridge's of the north-east, mark my words. Mrs Moore knows more French than she lets on, too, so if you get the chance . . . Goodbye now.'

She was gone, like the whirlwind she was, always rushing from one place to the next. She'd make someone a wonderful wife, she had once said, if she had any intention of marrying. But she wanted to be her own woman and she would be, once they had the vote.

Evie reached Old Bert's Field to find it thronged with people and music and laughter, and over everything there was the smell of suckling pig slow-roasting over the pit. The Easton and Hawton Colliery banner rested near the entrance. It had been sewn by the local women decades ago, and would have been blessed by Edward Manton and the Methodist minister at the start of the proceedings. They took it in turns, year on year, to be first with the blessing, and it made her mam laugh. 'Why they can't just do it together I'll never know, but even in religion someone has to win,' she'd said.

Evie felt in her pocket. Miss Manton had given her two guineas which were already in the savings pot but she had received her wages as well, a shilling of which would be spent tonight.

She almost hugged herself as she wove her way between her neighbours and friends, all wearing their best clothes and freshly greased boots, longing to tell them that soon she would be a cook of renown. The grass had been cropped by sheep loaned by Froggett so there was a fair smattering of sheep droppings but who cared, this evening was for fun. She ran through her plans again. She was going to work just five years for Lord Brampton, gleaning all the skills possible, and then she'd move to a hotel to get the experience she'd need for the future. The family could sell the house they would have bought by then and move into their own hotel. Her cooking would help bring them customers, and the men would never go in the pit again.

She laughed aloud. It had seemed a dream until today, but now it was going to become a reality. She was taking that first step and no one would stop her, not even Jack. She just had to make him see the sense of it, and about her da too. That was all there was to it.

She was almost running now, heading for the shooting gallery, for it was here that Simon Preston would be, or so Jack had said. She dodged to the right past Mr Burgess, whose waistcoat buttons stretched too tightly across his belly as always, and he hailed her. 'By, young Evie, you're a sight for sore eyes. Where's your da then? Need to buy him a pint. Celebrate Jack's win.'

She slowed but didn't stop, turning and walking backwards as she answered him. 'He'll be over by the pigeons. They're behind the beer tent, I think.' Ah, so the lad had won but she knew he would.

Then she was flying on again through the crowds, slowing only as the shooting gallery came into sight. She patted her hat, touched her curls, straightened her bodice, hating her corset as always. She fluffed out her skirt, checked her gleaming boots and walked slowly, looking everywhere but at the gallery, letting her breathing calm, hoping Simon Preston was there but not daring to search for him. The spring evening was darkening as the clouds built. Would it rain? She hoped not.

'Evie.' Jack was heading towards her from the direction of the beer tent, shouldering his way through, tipping his cap in apology. His face was bruised, his eye swollen, his nose looked broken: there was blood leaking from it. He had been drinking, his gait was unsteady. He was being slapped on the back by those he passed. He was close enough now for her to smell the beer on his breath.

'Evie, you should have put a bet on me.'

She said, 'Are you all right? Our da did put a bet on. He believed in you. He always has. You should believe in him.' His arm was round her. He pulled her to him and whispered, 'I always used to.'

He oozed sweat. She drew back.

'Evie,' she heard again. Simon was ambling towards them from the shooting gallery. 'Evie, Jack said you might be here.'

His red hair shone, his face was tanned in a way a pitman's would never be. Gardening suited him, the daylight suited him. He was beautiful. Jack turned, staggering slightly. 'Well, Si Preston, time you had a beer and swilled out the rotten taste of Easterleigh Hall.' He slung his arm over Simon's shoulders, winking at Evie. 'Or are you going to have a few minutes with our Evie because you're not let out much, lad, are you?'

Simon mock-punched Jack. 'You won, man. Never in doubt. I saw the end, by, you were on fire.'

Jack shot a look at Evie. 'Not to be wondered at, is it.' His voice was harsh.

'Jack,' Evie warned, wanting to pull him away now, wanting to take him home before he flared again.

'So, come on Evie, when do you start? Me da told me the news. Tomorrow, is it?' Simon was grinning at her. 'T'other one fell by the wayside, so they say. It's the talk of the servants' hall.'

Evie felt herself grow cold and then hot. She took hold of Jack's arm. 'I'm going to get him back to Mam, Simon. I'll come and find you later.' She ignored Simon's look of confusion. Jack was swaying, a frown gathering. He let himself be led a yard or two, but then he pulled free and lurched back to Simon, gripping his shoulders. 'When does she start what? Where? What servants' hall?'

Simon flashed a look of dawning comprehension at Evie who shook her head, her mouth dry. She half raised her hand, but to no purpose. She couldn't stop this now.

Jack shook Simon. 'What the hell is going on around here?'

It seemed to Evie that the music was pounding more than ever, that the raucous shouts of a group of pitmen nearby were even louder. Groups were gathering into tight knots, some talking, some tossing coins and betting on the outcome. Some had fallen silent as they watched them. One man, Martin Dore, Jack's marra, was walking unsteadily towards them, his face flushed, the drink in him. He had a glass in his hand, half full.

'Jack, not here.' Evie tugged him along, waving Martin away. People started to talk amongst themselves again, and always the music played. Jack hesitated and turned back to Simon. She dragged at his arm, speaking urgently. 'I have another job, that's all. I'm to be assistant cook for the Bramptons. I have a plan. I need Easterleigh Hall. I am going to use them. I want a training, for us. I'll explain but not here. Come on.'

Simon moved to help her. She stopped him. 'Howay, Simon. Let it be.' She held up her hand to Martin too, who had started to approach again. He stopped, uncertain. It was like herding a load of sheep, for pity's sake.

She thought she'd reached Jack because he let her lead him from the shooting range, well away, slipping through the throng. Some of the men they passed were smoking roll-ups, some of the children were eating toffee apples. Now the sweet smell of boiling sugar vied with suckling pig.

Jack let her slip her arm through his as they approached the swing boats but in the fading light he stopped, drew himself erect, staggered, pulled away and turned to her, stared and then spat full in her face. He wiped his mouth with his hand. 'You too, my Evie. You as well. And I had to hear it from someone else.' He staggered again. His nose was bleeding properly now. He wiped the blood away, but it continued to flow.

As he spoke again his teeth gleamed red. 'At least Da had the courage to tell me to me face. You're serving them, stuffing food in their gobs. You could go anywhere but you are working for that bastard. I don't have a choice but you do. You could go anywhere for your . . . training.' He was sneering.

She interrupted, 'I can't go anywhere else. I owe Miss Manton so much. I made a promise . . .'

He waved her silent, snatching off his cap, punching it into his other hand. 'You know how I feel about them. First Da and now you. Don't you understand, you've both tethered me? How am I going to fight the bosses now? If I do, you'll lose your job, because they'll know you're a Forbes, and Da'll lose his for the same reason and we'll be out of the house.' He drew breath, and now his voice was quiet and cold. 'I hate you, Evie Forbes. I'm glad you're going. You've got options, Da's got options, I've got bugger all.'

His spittle was rolling down her cheek, sliding on to her jaw, and then her neck, her collar. She wiped it and out of habit checked for black phlegm. It was clear. Simon came running then, pushing between them, panting, 'That's enough, Jack.' He seemed slight against Jack's strength. 'That's more than enough, man. Go and sober up.'

Jack's eyes were glazed and full of tears as he

stared at her long and hard and then turned away, walking erect, not a stagger, not a sway. She called after him, 'I'd already thought about my name, it's all right. I used Anston. Da's already explained to you what he will do when it comes to a strike. He'll resign. You can go on with your union work.'

Jack didn't break stride, just kept on walking, away from her. The crowds parted before him, and closed in his wake. Martin stumbled after him, catching him up, hooking an arm over his shoulder. Jack shrugged him off but Martin took no notice. They were marras. They worked the seam side by side. They belonged together, always. His arm went round Jack's shoulders again and this time it stayed.

None in the crowd looked at either Jack or Evie. They gave them their privacy because they were their marras and neighbours. The music was still pounding, laughter was in the air.

She wanted to call, to run after him but she felt Simon's arm around her shoulder, his sleeve wiping away the remaining spittle, his face close to hers, so close. She felt his breath as he said, 'Leave him for now. I'll follow and make sure he's safe, and Martin too. They're so drunk they'll end up in a ditch if they're not careful. I'll try and talk to him. I'm sorry, I should have thought but don't fret, none at Easton will give you away after this, pet. It will be Evie Anston, and most of the staff are from away and those that aren't I'll warn off.'

He was smiling, his blue eyes so kind, but Evie

couldn't think, not of anything. Not of the Hall, not her name, her mother's maiden name, the hotel or anything any more. Jack had spat in her face, her beloved brother had not only spat in her face but had walked away from her, and she felt as though her heart was tearing apart inch by inch.

Chapter Three

Evie sat in the armchair all Saturday night. It was her mother's turn to sleep in bed as there were no shifts and no pitmen coming in or going out at all hours, needing to be fed and bathed. Evie had not slept but had waited for Jack, who had not come, and now it was morning. She knew Simon and Martin would look after him and when Simon had to return to the Hall someone else would take on the role. It was what people did round here. But she wanted Jack. She wanted to talk to him before her father took her in the cart, an hour before midday. They were to have ham butties on the way as a special treat; ham her mother had boiled from the pig they had bred in the allotment. Then there would still be time for Da to turn the cart around and head to Fordington for sea-coal scavenging.

It was the first time she would not be with them, feeling the cold wind beating against her, tearing at her skirt and lashing at her hessian apron which would be black by the time they turned for home. Would Jack go? She checked the time. Eight o'clock. Everyone was sleeping. Sunday mornings were like that, but even more so after Gala day.

She brought in buckets of water from the communal tap, just missing Mrs Grant who was entering her backyard with a bucket in either hand. She crept up as silently as possible into the box room, changing into her best clothes. She made herself porridge and ate it. She went into the yard again, her shawl pulled around her. The trunk lent by Miss Manton was packed with her uniforms and her crisp white aprons as well as her hessian ones. She sat on the bench her father had made from driftwood and which he had set against the brick wall opposite the pigeon loft so he could hear and watch the loves of his life.

The spring sun was full on her face and she didn't care that it would darken her skin. The family rose, ate, busied themselves. No one came out to her. No one spoke of Jack. She sat alone, listening to the sounds of the street, watching the sparrows which fed on crumbs her mother put out every evening. 'So the wee ones could have their breakfast,' she would say. How long would it be until Evie was here again, really here, as part of her family? Could she ever resume her place if Jack hated her?

After the slowest morning of her life the grand-father clock struck eleven. Her mother had packed bait tins for her and her da, who was picking up Old Saul, the Galloway pony that they shared with Alec Preston, Simon's da. He would hitch up their shared cart at the allotment and return here. He would line the cart with sacking to try to keep the trunk free of sleck. She paced the yard but Jack still didn't come.

Her father came to the back door, a blanket over his arm to put on the cart seat to keep her skirt clean. 'It's time, hinny,' he said. The sun was warm, the wind gentle. It should have been a lovely day.

Timmie came into the yard, snatching off his cap and running to her. He hugged her so tightly that he squeezed the breath from her. She held him, and laughed. He was the image of Jack and her da right down to the black hair and the cock-bird bearing, whereas she was the dead spit of her mam with the same deep chestnut curls. Their eyes were all dark brown, though. She leaned away, their eyes on a level. When had he grown so tall? He was barely thirteen. 'I'll be back in two weeks, bonny lad, on my afternoon off so I'll be sea-coaling with you in the flick of a lamb's tail.'

'I don't want you to go, our Evie,' he said.

'I've got to, Timmie, you know we have to save to buy Froggett's house.'

He pulled away, kicking at the path. 'I'll be down the pit soon and earning more so there's no need for you to leave.'

She sighed. Mr Davies the pit manager had long ago told all the miners that they'd lose their houses if their sons didn't become Easton pitmen. It was this, as well as the freedom for Jack to press for better conditions, that had focused her on the future.

Her mother's arms were tight around her next,

her plump body as yielding as ever. 'Do as Miss Manton said and look after Mrs Moore, pet. Don't worry about Jack, the daft beggar knows he's in the wrong. All will be well in that direction, you mark my words.' All will be well was a family saying, but did it mean anything?

Her da was waiting on the cart. All the neighbours lined the street, waving as Old Saul clipped along the cobbles, jolting them this way and that. The conical slag heaps overlooking them were seething and fuming, the winding engines glinting in the sun, and over everything hung the smell of sulphur. She waved, smiled, but inside she was empty because the one person she was looking for had not come.

They left Jennings Street, turned into Norton Street. Her da placed his hand over hers. She kept the smile fixed on her face. 'Where shall we have the butties, Da?'

He didn't answer; instead he grinned and nodded towards the road ahead. It was Jack, walking in the street, his arms outstretched, flagging down the cart. He didn't look at her but went to her father's side. 'I'll take her, Da.' It was an order. Her da glanced at her and she nodded, her throat tight because Jack was pale and grim, and his two black eyes stood out, his nose was crooked, his lip was split. This she hadn't noticed yesterday. Perhaps it was a later fight. He had not once looked at her

The two men changed places. Jack tossed his father a purse. 'From the fight.' They nodded to one another, which was as good a rapprochement as one could wish for. Her shoulders sagged with relief. He shook the reins. 'Walk on, you daft beggar.' Her shoulders rose again at the coldness of his tone.

They took the high road out of the village, heading north. It was tarmacked for the convenience of the Bramptons' cars. Alongside the road, the river Tine ran thick and sleck-flecked. The journey would take an hour at Old Saul's leisurely pace. He was a pony not inclined to action unless given a good thwack across the rump. Jack merely held the reins and stared ahead. They'd need to come out of the valley, over the hill to the next hill on which stood Easterleigh Hall. Old Saul clopped along past the row of hawthorns which ended in the Cross Trees crossroads. There were three trees, and it was the tallest spruce, the middle one, on which highwaymen and poachers were once hung. Here, Jack flicked the reins and turned left. Evie spoke now. 'We need to stay on the road.'

Jack stared ahead. 'Not if we go to the beck. We need to eat.' It was where they often went. His voice was quiet and tired now. He rolled up his sleeves and they swayed and jerked with the progress of the cart, his hands moving on the reins. His knuckles were cut and swollen, his arm too. His ear was bruised. Her heart ached for him. He shouldn't have to do this, his job was enough, for God's sake. He had to come out of the pit, he had to. She put her hand to her cheek where his spittle had landed. He said, 'Forgive me.'

She said, 'Always.'

They jerked downhill, in and out of the ruts made by previous carts. Either side there were fields in which sheep grazed, fields that she and her family would de-thistle if required. Froggett always gave them first refusal because they worked so hard. It all helped the house fund. She turned. The slag heaps loomed behind them. What had been here before the pit and the village? Fields like this. Old Saul huffed, the cartwheel slid out of the rut again. She held the side of the seat, hesitated, then murmured, 'Forgive me.'

'Always,' he whispered.

The beck was only ten minutes further. At the end of the lane, by the gorse bushes, he pulled up and jumped down, tying Old Saul to the fence. Evie started to clamber from her side but his voice was sharp. 'No, wait.' She did. He came and lifted her, slinging her over his shoulder. 'Hey,' she shouted.

'Can't have you ankle-deep in mud for the gentry, can we?' He reached into the cart and took the wicker basket with the bait tins, and the blanket from the front seat. He carried her as easily as he would have carried a sack of coal and just as inelegantly. She started to laugh and he joined her, and it was almost like it had always been. It was only when he'd thrown the blanket down on the bank and poked it flat with his boot that he let her down. For a moment they looked at one another. 'I'd never hurt you deliberately, bonny lad,' she said.

'Nor I you. I will never drink like that again. I will never treat anyone as I treated you.' Somewhere he'd washed. Somewhere he'd had some sleep but not a lot, probably at Martin's house. She said, 'You'll drink again.'

He grinned. 'I won't treat anyone like that.'

'I know you won't. We hurt you. It's over.'

They sat side by side, his arm around her shoulder. The beck was clear and clean and trickled over the dam they had built years ago, so it was deep enough to swim. Across on the other bank willows draped their fronds into water and sparrows sang. She said, 'Miss Manton said that she could get me into Easterleigh Hall and her old cook would teach me all she knew. I have to go there because I have promised to protect Mrs Moore, whose hands are sore with the rheumatics, for as long as possible in return for Miss Manton's goodness. I want to go there too because I need to see you all as often as I can. I have to go there because I would have to wait for much longer to get a post like this without Miss Manton's influence. I need to go because I want you all out of the pit, Jack. You know I want us to get a hotel. I want us to be safe. I can do it. I can cook . . .'

Jack put his hand over her mouth. 'Enough. Enough.' He was laughing. Then he became more serious than she had ever known him. 'I was wrong. It's your life. I hate you working for the Bramptons but you know I don't hate *you*. I was just angry and

I've had my punishment from Mam.' He rubbed his ear. 'By, she'd win any damn fist fight with one hand tied behind her back. The thing is, Evie, I want to stay in the pit. It's what I am, a pitman. My marras are pitmen. I belong. It's my family as much as you are.'

He removed his hand from her mouth and she tried to interrupt but he drove on. 'What's more, it's my duty. Thanks to Mam and Da and Jeb I can talk the talk when I need to, to try and make sure the men have the best that they deserve and that the pit is as safe as it can be, and that we all earn what we should. There's so much to do and I can't, don't, want to walk away from that but neither do I want Timmie in it, so you're right. We have to get the house.'

He was picking at the blanket. The sparrows flew above the willows. The sky was blue and clouds skidded along in the breeze. She wanted to speak but knew he had more to say. 'I know why Da did it and if he can change the way management behave that's great, but I can't see it. What's more, he's putting himself in danger. He'll have to knock those damned props out of worked-out seams to be reused and as much as he tests the roof, it can come down. You know that. I know that. I don't want him hurt. Christ, his chest's bad enough without that worry.'

She said, 'He knows that too so he'll be careful or he'll have Mam to deal with, and you know which he'd rather face.' They were laughing, but not inside. This was all too serious, and this was also their goodbye. This was the talk they would not have again because it was a parting of the ways. She was no longer a child and their lives would be lived separately. She said just once more, 'I want you out of the pit.'

He shook his head. 'One day maybe but it's funny really, we're both in the lion's den, now, pet. You as well as me.'

She stared at him. Yes, she was, and another idea came to her. She gripped his arm. 'Listen Jack, I can pick up any gossip to do with the pit. I can use them in that way too.'

Jack turned from the beck and looked down at her, then nodded thoughtfully. 'Aye, there's that. But you just remember to be careful, bonny lass. I want nothing and no one to take your dream from you.'

They watched a kingfisher swoop down and tear along the beck towards the source. She had swum in it more times than she could count, with Jack, with Simon and with Timmie. Well, life could take away a dream, but not the past, and she started to cry and so did Jack. Against his shoulder she murmured her plans. 'In five years I want to be in the Vermont in Newcastle, learning that side of it so I get it right for ours.'

She looked about for the kingfisher while he told her that Ireland was preparing battle lines between Protestants and Catholics, that Germany was building battleships to challenge the British world domination, and that was not all: the British workers were realising they had power, 'By, we've a political party now. Can you believe it, the Independent Labour Party, and one day soon there's going to be trouble. Hell, there could even be revolution. You must enjoy every day for itself, Evie, for who can tell what's going to happen in the future.'

She read the papers too but wouldn't believe the rhetoric. 'War can't happen, we wouldn't be that daft, and anyway, if it does it will be between the Catholics and Protestants in Ireland, or if Germany quarrels with us it will be a fight between armies, not people. There won't be a revolution. I don't think enough workers are angry. My concern is that you, Da and Timmie stay safe at Auld Maud.' She gripped his arm. 'You continue your union work, but more importantly you must stay safe.'

Jack shrugged. 'That's down to luck.'

She gave up on the kingfisher and instead stared into the beck, hearing the water gurgling through the dam boulders, and murmured, 'It's down to listening to the roof and getting out before it falls, it's about taking no risks. And yes, it's about luck. So stay lucky.' They ate everything in the bait tins.

They arrived at Easterleigh Hall in good time. The Hall had been built in the era of George III, a monarch much maligned according to Miss Manton, who said he had not really been potty but had some sort of a condition. Easterleigh Hall had been designed by a young Italian architect who ran away to Florence with the lady of the manor, which had led to the lord selling it to his cousin and upping sticks to London. That line had died out, and the Bramptons had bought it five years ago.

Whatever the young architect's naughtiness, his sense of style was perfect, Evie had thought on the day of her interview, and thought it again as Jack drove the cart up the tradesmen's track. It was a track hidden from the gravelled driveway by yew hedges because, presumably, the sight of it offended Lady Brampton, much as the sight of Evie's rear would have done had she not backed out of her presence. The gravelled drive, visible through gaps in the hedge, ran alongside the huge lawn, in the centre of which grew a cedar tree. 'It was planted by the Italian architect and you'd have thought the cuckolded husband would chop it to the ground and use it for kindling. I would have done,' she murmured to Jack. He laughed quietly.

At the end of the track they arrived at the stable yard where lads darted from here to there paying them no mind, and then they clopped through to the cobbled kitchen yard at the rear of the big house. Simon was waiting to heave the tin trunk from the cart, which he did quickly, so that Jack, his cap pulled well down, could turn Old Saul around and head off again before anyone saw him and recognised him as the Forbes agitator. Jack leaned down and whispered, 'If you hear anything that can be helpful to the union, tell Simon.' Then he straightened and called loudly, 'Goodbye, Evie Anston.'

Simon nodded towards the steps that ran down to a door she had thought was a cellar when she came for her interview. 'You know the way, bonny lass. You've made up with Jack, I see.' Evie nodded, too edgy to speak. She was here at last, and her courage failed her. It seemed her feet wouldn't move.

To the right through the archway the stable lads were still darting, criss-crossing. One had a great sack of hay on his back, another a bridle over his shoulder which clinked over the sound of his hobnails as he strode forward. Behind her, garages edged the whole of the kitchen yard and cast shadows which just caught the tail end of Jack's cart as it passed into the stable yard.

Simon jerked his head towards the steps again, the strain of carrying the trunk clear on his face. 'This isn't quite the feather that you might think. Can we get into your new place of work so I can put it down?' He had put on a posh voice, and grinned.

She cast a last look at Jack as he disappeared along the track and followed Simon down the stone steps, opening the door for him, stepping back as he struggled into the corridor with the trunk, dropping it as soon as he could. It should be returned to Miss Manton within the week, her mother had insisted. 'Borrowers mustn't become keepers,' she had said. Simon had promised he would see to it. Then it was

Evie's turn to step from the fresh air into the darkness.

There were banks of bells on the left, with room names printed beneath. The floor was of stone slabs. It was spotless. There was some sort of a cross-stitch text on the wall. Evie didn't read texts, they were either biblical or improving, and a load of rubbish when the nobs were up there and she was down here.

The first person she saw was a girl of her own age, who wore a dark blue uniform and white pinafore and a neat little white cap. 'Hello Simon,' the girl called as she lounged in the kitchen doorway with a broom in her hand. 'She's not from here, she's Lancashire-born,' Simon whispered, then louder, 'Lil, this is Evie . . . Anston.' The hesitation had been slight and the girl noticed nothing. Simon added, 'Evie's come as assistant cook.'

Lil laughed. 'That's what she thinks, is it? Her Ladyship has decided to economise, taxes being what they are after the Liberals got in.' Lil's mouth was grim, her eyebrows arched in mock pity.

Evie studied her closely. 'What do you mean?'

Lil was turning back, beckoning her into the kitchen where Evie had had her first interview just a few days ago. 'Come on, Mrs Moore is expecting you. Hurry up. She said to keep an eye out. See you later, Simon.' She disappeared.

Simon touched Evie's arm. 'It'll be fine. Remember it's a training and I'm not far away – in the cottage down by the lake with the other under-gardeners. One of us comes in daily with the house flowers and sometimes the vegetables. I'll try and make it my job as often as possible. Lil's not too bad really, and you'll find Annie in the scullery.'

Lil reappeared and leant on her broom. Her fair hair had come adrift from her cap and framed her face. 'Are you coming or not? You'll have to look sharper than this with the housekeeper, Mrs Green, on the lookout. Did you meet her when you came before?'

'For a moment.' Evie took a step forward. Lil added, 'And Mrs Moore is in a right glucky mood. She wants you to do the clear soup straight after tea.'

Evie hesitated. She'd only done clear soup a few times. She'd thought she'd be setting up the utensils and chopping the vegetables until she found her feet.

Simon gripped her arm. 'It's just a training,' he repeated close to her ear. 'Train, learn.' She felt his breath, felt his hand and relaxed. Yes, of course. She was here to learn. It wasn't for ever. He smiled at her. She loved his eyes, such a deep blue. Loved all of him, always had. He had been in Jack's class, Jack's gang. At least, he was after he fought them because of his red hair. After that, they stopped going on about it. What was it about red hair? What was it about the bluest eyes she had ever seen? It was everything, that was what it was.

Once in the kitchen, she felt again the awe she had experienced on the day of her interview. It was enormous, with large ranges down the left-hand side radiating warmth, and internal windows on the right looking out on to the central corridor. On the other side of the basement was the huge servants' hall with similar windows looking on to the same corridor. Well, of course, she grimaced, what else when there was no expectation of privacy for servants?

One long deal table took up the centre of the kitchen. Pots and pans hung from hooks above it. They were copper, the kitchenmaid's responsibility, or the scullery maid's, but whoever it was, it wasn't hers and she was thankful for small mercies. Small mercies made her think of Jack, and home. She fastened instead on the plates that festooned the dresser on the wall behind which was the scullery. There were cups too, pristine in their whiteness. In the cupboards which ran around the room were, she suspected, many more utensils and endless crockery, and staff cutlery. The silver, though, and the good glasses and dinner services, would be in the butler's pantry.

She had been shown the knife cleaner and the knife sharpener in the far corner last time. The sharpener looked more like one of Old Dan's milk churns. Over everything hung the aroma of a bubbling stockpot.

Sitting on a stool at the table, her back to the

ranges, rubbing her eyes while her glasses rested on her recipe book, was Mrs Moore. Standing just inside the doorway, Evie could see the swollen joints and the pain etched on the cook's face. 'At last.' It was more of a growl, and Evie didn't blame her. 'Well, don't just stand there, you daft dollop. Lil, you help Evie take her trunk to her room. She's sharing with Annie. Evie, you get into uniform, then come straight back down. You can meet the other servants at tea, which you will prepare. We've more to do than I thought. Her Ladyship has returned early. We must be grateful that his Lordship has not, yet. We will be cooking for three upstairs, four when his Lordship returns. Mr Auberon is back from university, it seems for good. Lady Veronica is a fixture. Her Ladyship comes and goes, but you know that, if you've remembered our interview.' Her plump face was red, her eyes watery.

Lil hurried out with Evie in her wake. They each took hold of a trunk handle, Lil leading the way along the bell corridor to the back stairs. They climbed first one flight, and then the next, turning on each landing. To begin with the stairs were stone, but became wooden when they reached the first floor. Lil said nothing at all until they reached the third floor, then she muttered. 'Annie should have done this, not me. I'm house, not kitchen.'

Evie eased her shoulders and kept going, saying nothing beyond, 'I'm sorry.'

'So you damn well should be.'

They toiled up the next flight. One of the stairs creaked. Lil was panting as she said, 'This is the one to catch us out if we come back late. Step over it. A former head housemaid marked it when she was under-housemaid.' She nodded towards a mark low on the wall. 'Hope you're good at baking. Mrs Green's right partial to ginger cake, and Mr Harvey is too. It's quite his favourite.' Evie could hear the Lancashire in her voice.

As Mr Harvey was the butler he needed pleasing. Ginger it would be then, but the housekeeper usually baked the cakes for upstairs and downstairs tea, so why was it her job?

They reached the fourth floor. Lil nodded towards the door which led off the small landing. 'Toilet and the bathroom where you empty the tin bath, and make sure you clean it and the proper bath properly afterwards.'

'Bath?' Evie queried.

Lil's back bent lower to yank the trunk higher as she changed the position of her shoulders. Evie's arms and neck burned with strain as she took the weight. 'Tin bath, weekly, in your room. You'll have to bring up your own water from the kitchen. Only the head housemaid and Lady Brampton's maid can use the proper bath.'

At last they reached the final landing which had two doors and was dark as pitch, lacking even the small round windows of the lower floors. Lil dropped her end down on to the bare boards. 'Good God

Almighty, you owe me, so you do, Evie Anston, so be grateful to me.' Then she eased past the trunk and started back down the stairs. Evie called, 'Wait, where now?'

'Well, what about through the door with the picture of a woman on it. The one with a man is for the lads. Are you stupid?' She continued on down.

Evie called, 'Then where?' adding, 'Snotty little madam,' under her breath.

'Your room's second left.' Lil's voice grew faint as she clattered down at high speed but Evie could still hear her as she said, 'It's my rest time. I shouldn't have had to do this, I want a smoke. You can't have anything personal on display. We're invisible, us lot. We're not people, we're things. Mrs Green will check.'

'Thanks for the tip,' Evie shouted, dragging the trunk to her room. Annie's bed was clearly on the left. Her nightgown was folded neatly on the pillow. There were some pegs for hanging clothes and a chest of drawers to share. The bottom two were empty. There was one blanket per bed, and the mattress felt as though it was stuffed with rocks. She prodded it. 'Bloody hell, lumpy horsehair.' Her heart sank way past her feet.

She changed into the kitchen uniform of pale blue, pinning up her hair which had taken the opportunity to escape her bun during the journey. Well, she was here, and it *was* their escape, she just had to remember that. She felt Simon's hand on her arm again and

Jack's around her shoulders, and smiled, pinning the cap, then smoothing her white apron and gathering up a hessian one, just in case. Before she went she looked out of the attic window. The sky was a swirling grey and in the distance she could see the raging surf at Fordington.

The waves would be surging and throwing up the sea coal for her family, who would head for the coast the moment Jack returned. The thought that she could see where they would be warmed her, for there was little else that would up in this freezing ice house of an attic. There was a fireplace, but it was devoid of coal. She was unsurprised. Why would Bastard Brampton waste his coal on servants?

She searched the beautiful landscape for a moment longer but there was no sign of Easton, no sign of Auld Maud and its glowing slag heaps, hidden as it was in the folds of the hill. But it was there. By, it was there all right.

She clattered down the stairs in her turn, and into the warmth of the kitchen. She brought her recipe bible with her. Mrs Moore looked up. 'Good, you've had the sense to bring your recipes and I'll be familiar with those, I daresay. Our Miss Manton's a good teacher, I'll say that.' She was rubbing her eyes again and Evie hoped she'd wash her hands before she started cooking. 'I taught her, you know. I was her mother's cook. But that bairn, Grace Manton, taught me a thing or two as well. It seems a hundred years ago.'

Evie nodded. 'I can imagine.'

Mrs Moore stared. 'You can imagine I'm a hundred years old?'

Evie laughed, then saw that Mrs Moore was definitely not joining in. 'No, I didn't mean that, I just meant that it's a long time to be cooking.' She snapped her mouth shut. She was on a hiding to nothing.

Mrs Moore tapped her book. 'I think you've dug a deep enough hole for yourself, don't you?' She peered over the top of her glasses. Evie nodded. 'Quite deep enough, Mrs Moore. I can hardly see the sky from where I'm standing. By, I must be a pitman in disguise.'

There was a moment's silence, then Mrs Moore laughed. 'Away with you, pet. Perhaps we'll get along. Now, we've had a change, young Evie, since you came for your interview. As you know, Charlotte the assistant cook was no better than she ought to be and had to leave, so you keep your legs together if you don't mind, and now her Ladyship has taken it upon herself to move Edith the kitchen assistant over to second under-house-maid. So, sorry but you're to do kitchen assistant as well. There's your list of duties.' She removed her spectacles and pointed with them at two pages of writing that lay next to the mixing bowl on the table, opposite the middle range. 'Seems she feels economies must take place.' Her face was grim. 'Not that I would think there are many of them

51

economies going on upstairs, thank you very much.'

Evie clutched her recipe bible tightly. Kitchen assistant as well as assistant cook? She said nothing, but walked to the list. It started with lighting the furnace at 5.30 a.m. and don't forget the fender, plus scrubbing the kitchen floor, waking Mrs Moore with a cup of tea and also Mrs Green and Mr Harvey. It moved on to cleaning any copper pans left over from the night before – though they should _not_ be left, if you don't mind, Mrs Moore had added. This cleaning of the copper would be done to assist Annie. Evie was to cook the servants' breakfast, and help Mrs Moore with the upstairs breakfasts, before doing every conceivable chore anyone could dream up and then some more. She would also prepare the vegetables for the upstairs meals and cook all the other meals for the servants.

'I can't do all of this and draw breath,' she said, placing her book on the table, crossing her arms and bracing herself as she had seen Jack do so many times.

Mrs Moore looked up at her. 'Neither can you, bonny lass, so we'll muddle along together, you and I with young Annie in the scullery until they see sense. These gentry, you know, protect their stomachs like they protect their fortunes. We'll just have to make a few economies of our own and they'll come to heel.' She winked. 'They say we have to fade out of ourselves into them, so that we don't exist as separate beings. Well, they can say what they like but I say pooh to them, pet. We'll make sure that we come out all right, too right we will.'

Her thighs overhung the stool, her plump fingers were tapping the table, the nails spotless, her grey hair was tightly wound into a bun, her cap sat snugly, her stomach fought against her apron, her pale blue dress was smudged with flour, her sleeves were rolled up.

Evie felt every muscle in her body relaxing as she looked at the set of Mrs Moore's jaw. The woman was a hero, and Evie knew she would worship at her feet and they could cross-stitch that thought and stick it where their economies took them. Had Miss Manton influenced Mrs Moore, or was it the other way round? There would be plenty of time to find out.

Mrs Moore was patting the stool next to her. 'Sit down, pet, and tell me what cakes you'll make for the servants' tea and then I'll show you round the servants' hall which you must lay up for four o'clock. Now, don't you go getting irate or upset when the staff come trooping in saying nothing, but looking plenty. Just remember who you are. You're my assistant cook and without us the whole pumped-up ship would founder. So put them shoulders back and let's do some baking. Annie is getting herbs for the dinner from the gardeners but she'll be back for her cake, you mark my words.'

Evie smiled, knowing that though she could smell

the booze on Mrs Moore's breath it would be a privilege to protect her.

She asked where the ginger was kept. Mrs Moore heaved herself to her feet, wincing. 'Whatever for?'

'The cakes. Lil said . . .'

Mrs Moore shook her head. 'Spiteful girl, that one. Mrs Green and Mr Harvey have a particular disliking for ginger.' She nodded at Evie's book. 'I daresay you've a nice jam sponge in there. Miss Manton's father was one of the best bakers in Newcastle and he taught her a thing or two. Her mother was long gone when I arrived, French she was, pretty little thing, but she left our Grace with a thing about others speaking another language. Probably quite right. Her brother, Edward, was always destined for the Church and wouldn't know a good sponge cake if it came and hit him on the nose. Good sort but not of this world. Not quite sure how he manages to cross the street on his own.'

Evie was torn between amusement and intrigue. Miss Manton did not talk of such familiar things, only of the life to which women should aspire. Mrs Moore was watching her. 'She's a good woman. She particularly wants you to do well and that's why she asked me to take you under my wing. She wants to do well herself. Is she still going to them women's meetings?'

Evie was searching for flour and sugar in the earthenware containers lined up on a series of shelves at the end of the kitchen, and nodded. 'Yes.'

'So, are you going to them meetings too?' Mrs Moore asked.

Evie headed for the scullery to wash her hands and pretended she hadn't heard. She didn't know how much to trust people and bosses didn't like their servants talking of anyone's rights, let alone joining groups that did. Mrs Moore laughed gently as she returned, her finger tracing down her own recipe book. 'That was answer enough. I'll let you know the window that you can unlatch so you can get in if you're ever likely to be late. The doors are locked at 9 p.m. There's a creaky step that'll alert the new head housemaid who's a stickler for that sort of thing. Now, get on with the tea, we have just enough time. Them upstairs don't start their dinner till eight, and downstairs have theirs at seven. I've a couple of nice ham and chicken pies planned for the servants which you can make. It'll include upstairs' lunch leavings. I need you to make the clear soup for their dinner. Can you do that?' Her glance was keen. The glass-fronted cupboards reflected her movements.

Evie nodded. 'Yes, of course I can, Mrs Moore.' She felt sure now.

The cakes smelt good as the range did its job. She carried through a tray piled with the plates and cutlery into the servants' hall. Her back argued with the weight, but though there were several people sitting around in armchairs and sofas, some reading magazines, some sewing, some snoring, no one helped. Stuffing oozed out of splits in the old sofas. Some maids sat on benches at the table, sewing their lisle stockings even though the light was bad. What could you expect if you were underground? Two footmen sprawled at the other end of the table, playing cards. No one said hello.

By four o'clock the gas lights had been lit and the staff settled themselves at the table. Upstairs was electrified, but attic and basement were not. Still no one spoke, even when Evie came in with the tray of cakes. Mr Harvey presided at the far end, Mrs Green at the other. Mrs Moore sat adjacent to Mrs Green. Lil was smiling at Evie, patting her blonde hair and adjusting her cap. Evie placed a large jam sponge in front of Mr Harvey and another down Mrs Green's end. She placed another three along the rectangular table. She placed a small ginger cake in front of Lil. Lil looked at it, and pursed her lips.

Mrs Green poured the tea as slices of cake were passed around. Simon came in with the other five under-gardeners. The men moved up the bench to make room. That made twenty-four staff in total around the table. Simon smiled at her. She sat between Annie and Mrs Moore. Mrs Moore nudged her and smiled. No one spoke until the first bites were taken, and all the time everyone watched Mr Harvey as he savoured his. Evie almost expected him to spit it out as the wine experts did. Simon was grinning at her. Could he read her mind? She hardly breathed as Mr Harvey patted his mouth with his serviette. 'Splendid,' he said. 'How is your ginger cake, Lil?'

All the staff laughed, except Lil. Mrs Moore patted Evie's leg. 'Quick, eat up now. We have a dinner to prepare.'

Chapter Four

On Monday morning, 5th April, Jack slung his bait bag over his shoulder, grasped his pick and shovel and walked out of the backyard into the alley along with his da. It was the eight-to-eight shift and the spring morning was more like winter. There had been heavy snow from December to the middle of March and they'd had to dig their way through to the pit, and the cold was with them yet except for the odd good day. The east wind came across from the Russian steppes and it ruddy well felt like it, aye that it did.

He could feel not just the weight of his tools but the tension. The Gala had been a celebration, but would the men turn on his da now that they were streaming to the pit on a cold Monday morning?

As they passed down the back alley, pitman after pitman grumbled their way out with their tools and bait bags and joined them for the walk to Auld Maud, merely tipping their caps, just as always. Jack's tension eased, but looking at his da who walked at his side he could see that he had other concerns. 'I've got to check the pumps. They're old and struggling, lad.'

'Is that yourself you're talking about, you old bugger you?' called George who'd just joined them, dragging his feet as always. He was such a devil to walk behind in the pit, kicking up the dust as he did. His da laughed and the tension ebbed further in Jack.

Jack's marra, Martin, came out of his uncle's backyard, 6 Trelawney Way, letting the gate slam shut behind him, and slapping Jack on the shoulder before bowing low to Jack's da. His own had died of black lung the year before. 'Well Bob, our deputy, our God, you take care of us and the pumps, old man, and we'll take right good care of you.'

Bob Forbes laughed. 'Always, Martin. Always.'

Jack grinned. So far, so good, and only now did he take notice of the throbbing of his nose which his mother had pulled to straighten last night, but which still leaked blood. His eyes had almost closed up but he could see well enough, and in the pit it was almost by feel anyway. They were joined by Ben, his da's old marra, who'd paired up with his younger brother Sam. 'Been painting any more pretty pictures, our Ben?' Bob Forbes asked. Ben's slap on Bob's back was the same as ever, and so was the walk to the pit during which they heard about the problems of sketching when the wind was howling across the beach. They all knew about that wind because they went so often for sea coal, but they let him ramble on as no one felt much like talking on the way to Auld Maud on a Monday, except Ben. His words lulled them with their familiarity.

Jack, Alec Preston and Bob had done well at the beach yesterday, and Timmie had stacked the cart, wanting instead to be with his father at the surf's edge, but someone had to manage the loading. They had sold the lot to the wholesaler who turned up most Sundays with several carts. It was better than lugging it home and selling it on from there.

'Alec just had time to stable Old Saul before he went straight off on the backshift. Where were you, man?' Jack asked Martin.

'It was me da's birthday so Mam wanted to put some flowers on the grave.' They all fell silent, even Ben, as they toiled up to the colliery, the wind moaning through the winding gear. At the shaft head they waited, as ten by ten they prepared to enter the cages. Soon it was their turn to take a lamp from the cabin, and a token from the board to be returned after the shift, indicating they were up safely. Then it was time for the cage. After the banksman had rapped three times, they squeezed in.

Jammed among nine others like sardines in the cage, Jack always felt his chest constrict. At two raps they were almost ready to fall through the air, for that was what it was, just a falling. He swallowed.

One day he might not mind. One day his breath might not catch in his throat, but he wouldn't place a bet on it. Martin was humming next to him. He always did. At first it had set Jack's teeth on edge but now he'd miss it. Everyone coped in their own way. He waited for the last single rap. It came. He braced, and down they went, rattling and heaving. Ben eased his bait, knocking against Jack. 'Sorry, lad,' he said, but his words were almost drowned by the creaking and clashing.

Soon they'd be at the bottom, safe for that moment. With a jolt they were there, in the dust and the heat. It was his world. It was what he knew. He could read Auld Maud, the creaking of the pine uprights, and the coal, the roof, the movement of the air, he could almost taste her moods. He could smell the sleck. They all could. They were a band of brothers.

They waited for the lower banksman to come and release the barrier. The lamp hung from Jack's hand. A few of the others talked, some cleared the coal from their throats. Some were silent. Did they run through talisman thoughts as he did when they hit rock bottom? He earned good money, he had a marra he couldn't leave, he had other marras in his group that he couldn't desert for if he did how could he ever sleep easy again, knowing that they were down here, beneath the waves, beneath the fields? Each descent he thought these thoughts, and so far they had kept him safe.

Eric, the lower banksman, unlatched the barrier. Martin nudged Jack. 'Have you heard that the whelp Auberon Brampton is back? Soiled his copybook at university good and proper; failed his exams, too much boozing and gambling. Come on, Eric, we can't earn until we get there. Get the barrier back, for Christ's sake.'

Eric grunted and then whistled as he always did, and didn't alter his pace one iota. The men were shifting their weight from foot to foot. 'Eric, man, get a bloody move on.' It was Sam this time.

The barrier went back.

'About ruddy time,' Ben muttered, elbowing past Eric. They started their trudge to the coalface, but as they did Jack heard Eric call out, 'All right for some, going over to Deputy. There's a word for that.' Jack stopped. His da called him on. 'Leave it.'

Ben walked into him, pushing him forward. 'Howay with you lad, leave it to Sam.'

Jack heard Sam, one of the last from the cage, say, 'Sorry about that, Eric, did I kick you? Must have been something I heard. It would do you more good to keep your gob shut and your mind open.'

Jack snatched a look at Martin, who muttered, 'Well, who's Eric to pass judgement, daft bugger. We need a deputy on our side, that's what we think, so forget anyone else.' He lifted his head and shouted, 'You hear that, Eric?'

Yes, they were all in this together, and Jack smiled, really smiled for the first time since he'd opened his eyes this morning. They all pressed themselves against the sides as the full coal wagons passed, driven back to the cages by the putter boys who called out to their Galloway ponies to hoof it. It was the end of one shift, the start of another. Soon Timmie would be with the Galloways, but first he'd be a trapper on the doors, controlling the flow of air, and now Jack's smile faded. Trappers could fall asleep in the darkness which was lit only by the weak pool of light thrown by their lamps. If he slept he'd likely be crushed as a runaway wagon or a putter's cart tore into the closed gate. Jack had to talk to Timmie again, make him aware he had to get the gates opened in time.

Their lamps cast light only over the immediate area. Rats scurried, dust rose, the roof sighed, men shouted to one another above the clatter of the wagons, the neighing of the ponies, the noise which never stopped. Jack nodded to his father as they approached Fred Scrivens' old desk in his kist, or work station, a mile and half from the face. 'Howay with you then, Da.'

His father was carrying an axe and saw to cut new props or salvage others. It was the most dangerous job in the mine, and it was this that had taken off Fred's legs when he'd clawed out a prop for reuse and the roof had crashed in. He'd been lugged in a tub back to a wagon courtesy of a putter, a bairn who had vomited all the way. Jack grimaced; the sooner the lad got used to the bloody battlefield down here the better.

Fred was taking a long time to die in the infirmary, but while he lived his family had a house so he'd cling on no matter the pain. 'Has Scrivens' missus moved in with relatives yet?' Jack called to no one in particular. Sam replied above the shuffling, 'Last I heard her brother over Gosforn way was taking her in, and the bairns.'

Fred Scrivens would die now.

His da had not diverted to the kist but was still trudging. 'Have you lost your sense of direction, Bob?' Ben called from the back as they continued past the turn-off.

'No, I'm coming with you, Ben. From now on no one goes to their placement without me checking it out. How can I write a report if I haven't seen it?' He nodded back to his kist where he would produce his reports in between checking the props, checking for gas and airflow, keeping an eye on the water and pumps, checking that the trappers were awake as they sat in the dark opening and shutting the doors quickly, so as not to interrupt the airflow more than necessary.

Jack gripped his da's arm. 'Just make sure you check the roof if you're drawing out roof props. Don't die for the bugger's cutbacks. There should be no need to take out the real old ones, he knows that. It's never safe. The props were put there for a reason, course they bloody were.' He ended on a cough. Bloody dust. 'Don't kick up, Mart, for God's sake, man.'

'Hush your noise, Jacko,' Martin grunted.

'Don't take on about props, lad. It just "is", isn't it,' his da said. The lamps cast deep shadows on sepia faces.

On they trudged, another mile to go out under the sea. His da would make a good deputy, though it still stuck in his throat along with the bloody dust. Mart must have read his mind. 'So, Bob, have you joined the Brampton Lodge yet?'

He listened as his father grunted into the silence that fell amongst the men, 'I'll have to, but why not? I'll hear what's going on and what plans are being cooked by management.'

The others nodded and continued their talk of pigeons or quoits, whippets or painting while he and Martin discussed the negotiations for the eight-hour shifts that were due to start in January 1910.

Jack murmured, 'You just wait, Brampton'll cut the piece rate on top of cutting the hours. He's just waiting for any change that lets him slip it in. I don't know why they do all this squealing about the Liberals and their taxes, because they just pass their shortfall down to us. It'd be a different bloody tale if the taxes were raising money for them instead of pensions and medicine for us. That's if they get this National Insurance Act passed, it'll likely be hoyed out instead. Or should I say "thrown" in a posh voice?'

'Let's worry about one thing at a time, man. It's the shifts that come first right now,' Martin grumbled. 'The government means to help the workers, of course they do with the hours cut, but we need the twelve hours' money. Grand your da's on the inside. We'll maybe hear something useful to take to Jeb.'

Jack nodded. 'And then Jeb can feed it to the union agents. They're the ones doing the negotiating.'

'Aye, but they'll come back to us before they agree, won't they, man?'

Jack shrugged. 'God knows. If they don't, will we strike on a matter of principle? If we did, would we win? Would we hell.'

They paused as Bob led Thomas and George to their placement and hunkered down, waiting. Jack set his lamp down and touched his nose. The dust was on his swollen eyes, but not in them.

Martin muttered, 'You don't reckon Bastard Brampton'll take over the allocation of placements?' He leaned back on the wall of coal. He sat, rather than hunkered, as a prop had crashed on to his leg a couple of years ago, leaving it stiff, and he needed to ease it when he could. Bob returned and they groaned their way upright and trudged on, Jack taking his place alongside Martin, gripping his arm, his marra's words still resonating. It was something he'd never thought of. 'Take over the cavil? No owner ever has and none ever would. It's democracy in action, that allocation process is, bonny lad. We draw for our work stations and no bloody great lump is going to change that. You'd really be talking strike then.'

Jack stared ahead. The cavil was mining tradition, it was set in stone. Every quarter they all met in the Reading Room and held the cavil – each marra pair drawing lots for their work placements in the mine, with not an owner in sight. Just them, and Lady Luck. If you lucked out on a good seam on that cavil, then you'd maybe pick up on a better one next go-round. He said, 'It's sacrosanct.'

Martin spat into the dark as a huge rat was caught fleetingly in his lamplight, scampering past. 'Got one of the beggars.' Behind him some of the others who hadn't yet peeled off to their placements laughed. Jack nudged him, calling over his shoulder at the others, 'He'll be notching his hits on his belt soon, daft beggar.'

Martin jogged his arm so that his lamp cast chaotic shadows. 'Aye, maybe. And if you churn out any more long words we'll have to notch your tongue out. Too much reading under the covers is bad, lad. You'll go blind.'

Ben and Sam laughed from behind them. The floor dipped a few inches and they scudded up the dust. The roof was lowering, they were stooping. It was killing on the neck. It was hotter.

Bob peeled off to the left, taking another two to their placement. 'Keep going, I'll catch up.'

The roof was lowering by the stride. They could see little by the light of their lamps, but enough. 'Penny for 'em,' Martin grunted.

'More of the same. The bairns are going to be hungrier next year unless we hammer out a good deal,' Jack replied.

Da caught up as the roof became even lower and they bent double, kicking up crud with every step, and though they cursed they did so silently because to open their mouths invited a lungful of dust. Jack risked it for a moment. 'Jeb's mebbe coming to talk about it all at the end of shift when we head to the cage.' He ended up choking and coughing.

'Save it lad,' Luke called. 'See you later.' He and his marra peeled off.

It was so hot this far down, sweat was streaming off Jack's face and dripping to the ground. He grinned, not a bad idea, they could do with some damping of the dust. His nose still hurt but it wasn't the first time it had been broken and not the last, if he kept on fighting. But he had to. They were not far off what they thought would be the price of Froggett's house. OK they weren't there yet, but it was doable. Just look at the Gala fight – five guineas. There could be other purses that big and with Evie's pay . . .

His father squeezed past, panting. 'Time I took the front.' He was bent double as they all were now, and still the roof scraped their backs. More button scabs torn off. So what was new? His father set up a good pace. Deputyship needed men who cared, men who took safety seriously.

Ben shouted, 'Am I talking to myself back here? Or do I just eat your dirt to amuse myself? Keep your bloody feet gentle in front, won't you? What d'you say, Sam?'

His brother retorted, 'Keep your gob shut and you won't swallow so much.'

Da was at the turn-off to Jack and Martin's placement now, crouched down low. Jack's back was screaming as he followed, his legs bent. Martin was breathing hard and his leg must kill but you'd not hear a word from him. They changed to a crawl. His da was checking the props at the seam face, which was slightly higher. He was crouched on his knees, which was how the hewers would have to work. Jack eyed it up. Or maybe this shift would be spent lying on their sides. It depended how much they cut away.

'Martin, Jack, get alongside.' Bob pointed with his saw at the sides. 'I'll get some more props sent up. You'll need to set them as you cut away. The putters will have to push in the tubs for the coal and leave the Galloway wagons back where there's headroom. It'll slow you down, mark you, but don't be tempted to take bloody risks. You hear me now?' He looked up at the roof. 'Get back now, both of you.'

They did as he checked the roof. 'Right, lads, you're safe and sound.'

Jack and Martin grinned at one another. That was a new one – down a pit and safe and sound? His da saw them and shrugged. 'Make sure you keep it that way.' He pressed Jack's shoulder as he passed. 'You make sure,' he murmured.

'Same for you, Da.'

Jack and Martin had drawn a favourable placement in the cavil, so their piece rates were good. Martin had gone on to the face and was busy already, wielding his pick in short jerks. Jack shovelled the chunks to the rear as they fell to the ground. 'Putter!' he yelled. The tub came up as far as it could. Eddie shovelled the coal into the tub. Soon it could be Timmie doing that. Jack thrust his shovel beneath the coal as he thought for the first time, really thought, about a hotel. Well, why not, it was a grand idea, and Evie was a grand lass, as well as a grand cook. Timmie could work there, his da too. Well, *they* could. He couldn't leave his marra, never could he do that.

All morning they hacked with their picks and shovels in the light from their oil lamps. Would miracles happen, would the Bastard introduce electrics like some of the other pits? Would he hell. By bait time they'd stripped out of their hoggers and were down to their underwear, with sweat stinging their open cuts and running rivulets through their dust-coated bodies. They were lying on their sides getting at the under-coal.

Jack called a halt at midday, and they sat against the wall, pulling out their butties and casting great shadows on the walls of coal and shale in the yellow fluttering light. Jack's butties were stuffed with the remains of the ham, and for a moment he was at the beck again with Evie. She'd probably be serving up the servants' lunch now, and halfway through preparing the upstairs meal. How many courses would that be? At least she wasn't sweeping up the family's detritus or scuttling down the corridor to stay out of sight. What did the nobs think would happen to them if they cast eyes on a servant? That they'd turn to a pillar of salt? Beggars they were, but at least they were paying to aid her escape. He felt his mouth twist. There was a grand justice in it.

Martin handed him one of his butties. 'Cheese. Swap?'

'Aye, just the one.'

They swigged from their water bottles. 'How's your Evie?'

Jack shrugged. 'Si will look after her, if she needs it. But you know her, she's our Evie.'

Martin laughed, a piece of ham falling to his lap. He picked it up with coal-coated fingers and ate it. Jack could hear the crunch of teeth on dust.

Jack eased his back on the wall and felt the pain of torn scabs and the blood from the old and new running down into his drawers. All around was the thick smell of coal. It was a strange way to live your life, in the dark and always close to death. It changed you, gave you a different attitude which must be useful for something, but who the hell knew what.

Martin gulped at his water, wiping his mouth with the back of his hand. 'I was thinking. There's talk that the Brampton whelp could be coming in here to peer over Davies' shoulder. Bet it'll end in more cutbacks. Someone heard something from the office, so they say.'

Jack shook his head. 'They say a lot, but I can't see it, can you, man? That beggar Brampton's a businessman and it's not good business to put in a fool like Auberon. By, I'd give my right arm to go to the university, and for him to chuck it up . . . If he's a gambler, he'd have done well to put money on my fight. Just shows what a daft beggar he is.'

They laughed, then Martin coughed and spat. In this light Jack couldn't see the colour. Martin coughed again. Jack said, 'Stop smoking so many of those Woodbines would you, you daft beggar? Don't you reckon your chest has enough to put up with?'

Martin nudged him with his foot. 'Are you my mam?'

'Aye, haven't you noticed my skirts?'

Beside him Martin tossed his crust into the dark where there'd be a rat or ten waiting. Jack said, 'I'll ask Evie to see what she can find out. It's bound to be only gossip.'

Their bait time was over. It was back to work. They crawled to the face, then froze. Something . . . what? Neither moved, both listened. No creaks above, just the usual sighing. Then a rumble, shouts. Way off. Was it down the east seam? Martin looked at Jack. 'Bugger of a life, eh?' It was some poor sod's unlucky day but not theirs, this time. They'd hear whose soon enough and put something into the collection, but all they could do now was to get on.

They crawled on. They spent too much time on their knees, far too much. Too many workers did, from the dockers to the railwaymen, to the miners, to the domestics, and if this went on there'd be a revolution just as he'd said to Evie. Jack wielded his pick and felt the judder right into his shoulder, and settled in to hacking out the coal because he had enough to think about without straying into the land of maybe. He'd just listen hard and perhaps he'd hear the roof before it came down.

Chapter Five

It was her first morning at Easterleigh Hall. Monday, the day the miners hated. The clock chimed on the wall of the corridor outside Evie's bedroom. It was 5 a.m. and she'd barely closed her eyes, so worried had she been that she'd not hear the corridor clock chime the time and not be down to light the range furnace at five thirty. Annie was still asleep, the blanket pulled up around her head. She had put her two shawls over the bed for extra warmth, just as Evie had done.

Evie lay quite still listening for the noises of the house. There were none. At home in her box room she would have heard coughs from the men's bedrooms, a stirring from her mother downstairs, the barking of a dog further along the terrace. A sense of loss drenched her, but she had no time for that.

She crept to the washing bowl, the wooden floor like ice. She'd bring one of her mam's proggy mats and let Mrs Green try and stop her. She poured in bitterly cold water from the jug which she'd lugged up last night. It was midnight before she'd finished clearing the kitchen with Annie, but what did that matter when her clear soup had been acceptable, and her vegetable-chopping adequate, or so Mrs Moore had said with a smile before retiring to her room further along the corridor from the servants' hall.

The clock chimed five fifteen, by which time she was washed and dressed. She'd left her corset looser than was thought desirable, but she couldn't see the point of agony. She dragged on her boots, tied her hessian apron, then shook Annie. 'Come on, lass, time to get up and at 'em.'

Annie groaned. 'In a minute. It's your job to get the furnace going, not mine. So get it going.' She turned over, her face puffy from tiredness and her light brown hair a bird's nest.

Downstairs Evie hurried into the kitchen and mice scuttled in all directions. She froze, but within a few seconds they'd disappeared. 'Darned beggars.' She hated them, always had, always would. She dared the furnace to misbehave, though Mrs Moore had said it would be fine if there was a brisk wind to draw it. And when wasn't there hereabouts, even in the valley? Dropping to her knees, she cleared the ash into the buckets left by Kev the hallboy. She heard him coming in from outside with the coal. He slept in the bell corridor on an apology for a bed, but had told her yesterday evening that one day he'd be a butler, and he'd show his beggar of an uncle in Consett who'd wanted him in the steelworks.

'Here's your kindling too, Evie.' He had not

75

washed, or if he had the coal had worked its magic and left its usual coating. Paper and kindling laid, she carefully placed the coal, finding the familiar smell comforting. What was more, it was top grade, not a trace of shale anywhere. She opened the flue, lit the paper and prayed.

Kev laughed. 'You don't need that sort of help, the wind's fierce today.'

Annie said from behind, 'He's right, you know. It'll go like the clappers.'

Kev disappeared back into the bell corridor to clean the shoes, all twenty or so pairs of them including those of the upper servants. Annie had soaked the blacklead for the ranges overnight, and they worked until Evie's hair was sweat-soaked. Finally the ranges gleamed, but not as much as Evie's mam's. 'They'll do,' Annie groaned. 'Old Moore can't see too well, even with her glasses.'

They tackled the fender with emery paper and by then their hands were sore and smudged, their nails torn. At Miss Manton's, Susan from Hawton had sculleried for her and Evie realised just how lucky she'd been. The kettle was boiling and it was time for biscuits and tea for Mrs Green, Mr Harvey, and Mrs Moore.

As instructed, Evie left the sustenance on the occasional table in both Mrs Green's sitting room and Mr Harvey's parlour, which was opposite Mrs Moore. She tapped lightly on the cook's parlour door, and put her tea and biscuit on her table. It was a nice room but cold, with a fireplace laid but unlit, and photographs on the wall. Evie glanced at these as she headed for the bedroom. She saw a young woman who must have been Miss Manton sitting in a garden, alone, smiling into the camera. She radiated joy.

Evie kicked something as she was about to knock on the bedroom door. It was an empty gin bottle. Mrs Moore had asked her to make sure she knocked long and hard. She left the bottle where it was, because to move it would show that she knew. She knocked again, and again. At last she heard Mrs Moore call, 'Enough. I'm awake. Leave the tea, get out. Just go. Get out.'

She went, wanting to bang the door shut on the canny old witch, but did not.

Evie checked her list of 'things to do'. Some of the copper pans had been left from the night before, though Mrs Moore had written that they should not be. Annie had already started on them in the bitter cold of the scullery and Evie rushed in, dipping into the mixture of silver sand, salt and vinegar and starting to rub the largest, gasping at the stinging of her raw flesh. 'Quick, she's awake and not happy.'

Annie looked up at her, her face still puffy, a Woodbine hanging from her mouth. 'Never is in the morning. Don't know why, except I'm not either. She's got a touch of the rheumatics is all. No need to make such a do of it, is there. Don't worry, she'll be half an hour yet and by then she'll expect this kitchen to be on the way to being perfect, with the table laid up. But that's your job, not bloody mine. How it can all be done just by us two I don't bloody well know.' Her ash dropped into the pan, her cigarette clung to her bottom lip. How could she talk with it in her mouth? The same way Jack and his marras did.

They worked on, and any skin on their hands that had survived was soon as raw as the rest. Evie felt the stinging right up through her arms as far as her eyebrows. Nonetheless, by the time Mrs Moore appeared the pans were hung up on the hooks and gleamed enough to satisfy the pickiest of souls. But not Mrs Moore. 'They're a disgrace, take 'em down again and finish them properly and stoke up that furnace, for God's sake. And I'll expect them to be cleaned every time we use them today.' She had the same frown that Jack had after a night at the pub, the same faint tremble of the hands, and that smell.

She slumped down on her stool. 'We need the porridge ready for the staff, don't you forget that, Evie, and I'll have more tea. Miss Donant, the lady's maid, will be in hotfoot for her bloody highness's cuppa and then for Miss Veronica's, and Archie will have to take up Mr Auberon's now he's home, so hoy that down to the butler's pantry. God almighty, as though we don't have enough to do. And this table isn't laid properly. Get the ladle, or are you expecting Mrs Green to serve with her hands? But why haven't you stoked up the furnace, or is there something wrong with your lugs? Didn't I say sort it? Let's get some proper heat.' As Mrs Moore spoke she was flexing her hands, moving her shoulders, and her face was creased with more than a hangover. Pain was too mild a word. Well, Evie thought, flexing her own hands. Well, what about *my* pain?

She exchanged a look with Annie. Mrs Moore eased her back, rolled her shoulders more gently and glanced at Evie. 'Come on our lass, pour me a cuppa and ignore me for the moment. I'm sorry my pets, grumpy old woman, I am.' There was sweat beading her forehead as she sat.

Evie lifted the teapot, wincing at the pressure on her raw hands, and for a moment paused, her eyes fixed on Mrs Moore's swollen knuckles, and her heart ached for her. 'You've a right, I'd kick every cat in sight and so would Annie if I had your rheumatics.'

Annie mouthed, 'Stop buttering up the old hag.'

Evie poured Mrs Moore's tea, shovelled more coal into the huge furnace. Within moments the heat had upped enough degrees to ease a million joints, but as Evie looked more closely at the cook she saw what she had not seen before. It was not just pain, but fear. Evie remembered how she had felt on Saturday when she thought her da had lost his job. What would happen to Mrs Moore if she lost hers? Perhaps she could live with Miss Manton, or would it be the workhouse? Evie shook herself back into the moment. It wasn't going to happen; she, Evie Forbes, would not let it.

She put the kettles on to boil for the upstairs tea. Along the corridor between the kitchen and the servants' hall Lil was rushing towards the broom cupboard, tucking her hair into her cap. Archie and James, the footmen, were heading off towards the butler's pantry where Evie should by now have taken Mr Auberon's tea. Well, she couldn't do everything and kettles didn't boil while you watched them.

Annie had taken down the copper pans again, and was banging about in the scullery. Evie joined her, out came the mixture, along with the elbow grease, scouring their hands again as much as the copper while Annie's curses accompanied them.

'The kettles have boiled, so make that tea for Mr Auberon now, Evie, if you please.' Mrs Moore stood in the scullery door, her tone soft. Evie did so, and carried the tray to the butler's pantry. Young Archie nodded, his face one big scowl that leaked into his shoulders. In fact his whole being was crunched up into one big sulk. 'Afternoon tea, is it, for heaven's sake?' He raced off with the tray while Evie hurried back to the kitchen, wanting to kick him up the backside.

Miss Donant was there, by the kitchen table, tapping her foot, her hair immaculate, her face scrubbed clean, her mouth pursed into a sparrow's bum. 'I need that tea, now. This minute. Her Ladyship shouldn't have to wait.'

Mrs Moore was studying her recipe book and

without looking up said, 'If there's a problem then suggest to her Ladyship she reviews the employment policy, if you wouldn't mind.' Miss Donant's mouth pursed tighter still as Evie provided the tea, wanting to pour it over her head and to do the same to her Ladyship. 'I'll return for Lady Veronica's,' snapped Miss Donant. She swept from the kitchen.

So it went on until Evie and Annie had finished the pans, Evie had prepared Lady Veronica's tray, and both had swept the stone floor clear of mouse droppings, and then scrubbed it. It hurt Evie's pride as much as her knees. She rushed to collect up knives, spoons, ladles, bowls, plates, and checked everything against the list. They matched, heaven be praised.

She flicked a clean hessian apron from the hooks on the back of the door whilst Annie took the other along the corridor to the laundry. Evie made porridge for the servants' hall while Mrs Moore finished her tea, sitting on her stool with her back to the ranges, tapping her pencil against her teeth. At last she closed her recipe book and wrote up the lunch menu. At eight the house staff came down, having sorted the upstairs fires, and begun the brushing of the carpets. The dusting would continue during the upstairs breakfasts, along with all other chores that consumed the day.

Putting on clean white aprons, Evie and Annie spooned porridge into bowls for themselves and Mrs Moore, then lifted the huge earthenware pot and staggered into the servants' hall, setting it down in front of Mrs Green as instructed. Evie, Annie and Mrs Moore sat around the deal table in the kitchen eating their porridge, and all the while Evie waited for Simon and the other under-gardeners to arrive, for they'd have to pass through the kitchen. They didn't. Perhaps they cooked for themselves in the cottage? But they'd be back at lunchtime, surely?

Mrs Moore nodded at Evie. 'Good porridge, no lumps.' Annie grimaced. 'Better than Charlotte's, bloody hopeless she was.'

Mrs Moore tapped the table. 'No need for language, thank you Annie. At least Charlotte was another pair of hands.'

Annie shook her head. 'We can't manage, Mrs Moore. We need another two girls, or get Edith back at least. Look at her smirking with the housemaids, silly cow. Can't you do something? And anyway, you use language.'

Evie watched as Mrs Moore dug her spoon into her porridge again. 'I do and I shouldn't. So do what I say, not what I do. So less of the cow, Annie, less of your cheek and yes, I can do something, but at the right moment. Remember that, girls, you go in at the right moment. Until then we have to manage.' Mrs Moore's colour was coming back, her hands had steadied but were still so swollen that Evie winced again on her behalf, and almost forgot her own stinging pain.

They had twenty minutes for breakfast, and then

Annie and Evie collected the dishes from the servants' hall and Annie set to in the scullery washing yet more pots, plates and cutlery, sinking her hands into the soda-rich water, the very thought of which made Evie want to hug the poor wee bairn. Meanwhile she and Mrs Moore cooked bacon and eggs, sausages, kidneys, finnan haddock. 'We won't do kedgeree but we'll have to when his Lordship returns,' Mrs Moore told her.

'It's a feast,' Evie said, thinking of her family and those others in the village and all the pit villages around. 'It is indeed,' said Mrs Moore. 'For just two people.'

'Two?'

'Yes, her Ladyship takes hers in her room, just a slice of toast and "I'll keep my figure thank you very much", but Lady Veronica takes hers in the dining room, as she's not allowed the luxury of lounging about. That has to wait until she "comes out" and has done her duty by snagging a husband. Not to mention that we have Mr Auberon, so we have to fill the sideboard. Lady Veronica was happy with a kipper.' Mrs Moore had some of her smile back now. 'The lad's been busy with the demon drink and too fruity with the cards, I gather. He's wasted his father's money and that is the number one sin for this family. Can't say I blame him, poor him, poor Miss Veronica. They've been without their mother for so long, and then Miss Wainton, their nanny, who stayed on, died recently.'

Mrs Moore fell silent, her eyes filling. Kev brought in ice to replenish the icebox, clattering through the kitchen in his boots, then down the central passageway to the cool room. 'Off you go, pet. Fetch bones from the icebox for stock.' Evie did so before setting the stockpot on to the range and putting in water, bones, root vegetables and a small lump of salt. She then turned the bacon and tossed the kidneys, while Mrs Moore sniffed and sorted out the haddock and toast.

At eight thirty Mr Harvey, Archie and James took up the trays for the dining room and Evie set out the table again for Mrs Moore, who settled down on the stool and thumbed once more through her recipe book for dinner this evening, nodding towards the cupboards beneath the internal windows. 'Fetch us the sieves from there. We'll need them for luncheon, and the cutlery. Hurry up now.' Evie found big long carving knives, small ones for fruit, palette knives, huge spoons, small spoons, and dug out sieves from the bottom cupboard. She placed the wire ones and the hated hair ones side by side. It was anything but a labour of love to force meat or fish through those. She added flour sifters, egg whisks, graters, and in between fed the furnace. It went on and on and Evie felt she'd run a million miles, for she was indeed running, not walking.

'Draw breath, Evie,' Mrs Moore said, pulling out the stool next to hers. 'They won't be back down with the dishes for twenty minutes at least, then you'll have to start running again.' She pushed across the lunch menu while she continued to leaf through her recipe book. 'I said, sit down and have a look at these, they'll do for luncheon, don't you think? You get off and get herbs from Simon, Annie.'

Damn, Annie was getting Simon and she was left with clear soup, and what else? Ah, chicken in aspic and a cold dessert.

'No fish course?' Evie queried, her mind still on Simon.

Mrs Moore shook her head. 'Five courses at dinner, only three for luncheon. It's a different matter when they're shooting, or have guests, or Lord Brampton is in residence, but we'll sort that out when we come to it.'

Evie rested her elbows on the table but wanted to sink her head on to her arms and sleep for England, and the upstairs breakfasts weren't even down yet. 'Don't the under-gardeners eat in the servants' hall?'

Mrs Moore licked her finger and turned the page of her bible. Evie looked across at the chicken quenelles recipe Mrs Moore was perusing, and her heart sank. The hair sieves would have to come into play. But the page was turned and she sighed with relief and repeated, 'Don't the gardeners eat with us? And what happened to Miss Wainton?'

Mrs Moore placed her bible down carefully, looking out to the corridor. Evie followed her gaze, but there was no one there. Mrs Moore removed her glasses and rubbed her eyes. 'Miss Wainton brought them up after their mother died. Lady Veronica was ten and Mr Auberon was twelve when that happened. It was before they bought Easterleigh Hall. The family made their money with the steelworks really, and a brickworks, and then bought into the collieries. Mrs Brampton was a lovely woman, they say. Kind, sensible and brought those children up to be decent people, or she would have done. She got it started, let's say.' Mrs Moore hesitated. 'Now, don't go tittle-tattling this all over the place, young Evie. I'm telling you because I know Miss Manton is a good judge of character.'

Evie touched Mrs Moore's arm. 'I won't, I promise.'

'Well, as I say, she died. Miss Wainton stayed on and really mothered the children. She came with the family to Easterleigh Hall when that jumped-up bully was made a lord. Can't imagine what the Liberal Party was thinking of, but they say he gave them a big donation so that explains it. The Tories probably got his jumped-up measure and wouldn't play his game when he was toadying up to them. It's a disgrace, the sort of people who buy titles these days.'

Evie smiled. 'I can see you really like this man.'

Mrs Moore grunted. 'If I did I'd be the only one.'

Evie saw Mrs Green walking along the corridor from the stairs. Mrs Moore picked up the bible again and replaced her glasses. Evie fetched the chopping boards, saying quietly as Mrs Green opened the linen cupboard alongside the entrance to the servants' hall, 'Except for his present wife, presumably? Wives usually like their husbands, don't they?'

Mrs Moore laughed so loudly that Mrs Green turned round, her arms full of linen. Mrs Moore ignored her and Mrs Green continued on her way. 'You've a lot to learn, young Evie.'

'Oh, didn't you like your husband then?' The moment the words were out Evie knew they should have stayed in.

'A husband? Why would I want one of those? Not many men I could stomach looking at over the breakfast table day in and day out. All cooks are called Mrs. Don't know why and don't need to know why. No, this Lady Brampton is of the proper aristocracy and her family haven't a bean. She followed her nose and it took her to Brampton's trough. He wanted the kudos of marrying aristocracy so it's a marriage made in heaven you could say, except she didn't like Miss Wainton any more than did his Lordship, and when Mr Auberon went to university Lord Brampton gave the poor woman her cards. Last year it was. She . . . Well, she died. I miss her. She was my friend. The children lost their second mother and gained Lady Brampton. What a prize that must have been.'

Mrs Moore flexed her hands again and glanced at the clock over the dresser. It was nine fifteen. 'They used to come down for a cuppa in the afternoon with Miss Wainton, but not when Lady Hoity-Toity was in residence. Sometimes they still do, but not often.'

Mrs Moore crossed her arms and hitched her bosom. 'Now, have you finished the laying up? We have a lot to do. And no, the gardeners don't eat here. They have a good plain cook from Hawton who cycles over to do for them in Southview Cottage, except when we have someone new, like you yesterday, for them to gawp at. And don't go getting too stuck on one or you'll be out of your job. No followers allowed.'

The trays were brought into the kitchen from upstairs and still Mrs Moore hadn't told her how Miss Wainton died. Mrs Moore waved at the trays. 'Throw the leftovers into the bucket for the pigs, and make a start on these dishes, pet, until Annie gets back. She'll be chatting to the gardeners. Anything in trousers and she lights up, and I don't mean cigarettes, though she'll likely be having a Woodbine an' all.' Mrs Moore wiped her hands across her apron.

Evie wanted to run out and haul Annie back, well away from Simon, but took the trays into the scullery, disposed of the food in the bins and ran hot water into the sink, something that she still could not get used to. At Miss Manton's she had heated it on the range. In went the soda crystals, followed by her hands, and she winced but was glad because it took her mind off Simon, but just for a moment. Were his eyes on Annie's, his hand on hers? What would it feel like to hold a man's hand, to feel his mouth on hers? She shook her head and washed the plates and bowls first, and then the cutlery, determined to leave the pots until last, by which time wretched Annie should be back. She was, smelling of her cigarettes. She flounced into the scullery with a flea in her ear from Mrs Moore, replying, 'Well, I wasn't that long.'

Evie said nothing, just wiped her hands and left the scullery. She wanted to ask where she'd been but didn't want to hear the answer. There was rosemary and sage on the table, and Mrs Moore stood near the door to the internal corridor with her arms akimbo, her face grim, listening to Mrs Green who was whispering in her ear. Finally, she nodded and Mrs Green left.

Mrs Moore swung round. 'Evie, take all these things off the table and find a clean tablecloth from the cupboard drawer over there.' She hurried to the table, closing her recipe book and brushing her apron smooth. 'Be quick now, we have a visit from her Ladyship for which we must send up prayers of eternal gratitude.' Her sarcasm could hardly have been thicker.

Evie just stared at all the knives, sieves, spoons and Uncle Tom Cobley and all. Off the table? Mrs Moore clapped her hands. 'Come on, we can't have anything that reminds upstairs of the frantic little legs paddling away to keep them gliding on their bonny lake. She'll want to talk about a dinner party, it's the only time she deigns to visit the bowels.'

Evie felt her stomach twist with nervousness. Her Ladyship? Here? Soon a pristine white cloth covered the scarred pine. 'Evie, into the scullery with you now, and listen and learn how to get what you want. Did you hear that, Annie? Not a sound from either of you. Everyone else will stay out of the way until she's been.' Indeed, the corridor was deserted.

Annie and Evie silently dried up the dishes, leaving the door into the kitchen strategically ajar. Now they could see but not be seen. There was a brisk knock on the kitchen door and in her Ladyship swept in her elegant grey morning dress, her hair freshly dressed by Miss Donant. Evie and Annie stood quite still with the dishes and tea towels in their hands. Mrs Moore offered Lady Brampton the stool. She refused. Well, of course she would, Evie thought. She wouldn't want to place that upper-class bum on something used by the servants.

Lady Brampton stood tall, but rested a hand on the tablecloth and looked at Mrs Moore's forehead. 'Now, Mrs Moore, his Lordship will have returned in just under two weeks, Saturday, and I just wanted to warn you personally that we have dinner guests on that same evening. I have a few ideas for a menu. It could be twenty-two, but at the moment it's twenty. I have informed Mr Harvey that we'll need all the leaves in the table and I will discuss flowers with him. I would like colour co-ordinated food – cream and white.' She was speaking as though she was working her way down a list which only she could see.

Evie and Annie stared at one another. Colour

co-ordinated food? Cream and white? For heaven's sake, what next? Mrs Moore's face was a picture and her bust impressive as she drew herself up to her full height, which slightly topped Lady Brampton's. 'That is perfectly all right in theory, Your Ladyship, but I would like to think you have not yet sent out the invitations because I cannot guarantee to be able to cater for fourteen guests, let alone twenty-two.'

There was an appalled silence. Evie felt her own jaw sag. Lady Brampton looked as though she had been slapped around her chops. 'I beg your pardon, Mrs Moore? I don't believe I heard you correctly.'

'Let me repeat myself then. I cannot guarantee that we can any longer cater for fourteen guests . . .'

Lady Brampton gestured sharply. 'Yes, I heard that. But I don't understand.'

Mrs Moore crossed her arms and said firmly, 'We should have two kitchen assistants and two scullery maids at the very least. We are without one scullery maid and have no kitchen assistant. I gather it is a question of cost. May I respectfully suggest that we cease importing provisions from Newcastle and Durham which require packaging and cartage costs and return instead to supporting the local co-operative store and the farmers, not to mention Home Farm whose task and duty it is to provide for the house, rather than concentrating on your London and Leeds establishments. To buy locally would not only be cheaper but the produce is fresh and good. It will also act as a symbol of support from Lord Brampton to the area. With the money we save we can pay for three more girls, which should suffice for now. This will facilitate any number of dinner parties.'

An even more appalled silence fell. Mrs Moore was sweating: it beaded her forehead, cheeks and chin. Evie hoped that this wonderful woman would hold her nerve in the face of her outraged employer, whose colour was high. Nothing was said now, not by either woman. But then, Lady Brampton spoke, her voice high and tight as though someone had stuck a pin in her bum. 'Yes, very well, you will organise the change in delivery arrangements and discuss with Mrs Green and Mr Harvey your staff requirements, and be mindful that they must be in place by the end of April. I will approve two new staff, not three. One kitchen assistant only.' She marched to the door and then stopped, turned. Evie held her breath. 'I will expect exemplary food from this moment forth.'

'You will receive exemplary food, Your Ladyship, as always. Colour co-ordinated for the dinner party.'

Lady Brampton swept from the room, clutching her skirts close in case she brushed against something or someone unpleasant. For Evie this was one of the best and most triumphant moments of her life, and proof that the lady of the house would do anything to keep a cook who created *exemplary* food. Annie nudged her and they grinned. Annie whispered, 'Better not let the food go downhill.' Well, it wouldn't, for no matter how bad Mrs Moore's rheumatics became she, Evie Forbes, would cover for her and keep the standard as it should be. At that moment Simon entered from the bell passageway with a basket full of flowers.

Evie came from the scullery, smiling at Simon. Mrs Moore asked her to clear the tablecloth. Conscious of Simon's eyes on her as she did so, she said, 'I'm sorry you will only have two more girls.'

Mrs Moore tapped her nose. 'Always ask for more than you need. They'll never agree and will always offer under, it makes them feel they've won, when in fact we have. We only needed two, I can't have silly girls cluttering up my kitchen.'

Evie laughed, Simon too, though he looked puzzled. 'What's the joke?' His eyes really were the most vivid blue.

Lady Veronica sat in the window of the Blue Drawing Room overlooking the formal gardens at the back of the house. The cherry blossom was wonderful after such a winter, but when wasn't it harsh? She looked beyond the box hedges, seeing daffodils and plants that had yet to flower. She loved it here, harsh winters or not; however, she did not love luncheon with her stepmother. She did not love luncheon full stop. What on earth was the point of trying to stuff three courses into a gut that was pinched into nothing by a ridiculous corset? It was not something Wainey had thought sensible or right; she had hooked her own and Veronica's stays up as loosely as possible.

At the thought of Wainey she swallowed, hardly able to bear the misery. Why had she done it? Her vision blurred and she could no longer see the balcony outside the long windows. In the summer it had always been glorious to sit there as the last of the heat fled the day, but she didn't know how she could ever enjoy it again.

She turned at the sound of her stepmother's voice. 'Really, where is your brother? There is no need for him to slouch so long over the luncheon table after we withdraw. Look at the time, it's now early afternoon and he could be occupying himself in some way.'

Veronica said, 'I expect he is occupying himself, probably enjoying a cigarette.' Her voice was carefully neutral.

'He enjoys a sight too many things, and always at the expense of others.' Lady Brampton was sitting at the end of the sofa, reading *The Times* while she drank her coffee. Veronica said nothing. What was there to say?

Her stepmother lowered the newspaper, peering at Veronica, the hint of a scowl beginning. 'Is that a sullen silence, my dear? If so, it's not as a lady should behave.'

Veronica said, 'It is merely a silence. I have nothing to contribute to our scintillating conversation.' She wondered if her stepmother noticed her hatred, or if she did, whether she cared, so preoccupied was she with herself. What on earth would her mother think of her husband's choice of a wife who was everything that Wainey and her mother had considered a disgrace to women? Auberon had told her that their mother would have stood her ground on the purchase of a title and asked how one could possibly buy status, because such a thing needed to be earned? Veronica wondered if perhaps their father had earned it with his various businesses, because for all his faults he was a worker. She thought not and returned again to the views over the garden.

Her stepmother hadn't finished. 'Veronica.' It was a command. Veronica turned. The newspaper had been left to fall to the floor. No doubt some wretched minion would be expected to pick it up, re-iron it and leave it on the table in case it was required later. Lady Brampton said, 'I see my task as bringing you up to par. Miss Wainton was too lax, too full of silly ideas and has let you down. We need to determine on a schedule of visits to your Northumbrian contemporaries and not lose sight of the fact that within two years you will come out. We will, at that time, circulate you amongst your London contemporaries to be viewed. Nineteen will be ideal. We'll have to find you a husband, one with prospects and a suitable rank.'

Veronica stared anywhere but at this impossible woman with her immaculate hair and clothes, sitting there as though she was a set piece in this house she had refurbished as a backdrop to her own perceived brilliance.

It was a house that was too big, too unlike anything Veronica or Auberon needed, or in which her mother would have felt comfortable. 'I don't want a husband,' she said. 'I want a life. I want a career but I just don't know what yet.' She stood and walked to the window, longing to rush down the stairs and outside, to run across the lawn as she used to before this woman became her stepmother five years ago and forbade such unladylike behaviour.

Her stepmother was staring at her, leaning forward as though to hear better. 'I don't believe I heard correctly.'

'I'll repeat, then. I don't want a husband, not yet. I want a life.'

Lady Brampton shook her head, her eyes narrowing. 'That Wainton woman has a lot to answer for, indeed she has. I mean, just what do you intend to be, a shorthand writer? How absurd you are, and how can you consider taking a job from someone who has need of it? I absolutely forbid it, Veronica, and don't want to hear any more about it.'

The door opened and Auberon entered. Veronica shook her head in warning. He nodded, walked to Lady Brampton, bent over her hand and said, 'Delightful luncheon, Mama.'

It was water off a duck's back. Lady Brampton leaned away from him. 'I can smell brandy. Sit down and be quiet. You deserve bread and water when I think of the way you've behaved, and how on earth can you put your father through this endless worry and embarrassment?' She was now waving him from her, her eyes as cold as ice. But when weren't they, the witch. Was that why she had been a spinster for so long, wondered Veronica, not for the first time. Or had her heart been broken somewhere along the line? But no, that couldn't be so, for that would assume she possessed such a thing.

Auberon sat opposite his stepmother on the other sofa. From the set of his head Veronica knew that he was only a short step from disaster. She intervened, walking towards them and taking her place alongside Auberon. 'How long are you remaining at Easterleigh, Mama?'

'Don't change the subject.' Lady Marjorie Brampton had a ramrod-straight back and it was the one thing Veronica admired about her. Her stepmother continued, 'Auberon, you insisted on university and I supported you because it's so much more suitable than the grubby world of business, but you've made me out a fool. Therefore this is where you'll remain. There'll be no more drinking, no more gambling. How dare you when we are economising, when we are threatened on all sides by this lunatic Lloyd George who is attempting to redistribute our wealth to pay for his absurd welfare reforms.'

'But Stepmama . . .'

'Do not interrupt, Auberon. For heaven's sake,

boy, can't you understand the severity of the situation? They demand a much higher income tax from those with our wealth, plus an inheritance tax, and land tax, and all for these workers who threaten us on all sides, wanting more. If it isn't your father's steel workers, or the brick workers, then it is the miners, and it's not just *his* workers. Read the newspapers. What is the world coming to?'

'We're hardly threatened, Mama. We have more than a little bit in hand, haven't we?' Auberon's tone was dry.

Veronica knew it was the brandy talking, but whatever it was it was a step too far. She spoke loudly to gain her stepmother's attention. 'Have you received replies to your dinner invitations?'

Lady Brampton forced herself to turn to Veronica. 'Yes, I have indeed and I think that you must attend. You are not yet "out", but Lady Esther will be coming with her parents and perhaps Lady Margaret with hers. They are both from good Northumbrian families and it really is quite time you learned some polish. That dreadful Wainton has quite worn out your brain with all this book-learning.'

Veronica stared. Next this stupid woman would be telling her that to think would leave her in a state of hysteria. Find the crinolines immediately.

Lady Brampton continued. 'Listen well, Veronica, because you will one day have a household of your own to run. I have solved the latest servant problem and have suggested that we change provision suppliers in order to budget for the full complement of kitchen staff.'

She rose, brushing past her stepchildren with her usual disdain. 'I will change and then I am to call on Lady Taunton. Tomorrow, Veronica, we will both call on Lady Margaret while her mother is in Paris. Let me repeat myself. When you are nineteen you will come out, and you, at least, must, and will, enhance our family name. I expect you to marry well.' She swept from the room.

For a moment neither Veronica or Auberon spoke, then she turned to her brother. 'Don't inflame her. You have ground to make up. It doesn't help, it really doesn't.'

He sighed, his fair hair flopping across his left eye as it always did. He brushed it aside. 'I can't help it.'

'Yes you can, it's simple, just don't open your mouth.' Veronica shook his arm. He shrugged. 'Then it's called dumb insolence.' They both laughed.

'What's wrong with putting a few crinklies on the horses, Ver?'

She shook his arm again, exasperated. 'You know what. And what would Wainey have said?'

'Leave her out of it.' His voice was sharp and he looked into the fireplace. It had not been lit and wouldn't be until four o clock.

'Why, when she's at the heart of it? You've got to move on, you simply must, this is not what she would want.'

He gripped her hand, which still lay on his arm. 'Why did she do it, Ver? You were here, did she say anything? Yes, she was asked to leave but we would have made sure she was all right, we would have stayed close. Why would she jump, and from the balcony?'

They both looked towards the long window and the balustrade over which their father said Wainey had flung herself.

Auberon let go of her hand and leant forward, his head in his hands. His voice was muffled. 'It's my fault. I went away, and to get their own back they dismissed her. If I hadn't gone . . . How could he say she wasn't needed? She was part of the family, for God's sake. You know, I sometimes wonder if she didn't jump, but . . .' He stopped, straightened up and stared at the gold clock on the mantelpiece which his stepmother had brought with her from Headon Hall, her decrepit family pile. 'I'm sorry, Ver. I shouldn't go on, and I won't, not any more. It's over and he'll be back soon and then I'll really have to face the Furies.'

'She jumped, of course she did, Aub, don't be a fool.' Veronica was pulling him towards her, stroking his hair. 'Dearest Aub, anyone faced by him might if he was raging, and if their heart was breaking. So, never think anything else. It was just one of those terrible moments in a person's life. One day things will be better.'

She held him as though she could somehow keep

him safe, because it was all she wanted: Auberon safe. She loved him and God help her, he kept the rage of their father fixed on himself, not on her. Before Auberon, had it been her mother who did this? She could bear none of it. For a moment she thought that she would cry with fear and anguish but that must not happen, for once she started she didn't know how she would ever stop.

Chapter Six

Almost two weeks later, on Saturday, Evie prepared the breakfast porridge as usual. It was the dinner party in the evening, and Lord Brampton would arrive for luncheon. There was a degree of tension in the air that was quite new to her. Mrs Moore had not smiled once and her tone had sharpened. Twenty guests and Lord Brampton home. The air seemed too tight for anyone to breathe, but at least they had a new scullery maid and kitchen assistant.

'Colour co-ordinated food indeed,' muttered Mrs Moore, rattling the pan in which kidneys for the upstairs breakfast were being sautéed. 'Never heard the like.'

Evie had written out the menu cards as she had better hands and French, said Mrs Moore, some days before, refusing point blank to spend time chatting in the lingo just to help Evie keep hers up to scratch. Instead she'd said, 'One day you'll be hearing quite a bit of it, and that will do the job rather well, lass.' She had refused to elaborate but pointed to the sieves. 'The quenelles are calling you, and I have enough to do without teaching you extra,' she'd said firmly.

Tonight it would be clear golden soup using veal stock removed by turbot and cream sauce, removed by compote of pigeons at Lord Brampton's insistence which could hardly, even by the wildest stretch of the imagination, be called cream-coloured. On and on it went until eight courses, frequently with a cream sauce to keep within the colour parameters of cream and white, were prepared. 'To be devoured by the less than starving masses above stairs,' Mrs Moore grimaced.

'Well, good luck to those corsets, all you lords and ladies,' Evie grunted, stirring steadily as the heat from the range beat at her. The kitchen staff had been up at four thirty this morning to start and stoke the furnace, check the pantries, and get an extra hour out of the morning. The house servants were up with the lark also but the upstairs and downstairs breakfasts were at the usual times, as upstairs routine could not be disturbed.

Mrs Moore was now placing the kidneys in a pan and snapped, 'Never mind your clever remarks, Evie Anston. Stop fiddling about with the bloody porridge and do something useful. Millie, take over the porridge and get it to the servants' hall and be quick about it, if that's within the boundary of your under-standing?' Millie was from Easton, which had alarmed Evie, until her mam sorted out the need for secrecy with Millie's family. She'd been employed as the new kitchen assistant after the job had first been offered to Annie, who had refused, preferring to stay in the scullery because there was too much learning that went with cooking. Evie had said they would teach her, but it had done no good.

Evie said to Millie, 'After that lay up bowls for us and we'll have them down at the end of the table . . .'

Mrs Moore cut in, 'Evie, we'll need all the knives, sieves, every bloody thing, but pour me a cup of tea and check that those damned rabbits are on their way.' Her hands were shaking, her face pale. There was a sheen of sweat on her cheeks, her hands seemed even more stiff and swollen this morning as she tucked a strand of hair beneath her cap.

Evie wondered if she had suddenly grown an extra pair of hands to be here, there and everywhere, but the only thing she could do was to take it steady, and that was that. Millie was stirring the porridge so slowly it was painful. Evie helped her tip it into the earthenware pot leaving sufficient for the kitchen staff, then tapped the ladle on the side, resting it on the plate on the side of the range.

'It was right canny seeing Simon the other day, wasn't it?' Millie said, wiping round the edge of the pot. Evie nodded. The gardeners and stable lads had come for tea a week ago when Millie and Sarah, the new scullery maid, had joined them. Poor Sarah's hands had the look of raw beef within two days.

'Take it through now and you still haven't laid up for four down the table end.' Evie poured a cup of tea for Mrs Moore, who was rattling the pan on the range. Millie nodded, and she and Sarah took the porridge through to the staff. 'That girl can hardly be bothered to be lazy, and where's me biscuit?' snapped Mrs Moore.

Evie hurried to the biscuit barrel and popped one on the saucer for Mrs Moore. There had been another empty bottle of gin in her sitting room this morning, which meant Mrs Moore had gone through a whole one over the last two days. Perhaps it was worsening pain, perhaps the stress of the dinner party.

Evie took over the pan. 'Leave these and have your tea,' she insisted, nudging the woman away and on to her stool. They were running late but Mrs Moore needed a pick-me-up, and that was that.

Millie was back, standing by her side, looking lost. 'Now what?'

Evie snapped, 'Just put our four bowls on the table and fill them with porridge, for the third time.'

Millie flushed. 'What's the matter with everyone today?'

Mrs Moore shouted, 'What do you think, you daft bairn? We're busy with their breakfast and have to think of their luncheon as well, because his Lordship is on his way and has requested rabbit pie. Rabbit pie on a dinner-party day, I damn well ask you, not to mention a colour co-ordinated dinner for twenty-four, cream and white. What can I do with that? Cream and white and just the odd spot of colour, and you stand there . . .'

Evie interrupted, 'Just serve our porridge, Millie, and then take the pan to the scullery. Try and remember what you learned when you worked for Mrs Fredericks, that was her name wasn't it, at Gosforn? It's the same here, just a bit busier. We know you're trying to get used to it.'

She forced herself to be pleasant as she tipped the kidneys into a serving bowl, grabbed a thick cloth, jerked up the handle of the warming oven and slid in the dish. Millie slopped across to the scullery while Evie wondered why on earth Lady Brampton insisted on sautéed kidneys when they could be cooked just as adequately in the oven and she didn't eat them anyway. Today instead of toast in her room she wanted fresh fruit, a boiled egg and soldiers, for pity's sake. Soldiers? She felt her shoulders rising, felt herself on the verge of tears. They'd never do it, never get everything done.

Millie flounced out of the scullery and stood with her hands on her hips, calling, 'Anyway, our Evie, you never could count at school.' Evie swung round, tucking the oven cloth on the fender. 'There are five of us not four, so it's as well I've just put out five bowls if you cared to look, or you'd go hungry. So stick that in your pipe and smoke it.'

There was a silence as Evie stared at her, then at the five bowls, and then at Millie again, so slight, so flushed, her brown hair refusing to be imprisoned by her hat, and she remembered who she was. Evie Forbes, a miner's daughter who could handle whatever came her way because she wasn't in a bloody pit expecting the roof to come down whenever it chose. She felt the laugh begin, along with a great explosion of joy. It was only a meal. Yes, she could be dismissed without a character, but it was only a meal and they were all in it together. She roared now, and heard someone else laughing too. It was Mrs Moore. They were joined by Millie, whose relief was written all over her face, and behind her were Annie and Sarah, smiling, too tired to laugh. Poor wee lasses.

Mrs Moore slammed down her tea cup, removed her glasses and wiped her eyes. 'By, we needed that. Not the tea, the laugh.'

They all ate their porridge, the atmosphere relaxed and for Evie everything became possible, even a meeting with Simon at last, for she still had to check on the rabbits.

She and Mrs Moore finished the upstairs breakfast. Archie and James and Miss Donant collected the trays. Evie and Millie began to lay up the table for Mrs Moore and, glory be, the lass remembered at least some of the utensils. 'Good girl,' Evie murmured, 'I'll leave you to it and get the stockpot on.'

She scooped bones from the icebox, and vegetables. These she cleaned before adding them to the stock. One of the bells in the corridor rang. Millie ran to see who it was: her Ladyship. Evie said, 'Tell Miss Donant it's time to bring the tray down, she's eaten her soldiers. Likes her flesh, she does. Reckon she'd eat any one of us at the flick of a duster.'

Mrs Moore shook her head at Evie but waited

until Millie ran off to the servants' hall to find the lady's maid, then murmured, as she checked her utensils, moving the vegetable knives into one group, 'Be cautious, Evie, trust no one. If that remark about her Ladyship liking flesh goes upstairs you'll be out. Make the servants your friends, they're the only family you've got while you're here, but keep your opinions to yourself or you won't get to where you want to be.' She didn't look at Evie, but her voice was firmer than Evie had ever heard it.

'Where do I want to be?' Evie heard herself asking as she reached for her shawl. Could Mrs Moore know she was only using the Bramptons for her own ends?

'Well, perhaps somewhere the equivalent of Claridge's.' Mrs Moore sounded tired. 'You see how information travels.' She looked at Evie with a gentle smile.

Evie slipped round the table and hugged her, half expecting to be shrugged off. She wasn't. The woman just nodded, patted her hand. 'Claridge's will happen, I know it will, but you have things to learn, not just cooking, pet. Now get the rabbits and show Millie how to skin them. We need to work harder on her training. Heaven knows what Mrs Fredericks ate because there's not much sign of ability in that young woman, or is it willingness? Well, you did warn me when she came for her interview that you remembered her behaviour from school, but I thought I knew better. Ah well, she might smarten up and want to own a hotel. Stranger things have happened.' Evie grimaced and Mrs Moore laughed. 'I tell you what, our Evie, if I had the money I'd probably stay in yours, but . . .'

Evie squeezed her. 'You'll never have to pay.'

Mrs Moore laughed softly. 'Off to those rabbits and young Simon, then.'

Evie hesitated. Mrs Moore whispered, 'Remember to be cautious. Reckon even the vegetables have ears. No one's allowed to "walk out" here.' Her look was kind. Evie nodded. 'Thank you. I have remembered.'

Across the corridor the servants were bustling to their duties. Millie returned carrying a trayful of bowls which she took straight to the scullery. Above the clatter of the dishes being almost hurled into the zinc-lined sinks, Evie called, 'Millie, after you've fetched the earthenware bowl – and remember to put the scrapings into the bin for the pigs this time – would you come and help Mrs Moore, please? I'll be back with the rabbits and then I'll show you how to skin the little beggars.'

Evie headed for the door, eager to see Simon, although she knew she must hide her feelings. She'd be careful, very careful.

As she left Mrs Moore called her back. 'You'll use last evening's leftovers from upstairs for staff lunch as usual, will you? I think there's sufficient but if not there're some hocks of bacon from Home Farm.'

Evie nodded. 'I was going to make a bacon and

chicken stew with dumplings, and I'll make the pastry for the rabbit pies as well.'

'Good lass.' Mrs Moore was bustling to the pantry. 'We'll have ours here and Mrs Green will just have to put up with it. She thinks if we eat in here we're giving ourselves extras. Silly woman, we have all day to stuff our faces if that's what we want to do.' She turned and winked at Evie, for that was indeed what they wanted to do, and often did.

Evie laughed and almost ran down the bell corridor and out into the backyard, past the garages, skidding round the coal shed, past the garden store at the top of the brick path leading south along the walled garden. In the distance was the under-gardeners' house, hung with wisteria. Soon it would be in bloom, Mrs Moore said.

She had only seen Simon in passing when he brought in vegetables or house flowers but he always smiled, always looked for her. She was sure he did. She rushed down the path. It was colder here in the shadows cast by the wall and the breath jogged in her throat as she ran. The wall ended in a brick-built store. She slowed, and forced herself to approach casually. Perhaps it wouldn't be Simon who had caught the rabbits, it might be Alf, or Bernie. She called quietly, 'Hello.'

Simon stepped from the store, holding up four rabbits which hung from his hand on a string, their eyes glazed. His were as vivid blue as always and his hair as red as ever, and she had never seen him smile so broadly. 'Well, if it isn't our Evie. I thought it might be Annie or Millie yet again. Have you been avoiding me? Why do you always send *them* for herbs? Little talkers, those young madams are.'

She stopped within a yard of him. 'I don't send them, Mrs Moore decides, or they nip out before we can stop them. Anything to get away from the work.' He just laughed, and said, his voice hardly more than a whisper, 'Then you nip out instead, dead quick or we'll never get to talk and I can't tell Jack anything he might need to know.' Her smile faded. So it was only because he wanted to pass on her messages.

She brushed past him into the store, her head high, her voice low as she said, 'I've heard nothing that can help him. Brampton's not back until lunchtime. I'll do what I can then but I don't see how I can hear anything useful ever. We never mix. Mr Auberon's here, that's all I know.' She reached for the rabbits. He swung them away from her. 'I'll walk them back with you. Not a job for a lady.' A trickle of dried blood ran from the rabbits' mouths.

Perhaps he said this to the other girls too. She avoided his eyes and set off back down the path, glancing over her shoulder at him. 'I'm no lady, I'm the cook.' There was no laughter in her voice, or in her heart.

He hurried to catch her up, grabbing her hand well before they reached the top corner store. 'You listen to me, Evie Forbes.' He pulled her to a stop;

they both looked around. There was no one in sight, and no sound from the other side of the wall in the vegetable garden. 'You listen to me, Evie Anston, you're as much a lady as any of them.' His grip was tight as he raised her hand and kissed it. His lips were soft and warm. 'I used to pull your plaits, and I still want you to play tag with me. I really like you, Evie Anston. Really really like you.' His smile was wide but not as wide as hers, surely.

She wanted to stay here for ever, but they both turned as Millie called from the corner. 'There you are, we need herbs as well, and Mrs Moore says that at this rate the bloody dinner will be over by the time you get back and then where will we be, the bloody workhouse. Those were her real words, Evie.' Millie's colour was high, her eyes frightened. 'Hurry.' She turned and ran back to the house.

Simon dropped her hand, giving her a push. 'You get back with the rabbits and I'll fetch the herbs.' She began to hurry away but he called to her. 'No wait.' He came closer, talking quietly. 'Two things – tomorrow, Sunday, it's your day off, are you sea-coaling? Jack brought up your bike last week and I haven't had a chance to tell you. I'll show you where. I didn't want the kitchen to hear me mention Jack . . .' He trailed off. 'I'm going too.'

Her heart soared. 'Yes of course I'm going, man, where's my bike?' She was walking backwards, the rabbit string cutting into her fingers, they were so heavy.

'In the bothy by the big gate. It's all right, it's where we keep the gardeners' bikes and no one will notice there's an extra one. There are a load of mowers, tools and the like. I'll meet you there at three.'

He went on, 'One other thing, the valet will be back with Lord Brampton. Watch him, he thinks he's God's gift to the women and has a right to whatever, or whoever, he wants. He'll be gone in a day or two because his Lordship hardly ever stays more than that, so do a good job at ducking and diving, Evie. Any trouble, let me know.'

She recognised the frown, the thinned lips, from the playground when he'd had to fight his way into Jack's gang, and she laughed. 'I'll be fine.'

He nodded, she too and then he hurried back down the brick path, turning right towards the walled garden. 'I'll get the herbs and will be bringing the flowers for the table, the colour co-ordinated ones.' Bernie stood at the entrance. 'Where you been, lad? The boss's foaming at the mouth.'

She ran to the kitchen, the rabbits bumping her legs, their clotted blood catching on her apron but she didn't care, because he did, or seemed to. Once back she hung her shawl in the corridor and wiped her boots, hurrying into the warmth. 'Here they are,' she called, holding up the rabbits, then slowed, for Annie, Sarah and Millie were standing close to Mrs Moore, who sat on her usual stool, and beckoned to her.

'Hurry up, I need to tell you all something even though I'm too busy, but Mrs Green wants you to know, so know you will. You will not even mention that it has been said, is that clear?' Her lips were as thin as Simon's had been.

The younger girls looked at Evie and their anxiety was clear. Were they to be sent away when they'd just arrived? What on earth had happened? Evie stood with them, the rabbits swinging on their string, her fingers white and numb. Mrs Moore murmured, keeping her finger on her place in her recipe book, 'His Lordship is back with Roger, his valet, though he is no longer his valet.'

The girls tried to follow what they were being told. Millie moved her lips as she repeated what she had heard. 'What do you mean?' Annie asked.

Mrs Moore snatched a quick look at the list of chores she had drawn up for the dinner, then back to the girls, frowning, preoccupied. 'I'm getting to that. The valet has been told he is to remain here as Mr Auberon's valet. Annie, you know that we have a slight problem with Roger.'

Annie nodded. 'He can't keep his bits in his trousers.'

Mrs Moore shook her head in exasperation. Evie laughed. Mrs Moore snapped, 'And that's enough from you, Evie Anston. What I'm trying to say is that you mustn't be swayed by any soft talking. Remember, you will be dismissed out of the door if there's any of those goings-on. It's never the men, always the women who are left with the bun in the oven and you'll go, with no character and a babe on the way, and end up on the streets or in the workhouse.' Millie moaned, and started to cry. Evie put her arm around the girl. 'It won't happen to you, Millie, if you listen.'

Mrs Moore shook her head impatiently. 'The point is, apparently Roger's in a real fret at being passed to Mr Auberon. He sees it as a right slight, which it is. So stay out of his way in case he tries to prove he's top cock-bird.'

Millie looked even more scared, but then she had been a scaredy-cat ever since her da had been killed in a pit explosion when she was a bairn, and who wouldn't be, Evie supposed. It had taken off her brother's arm too and now, rather than the workhouse, they lived with her mam at an aunt's. Her mam cleaned for the head clerk at Hawton Pit.

Evie held up the rabbits. 'Come on, Millie, we have important things to do. Let me show you how to skin a rabbit, and if anyone is a nuisance to us, we'll nip off his tail and skin 'im.' Everyone laughed and the mood was broken. What a fuss about nothing. Evie scooted Millie along before her to the cold room, and the heavy piece of slate on which they'd skin the rabbit.

Auberon left the safety of the Blue Sitting Room and approached the library, which was further along the landing at the front of the house. He had been summoned by his father after a lunch of mushroom soup and rabbit pie and no dessert, just fruit and cheese as per Lord Brampton's instructions. Auberon hated rabbit but had eaten well, for his father couldn't bear people poking and prodding their food like namby-pambies.

He stopped on the landing, looking out over the front lawn to the old cedar tree. The sun was shining across the Indian carpet on which he stood. He studied the pattern, breathing deeply, squaring his shoulders, and was about to knock when Veronica called softly, 'Aub.'

He spun round. She was tiptoeing towards him, her hair fluffed and radiantly blonde, like a halo. What on earth had she done with it? He'd wondered that at lunch, but had decided against a remark. One didn't make remarks when his father was in residence. She said, 'Remember what Mother said. Listen to him, agree with him, and then find a way to do what you feel is right, regardless. All will be well.'

Her hand was shaking as she touched his arm. She added, 'Please say you haven't been drinking?'

'Only a brandy. Could you face the bugger without one?'

'Shhh.' She held up her hand. 'Be quiet, he'll hear.'

Auberon felt his legs go to jelly. It was the usual feeling. He checked his watch. Three o'clock. On the dot. It had to be on the dot. Veronica faded away, up the stairs to her bedroom, to change, to hide, perhaps to do something with her hair? What the hell was he doing, thinking of hair? He knocked. At the sound of his father's voice he entered, shutting the door behind him, holding on to the doorknob for a moment, feeling he'd fall to the floor if he let go.

His father stood in front of his desk, facing him across what always seemed like a huge expanse. The window overlooking the front lawn was behind him, and the other walls were lined with books. Had his father read any? He knew he had not. In their old house they'd had a library and Auberon had spent hours there every evening, reading about the past. His tutor, Mr Saunders, had shared his passion for history until his father had dismissed him and sent Auberon to a public school to make a man of him.

'Stop slouching and get over here.' The voice was cold, but when wasn't it? The face was fierce, but when wasn't it? Auberon walked across the carpet. It was also Indian. No two patterns were the same. Why was he thinking of such trivia?

He stood facing his father and never saw the hand lifting, so fast was it. He just felt it backhanding across his face. He felt his lips burst. His father said, 'I will not be called a bugger. I will not be shown any lack of respect in my own house, is that quite clear?'

The blow was no surprise. Why would it be? 'Yes, that's clear, Father.'

His lips wouldn't work properly, but that wasn't a surprise either. He braced himself. The next blow caught him in the ribs. He felt the crack, and the pain. 'I will not have my money spent by some idle drunkard who is presumably weeping and wailing because his little Wainey is no longer here, and whose fault is that, may I ask?'

The next blow caught him above the kidneys as his father stepped forward quickly, and then retreated, on his toes, like a boxer, or a ballet dancer. Should he share that thought? He almost laughed, but felt too sick, and fought to stay upright when all he wanted was to crumple to the floor. His father moved again and he was backhanded again across his face, the signet ring catching his cheekbone. He usually kept his blows to the body so no one would know. He must be very, very angry. 'I asked you whose fault it is?'

Auberon tasted the blood from his lips. 'Mine,' he murmured, wanting to groan.

'Why?' His father lifted on to his toes and Auberon flinched but no blow fell, instead those hands, so large, so hard, remained by his sides. Auberon's grandfather had such hands too, but he had never lifted them against his grandchildren. Had he against his own son? Well, who was going to ask that question of his father? 'Why?' his father bellowed.

Auberon made himself focus, stay in the moment, stay upright. His voice must not shake. He said, 'I asked to go to Oxford. I insisted. I said I had some money from Mother if you wouldn't pay. I went. You dismissed Wainey because I wasn't here. If I'd stayed and not been selfish she would not have . . . She would not have died. There would have been no reason.'

His father nodded, head on one side, listening. His mother had been right. Say what he wanted to hear, but the devil was that it *was* his fault. He should have stayed.

His father lounged back against his desk, crossing his arms. The knuckles on his right hand were bruised. 'Finally, is your mother's money mine, or yours?'

'Yours, Father.' It wasn't. It had been left by his maternal grandfather to his daughter, and thence in trust to Veronica and Auberon. There had been a substantial bequest from his mother to Wainey too, in gratitude for her enduring role of support which she had never received. He looked beyond the man he hated to the sea in the distance. One day he would set sail for France and never return until his father was gone from here, hopefully in a wooden box, utterly dead.

Yes, he would take a boat across the Channel and then a train to Paris. From there he would head for the river Somme, which Mr Saunders had said was the Celtic name for tranquillity. He wanted to feel tranquil, just once, and he thought perhaps he would there. A wide river, meandering . . .

'Listen to me, boy.' It was a growl.

Auberon could barely breathe because of the pain from his ribs. They were cracked, he knew because they'd been cracked several times before, and the throbbing from his kidneys and face was beating in time with his heart. 'You are a disgrace but seem to have no shame. Am I going to have to get the belt?' His father was upright, balanced on his toes again.

Auberon almost laughed. The belt? He wasn't a child but when had that made a difference? At least his father had never laid a hand on Veronica. How strange. Women, it seemed, were exempt from his father's moods, or were they? Again he thought of Wainey. His father dismissed her, so had she argued? Did he become angry? Did she back away from him out on to the balcony? Did he come closer, closer? Did she tumble over the balustrade or did he forget himself and push her? Or did she really jump? He had to stop this. Stop. Stop. His father said again, 'I repeat, do I have to get the belt?'

'No, Father, you won't have to get the belt. I am listening.' It hurt to speak. Everything hurt, it had hurt for rather a long time. Again he almost laughed. What was the matter with him? He used to cry.

His father moved to stand by the window. Auberon dared not move though his back ached, and his legs trembled. He shifted his weight from his toes to his heels and back again as they'd been taught in the Officer Training Cadet Force at school.

'You will not return to Oxford. Instead you will

become a man here, under my guidance. Rustication is no laughing matter.' His father glared.

Oh God, was he laughing after all? Apparently not, for his father continued. 'You have wasted my money, heedless of the pressure these cretins are bringing to bear with this People's Budget. But just wait, the House of Lords will wipe the smile off their faces because no damned idlers are going to get pensions paid for by us.' He was banging his fist into his hand as though he was in some music-hall melodrama. 'Meanwhile I can do without pathetic creatures like you adding to my problems.'

Auberon nodded. 'I understand, Father.' Say what he wants to hear, he prompted himself, trying to move his lips as little as possible. He swallowed down the blood. He knew his words were slurred. His father was waving his hand as though conducting a ruddy orchestra as he continued.

'You will recover the money you have cost me by sitting on the shoulders of Manager Davies at Easton Colliery. You will learn the business. There is trouble coming because I'll screw down the wages on the back of the Eight-Hour Act. You will teach them a lesson if they dare to strike. In addition you are to cut back on props, on anything you can find, to make the bloody place more efficient, more productive. And don't forget Froggett's three houses. They are to be bought immediately because they're a loose end, and I want it tied, and I want it tied cheaply. They will not go to any pitman, is that clear? I want the workers tied to their cottages, I want them scared of eviction, I want them working like bloody maniacs. So I don't care what you have to do, but get those houses.'

He was stabbing the air now, aiming at Auberon's face. His father would make a good killer. Oh yes, indeed he would. Again he thought of the balcony.

'There will be no shooting, hunting, or the season. I will return here more often.' His father left the window and approached. Auberon felt the fear overwhelm him. More often? How often? Closer and closer his father drew until he was against him, his breath full on Auberon's face. It was then that his father smelt the brandy.

The fists came again, faster and faster but on his ribs because there was less to be seen, and this evening there was a dinner party. That was what he thought of as he tasted his tears. It was then his father stopped, triumphant. 'You are a coward and an appalling failure.'

Auberon was dismissed. He found the door somehow, and looked to left and right to check there were no servants about, but they never were, they knew their place and he must know his. He made himself climb the stairs to his room, the pain catching him with every step, and he knew he must make a success at the mine. What the hell would happen if he didn't? He pushed the fear from him and instead drew in France, drew in the Somme.

Were there kingfishers? He would take a boat. He would fish. Nearly at the top of the stairs now, thank God.

Mrs Moore struggled to her sitting room once the dinner had been cleared and the pots, pans, utensils and plates were being washed. It was midnight and the visiting chauffeurs had gone, the servants' hall the poorer without their uniforms and boots. The footmen and housemaids were washing the glasses and silver in the butler's pantry but were also still on duty, should hot chocolate be required by the family.

Evie wiped down the table for perhaps the final time that day and slipped out into the night for a last long breath of air, knowing that her cooking had helped to create a success and she had many more tips for her recipe book. She felt proud and satisfied as she tugged her shawl over her head against the chill and held it close around her neck, gazing up at the stars. Would Jack and Timmie be sleeping, or were they struggling in from their shift? Was Simon sleeping, or standing somewhere, stargazing too? There were owls hooting and from the stable yards came the huffing of the horses, and the clip as they moved from hoof to hoof.

She walked quietly across the cobbles heading for Tinker, Lady Veronica's old pony Evie had taken a carrot from the pantry for her. As she entered the yard she saw a stable lad standing beneath the oil lamp that hung on an upright near her stable. What's more, for God's sake, he was smoking. She called, 'What d'you think you're doing, man? Put out that cigarette or you'll have the place in flames. Think of the horses. You'll be dismissed, you fool.' She was running across, slipping on the cobbles, turning her ankle more than once. 'Put it out.'

As she ran, Lady Veronica's two dachshunds started skittering across to her as they rounded the corner from the drive, yapping and snarling. Good grief, it was turning into a riot. She slowed, trying to hush the dogs, who continued to rush about like creatures possessed. The lad was ignoring her so she snatched the cigarette from his hand as she reached him, stamping on it. 'You'll be dismissed, why don't you listen? Lady Veronica will be here in a minute after the damn dogs.'

Tinker was neighing now and jerking her head as she looked out of her stall. The lad stumbled out of the pool of light as he turned, swearing, treading on one of the dachshunds. It yelped, and both dogs ran back towards the front of the house, then one returned. Oh God, the last thing they needed was Lady Veronica swanning round the corner. Evie managed to catch the lad, holding his arm, keeping him from falling. In the gloom she couldn't see who it was.

'You smell of booze, get to bed and pull yourself together, you stupid beggar. You'll not be up in time to sweep the damned yard for this lot of idle layabouts, and think of the horses. What if they'd gone up in flames? Come on, hurry up. Her Ladyship will be here, hot on the trail of the sausages.' She was tired, it was cold. She needed her bed. The dog was jumping up at her.

He wrenched himself free, and for a moment it looked as though he would strike her. Evie stepped away but then he dropped his arm, saying, 'How dare you speak to me like that, or at all? How bloody dare you?' Evie froze. This was no stable lad, it was Brampton's whelp. The second dog came rushing round the corner, yapping, and now both were running in circles around Evie and Mr Auberon. Lady Veronica was calling, almost hissing really, 'Currant, Raisin, come here. Aub, where on earth are you? Come in and don't make it any worse.'

Mr Auberon said, '*Il faut parler français, nous avons des serviteurs ici.*'

Did he really think Evie wouldn't understand that he was warning his sister to speak in French in front of the servants? Thank God for Miss Manton. Evie turned, modifying her voice, hoping it was unrecognisable, hoping he was too drunk to remember the sight of her. 'I'm sorry, sir.' She should say that, she thought. Perhaps she should also explain that she had thought he was just a stable lad, but she was damned if she would. No one was 'just' anything.

'Aub, come on,' Veronica hissed. '*Vite.*'

As he turned to leave she saw his face, at last, in the lamplight, his poor battered face. She watched as he managed to pull himself upright, ease back his shoulders and call Currant and Raisin softly to him. 'Come on lads.' He left without a backward glance. They had been told that Mr Auberon had been unwell and unable to attend the dinner, so his place setting was to be removed. Mr Harvey had been unamused. 'Too much brandy, no doubt,' he had muttered. 'Now we have to measure up the place settings again.'

'Too much something, but it wasn't brandy,' Evie muttered to herself as she turned away, because she had seen the result of Jack's fist fights too often not to recognise the result of blows. She had heard the gossip and here it was, confirmed. She shuddered that a father could do that to a son as she made her way back to the kitchen, where the light and warmth comforted her. Millie came out of the scullery with the broom, almost dropping with tiredness. 'Is it good enough?' Millie's anxiety was palpable as she pointed to the floor. Annie and Sarah were just behind her, pale as ghosts.

Evie took the broom from her. 'It's good enough, and that's all that's required. You've done well.' There was too much fear about the place tonight. 'I'll swab the floor, you put out a pan in case hot chocolate is required, and then you can change into your ball clothes without the aid of a fairy godmother and fly on up to bed.' Millie laughed.

Evie let them all go to bed and she reached hers by two in the morning almost insensible with tiredness, but in spite of that she merely dozed: would tomorrow bring her dismissal? And how was that poor young lad?

Chapter Seven

The next morning breakfast came and went with no summons from Mrs Green, or Mr Harvey. Mrs Moore shouted at her as she burned the kidneys, and took her into the ice room, asking what the devil had got into her. 'Devilled kidneys they wanted,' she continued. 'Not Auld Maud lookalikes, you silly lass.'

Evie told her. Mrs Moore flushed. 'We'll know by luncheon. In the meantime work and say nothing. And concentrate. Always concentrate, it will get you through most things, pet.'

The morning dragged. She collected herbs from the gardeners' store but it was Sidney, not Simon, who was there, checking the baskets of flowers, and Evie could have stamped. She hurried back towards the kitchen. As she crossed the yard towards the steps down to the basement Roger, the valet, emerged from the bell corridor and mounted the steps. He pressed himself to one side as she passed, but reached out, holding her back, his hand on her arm. She dropped some rosemary and it fell on to the lower steps. She pulled away, stooping to gather it, and he stooped with her, his head too close, his hands brushing hers as she scrabbled for the herb.

'Let me,' he said. She shook her head. 'It's my job. Please don't.' Her voice was sharp. He laughed, his breath, peppermint-flavoured, in her face.

'Life isn't just work, you know, Evie. It is Evie, isn't it? Perhaps we could have a little chat soon, get to know one another better?'

Evie gathered up the last of the rosemary and rose quickly, so quickly that he staggered. Let's not, she wanted to say. But she remembered to be careful; after last night, would she ever forget? Last night: had Mrs Moore heard anything? 'I must go,' she said, rushing down the remaining steps and into the kitchen.

Mrs Moore shook her head, mouthing, 'You'd have heard by now, so stop worrying.' But it was only when an earlier than usual luncheon of mock turtle soup, removed by dressed salmon and dressed cucumber, removed by rump of beef à la jardinière, removed by jelly in glasses and damson tart was served that she could relax, and she felt as though she would never worry about anything again because nothing could be as bad as those last hours.

Evie baked scones and fancies watching the clock on and off, for her free afternoon began at three. 'Do extra and take them to your family. Sea-coaling is hungry work,' Mrs Moore murmured before she went to rest. 'No need to mention it to the others.' She winked as she took a cup of tea and left the kitchen. She reappeared to check that Millie had cleared the table in the servants' hall, and looked in on the scullery maids who were clattering the pots and pans. 'I'll unlatch the pantry window if you're late back, but remember the creaking stair,' she whispered to Evie as she limped out again.

She must hurry. She had sieved the flour and now rubbed in the butter, watching Mrs Green through the windows as she busied herself checking that her housemaids had completed their tidying of the sitting rooms while the Bramptons took luncheon. It was Mrs Green who should be making these fancies for the upstairs afternoon tea, but Mrs Moore had taken over the task when originally faced with the sad little lumps which masqueraded as scones and fancies under the housekeeper's heavy hands. The task had been passed over to Evie, pretty smartly, when she arrived. No mention must be made to Mr Harvey though, Mrs Moore had said, with a finger to her lips.

At last everything was baked and cooled, and as she changed into her home clothes the relief of not being dismissed made her feel as though she weighed a mere few stones and to crown it all, Simon had said he'd be waiting from three. Stopping only to pick up the bag of hessian aprons, cakes and scones she ran down the back track, but only for the first hundred yards, at which point the breath was jagged in her chest and her legs felt as heavy as Mrs Green's fancies. Instead she walked as briskly as she could, with the clouds racing across the sky and the wind strong enough to throw up huge waves at Fordington. The sea coal would be grand.

To her right, in between the silver birches, she could see the lawns stretch for what seemed like miles, and in the centre the cedar tree stood majestically. Further over, beyond the sweeping drive, the arboretum was threatening to burst into leaf. Did Simon prune those trees? Or did he put leather shoes on the horse, hitch up the mower and take care of the lawns? Or maybe both jobs, maybe neither? She realised that she knew so little of the lad she was sure she loved.

There was the bothy over to the right of the gates, thatch-roofed and almost hidden by rhododendrons and there, too, was Simon, holding the handlebars of her bike and his own. He walked out from the trees, looking from left to right, for bicycles were not approved of for the female staff. Presumably they were to walk everywhere, unless they caught a lift on a cart.

She ran again, snatching off her felt hat and waving it. 'I'm free,' she laughed. 'Free!'

His face was alight with mirth. 'Then let's get going. Did you bring your apron? You'll need it.'

'Two.'

He pushed her bike towards her. 'That's my girl. Saddle up.' For a moment she was reminded of the stable yard last night, but the sun broke through the clouds and Simon pedalled away, down the road leading to Easton, leading home. My girl, he had called her, my girl. She adjusted her hat, took to the saddle and followed him, relishing the sense of freedom that speed brought. 'Wait for me,' she called, pedalling hard, head down. As she did so she decided to say nothing of last night and Mr Auberon. She had been a fool. She would learn by it, and the fewer people who knew about it the better.

Half an hour later they sped through Easton and on to the road leading to Fordington. It was easy going over the tarmac surface and Simon called across to Evie as they puffed up the hill together, 'Economies, eh? But new smooth roads for the Rolls-Royce, eh?'

Once up the hill the tarmac road turned off for Gosforn and in due course to Durham, but Evie and Simon continued towards the sea along the rutted track, settling into a steady but jolting pace with hedges and verges either side. They talked of their jobs, of the Brampton family, and Simon told her that the talk was that the whelp Auberon was going to be taking over some position at Auld Maud as a punishment for his debts, boozing, and being chucked out of Oxford University. 'That comes courtesy of Roger the Dodger. When we know for sure we should let Jack know, or perhaps we should do that today?' Simon said. 'By the way, lass, has Roger made a play for you?'

Evie shrugged. 'He just offered to help. I was in a rush and ignored him.'

'Keep it like that.' He looked angry for a moment. 'He's just trouble, as that daft lass Charlotte found out. She's not the first by a long shot, so they say.'

Evie was unconcerned because she could handle any man, having grown up with a brother like Jack who'd shown her how to fight. But she had something she needed to ask after last night. 'What's Bastard Brampton really like?' They pedalled over a bridge, the stream high because there had been a great deal of rain during the week. There were sheep up on the hills. Over to the south there were the workings of Sidon Colliery and to the north, Hawton Pit. Slag heaps were dotted like smoking sulphuric tussocks as far as the eye could see. Her father said that the Empire was built on coal, and one day she'd like to make sure the bloody Empire knew it was her family's backs that had hoisted out that coal. She realised that Simon hadn't answered her. She looked at him, at the length of his eyelashes, the set of his jaw.

He looked at her now. 'He lives up to his name, let's just say that, handy with his fists and not the person to have as a father. He's black as coal right through to the other side. Heard it said by Miss Wainton that his first wife was different, fair, good to her staff. His money came from his father, who rolled up his sleeves and set up the steelworks and then the brickworks. It was this Brampton who bought up the two collieries on top of all that, so I suppose he wants to prove himself by milking them for all their worth. Money is his god. The present lady of the manor has the same focus, so Miss Wainton said. Money and power.'

Ahead there were some cattle on the road, being herded by a farmer with two sheepdogs and a whippet that was off doing its own thing. They stopped and hauled their bikes on to the verge as he drove the cattle past with calls of 'Hoy-ah'. The beasts' coats steamed and they seemed to veer towards them, and then away, nodding and huffing at Simon as though in approval. Evie grinned, snatching a look at Simon, only to find him smiling at her. 'They like you,' he called above the noise. They waited until the dogs, the farmer and his charges had passed along, and then set off again, but Simon hadn't finished.

'Bastard Brampton's getting a bit of a smile growing on his chops these days, Roger the Dodger says, because them Germans are building all these ships, which means we are too, and who'll be providing the steel? Could it be Brampton's got his head in the trough? Aye, he most certainly has, so he'll get richer, and you just wait and see, we'll get poorer. Not a nice bugger to be working our fingers to the bone for.'

Evie nodded, swerving to avoid a huge hole. 'I thought you liked the gardening?'

The sun was shining now. It was only another few hundred yards to the beach and they'd be in time to help bring up the coal. Simon said, 'Aye, I do but

I miss being part of a marra group, having someone watching my back. I'm an outsider. You'll see when we get there; I'll be welcome but not part of them, not in the gang. They went one way, I went the other, our Evie.'

Evie understood, because it was true. She said, 'You can be in my gang, lad.'

He laughed, throwing his head back so far he nearly lost his cap. 'I intend to be, bonny lass.' As they entered the beach, her heart soared as high as the gulls which were tumbling and rising in the chaotic wind.

They left their bikes propped up on the dunes where others had tumbled theirs and traipsed along to the north, looking for the Forbes and Preston cart. The wind was so brisk that she snatched her hat off and rammed it into the pocket of the tweed coat Miss Manton had passed on to her last winter. Simon did the same with his cap. They searched until they saw them, down near the surf, and ran, Simon leading then stopping, waiting for her to catch up. 'By, you need to get a bit of steam up, lass.'

'Steam up yourself,' she said, pushing him so that he lost his balance as she took off again towards the sea. 'I'll beat you,' she called, running as though her life depended on it, but she heard him panting, heard him in pursuit, as she slipped and stumbled through the dark coal-solled sand, until he was abreast of her. Her father was looking at them as he emptied a sack of wet coal into the back of the cart, and laughing. They arrived together, though Simon could easily have sprinted yards ahead.

'I've missed you, Da,' she called as he jumped down from the cart, threw down the sack and held out his arms. She ran into them, smelling coal, smelling home. 'Aye pet, me too. Your mam's over by Miss Manton,' he said into her hair. 'And where's your hat, there's a bite in the air.'

She pulled away. 'Miss Manton?'

Her father grinned and raised his eyebrows. 'Aye, that brother of hers thinks that we're heathens who need to be gathered up and lugged off to church, or something like that. Perhaps he needs to talk to Brampton about our woes, because he thinks he's God, wouldn't you say? Your mam's been waiting for you, get yourself over there.' Her da held out his hand to Simon. 'You giving us a hand here, lad? Your da will be pleased to see you, but that's not to say we're not.'

Evie headed for her mother, who was wearing a coat, and had slung a shawl around her head. Evie recognised the coat as Miss Manton's mother's that had hung on a hook in the vicarage hall for years. Pure wool it was, lots of warmth in it. By, that Miss Manton was a grand woman. The gulls were screaming, the surf was pounding and all around were the calls of the men and the clatter of coal as it was poured from sacks into carts, and shovelled to one end.

She waved, running now, back up the beach, her

arms outstretched, to her mam. It was so good to be here, to have Mam's arms around her, to say into her neck as her mam kissed and kissed her, 'I baked extra scones and fancies, Mam. Mrs Moore said why not but don't shout about it. She's so nice, she really is.'

Her mother laughed. 'Draw breath, pet.' She patted and then released her daughter. 'Say hello to Miss Manton.'

Evie turned, not sure whether to shake her hand. What would be correct, with a former employer? Miss Manton took control, stepping forward and kissing her cheek. She smelt of lavender water, whereas her mother smelt of soda crystals and toil. 'Evie, you look so well, a bit tired but that's to be expected I suppose, and of course Mrs Moore is a nice woman. Do you think I would have sent you to an ogre? But how is she?'

The wind was whipping much harder and the sand stung their faces. It was tearing the words from their mouths and over everything was the crash and roar of the surf.

Evie hesitated. Miss Manton said, 'The truth now.'

Evie shouted above the wind. 'She's drinking, and her poor joints are swollen, but she's doing her job and she's just lovely, and I'm learning such a lot and Millie's standing in for me this afternoon, and I stand in for her . . .'

Miss Manton laughed. 'Slow down.' But then she waved to someone behind Evie, who turned. It was

Jack, lovely lovely Jack. She flew into his arms, and he lifted her up and spun her round. 'You look grand, bonny lass, just grand. But we've missed you. Haven't we, Timmie?' He put her down and she saw Timmie was running up behind him. He lifted and spun her round too. Surely he'd grown? But it had only been a couple of weeks, so he couldn't have.

'Evie, I'm down the pit now. I'm a trapper,' he said, putting her down, giving her time to find a smile, to find words that wouldn't be a shout of rage. 'That's grand, bonny lad, just grand.'

She looked at Jack, who shrugged and mouthed, 'His decision.' Timmie was grinning, and she saw him properly for the first time for months and months. Of course he was down the pit, he was not a bairn, he was thirteen, tall and solid and strong, like Jack. He had chocolate eyes like Jack, and shoulders like Jack, and now there'd be scars, blue-black scars. Jack nodded, knowing her thoughts, knowing the sadness.

She took Timmie's hands in hers. 'I was ignoring the fact that you are old enough and bad enough to be a pitman.' Everyone laughed, she grinned, then looked at her mam. 'I just didn't want to see it. He's our baby, isn't he, Mam, and he's to be careful, very careful.'

Her mother was standing close now, and shouted as the wind banked up, 'He's no fool, are you, lad? You'll listen to your da and your brother or you'll feel my hand at the back of your head.' She laughed and it reached her eyes, because she was a pitman's mother and a pitman's wife and you had to believe in their safety until you were shown otherwise, or you were no good to man or beast.

Her da was calling to them and beckoning. Jack pulled her arm. 'Come on, get your apron on and give us a hand. The wholesalers are all here so we'll do well. What about you, Miss Manton? Are you coming to heave some coal?' He was laughing, her lovely strong big brother was laughing, and Timmie too. Carbon copies they were. They all started to head to the cart except for Miss Manton, who held up her hand and shouted against the noise. 'I'll go and support Edward. He feels that if the mountain won't come to Muhammad then Muhammad must go to the mountain.'

Jack shouted back, 'Aye, well start by telling him he's flogging a dead horse, that most of them are chapel, if they're anything.'

Miss Manton was pulling a shawl tightly around her coat as she set off towards her brother, who was about two hundred yards along the beach towards Lea End. 'It's the anything he's after,' she smiled.

Jack watched her go, snatching a look at the parson, and then saying quietly, 'God damn it.' Evie caught the concern and saw its cause. Jack raised his voice and sprinted after Miss Manton. 'Look, tell him to turn back this way. He doesn't want to go any further down that end. The Lea End lot are rough, they're after the coal, not fire and brimstone, and they'll be drinking themselves daft. They won't take kindly. Let me go, I'm quicker.'

Miss Manton held him back, her gloved hand on his arm. 'You're kind, but I'll do it. Get that coal on board your cart, the Prestons are hard at it, and they'll be letting you know that any minute now.' She plodded on.

Evie and her family hurried down to the cart where Simon and his father Alec were shovelling and stacking. Jack punched Simon on the arm. 'Here to do some real work for a change then, Si?'

'Need to help those less able to help themselves, bonny lad,' Simon said with a grin, taking another sack from his father and shovelling hard. Evie took one from her da who was up on the cart. He gave her thick gloves too. 'You need to keep your hands clean, lass, and should wear them anyway now you're an adult.' Her father jumped down from the cart.

She ignored him and snapped at Jack, dragging on the gloves, 'Pitmen aren't the only workers, you claggy waster. Simon's at it for hours, he was hedging and ditching all week.' She strode off across the beach, harvesting coal as Jack's laugh followed her, and his words. 'Si, you've a defender there.'

She looked over her shoulder at Simon, who was grinning again. 'Never hurts to have a gang,' he said. He looked at her and nodded. She returned to her work. Aye, they were in a gang together. All was well, very well.

They worked for an hour before Mam called a halt. She'd fetched the fancies and scones from Evie's rear-wheel box, and her own bread and jam butties and beer, and they all huddled in the lee of the cart. Alec looked tired. He'd drawn an abnormal placement in the latest cavil, just about the worst seam in the pit, the hardest and the least productive. He shrugged when Simon commiserated. 'Well, next time we draw lots my luck'll change. It could be Jack's turn.' He nodded towards Jack, who laughed. 'Ah, we'll see, man. Lady Luck'll decide.'

Alec's marra Steve was picking up coal nearer the wholesalers with his family and waved, calling, 'Any leavings from them cakes, send 'em across.' Simon looked at Evie, who nodded. Her mam packed a few fancies into some greaseproof paper. Simon took it, the wind whipping his hair. He turned to go, then swung back. 'Grand cakes these are, Evie. But Da, or Bob, isn't there a better way than the cavil?'

Timmie answered, 'Only someone who's not a pitman would ask that. It's democracy in action, lad, and don't you forget it.' He was stuffing a third jam butty in his mouth and spat crumbs as he said, 'And don't get the old 'uns on to the pit today, Si, or you'll have 'em both tub-thumping and it's too cold.'

Simon laughed, then sprinted across to Steve's family while Jack and Bob cuffed Timmie gently. Mam shook her head at Evie. 'Nothing changes, bonny lass.'

She was sitting on an upturned orange box, with

her feet set firmly on the sand, and Evie knew that she would never forget this scene. How she had missed them all, how thankful she was that nothing had changed – all the men were here, and in one piece. She'd have to talk to Timmie about Simon not being a pitman, but not now.

'How're we going with the savings, Jack?' she asked quietly as he came to stand by her, viewing the sky, measuring how much daylight remained. They would travel back as late as they needed, but it grew hard to gather the coal beyond a certain time.

'Not there yet, pet,' her brother said. 'It'd be canny to get another big fight, the smaller ones are all right and give us a little and it's good Da's on a better wage, not piecework, so that's putting more into the pot. But I reckon there'll be a strike when the eight hours comes in.' He took a gulp of his beer before setting it down in the sand. Around them some were eating, drinking, others were still working. 'But you see, lass, if we go out, we'll need the house right enough because I'll be earmarked even more. Jeb's all right because he lives outside the village, on his own land.' Evie could see from his knuckles and black eye that he'd fought again.

Her mother was handing out the remaining scones. Evie refused. She could always have them, her family couldn't. Simon and his father were talking quietly as they sipped beer. Jack ate his scone in one mouthful and wiped his mouth with the back of his hand. Timmie was drinking water, as Da wouldn't allow him beer, and he grimaced as he slurped. 'It's not fair, I do a man's job, them trapdoors are heavy, and we have to be sharp and quick so's not to disrupt the airflow, but still let the wagons through,' he muttered to Jack and Evie.

Jack laughed. 'You deserve a slurp after such a long grumble. Here, have some of mine, but take it steady.' He handed the tin mug to his brother. Evie smiled as Timmie took a gulp, coughed, choked. Evie thumped him on the back, turning to laugh at her mam who was calling, 'That'll teach you, lad.' But as she did so she saw Miss Manton about a hundred yards away, running towards them, waving, her hat falling from her head. It was bowled along the beach by the wind but Miss Manton didn't stop, she just kept waving, and calling. But what? She was too far away, the wind too strong, the gulls too noisy and the surf was raging and thudding into the beach far more violently than earlier.

Behind her, a good seventy yards or so, there was something . . . What was it? Men dragging something . . . No, perhaps not something, was it someone, towards the sea? She looked from that to Miss Manton, who was nearer now but still indistinct. Where was the parson? He'd been further up that end, hadn't he?

Miss Manton was still calling. And where *was* the damned parson? Evie remembered Mrs Moore telling her she was surprised he even managed to cross the street on his own. Evie gripped Jack's arm,

143

pointing, words not coming because she didn't know what it was she needed to say. Timmie and Jack turned. Jack looked from the running woman to the scene behind her, far behind her.

He shook off Evie's hand, shouting, 'Stay here, you too, Timmie. Da, come *now*, it's the parson. We're needed, so call your marras. Ben's away by the surf, and what about Sam?' He glanced around. 'Alec, get Steve and the marras, looks like the parson's gone where he shouldn't, bloody fool, and why the hell he doesn't listen . . .' He was already running, with Timmie close behind, and Evie. 'Stay here, I said,' he threw over his shoulder.

Timmie and Evie exchanged a look and didn't break stride.

Jack dug his toes into the sand, forcing himself ever faster. Bloody fool, bloody churchy fool, he chanted in his head. Didn't I say don't go down there? He was pumping his arms, searching for Martin. He saw him at his cart, nearer to the dunes. He called, beckoning him to follow. 'Get the others, parson's in for a ducking,' he shouted. Behind he could hear the breath of pitmen who were not used to running and didn't have the chests for it but they'd keep up with him, because that's what they did.

He passed Miss Manton who was crying, bowed over, her hands on her knees, struggling for breath, hair streaming from her bun. He didn't stop as she reached for him, but tore himself free. Behind he heard Evie call, 'Go to my mam.' Her voice was ragged, her breath harsh. He hadn't time to tell his sister yet again to go back, and what good would it do? He half smiled. They were closing in on the group, who were shouting and singing as they dragged Parson Manton nearer and nearer to the surf. If they threw the man in there, God help him. Jack laughed harshly at those words. Well, the parson was the right person to ask for that sort of help. The rest of them were a lost cause.

He snatched a look behind. The marra groups were with him, and others had stopped their work and were joining them, leaving the coal to the women. And there, behind Evie, was Simon. Well, he wouldn't be in the first wave, he'd see to that. He wasn't going to jeopardise anyone Evie loved, and no way could the lad go to work with a face like a bruiser. It was a shame, he was a canny fighter.

The sea-coalers from Lea End had spotted them and were fanning out, creating a jeering barrier between the parson and the oncoming Easton and Hawton pitmen. Jack knew they'd be drunk, they wouldn't be thinking clearly, they'd be easy. He headed down to the surf to flank them and get at Manton. His da would know to spearhead the charge on the right flank. He gestured to his own marra group. 'To the left, the left, we need to break a way through near the surf, because he won't survive the waves, they're bloody giants.' He heard them behind him, heard Simon call to Evie, 'Stay back, let us do this. You too, Timmie.'

Jack swung round. 'Not you, Si, stay with Evie and Timmie, keep them back.' He nearly tripped, staggered, felt his knee twist, but righted himself. His group were with him, his father was pitching into the barrier higher up, arms swinging, the others on his heels roaring head down into the melee.

Jack used his fists as they tore into the lower section and had the parson in his sights. Martin closed up on his right, some others to his left. The Lea End mob were lifting Manton's legs now. They were just a yard or two from the surf. They dropped a leg and fumbled before grabbing it up again. He could hear their laughter, their shouts. Manton seemed lifeless, he wasn't struggling at all. Surely the bugger wasn't turning the other cheek? God in heaven, there was a time and place, the daft beggar.

Jack punched and kicked, grunting as a damn great stick broke across his shoulders. He felt more blows land as he forced his way through with Martin at his side, while Joe and Andy and the others exchanged blows of their own. The parson was being swung backward and forward, and again, and then once more as the bastards stood knee-deep in the surf, the waves breaking and crashing waist-high. As Jack reached them they threw the parson high into the air and into the waves. 'Let your preaching help you now, you daft bugger, and stay away from us,' one of the men called, trying to throw Edward Manton's hat in after him, but the wind took it.

Jack barged through the group, using his shoulder and his fists, which were already bruised and swollen from last night's fight. How long could he go on doing this? He was through now and skirting the surf, leaving Martin and the others to beat the group back. He tore his jacket off, searching the waves. He grappled with the laces of his boots. Where was the daft bugger? Where?

Breathe deep, calm down, he insisted, trying to ease the knots, knowing that Martin would protect his back. Evie rushed through the surf. 'Don't, Jack. It's not the beck. Don't.'

He must. What else could he do? He yelled at Simon, who was wading into the fight, 'I said look after her, damn you, and where the hell's Timmie?'

His boots were off and he forced his way through the breaking waves, which snatched at him, slowing him. The cold took what was left of his breath and he caught his foot on some coal, and lurched forward. He tasted the salt, sinking beneath the oncoming waves, swallowing water, feeling the coal cutting into his feet as he struggled up, only to see a bigger wave roaring in, bowling him over again. He struggled to the surface, standing firm. The water was up to his waist.

He dived through the next wave, and the next, searching, out of his depth now because it was here that the beach shelved, making it a poor place for sea coal. The light was already fading and the current was taking him back to shore, and the cold was seizing up his limbs, so what was it doing to a namby-pamby like Manton? He snatched a look around. Nothing. He beat his way back out to sea, swimming hard, throwing himself upwards again and again, searching before breaking through the next wave.

He could see the fighting on the beach as the Lea End men were forced back towards the dunes, he could see Evie with Si at the edge of the surf holding back Miss Manton who was struggling and hitting out at a passing Lea End man. By, the Manton lass had courage. But where was Timmie? He flicked his hair out of his eyes, treading water. Where was the bloody parson? A wave hit him and dragged him down, sucking him to the depths, tumbling him in the water. He hadn't been ready and had no breath. On it went, tumbling him over and over, his lungs bursting, and then he felt a tug. Something changed, slowly he was being hauled out of the rip, but he still mustn't breathe or he would die, but he must take in breath because his chest was on fire.

The tugging went on, he kicked, helping, he was breaking through the surface coughing, choking and Timmie was grinning at him, holding him up by the armpits. 'You know I swim better than you ever did,' he shouted. 'You go left, I'll go right. Evie, Si, and Miss Manton are looking out for the parson. Keep an eye on them.'

As he stroked away Jack searched the sea yet again, checking with the shore, swimming off to the right, lifting and falling and diving through the waves, and then he saw something black further out. He swam towards it, ducking beneath a wave again. He saw an arm, lifting, then it fell, and yet another surge dragged at him. He kicked hard, swam out of it, stroking the moment he broke the surface.

He yelled after Timmie, who glanced back. Jack pointed, then stroked as though his life depended on it, but it wasn't his life, it was the daft beggar's who hadn't listened. How had he ever heard 'the call'? He thought this again and again, maniacally laughing, then stopped. No. No. By, it was so cold.

Jack's arms were heavy, his legs too. His body was beyond numb. He forced himself on, rising to check on the position of Manton. There was no outstretched arm, but he could still see something black, lolling like a clump of seaweed. Timmie was alongside.

'It's him,' he said, crawling stroke for stroke with Jack, both spitting with every turn of their heads. The sea seemed to be lifting and falling as though in the grip of a cauldron and the wind was howling. If they didn't get out soon they never would.

They were closing, they were there, but Manton was face down. Timmie dived and turned him, Jack grabbed the parson beneath the arms and dragged him. Together they struggled shorewards with Timmie sidestroking beside him, hauling for all he was worth. The waves continued to surge and boil, and now the rain came, stinging their faces. Timmie coughed but they were making headway because the tide was turning and the waves were with them, at last, but it was too late. He had to let go, had to sink, had to give up, he must, but then the waves were breaking on them and he felt sand beneath his feet, and they were in the shallows as Timmie took over.

Exhausted, Jack felt his body give up. He rolled on to his front and crawled towards safety, but he couldn't think because of the noise and the deadness of his body. Then Simon and Evie were in the sea beside him, hauling him towards safety, but he couldn't stand, damn it. He had no strength, no feeling, and was so cold he thought he'd never be warm again.

Evie was saying, 'Come on, Jack. Help us, get those legs moving, bonny lad.' He tried, stumbled and stood, but only for a moment, for he had no bones, only jelly, only numbness. He fell to his knees, and the surf still crashed over and around him, and over his sister and the man she loved. They dragged him out of the water as Timmie and Martin dragged Manton.

His mam was there and threw her shawl over him as he lay scarcely able to breathe, and what air he sucked in barely reached his lungs, though he could hear it rasping. In and out. In and out.

Evie was rubbing him, his mother too, but all the time he searched for Timmie and Manton, and saw them higher up on the beach with Miss Manton and two pit wives rubbing and drying them both. His father and the Easton men were returning, leaving the Lea End gang fleeing. Da was helping Timmie and Martin move Manton on to his belly, while Si's da, Alec, took over from the women. Evie was crying, his mam was crying and stroking his hair. Miss Manton was crying. It was bloody bedlam.

He watched his da thumping Manton on the back. Was that what you did when someone had drowned? Was he dead? Was there any hope? Simon was running towards Manton, taking over from Da, whose nose was bleeding, and Alec's too. By, that must have been some fight. He knew his own head, nose and fists would be sore if he could feel them. Over by the dunes the Lea End group were turning around their carts and leaving. They should be reported, but you didn't report one of your own, for they were pitmen from Sidon Pit.

Evie and his mam were helping him to his feet and urging him away from the surf and the spray. 'Come on, Jack, let's get you safe, the tide's coming in.' He was shivering so much that he couldn't speak and his legs didn't seem to belong to him.

It was then that his da turned and held up his arm, shouting. 'We've got him back, the daft bugger. We've got him back.'

Miss Manton was on her knees, not praying but cradling her brother. Jack grinned inside but his face wouldn't move. Daft bugger, oh yes, he was. Timmie came across, hauling him up. 'Thanks, Timmie,' Jack whispered. 'You saved me.' He was slurring his words. 'You led me,' Timmie said and then his legs sagged and they both fell back on to the beach.

The marras carried all three men to the dunes near their carts where there was some degree of shelter, and then they carted the coal to the wholesalers. Evie and the other women stripped Jack of his shirt, forcing his arms into his father's old spare shirt, which he always brought in case of accident. Then they helped him into his jacket while his da removed Jack's trousers, and changed them for his own. Alec did the same for Timmie. They wore the wet ones. Jack was barely conscious, but Manton was even less so. Alec had found several blankets and was wrapping them around the parson, whom he had stripped. 'We must get the bugger to the infirmary,' Jack croaked.

Miss Manton came across then, bending over him. 'How can I thank you, Mr Forbes?'

'Keep your brother warm,' Jack murmured as his da arrived, looming over him.

Jack grinned. 'I've been given your old shirt, man, so I'm not good enough for your better 'un, I suppose.'

His da grinned too, and gripped his shoulder. 'You got that right, lad. I'm right proud of you both.'

Jack pulled his father close. 'Let the bairn have a beer, for God's sake. He's a man now.'

Evie and Simon pedalled back, following the cart

and the trap to the infirmary. They left Mr Manton there, but Jack wouldn't stay in after he'd been examined. 'I need to work,' he said to Miss Manton. Timmie nodded. 'I need to work too.' He smelt of beer. Jack grinned at his father. They'd be in the pit again tomorrow; sickness was a luxury they couldn't afford, especially with trouble looming. The grin faded. He hadn't done enough. They didn't have the house.

Night was falling and Evie and Simon set off for Easterleigh Hall, pedalling slower with legs that ached. Simon barely spoke, but Evie was tired too, and wet, and as cold as he was. She would take a hot brick up to bed, wrapped in sacking. In fact, she'd take two, maybe even three. Simon checked his watch in the light from the moon. 'We'll be in time,' he said.

Evie nodded. 'Thanks for your help, lad. Make sure you take hot bricks to bed.'

He said nothing for a while. Then, in a distant voice, he murmured, 'You see what I mean. I was sent to stay with you and Timmie when I could have helped beat back the Lea End lot.'

Evie shook her head, a surge of irritation washing away her pride in her brothers. 'It saved you turning up for work with a face looking as though it had been through a mincer. Jack will have worked out that you need to keep your job. We're not outsiders, we're just . . . well, we made a different choice, Simon.'

'You mean my father made a choice. He wanted me out of the pit.'

She pedalled hard to keep up with him as they rode up the hill. 'We each had a part to play. We saved a life.' He was being a daft beggar. He was cold and wet and he'd pick up soon.

She laughed suddenly. 'Don't forget, we're a gang, and we stayed together, worked together. We got Jack back.' She freewheeled down the hill and in a moment he overtook her, laughing at last. 'Heaviest gets to the bottom first.'

She braked steadily. 'Then I'm way behind you.' His laugh rang loud and clear. Before they'd left the infirmary Miss Manton had said, 'Evie, I think you might have forgotten the Suffragette meetings. Why don't I pick you up at the crossroads near Easterleigh Hall on your afternoon off next Wednesday? In fact, I'll be there every Wednesday and Sunday until you come. I owe your family everything, and you owe yourself – well, something of the utmost importance.'

Chapter Eight

Evie woke during that same Sunday night with a searing sore throat, aching limbs and thumping headache, but she and Millie were up at five thirty as normal. She'd only been here a couple of weeks but already the pattern of her days was set firm, as though there'd never been anything else. She eased her aching body down the back stairs into the kitchen, starting the furnace, then boiling the kettle while Millie leaded the grate and the scullery maids attacked the copper pans. It was becoming a daily occurrence that they were not completely finished the night before, but Mrs Moore had made no comment beyond, 'There are only so many hours in a day.'

Tea was delivered to the upper servants, and Mrs Moore's gin bottle was only half empty. A good sign? Hopefully. Back in the kitchen, Evie left the servants' porridge to Millie and set the table with all that was needed for breakfast preparation, though it was too early to start to sauté the kidneys. She checked Mrs Moore's lunch menu for today. Parsnip soup removed by boiled turbot and lobster sauce, removed by forequarter of lamb, removed by apricot tartlets and rhubarb tart. She set the stockpot brewing, dragged on her shawl and told Millie she was going to the gardeners' store to collect the parsnips. Millie smiled as she stirred the porridge. 'Say hello to Simon for me.'

Evie croaked, 'I don't know what you mean. Remember, no friendships like that are allowed.' Millie looked scared. 'I'm sorry, right silly I am.'

Evie went to her. 'You're not silly, pet. It's the rule that's daft. Just be careful what you say.' She patted her shoulder and called through to the scullery, 'Annie and Sarah, there's a note here from Mrs Moore: *don't forget to wash that floor.*'

Then she was gone, out across the yard feeling as though knives were cutting into her throat, drawing her shawl across her head to protect it from the cold morning breeze, her legs feeling like lead, with each step jolting her head. She turned on to the path. She'd find some dried bergamot in the vegetable store at the back, where a small furnace kept the air dry. She would infuse the herb with honey, and it might help her throat. She couldn't see Simon anywhere. Once she arrived it was Bernie who was sorting the root vegetables, and her heart sank. He grinned. 'Parsnips today, Evie. Your Mrs Moore gave me the list yesterday. I'll bring 'em up as usual so no need for you to come down.'

She stood in the doorway, clutching her shawl at her throat. 'I know.' Her voice was barely more than a whisper by now. 'Just thought I'd get some air and some bergamot.' Bernie cut some down for her. 'What's going on round here? Simon's voice has gone to the wall and I reckon he's got a fever. Could it be anything to do with a certain afternoon off?' he asked.

She decided on a half-truth. 'I was sea-coaling and Simon was there helping Alec, his da. It rained.' Her voice ended on a squeak. She took the bergamot and almost crawled back up the path, and was turning into the yard when Roger stepped from the garage. She increased her pace, conscious of his smile as he pinched out his cigarette. He called, 'Slow down, not a race is it?'

She croaked, 'In a way. I need to start the breakfasts and you have duties too.' She made to sidestep him but he stepped with her. She stepped to the right, and he too. 'Mrs Moore is up and sorting out the breakfasts, let's walk in together, why not?' His smile was crooked, his grey eyes as cold as the sky, his hair short and straight and it looked as though it was slicked down with something. His black suit and tie were pristine and his shirt so white it could have been called blindingly so, if one wanted to impress him. She didn't. He repeated, 'Why not, we can get to know one another rather better.'

Why not? Because your reputation goes before you, man, she wanted to shout, but he was an upper servant and she knew better than to say what she thought. She smiled, but looked towards the kitchen. He stepped closer. She put up her hand, firmly, and retreated. His jaw set. She pointed at her throat and forced some words out. 'You can hear I have a right bad throat. You don't want to fall ill so soon after being set on as Mr Auberon's valet.'

She knew the moment she said it that it was a mistake. His smile disappeared, his face flushed. She added, 'It must be interesting to valet for someone who needs your experience, it's important for Mr Auberon to learn from you.' To her left she could see Len the chauffeur in the doorway, watching, and behind him, deep in the shadow of the garage, the Rolls-Royce. Len was moving closer for a better view. What was she, a music-hall act? Her headache was thumping.

Millie called then, from the doorway of the basement. 'We need you, Evie, get a move on. Mrs Moore is . . . Well, she's after hurrying you up.'

Thank you, thank you. 'I have to go,' she said, though her voice had almost gone completely. For a moment Roger watched her, as though he was assessing produce on a stall. He'd start to feel if she was ripe any minute now. Her head was spinning. He stood to one side and bowed. 'On your way, Evie Anston. I'm sure we'll have another chance to chat, when you are in full voice, and remember, I valet for both, while Lord Brampton is here.'

She felt that she scuttled away, and hated the surrender. She dragged herself into the kitchen with the bergamot. Mrs Moore stood with her hands on her hips, waiting. 'You do not go out until I say you may. You do not leave Millie in charge of porridge and quite alone, so what have you to say, Evie Anston?'

Evie knew it wouldn't be much, but she tried. There was no voice left. Instead she waved the bergamot. Mrs Moore looked from her to the herb. Millie said, 'She's right poorly, she is. It's her throat. She was sea-coaling, with . . . With her family.'

Millie flushed. It was one of the longest speeches anyone had heard from her, and Evie thought she deserved a hug. Mrs Moore snatched at the bergamot. 'Well, sit down here, on the stool, near the range. I'll make bergamot tea with honey, and just a little something else. I'll be back in a moment.' She picked up a cup from the dresser and headed for her rooms. Evie reached across and patted Millie. 'Thank you,' she whispered.

'I saw you with that valet,' said Millie. 'He looks right bonny. Bit like me da. I don't know why everyone's being so nasty about him.' Evie had no voice to say that he was anything but nice, and no energy left to even try.

Mrs Moore returned with her cup and added leaves of bergamot and honey, and lastly the hot water. She drew out a stool, pressing Evie on to it, forcing her to sit while she sipped; she almost choked on the gin Mrs Moore had added. Mrs Moore shook her head in warning while bustling to the range. 'I'll finish the breakfast, you get some energy back. It's a chill, it'll pass. I'd like to send you back to bed but it's warmer here. Rest when you can but, for land's sake, we're to have that Mr Auberon down here, and Lady Veronica, after their ride, for tea, so I'll need you to make extra-special fancies.'

'Down here?' Evie mouthed, her head swimming even more. Next to her, Millie and Annie almost spilt the porridge they were pouring into the earthenware bowl.

Mrs Moore was whisking the scrambled eggs for upstairs, her swollen wrists slowing her. Evie drained her cup to the dregs, then took the whisk from her. 'I'll do it, you sort out the kippers,' she mouthed. Mrs Moore patted her shoulder. 'You're a good lass, and Millie, get that porridge across the way.' She added in a whisper, 'The medicine I put in will help you sweat it out.'

The staff streamed down the central passageway chattering and nudging one another, with Lil almost last. Behind her came Roger. Lil was preening herself. Well, she was welcome to him. Just then Evie saw Mrs Green draw Lil away from the others, her face stern.

Millie and Annie lugged the huge earthenware bowl through to the hall, puffing and panting. The kippers were cooking, the bacon already done. The heat from the range was healing, the heat from within her was helping too, because her clothes were damp with sweat and her throat had eased. Mrs Moore looked across at her. 'I told you Mr Auberon used to come with Wainey, and Lady Veronica too, and they've come on and off since then if they can escape from Lady Brampton's beady eyes. I expect Lady Brampton will be resting after the exertions of the dinner party. Worked her fingers to the bone, I don't think.'

Mrs Moore was wiping the table with a damp cloth, and they both laughed. 'I reckon they need some home comforts. They get none up there. They'll talk in French if they have something they don't want me to understand. Bloody rude but then they're from upstairs so know no better. You can go into the pantry to stocktake and brush up your language. It'll be boring, mind.'

She swiped the crumbs on to the floor. 'You sweep those up when you've got yourself in hand.'

Somehow Evie struggled through the chores, making and serving a mutton casserole from a mixture of the leavings from upstairs and mutton from Home Farm. She had little appetite. Roger sat on the male side of the table. He smiled at her. Millie nudged her. Evie ignored them both. Before the lunch was finished she left, and prepared the soup for upstairs, slicing the parsnips with shaking hands, feeling that the heat from her body could melt the butter that was in the pan. She tipped in the parsnips and sautéed them until almost tender. She added the stock and simmered the whole damn lot for half an hour, wanting to lie on the floor and just sleep.

Millie and Sarah cleared the servants' table while Evie sat on the stool, her head throbbing, forcing the soup through the sieve, and then the hair sieve, her arm aching. How was Simon? At least she was in the warm. Jack would be warm and exhausted as he hacked at the coal down in the pit. Timmie would be warm too, sitting at the trapdoor in the dark, waiting for the tubs and wagons, opening just at the right time, and shutting it straight after. He must stay awake. She shook herself to alertness too.

She added more stock and the soup was ready to serve, timed to perfection. Archie took it upstairs. Mrs Moore had prepared the forequarter earlier and it was roasting gently. They cooked the vegetables. She made the tarts and placed them in the second oven. The scullery maids kept up with the dishes and implements, washing and replacing them. Luncheon over, Evie baked cakes and scones while Mrs Moore rested in her room. When she returned she came with jams from Mrs Green's preserve cupboard. 'For the scones,' she said. Gin was on her breath. Evie made a pot of tea; it would disguise the smell. She held out a cup to Mrs Moore and poured for all the kitchen staff. They sat around the table and Mrs Moore nodded and smiled at her. 'You're a good lass, Evie,' she said. The others wondered why.

Millie brought a tablecloth when they were finished and set the table to Mrs Moore's instructions. The sponge cakes, fancies, and scones were fulsome, the selection of jams plentiful, and Evie whipped cream in case Mr Auberon cared for some on his scones. The house servants had been warned

162

to stay in the servants' hall facing away from the kitchen, for no servant must watch, or cross the path of, the master. Evie felt rage filling her at the thought. It was bad enough that this was the rule upstairs, but downstairs was the servants' domain. She shut down the thought and rose, standing on legs that seemed empty of life. Mrs Moore sent her to the big pantry for the stocktake, and the others to the ice room, or the preserve pantry as requested by Mrs Green, to scrub the shelves and floor.

Mr Auberon and Lady Veronica arrived at four o'clock on the dot through the bell corridor. The pantry door was sufficiently ajar for Evie to see their faces flushed from their ride, their clothes mud-spattered. The lad's face looked worse now the bruising was coming out. They apologised for their attire, saying that they had ridden for too long, so glorious had the ground been for cantering.

Mrs Moore was allowed to sit and from the pantry where she ticked off the supplies of sugar, flour and other dry goods, Evie listened and watched. She heard them ask Mrs Moore to thank Mrs Green for the quality of the cakes, for it was she who should have made them. She heard the desultory discussion of the weather, the loss of Wainey, the coming of warmer weather. 'Surely it will arrive soon,' said Lady Veronica. 'Spring seems late this year.' Mrs Moore was asked about how she was and she assured them that she was perfectly well, thank you very much, Your Ladyship.

Evie was lulled because she was hearing what seemed to be real people, nice people, caring people. There was a pause and then Lady Veronica said, 'Aub, *as-tu pensé aux économies qu'il faut faire dans Auld Maud?*'

Evie shook her head. Mrs Moore would understand they were talking about the economies which Auberon, it appeared, had to bring in at the mine. How rude, as Mrs Moore had said, but how interesting.

Mr Auberon replied in French, his lips swollen and his words slurred. 'Yes, as I said on the ride, we'll have to cut back on the pit props for a start so I'll get Davies to pass the word down the line to the deputies. And yes, Ver, I really have thought. I know you think I should stop this, but how can I, so just stand back a bit, will you.' It wasn't a question. 'They'll have to make do with hauling out the props as seams are worked out. There're to be no new ones. They know their jobs, it should be fine. I'm discussing my other plans with Davies but those we can bring in as time goes by. Davies argued, said the men wouldn't be happy about the props. They're being paid to do a job, I said, not to be happy. It's none of their damn business how the mine is run and I'm not sure it's yours. We're putting work their way, and bread into their families' mouths. They should be glad, Ver.'

Lady Veronica played with her fancy, peeling the icing off and eating it with her fingers. She, too, spoke in French. 'Sounds to me just what Father would have said? Where's the real you in all this, Auberon? What about the men? They'll be at risk, won't they?'

'For God's sake, Ver, do we have to keep on talking about this? We did enough on the ride, surely. For the last time, the props are perfectly serviceable and we use too many. The deputies just need to withdraw more, and send them along the line to be used elsewhere. Miners are always saying they're skilled, so they'll know if the roof's coming down and they can get out of the way, and then clear the coal. It saves them hacking it out.'

At those words, Evie felt the breath leave her lungs. How dare he? He was talking about her family, her friends, all the pitmen. He pushed away his plate, his cake uneaten, his lips evidently hurting – Evie hoped they stung like the devil. Lady Veronica said, still using French, 'But think of the accidents, there are already so many every month. We should be doing more, not less, surely. How can we do this?' Evie chewed her pencil, looking with new eyes at the young woman.

Mr Auberon drained his cup of tea, banging it down into the saucer, wiping his chin, his lips not fully under his control. The teaspoon rattled. Mrs Moore was smoothing out her serviette, the colour rising up her neck. Mr Auberon looked up, straight at the pantry. Evie froze but there was no need, the door was only ajar, and his glance continued around the kitchen. He smiled at Mrs Moore while saying to his sister, still in French, 'I can't go on and on with this, so just stop, Ver, and would you like to be the one to tell Father that the men are more important than his bottom line?'

Nothing was said for the moment, then Lady Veronica slipped into English. 'We mustn't keep Mrs Moore for much longer, Auberon. Her Ladyship will be back soon.' And so, the talk became mundane again, but there wasn't much trace of relaxation and homeliness, was there? Isn't that what Mrs Moore said they sought from the kitchen teas?

Evie moved along the shelf, finishing the counting, knowing she must get word to Jack, but what could he do about it? This was no more or less than the way owners had always acted. But it was always best to know, surely? She knew she was angry but couldn't feel it beneath the hammering of her head, the soreness of her throat and the aching of her limbs.

Mr Auberon and Lady Veronica left at four forty-five on the dot, promising that they would be down again tomorrow. Well, Evie thought, how can we canny lot down here manage the excitement? Do you think we really like you here, do you think we should lay out a bonny carpet for you? And would she let Jack make such decisions? Would she hell. She'd rage, not argue, but what would she do if her da beat the living daylights out of Jack if he went against him? Her head was hurting too much to think.

She came out of the pantry with her completed list and the kitchen staff ate some of the remaining cakes, and put the others into the tin for whenever they needed sustenance. Mrs Moore looked at the clock; weariness had drained the colour from her face. 'Time to prepare dinner.' She added quietly to Evie, 'He's crushed, that boy is. He'll do what his father says or have another beating. His face . . .' Evie thought of her own da, clawing out the props to be used again, her brothers, and the increased spaces between the props. They could be crushed, *really* crushed, and any sympathy she had felt for Brampton's whelp after the night by the stables was long gone.

She tumbled into bed at midnight with hot bricks and again she wondered if Simon was warm, and were her da and brothers safe, and would they be safe tomorrow, and the next day and in the weeks and months to come?

In the morning she slipped from the house again, across the yard and down the path to the vegetable store. She had asked this time, and Mrs Moore had simply said, 'Take my shawl as well. Keep warm.' Evie's voice was still a hoarse whisper and she felt that she was barely conscious, so high was her fever. Simon was in the store and she handed him a list of necessary vegetables from Mrs Moore because her voice was no stronger, even after three cups of tea.

Simon grimaced, and whispered, 'You've lost your voice too?' His was just a hoarse squeak. He was flushed and his hands shook. 'We should be in bed,' she said, speaking barely above a breath. He looked at her and laughed. 'My, bonny lass, what would your da say?' Again it was a squeak but this time it ended in a cough that shook his body. She was glad of the distraction. What was she thinking to say things like that? For heaven's sake, she urged herself, take the bergamot and run.

She pointed to the bergamot on the list. 'I need this now,' she mouthed. 'Come to the kitchen and have some too. Mrs Moore puts gin with it.' He was watching her lips. She pointed to her throat and mouthed again. 'It doesn't hurt so much if you don't try and speak. I wonder how Jack is?'

He nodded, his eyes immediately distant. 'Keep warm, lass. I'll be in later.' She reached out but he turned away, busying himself in the back room and coming back with bergamot. He didn't look at her, just handed her the herb. 'I must get on,' he whispered, and she looked at the back he turned to her. She'd mentioned Jack, so it was still the marra nonsense.

She had been going to ask him to tell Jack of Auberon's plans but instead she turned on her heel and strode off, flicking a glance over her shoulder. He had gone. Immediately her energy disappeared and she almost tottered to the end of the walled garden, past the top vegetable store to the corner where she stopped, leaning back on the wall, her head spinning. The bricks were cold, pressing into her shoulders, steadying her. She concentrated on this, trying to make her head settle, somehow.

She forced the breath in and out of her chest, and for a moment it seemed the world had fallen silent, the wind had calmed, but then she heard voices around the corner, in the kitchen yard; something else to concentrate on, something else to stop the spinning. She pressed harder against the wall, wanting the pain of the bricks, anything to steady herself. She made herself listen to the voices. One was the chauffeur's, the other, louder, was Roger's. He was shouting. Her head was settling. She should get back, but . . . She stood up straight then sagged, because the spinning began again. The wind was nipping at her clothes. Wait, just wait, she told herself.

Roger's words became clear. 'No, I haven't bloody been demoted. Lord Brampton wants a wise head for his son, that's all.'

The chauffeur said something and laughed. Roger's voice was loud and savage. 'Well, I'm more than a few steps above you, you oil-rag minion.' She could picture the valet, the angle of his head, those eyes like ice. Any minute now he'd be strutting up and down, but the chauffeur was getting louder now too. Good for him.

'Prove it. What the hell can you say to help someone who's clever enough to go to university, and you're not even one step above me, I'll have you know. I'm a chauffeur. And don't even think of using your fists. I box in me spare time.'

Evie stood upright now, the spinning quite gone, wanting to peer round the corner to see Roger being rounded on. She stepped forward and kicked a watering can. It fell against the wall with a clang. She froze. Both men fell silent, then Roger began again. 'I wasn't going to do anything, don't be so damn stupid. I've more important things to think about than brawling with you. Just this morning I was giving advice.' His voice was lower now, but clear. 'Property advice, local houses needing to be bought pretty damn quick to scupper any of these bloody miners getting their mitts on them. Can't tell you more, Len. I reassured him that all he needed to do was emulate Lord Brampton, act swiftly and his life would be full of success.'

The chauffeur's laugh rang out loud and clear. 'Bloody hell, you swallowed a dictionary or something? So that's wisdom, is it, using long words and slimy talk? You didn't give any advice, you overheard him, you daft bugger, so sod off. I've an engine to look after, at least that's clean dirt.'

Evie pressed back against the wall. Property? Froggett? It had to be Froggett's. Now she could hear Mrs Moore shouting from the doorway of the kitchen. 'Evie? Where *is* that girl?'

The men had fallen silent again. Had they gone? Evie pushed herself upright and almost fell as the world seemed to swing in an arc right round her body. She reached for the wall, steadied herself, took a deep breath and walked into the courtyard. The chauffeur was throwing a rag into an old box at the entrance to the garages and Roger was pacing backwards and forwards. She tried to hurry over the cobbles heading to the steps, every step jolting her aching body. 'I'm coming, Mrs Moore.' But it was just a squeak.

Roger watched her, braced his shoulders and smiled at her, making for the head of the steps. He arrived as she did. He blocked her. She looked up, pointing to her throat in warning, and sidestepped him. He moved with her. She heard the chauffeur laughing. At her, or Roger? She saw Roger's face harden. He came closer.

The breeze carried the barking of the dachshunds, Currant and Raisin, and then they skittered into the stable yard to be hoyed away by well-hidden kicks from the stable lads. Roger gripped her elbow. It hurt. 'Well, how delightful, I hoped we'd have the chance of a chat again and soon.' She nodded but didn't speak, couldn't speak, her throat too sore and swollen. She longed to be in the kitchen, brewing bergamot tea with perhaps some gin. It did seem to help her get through the day, and her understanding of Mrs Moore increased further. She longed to be with Jack, telling him what she'd learned. Thoughts were whirling and chasing around in her head. She felt sick.

The chauffeur called, 'I'll be in for lunch later, you tell your boss that. I like big helpings.' She turned. He was wiping something with an oil rag and lounging against the garage door. In his working clothes with oil under his nails he wasn't the pretty picture that he was in his uniform and polished boots, and Lil wouldn't be impressed. She shook her head to clear it. Shut up. What did it matter about Lil, but that thought whirled away too.

Roger was looking at her intently. What had he just said? Was her expression suitably impressed? She knew it was not. She coughed, hoping he would not want to risk being infected by her. He stepped away but then drew close again. 'Did you shake your head? Not eager to be seen with me? Hard to get, eh? Clever girl. Let me walk you to the kitchen.'

He was walking her to the steps, gripping her elbow. She could hear the clatter from the kitchen and see Lil bustling along the bell corridor towards the back stairs with a broom in her hand. She'd be on her way to the sitting room while the family were still in bed. Roger was slowing, loosening his grip.

She wrenched free, almost running down the steps, one thought taking root and dispersing all the others. They were not ready to buy Froggett's house and Jack should have this news, but why? It would break his heart. And should she tell him of the props? What could he do if she did?

The kitchen was warm, the kettle was steaming, and there was a cup with gin in it. She hung the shawls on hooks on the back of the pantry door and sat on the stool whilst Mrs Moore tutted and added bergamot and honey before pouring in the hot water. She then made her hold the cup with both hands and sip slowly. Evie knew that tears were streaming down her face and she let the kitchen staff think that it was due to the chill that was racking her body.

Evie cycled to the crossroads the following afternoon to meet Miss Manton, if indeed she came as she had said she would. She hadn't seen Simon since yesterday when they had met over the bergamot and she had barely noticed, so poorly had she felt. She was marginally better today and was free now until nine thirty in the evening. She hoped her head would clear so that she could work out what message to send Jack, or whether to send one at all.

If she was held up at the meeting Mrs Moore had said there was no need to fret, for she would unlatch the big pantry window, as she had promised last Sunday. She had made bergamot tea again, but without the gin because Mrs Moore had said that it didn't do to make a habit of it. Evie thought of this as she wedged her bike behind the wall and waited for Miss Manton's trap. Did this mean that Mrs Moore would stop drinking? She shook her head; don't be daft, she told herself, habits aren't broken that quickly. She tried to think of what was best to do with the news she'd had but it all just continued to go round and round, and the wind was buffeting, making her cold, making her want to curl into a ball and sleep like any sane person would, on their afternoon off.

She heard the sound of the pony's hooves before she saw Sally, the bay mare, pulling the trap. Even before Evie settled Miss Manton reached across and squeezed her hand. 'I don't know how we can ever thank your family. Edward has pneumonia and will be home within a week or two, but without Jack and all of you he might never have returned.' She choked off her words, working her throat against tears. 'I can't bear the thought of life without the silly old fool. I called on your family. They have chills but are working, though whether they should be, I doubt. Edward will want to see them on his return.'

'As long as he is still with us, that's the main thing,' Evie said, her voice still no more than a whisper, her throat still swollen, sore and dry. She fell silent, and Miss Manton accepted that she was too unwell for chatter. Evie did hope that Edward wouldn't take the opportunity to try and lead Jack on to the path of righteousness. She knew the parson abhorred fist-fighting, but how else would Jack earn . . . ? She stopped. There was no house now to buy. There would soon be insufficient props. There was the Eight-Hour Act, there could be a strike. No, no more whirling thoughts.

The meeting hall was full and the speaker told of the People's Budget which had just been announced, which was intended to raise taxes to provide welfare and pensions. There was a collective murmur throughout the hall and it was the first time that Evie's heart had lifted even an inch from the floor since she had heard Auberon and Roger's news. At last they were on the road to equality. It was then that the speaker, a smart young woman with a feathered hat who was introduced as a friend of Emmeline Pankhurst, held up her hand for silence. 'Of course, we will protest to the government at their prioritisation. We are women and must have votes before taxes.' There was rustling from the front ranks, a nodding of smart hats. Evie just stared, shocked, then looked down at her hands which she had clenched into fists. Even here, amongst these women, the upstairs was present, was in control.

She sighed, too exhausted to fight any more, feeling too ill to protest. Miss Manton pressed her arm with hers and whispered, 'This can't be right.' Elsewhere many others were whispering. What were they saying? Were they for or against?

The speaker continued. 'Once we have the vote we can change life for our sisters and brothers in so many ways. We can pressurise the Liberal government to address all manner of things. Just think, a regiment of women using their vote to alter society. The People's Budget should wait, we can't.'

Cheers erupted. 'We insist on the vote this session,' the woman declared. 'For too long they've ignored us, or issued false hope. Enough. Our brains are not weak as they say. We go to university lectures but are not given degrees, we have businesses, and brains. We will not be moved.'

The cheers were louder now. Outside the men would be congregating to jeer them on their way home, jostle them, spit. They seemed to be able to produce saliva at will. Evie's mouth was dry as she touched her badge of purple, white and green. There were so many changes that had to happen, but how? At every turn they were thwarted – her class was always thwarted, even here, by the Pankhursts, by fellow suffragettes. Was she the only one to see the injustice of protesting the People's Budget?

The speaker left the stage to the stamping of feet. It was contagious. Many joined in. She and Miss Manton did not, and there were others, their faces tired, their clothes even more tired, their felt hats colourless, who did not. They drank tea, gathering kneeling on the floor, preparing to paint placards and banners while discussing priorities. Evie took the placard handed to her group of four. She looked around. Some weren't on their knees, some sat on chairs around tables, their smart colourful hats jostling as they painted and laughed. Did they think it was a game, something to fill their time?

The chairwoman, Mrs Dale, a widow from Gosforn, said from the stage, 'Votes before taxes, that's the message please, ladies. When we have votes we will be empowered to vote in those who will do our bidding. We can then address the ills in our society.'

Evie wondered if Miss Dale spoke to her family as though she was exhorting the masses. How tiresome it must get. She stared at the placard on the floor. There were brushes and black paint near Miss Manton, who handed a brush to Evie. Susan and Miss Lambert who usually sat in the back row were with them. Evie stared as Miss Manton drew the outline of the words as though she was teaching at Sunday school, big round letters, and neat, so neat.

Evie didn't want to pick up the brush, didn't want to begin painting words of which she disapproved, or did she? Would it be better to get votes first? Could they do more good that way? Slowly, reluctantly, she began.

When the placards were finished they left, forcing their way through the men who clamoured outside the doors and who stank of booze, grabbing at their hats and clothes. One spat at Evie, but missed. He was no pitman. A pitman would have made his mark. She stood still and started to laugh, a strange, almost silent laugh. Miss Manton pushed her from behind. 'Come on, Evie, don't stop, not here.'

Evie jerked herself back to the moment, and followed the woman in front of her, rushing to catch up, slapping away the hands that reached out. She wanted to hurt them, beat them, smash their sneering faces. Perhaps it was right that votes should come before taxes after all? What was right? Was this confusion what Mr Auberon and Lady Veronica experienced?

They struggled to the edge of the crowd that had spilled into the road. If the police came it was the women who would be arrested, not the men, so most hurried away, only lingering if they wished to create headlines by being arrested. Evie and Miss Manton were amongst those who left. They had lives to live, money to earn, brothers to look after. It was then that Evie broke down, crying hoarse sobs, stumbling along the road which led to the trap waiting for them at Miss Manton's friend's stables.

Miss Manton swung round. 'Evie, my dear.' She reached out, supporting her, urging her forward. 'Come, we need to be away from this area.' Behind them the men were shouting and jeering, some following the women who were hurrying along with them. Miss Manton helped her into the trap, urging Sally to trot briskly away. 'Evie, my dear, are you that unwell?' she asked.

In hoarse whispers Evie told her of the steps that they had been taking to buy their own small house to be free of the tied system. 'It's why Jack fights, it's why they work extra shifts, it's why we collect sea coal, sell Da's leeks, breed pigeons to sell, and now the Bramptons are going to buy the houses from Froggett. I heard the valet tell the chauffeur, and of course they are, why wouldn't they? How could we be so stupid? Then they'll own the whole village. We should have known, realised. They are going to reduce the props in the mines. The deputies have to reclaim the old ones. The gaps in between will be wider. The pitmen won't hear the pine creak before a roof-fall. I can't think, you see – should I tell Jack? He can do nothing about any of it, so what's the point?'

While they trotted along, their lantern hanging from the trap, she sobbed and Miss Manton gripped her hand and made soothing noises. It was only when they reached the wall behind which Evie's bicycle was waiting that she spoke. 'You must stop calling me Miss Manton, it's quite absurd. We owe you everything. My name is Grace. Please call me that. You are my friend. You are all my friends. Now, Evie, say nothing to your brother about Froggett, all you have to do is decide whether to tell him of the props. Let me think about the houses; there is often a way around problems.'

Evie shrugged, because there was no way round, though she knew that Miss Manton's heart was good and she would turn to the power of prayer. Irritation caused her to jump from the trap to the ground. How could she call her previous employer Grace? She'd known her as Miss Manton for too long to call her anything else.

She nodded up at her. 'Thank you. Your prayers will be helpful.'

Miss Manton laughed. 'You underestimate me, sometimes prayers need a bit of help. Try not to worry, Evie. Just get better.'

Chapter Nine

Evie was laying up the table the next morning for Mrs Moore, whose hands were so puffy they looked like the butcher's sausages. The servants' breakfast was finished, the upstairs was under way. Evie murmured, 'I'll do theirs on my own and the lunches today, you just talk me through. No one will know. Millie will think you're training me, and you will be, after all.'

Mrs Moore nodded, her face tense with pain. 'It's my back and knees too, lass. Some days they are just bad, really bad.' Her eyes were full of unshed tears. Evie swallowed back her own. At last the aching in her body was easing and her headache just a niggle. Her voice was recovering, too. She reached for the sieves in the low cupboard. At least she had a family; Mrs Moore had no one. Aye, well, that wasn't right. Mrs Moore had the Forbes family now and that was that.

But what good was that without a family home? Evie threw the sieves on to the table in a frenzy of helplessness. They slid to the edge. Mrs Moore grabbed and missed. They fell to the floor.

Millie was carrying back the empty porridge bowl

from the servants' hall as this happened. 'Wrong side of the bed this morning, Evie?' she enquired.

Mrs Moore just stared at Evie. 'They'll need a wash now. Take them into the scullery and come back with a smile on your face.' She wasn't cross, but concerned. Evie flushed with shame and did as she was told. The scullery was cold, Annie's and Sarah's hands were as raw as ever, their sleeves rolled up as far as their elbows. 'Sorry pets, they slipped out of my hand.'

Annie just nodded. 'A few more sieves is neither here nor there, I'm surprised a few more things don't get thrown in this bloody place.' They all laughed, even Mrs Moore, who had limped to the scullery door.

Millie was behind her, balancing the earthenware porridge bowl on her hip. 'Can I help with breakfast tomorrow, Mrs Moore, when I've finished the porridge? When his Lordship's in residence they have a lot, don't they? I could be learning, you know.'

Mrs Moore glanced at Evie. 'Aye, they do that, lass. And most of it goes in the waste for the pigs, save for the cold meats which he's requested for breakfast this morning. He should have gone yesterday but here he is, still.' The look on her face said it all. 'Evie, take the tongue and ham back to the cool pantry when it comes down with James and Archie. The omelette and whiting will go in the swill bucket along with the kedgeree. Pigs don't seem as fussy as humans.'

Lil hurtled through the kitchen, skidding to a halt behind Mrs Moore. 'Why's his Lordship still here? It makes her Ladyship fuss like the Queen when he's around. I reckon she runs her fingers along the surfaces too. I've just had Mrs Green on my back. I need some tea leaves for the carpets, Evie.'

Evie slipped past Mrs Moore who hobbled back to her stool, pulling her recipe book towards her and Evie's too. Lil took the tea leaves which were tipped daily into a special sieve suspended over a bucket. She tested them for dryness, waved at Evie and ran back out and up the staff stairs. She'd sprinkle tea leaves on the carpets to attract the dirt before sweeping up with the other maids while the family were having breakfast.

Mrs Moore looked at Evie. 'Why are you murdering the knife cleaner this morning? What's happened?' Evie realised that she was stabbing a vegetable knife in and out of the knife cleaner, and couldn't even remember walking to it. She shook herself but before she could answer she heard a knock at the kitchen door, heard it open and Simon call, 'Flowers, ladies. Are we colour co-ordinated today, do you think? I've only got daffodils and tulips. Bit of a mixture.'

His voice was strong again. She could have run across the kitchen and hurled herself into his arms, but she sauntered across instead, standing by the table as he placed the basket of house flowers from the spring garden on the chest of drawers near the scullery. He said, 'I'll take them through to Mrs Green, shall I?'

Mrs Moore laughed. 'Why wouldn't you, lad? It's what you always do, or are you after a cup of tea? You gardeners usually are. Pour the lad a cuppa, Evie. Seems he's recovered from the chill too. Oh my.' Her look was knowing.

Millie came into the kitchen and took over the laying up of the table.

Evie busied herself with the teapot, replenishing Mrs Moore's cup and taking one to Simon, who had taken off his boots in the corridor rather than risk a clip round his ear from Mrs Moore. He smiled, his fingers looking huge around the cup handle. 'Take a look at these beauties, Evie. What do you think of the ragged tulips? They're the head gardener's pet project.' He was nodding towards the basket, his eyes more insistent than his voice. Puzzled, she looked at the basket and there, tucked between the daffodils and the tulips, was a piece of paper. 'They're lovely,' she said, looking up at him. He nodded. 'Touch them, they feel like satin.'

She reached forward and lifted the paper slightly, seeing Jack's writing. She felt anxiety grip her. What had happened? Who was hurt? Hiding her movements, she slipped the note into her apron, nodding her thanks just as Mrs Green peered into the kitchen from the central passageway. She knocked on the window. 'Bring those flowers at once before they wilt in that heat,' she mouthed to Simon.

Simon handed back the empty cup. 'Thanks for the tea, ladies. I will see you when I see you.' He tiptoed to the door and followed Mrs Green to the cool flower room. He would have to return via the kitchen to collect his boots. 'I'll bring the flour from the pantry, shall I Mrs Moore?' Evie asked.

'Of course, Evie, or do you think you can make a luncheon soufflé without it, and why we have to have a soufflé at all I don't know. By the time that Archie gets it up the stairs it will be as flat as a pancake. Bring suet as well, you can make suet puddings using the remains of the upstairs beef bourguignon. Chop the ham and add that too. Put in some kidneys as well, it will reinforce the gravy, but slice and sluice them first. We can use up the upstairs desserts but make a rice pudding as well, or some will go hungry.'

Evie was already in the pantry. She half closed the door and made a pretence of collecting the food-stuffs, but instead drew out the note and made herself read it, not wanting to, but knowing she must. Which one had been hurt? Was it Da or Timmie? It couldn't have been Jack, for how could he have written?

For a moment she couldn't understand what she was reading, and had to slow down, take a deep breath and read it again.

I need to see you. Miss Manton has been around with word from the parson. They have told me the

*news about our dream. We should have guessed,
shouldn't we? Anyway Miss Manton has a
suggestion. We have said no but she says we can't
refuse until we have talked it over with you. Meet
me at 3 at the bothy. Si says it's easy to slip out
then when you all have some time free. Jack Anston*

On his return Simon fixed her with his eyes.
She nodded. 'I meet him at three in the bothy,' she
mouthed. 'No one is hurt.' He smiled, and she walked
to the big pantry, close by him. Millie was in the
servants' hall, the scullery maids were in the scullery, and Mrs Moore was studying the menus for
this evening. He reached out and held her hand.
'I'll try and be there,' he whispered. 'I've missed
you. I wasn't feeling well, I was moody. Forgive me.'
'Always,' she said, wanting to feel his arms
around her. How would it be? The only men to hold
her had been her da and brothers. She blushed. He
left.

The morning passed much as always. Evie prepared
stock for soup. She checked the menu and frowned
at the mayonnaise for the cod. 'A particular favourite
of his Lordship,' Mrs Moore muttered. 'If the wind
changes, Evie Anston, your face will stay like that.'
They both laughed.
'I'll make the mayonnaise. I think I can manage
that,' Mrs Moore said, setting herself more firmly
on the stool and picking up an egg. She winced as

she tried to separate the yolk from the white and the yolk broke on the shell. Evie said, 'Let me.'

She called Millie over. 'Clean the eggshells and put them in the stock please, and whisk it vigorously. You'll see that the addition of eggshell will bring the scum to the surface. You can then spoon it off.'

She cracked another egg open, and tipped the shells from side to side until the albumen had separated from the yolk. She summoned Millie again. 'Put these shells in too.' She obeyed. 'Separate the next egg yourself.' Millie did so, frowning with concentration. 'Excellent. Take the shell and whisk quickly now.'

Mrs Moore smiled at her, sipping her tea which was laced with gin. Evie wished she wouldn't do this, for someone would notice, one day. 'You're a good teacher, Evie.'

'That's because you are.' Evie stirred in the olive oil one drop at a time. What had Miss Manton said to her family? What? She stirred, watching the clock, seeing the hands crawl round, trying not to see Roger peering in through the window as he passed along the corridor.

She made mushroom soup while Millie prepared the vegetables and checked on the suet puddings that Evie had made. Mrs Moore talked Evie through the drying of mushrooms while the puddings simmered. Evie next passed the mushrooms through the wire sieve and then the hair sieve, which was like ramming a camel through the eye of a needle. Millie groaned, 'I couldn't do that.'

'It's all down to elbow grease, and you must do it if you want a good mushroom soup,' Mrs Moore insisted.

At last it was the servants' lunchtime. Evie barely tasted hers. Roger asked Mr Harvey if he didn't think it was quite the best beef pudding he had tasted. Mr Harvey said, 'On this occasion I do have to agree with Roger.' Evie thought Mr Harvey looked as though he had sucked a lemon as he concurred with the valet.

Then luncheon was ready to be taken upstairs, with the soufflé looking encouraging as the footman took the tray. It didn't last the distance, Archie told them when he returned with the empty dishes. Mrs Moore shook her head. 'Empty plates tell their own story. It might have lost its bounce but not its flavour – just the right hint of cheese, Evie, clever girl.'

The fish was transported heavenwards, and still Evie watched the clock. Apple tart, fruit and cheese followed, then coffee. At last it was two thirty.

Mrs Moore retired to her room. Evie had already prepared the scones and fancies for the afternoon tea. Mr Auberon would not be down today but would be at the colliery with his father. Lady Veronica and Lady Brampton were visiting friends in Gosforn but would return to take tea at four in the drawing room.

Evie said to Millie, 'I must have some fresh air, I'll be back by quarter to four.'

She rushed from the kitchen, up the steps and out into the yard and there was Roger, lounging against the wall. He straightened. 'Ah, I hoped you'd come.'

Behind him Simon appeared. He came forward, saying, 'Roger, I wanted to talk to you about the duties of a valet. You must be pretty good to be entrusted with the care of Mr Auberon. I want to better myself. Can you help me, just for a moment?'

Roger hesitated, irritation clear, but then he smiled at Evie. 'We'll talk later,' he said.

Over my dead body, she thought and slipped across the yard, smiling her gratitude at Simon. She hurried down the path to the side of the walled vegetable garden rather than through the stable yard to the path alongside the yew hedge, for with Roger on the loose it was as well to disguise her destination. She then cut along through the silver birches and primroses to the bothy, checking all the time that Roger had not slid away from Simon and followed.

Jack was in there, standing by her bike, smoking a Woodbine. She ran to him. 'I was so afraid,' she murmured. 'I thought you were hurt.' It was then she saw Miss Manton standing in the lee of the entrance, in shadow. She was also smoking. Evie was speechless. Miss Manton held up the cigarette. 'A secret vice,' she said. 'I succumb under pressure and Jack was good enough to oblige.'

Evie checked outside again. No one was coming. There was just the blue sky which she had not noticed before, and the blossom on the cherry trees which intermingled with the silver birches and which she must have run past without noticing. She looked from one to the other. 'What's going on? I have to be back soon. Please, someone tell me.'

She stepped towards Jack but now her lovely strong brother was crying. She was scared. She went to him, but Miss Manton called, 'Evie, we need to talk.' She was stubbing out her cigarette beneath her boot.

'Edward and I need an investment. We have money from the sale of the bakery and we have decided to buy the three houses from Froggett. Well, two actually. We intend to lend you enough to make up the shortfall from your savings so that you can buy the end one, the one with three bedrooms. It will need work, but the one you were thinking of is too small, the middle one is too big.' Miss Manton was talking so quickly that she ran out of breath and stopped.

Evie tried to catch up with her words and when she did she could see why Jack was crying. They had been offered a chance that they couldn't possibly accept. It was worse than no hope at all. Miss Manton had found the breath to speed on again, snatching off her modest felt hat as she did so, waving it at them both. Her auburn hair fell to her shoulders. Something had given way in her bun. 'You gave us back Edward's life. How can we accept that gift unless we give you one in return? How can you be cruel enough to expect us to live with that huge obligation? The loan will be interest-free. Your family call it charity, Evie, but can you see that it is not? It is a transaction. A life for a life.'

Jack shook his head, dragging his sleeve across his face, his voice hoarse from his fever, and aggravated by coal dust. He must have been on the backshift to be here now, and was exhausted. 'But can't you see, Miss Manton, it wasn't just our gift, it was all the pitmen. They held the Lea End lot so your brother could be saved.'

It was what had been in Evie's mind too. Miss Manton slapped her hat in her hand. 'You and Timmie risked your lives, they did not, and how selfish you will be if you deprive the others of the use of the other two houses by continuing to refuse our proposal. Do you think the Bramptons will use the houses to help the miners, as we intend?'

Evie's tears had stopped with Jack's and now they both stared at her. She continued, 'Now listen, Easton needs those houses and it's time we did something. Edward and I realised that we had made a mistake yesterday evening not to inform you fully of our plan. I wanted you here, Evie, because you will lend your weight to the right decision. We propose to use the other two houses as retirement homes for the miners of Auld Maud, or emergency accommodation should they be evicted, or should strikes cause hardship, or somewhere to convalesce is needed. It is our duty as Christians and it makes us happy.'

For a moment no one said a word. On the hills the sheep were grazing, the gorse was brilliant in the sun. Miss Manton was explaining that the property purchase would break the Bramptons' stranglehold, and prevent fear of the workhouse for so many. The decision was Jack and Evie's. 'If you say yes, then we go ahead. If you say no, then . . . I need a decision. This is undoubtedly blackmail and I make no apology for it. I know you need your sleep, Jack, before you go on at eight this evening but I fear if we leave it any longer we will be too late. Who knows how soon Mr Auberon will arrive at the Froggetts with a tempting offer? Please think of yourselves, the others and Edward, and accept.'

Jack was standing beside Evie now, his hand gripping hers. Evie watched the breeze rattle the blossom. A few petals drifted to the ground where the primroses grew. It was so beautiful, so very beautiful, which she hadn't realised before. She had never felt so happy in her life. They were going to be safe. They were going to be free. They had to do it for the others, as well as themselves. He said, his voice so hoarse and weak she could hardly make out his words, 'What do you think, pet? Can we say yes?'

She squeezed his hand, feeling the calluses, the ridged scars. 'If we have the house we can repay the loan, of course we can. You'd feel safe when you have to speak out against the management. The old and sick or evicted can go to the two houses, not the workhouse.' She stopped. 'But how would that be funded, Miss Manton?'

Miss Manton laughed, moving into the doorway too. 'Leave that problem to us, Evie. The world doesn't rest on your shoulders alone, you know.'

Evie grinned, and shrugged. It truly didn't, and nothing mattered if only they had a house. Nothing. She could continue with Mrs Moore and in just a few years they could set up a hotel. They'd be out of the pit in maybe . . . Well, maybe in just five years. Yes, she'd aim for 1914. Her heart soared with hope. She hugged her brother and whispered, 'Yes, if we pay interest. Do you agree?'

'Just what I was thinking, bonny lass.' She knew that from his face, and his strength as he lifted her up high into the air. 'Just what I was thinking.'

'I'm taking this as a yes. You must go back to work, Evie. And we must hurry.' Miss Manton was picking up her cigarette stub and Jack his. 'We must beat Mr Auberon to the Froggetts.'

Jack lowered Evie to the ground, kissing her cheek, then asking, 'Where are the Bramptons this afternoon?'

'Archie said that they were off to Auld Maud. You know Mr Auberon's coming to run the pit?' Jack nodded. 'Simon told me.'

'Did you know they're only to use reclaimed props, and the space between is to be greater? I heard it from Mr Auberon himself when he came to the kitchen for tea. He didn't know I was listening, of course.'

Jack's look was intense, then it cleared. 'He won't know how much space there is between the props and neither will Davies. Da will talk to the deputies and they'll just have to be clever about it. We can't do anything else. I'll tell Jeb, don't worry. And thanks, Evie, but be careful. I don't want anyone to know you're listening to all that's being said.'

Miss Manton shook Jack's arm. 'Enough of this, we must go. Let's get to the trap. Auberon could visit Mr Froggett on his way back from the pit.'

Evie ran back to the basement. Nothing was any trouble any more. If Roger was there, she'd leap right over him. He wasn't, Simon was. She hurried into the corridor with him on her heels. Quickly she told him and he shook his head. 'That's wonderful. Just to have the two houses for the others will be such a gift. I worry about my da and mam when they're old. I might have enough to look after them but you just never know, do you?'

He held both her hands and for a moment they paused, then Simon dropped her hands as Millie shot out of the kitchen. 'Come on Evie, Mrs Moore is trying to grate the suet for small herb dumplings for upstairs and her hands are sore. She wants you, not me.'

Simon smiled. 'I'll bring those marrows, Evie, don't worry. We've some stored.'

Millie was gone. He lifted her hand and kissed it. She paused, wanting his arms around her. He moved just a fraction closer, his eyes on hers, his arms lifting, but then Mrs Moore called, 'Now, Evie, right now.'

Simon laughed and she slipped past him into the kitchen, hearing him clatter up the steps. Life was so good, even when grating suet.

Jack took the reins from Miss Manton at her request. She wanted another cigarette. He handed her his Woodbines and she cupped her hand against the wind as she lit one. 'One for you?'

She leaned across, putting one in his mouth, and pressed her cigarette to his. He sucked, feeling strange. He'd never been with a woman who smoked, he'd never driven a trap, only the cart. He wasn't used to sitting sideways to the way he was going, or sitting opposite his passenger. He wanted to break Sally into a gallop but he made do with a fast trot, while the wind burned down his cigarette at a rate of knots. They had to be in time. Until they had sealed the deal it was too painful to even think about it. Perhaps they should have said yes to Miss Manton yesterday. What if they were too late and the whelp Auberon was there first? If they got it his parents would be ecstatic, and Timmie . . . Well, Timmie would want another beer and Da might just let him have it. If they didn't . . . No. Don't even think that.

'How much further?' Miss Manton asked.

Jack brought himself back to the present and pointed ahead. 'Froggett lives in the lee of that hill. It's called the Stunted Tree. You can see why.'

There was a windswept hawthorn on the top. It was a natural hill, not a slag heap that oozed filth and heat, but one with grass and gorse, and sheep dotted here and there right up to the summit. Froggett's farm ran up to the Bramptons' land, and he would not allow anyone to survey his property because he didn't want any of that bloody colliery rubbish on or under his land, he always said in the club.

The three houses were just within his land, a little spur that was an anomaly which ran almost up to the village. It was a salient, which Bastard Brampton had tried to acquire once he'd sunk the colliery. He'd tried again when he took over Easterleigh Hall. It was a thorn in his side. It threatened his total control of the miners and the village.

Miss Manton begged yet another cigarette. 'Light one for me too, bonny lass,' Jack said as he concentrated on the track, steering Sally away from a pothole. Miss Manton's laugh made him realise what he'd said. 'Sorry, Miss Manton.'

He took the lit cigarette from her and drew on it. The end was slightly damp from her lips. It would have been all right from Evie but Miss Manton was a stranger, and older what's more. Hell, she must be quite thirty and had been Evie's employer. He snatched a look at her. Her hand was shaking as she held the cigarette. 'We've got to be in time,' she said.

'We will or we won't be. Try and relax.'

'How can you be so calm?' Miss Manton drew deeply on the Woodbine, which was glowing in the wind. At the rate she was going she'd want another in a minute and they had to do him for the week, and by, it still seemed strange that she was smoking at all.

He shrugged. 'If you worried about things you'd never get through the day in the mine. You have to do your best, keep alert and hope your luck's in.'

'You could pray,' Miss Manton said, holding on to the handle of the trap as a wheel lurched into and out of the rut. The hawthorn hedges were almost in flower and were no longer neatly trimmed, which meant they were out of Brampton's land and into Froggett's. Jack knew the farmer didn't cut back his hedges until May was out, and neither did he cast a clout. His vests were a national treasure, or not. On either side of the track yet more sheep grazed.

There were a few lambs, jumping straight up into the air. Jack loved to see that. He loved the fresh air, but if you were a pitman you were in the pit by eight in the morning or night and down for the next twelve hours, though the hewers worked shorter shifts. What would the Eight-Hour Act bring? Would overtime be paid, would piece rates go up to compensate for the shorter shifts? So many questions.

He was conscious that Miss Manton was staring at him, waiting for his answer, but his God was his own business and he called it luck, and it didn't owe anything to church. It was something between himself and the other, whatever that other was.

'You could also call me Grace, please, I'd prefer it. Miss Manton makes me feel too old. I've asked Evie and if you did, she would. You should all call me that because I am your friend and you have done me the most immense favour.'

In the distance Jack could see the farmhouse. 'He'll be in the lambing shed. You were her employer first, so she won't feel easy calling you anything but Miss Manton.'

Miss Manton laughed. 'But I'm not now, so let's get over this. Try it. Grace. Grace. Edward, Edward. Go on, it's easy.'

It wasn't, that was the thing, Jack thought, irritated. 'Grace,' he said in the end as they approached the first of the six gates, keeping his eyes fixed firmly on the way they were going, not on her as she sat back and crossed her legs, her boot grazing his leg as she did so. If equality was what she wanted, then she was going to get it.

'Grace, would you jump down and open the gate?' he said as he turned to her. She looked at the gate, surprised, and then saw his grin and burst into peals of laughter. She hopped down and waited until he was through, then closed it. But then she called to him. 'There's rope under your seat. Pass it to me, please.'

Jack leaned down and felt beneath the seat. There were several coils. He brought one out and tossed it to her, puzzled. She tied the gate shut, creating knot after knot. 'That should hold him for a bit.'

She ran to catch up, climbing into the trap. He held out his hand to pull her in. 'Mine is the next gate,' he said.

'You're absolutely right, it most certainly is.' They were laughing and had almost forgotten the rush they were in. Almost. Jack shook the reins and Sally broke into a trot. Grace checked her watch. 'If Auberon is at the mine he might leave early. Will he bring his father, because if so they could come in the Rolls-Royce, and be here in next to no time?'

Jack shook his head. 'He wouldn't risk the car on these tracks. They'll come in a carriage or trap but whether Bastard . . .' He stopped. 'Brampton, I mean. Whether Brampton will come at all I'm not sure. He might just send his son. I gather he's trying to toughen him up, or that's the talk around the mine. Just send the little beggar down the pit, that'd toughen him up soon enough.' He shook the reins again to chivvy Sally along. She flicked her tail.

Grace said, 'She's not used to this terrain, or a man handling her.'

Jack grinned to himself. He had thought she would think him a boy. He sat straighter. Then he said, 'Perhaps he's ahead of us. We've no way of knowing.'

Silence fell, and all they could do was to take it in turns to open and close the gates until they finally drew into Froggett's yard. There was no horse there that could have belonged to Auberon, and relief caused them to look at one another and grin. He saw that she wasn't really old, not at all. He'd just never looked at her before, not really looked. Her eyes were almost green and she had freckles, and that hair of hers was so rich and thick that a man's hands could get caught up in it and not be in a hurry to be released. He shook his head. Was he mad?

Grace jumped down and stood uncertainly. Jack came round the trap and beckoned her towards the barn from which came the sound of sheep calling, and the higher pitch of lambs. He knocked hard on the barn door but there was no reply. He smiled at Grace. 'Could you hear above that racket? We'll go in.'

The lambs were penned in rows behind slatted wood and on straw. Froggett had said in the Working Men's Club on Saturday that he liked to keep some of the ewes undercover in case there was late snow, because he was sick of losing the lambs in drifts. Jack had slapped him on the shoulder and said, 'It's April.' The older men had shouted him down, waving their beer at him. 'You never know until May, man.'

Grace stepped carefully over the scattered straw as they headed for Froggett, who was in the far pen. His dog, Star, lay in the passage between the parallel rows. Jack breathed in the scent of the straw, and the warmth of the animals. Star turned at the sound of their footsteps and bounded towards them, his tongue hanging out. Froggett saw the movement and turned, yelling, 'Get ya back.'

Star obeyed instantly, slinking along and lying as before. Froggett shoved back his cap and stared from Grace to Jack. He stepped over the barrier and walked towards them, removing his cap. 'Well, young Jack, surprised to see you out here, and how's parson, missus?'

Jack explained about the houses and their wish to buy all three as Froggett ushered them out, and across the yard and into his kitchen. Mrs Froggett was preparing vegetables and a simmering kettle hissed on the range. She was more than plump, she was built like a bloody dreadnought, and the government should stop the naval race with Germany and just send the missus, or so Froggett would say with monotonous regularity after a few beers at the club; and every inch of her pure gold.

She showed no surprise at their arrival, or at Froggett's explanation, but insisted they sit and eat. 'Can't talk business on an empty stomach, pet,' she said, pointing Grace firmly to the chair at the head of the table. Grace removed her coat and hung it on the back of the carver, and placed her gloves on the table. Jack wondered if Mrs Froggett had ever had an empty stomach in her life. Froggett took the chair at the other end, and Jack turned his cap over and over in his hand, wondering where he should sit. Froggett turned to him. 'Stop cluttering up the place, lad. Take a pew, and the parson's getting on all right then, missus?'

Grace nodded and smiled, but then grew serious. 'He's recovering well, thank you Mr Froggett, but we needed to come and talk to you, quickly.' Jack felt Mrs Froggett's hands on his shoulders, pushing him towards the chair on Froggett's right. On the dresser to his left was a photograph of Danny, their son. He had chosen to go in the pit when he was thirteen because his elder brother wanted to stay on the farm, and it wouldn't support them all. Danny had been killed in a tub accident last year when he was trapping the doors. His body had been slung into a sack, then a cart and just dumped here on the kitchen floor by Davies' special few. It was not unusual.

Jack made himself listen to Grace because he mustn't think of Timmie trapping. Scones were placed before them, and rich yellow butter. The scones were still warm and the butter melted into the white soft dough and then did the same in his mouth. He wiped the crumbs from his lips and slurped his tea. Mrs Froggett laughed and pushed the plate towards him again. 'I'll put some together for the family. How's young Timmie doing?' Her eyes shadowed.

'Belting,' Jack said, trying not to see the quivering of her lips and the filling of her eyes, but how could you not? Mrs Froggett turned from him, and swept the vegetables that were scattered on the range side of the table into a large pan before seating herself.

Grace had finished by asking for a price for the houses, her voice high-pitched with tension. Jack checked the clock on the wall near the range. Was Auberon on his way? Would the rope knots hold him up? By, she was a canny lass, this Grace Manton.

Froggett studied his hands and looked at Mrs Froggett. It was then that Jack said, 'We need to tell you that the Bramptons want the houses too. It's only fair. We think they're on their way here any day now, and I bet they'll top any price you ask from us.'

There was a silence. He knew that Grace was studying him, and saw Mrs Froggett was looking at her husband. Jack's heart was beating in his throat because he might just have taken the future away, not only from his family, but the other miners. But he had had to say what he just did, for when the Bramptons came, and he knew they would, the Froggetts didn't deserve to be cheated. Losing a son was more than cheat enough.

Grace nodded at Froggett and said, 'Jack is quite right.'

Mrs Froggett pushed the scones towards Grace. 'Aye, them Bramptons speak to us often about it. Eat up, pet, we need to think about this and the lambs need checking.' The Froggetts rose and went out, leaving Grace and Jack looking at the scones, and then one another. She reached across and laid her hand on his arm 'You did well. I should have said something and didn't. I'm ashamed.'

He looked at her hand: it was so pale and so soft.

That would be because it did no work, but he couldn't feel angry. She snatched back her hand and attacked a scone. He said, 'No need to be ashamed. It's just fair, that's all.'

She was concentrating on the scone, heaping it with jam. Perhaps he'd try another too. He was spreading the jam when the kitchen door opened again and the Froggetts trooped back in, with Star. It must be a special occasion for the dog to be allowed in the house. He curled up in front of the range, on the proggy mat.

Froggett took a pencil and two slips of paper from the dresser, and wrote some figures. He showed one slip to Grace, and the other to Jack. On each was the Froggetts' price. Jack could hardly stay still. The amount was very little more than they already had, so they would only require a very small loan.

Clearly Grace was as delighted, but said, her voice firm and serious, 'This is more than reasonable and I must tell you that we would pay more, and don't forget the Bramptons. They most certainly would. You have a son to consider.'

The Froggetts were standing at the end of the table. Mrs Froggett nodded. 'Aye, you're quite right lass, we do have a son to consider. We should have two. I want the Forbes in that end cottage and I want them to fight for better conditions in Auld Maud so fewer folk have to unwrap a sack from their son's ruined body, in front of the range, staining their proggy mat, with not even an apology.'

At that moment Star stirred and barked, rushing out of the door and into the yard. A horse neighed. Froggett glanced out of the window. 'Well, speak of the devil.'

Jack peered out. It was the whelp, dismounting from his horse. He carried a whip which he tucked under his arm as he stood looking at Grace's trap. The day was darkening and the stunted tree was flattening in the wind. Auberon smoothed his fair hair and straightened his hacking jacket. He must have driven his trap home from the colliery, and had his groom saddle up straight away. There was a fair lather on the bay, who was tossing his head as Auberon tied him to a hitching post. The lad looked as though he'd walked into a door, or a fist or two. It would be the Bastard, of that Jack was sure.

He looked at the figures on the paper again. Perhaps Froggett would change his mind when actually faced with such power, such wealth. The farmer was at his side now, and spat in his hand. 'All done, lad?'

Jack looked over his shoulder at Grace, who was by the table, peering out of the window on tiptoe. 'Are you sure?'

Mrs Froggett nodded. 'We're more than happy, lad.'

Jack looked at Grace. 'Are you happy, Grace? I'm buying mine, are you buying yours or should you ask the parson?' Grace shook her head. 'No, I answer for us both. We're buying them. I'll see the solicitor and you will have your money within the next two weeks, Mr and Mrs Froggett.' Jack spat in his hand and he and Froggett shook. 'That's done then. It's right canny,' Froggett said.

He turned to Grace who looked uncertain for a moment, lifted her hand and seemed about to spit in it. Mrs Froggett laughed and shook her head. 'Not you, Miss Manton.' Mr Froggett held out his hand to Grace and they shook. 'That's you done too.'

Mrs Froggett was wrapping scones in greaseproof paper and tying the parcel with string.

The knock on the door came. 'You can go out the back way, lass,' said Froggett. Grace shook her head. 'The trap is out in the yard and I'm not creeping around for anyone, are you Jack?' Her eyes were challenging, which just went to show that she didn't know him very well.

'I never run away,' he muttered. Froggett laughed. 'Come on then, both of you. I'll see you off and entertain myself with young Mr Auberon.'

He led the way out of the kitchen, into the stone-flagged corridor. Mrs Froggett kissed Jack. 'Tell your mam I'm right happy she's to have a home of her own, right happy I am. We'll almost be neighbours.' He hugged her, unable to stop himself. She was soft and smelled of baking, and he wondered what Evie was doing. Was she baking, or cooking for the whelp? What did it matter, she was learning, she was near Simon, she was happy and would be happier when she knew the news.

He stood back to allow Grace to leave before him, but she shook her head. 'I think I'd rather you led, if you don't mind. I confess to feeling a little nervous. I fear there might be a tantrum. What is the matter with his face, do you think?'

Froggett was opening the door and there was Mr Auberon, his hand raised to knock again. He removed his kid gloves and stretched out his hand. Froggett hesitated and then took it, but didn't ask him in. He stood back against the wall as Jack and Grace reached the door. 'I'll see my solicitor tomorrow. We'll get the sale of the houses signed up nice and tidy.' Jack and Grace nodded to him, and to Auberon, who was standing as though struck by a heavy weight. He had paled and his expression was one of despair. For a moment Jack paused. The bruises on the lad's face were old but still stark against his pallor, and his lip was split. Poor bugger.

Grace pushed him from behind and Jack still hesitated, but what could he say? He stepped past Auberon, pulling his cap down and nodding. Star pushed out with him and ran ahead, barking and jumping, looking as though he was smiling, with his tongue lolling out. Jack laughed. 'He's such a daft beggar.'

They hurried to the trap, for they must get back before darkness fell and his shift began. As he handed Grace into the trap Jack heard Auberon say, 'But we can offer more, we'll top anything.'

Froggett said something Jack didn't hear as he

helped Grace up into the trap, but what he did hear was Auberon saying, 'Forbes, Jack Forbes, you mean?'

Auberon was waiting outside the library for his father's summons. He had to tell him that he had failed and he knew the price he would pay, but all he could hear was Jack Forbes' laugh and the words, 'He's such a daft beggar.' How dare he? How dare that rabble-rouser call him a daft beggar.

It was only after he staggered up the stairs later, tasting blood, aching from the blows, that he wondered who had told Froggett of his intentions. Someone had, someone had just ruined his life. It was his father's parting words that had burned the thought into his brain. 'You need to keep your trap shut. Someone knew our plans, you complete and utter fool.'

Chapter Ten

Auberon stood at the window of his dressing room the next morning, still tousled from bed, half dressed, his braces hanging down, his feet bare. He wore a suit for the colliery but it was bloody ridiculous because the air was thick with sleck dust as the manager called it, thick and stinking, and his shirts became so too, within an hour. He fingered his buttons but the trembling was too violent to do any good.

Where was the bloody valet? What was his name? He tried to clear his head which was still thick from the beating, the haranguing, the pain and shame of failure. He took deep breaths, concentrating on the valet. His name? What the hell was his name? For God's sake, Roger, that was what it was, all his father's valets were known as Roger, and why not. There were too many other things to think about without worrying what to call the bloody servants. Archie and James were the footmen, Roger was the valet, and the housemaids were Ethel, all of them were just Ethel, though there was a Lil, wasn't there? God, he couldn't think. He shook his head, and slowly he recaptured his mind.

He looked out into the grounds. He was glad his suite of rooms faced this way, with the spotless sweeping drive, all weeds hoed up by the staff. And what were *their* names? He didn't need to know that. He steadied himself against the window frame, aching and wanting to crouch down and groan, but he made himself look out of the window. He insisted to himself again that he was glad this was his outlook, and at the thought he pushed back his shoulders and lifted his head, for how could he have lived in rooms that overlooked the terrace on to which Wainey had plunged? He almost welcomed the deadly strike at his heart. It focused him. It was the same pain that had knifed into him when his mother just faded and died of consumption.

When would it fade? The pain of their deaths just seemed to get worse. He felt his shoulders slump again and the tears build in his throat, but men didn't cry. He straightened, forcing his head up. Tears were only acceptable at the end of a beating. He had learned that on the day of his mother's funeral when he had wept and his father had invited him into his study that evening, but when hadn't he been invited into the bloody place? One day he'd blow it up with his bloody father in it.

He needed air, and he needed his bloody shoes. He opened the window carefully, working around the pain. There had been no more damage to his face, because the bruises from last time were too obvious.

Good to know that even his father could slip up. His laugh was harsh.

The sun was out and the blossom was drifting to the ground in the wind. There were long shadows cast by the cedar tree in the centre of the lawn. It was reputed to be sixty years old, and from its height he could believe it. It had been planted by the father of the present head gardener, apparently. He wondered what their gardeners thought of working for a nouveau riche instead of a true blue.

But then, so many of the true blues had sold off or even burned down their houses rather than maintain them after the level of taxes continued to rise, so maybe the servants were glad of people like us, he thought. He leaned out of the window and breathed in the fresh morning air, filling his lungs before those hours at the colliery. There was a stiff breeze, ignored by the cedar. Auberon smiled. The bloody tree barely swayed in whatever wind blew, and perhaps one day he would achieve that level of solidity. Perhaps, but in the meantime where were his bloody shoes?

He moved carefully to the bell rope to the right of the doorway which led to his bedroom, guarding his ribs, trying to ignore the crushing pain, and pulled, returning to stand in front of the full-length mirror. He tried to do up his top button, but his fingers were still trembling too much. Roger should be here, for God's sake. He'd have finished with his father by now. Then he let his hands drop. Of course.

Of course. He stared at himself, realisation dawning at last.

He'd only mentioned the need to buy the houses to Veronica before breakfast when she'd visited his suite of rooms, and she would not have repeated it. Roger had been tidying the dressing room at the time. His father could have arrived at the same conclusion, for why else would his valet be late?

At that moment there was a knock on the door and Roger entered, a smile, as rigid as any Brampton steel girder, fixed to his face. 'You rang, Mr Auberon?'

Evie's day had begun at five thirty as always, and as she wished. She enjoyed being first down into what she considered her territory. In the kitchen the mice scattered at her arrival, also as always. Things never seemed to change, but perhaps today, they would. As she lit the furnace Annie, Sarah and Millie entered. Millie began to blacklead the ranges, saying, 'You're bloody mad smiling at this time of the morning, Evie. You're just mad.' She had bags under her eyes, as though she was the one who hadn't slept last night. Evie herself had not wanted to sleep away the joy she had felt.

Sarah and Annie were crashing and banging the pots in the scullery as Evie shook her head. 'It's spring, Millie, the primroses are out, the cowslips are in the fields, I saw them today from the bedroom window. There are swathes of them, haven't you seen?'

'Oh, get on with the tea for the upper servants, and that old drunk.'

Evie had been about to lift the kettle on to the range but now she banged it down, marching over to Millie, who was on her knees. 'What did you say? And stand up when I'm speaking to you.'

Millie stared. 'Who are you to tell me?'

Evie grabbed her elbow and forced her to stand. Millie dropped the blacklead and tried to wrench free, her face pale with shock. Evie risked her recovering throat by shouting, 'I'm your senior and if I ever hear you talking of Mrs Moore as you've just done I will have you dismissed. Do you understand? You'll be out of the bloody door without a character.' Millie nodded, her eyes full of tears, but when weren't they? 'Mrs Moore is in constant pain and occasionally she has a nip of gin and I repeat, *occasionally*. It's what any canny woman would do and you are to keep your gob tight shut, do you understand?'

She was shaking her. Tears were running down Millie's cheeks and suddenly the heat went out of Evie. She snatched the girl to her, holding her tightly, squashing her cap. 'I'm sorry Millie pet, but you must be more careful. What goes on in this kitchen stays in this kitchen and it isn't talked about, not here, not anywhere. What if we blabbed to Mrs Green about your mistakes? How long do you think you'd last?' For there were numerous 'Millie errors', as they were called. The girl stopped sobbing and Evie released her. Millie rescued the blacklead from the floor and sank again to her knees.

Evie said, 'I'm away to do the teas, and the ranges need to be finished.' Millie's nose was red and her eyes even more puffy, but she had to learn. Once the teas were safely delivered Evie gathered up her shawl and told Millie she was off to fetch the eggs. Millie stood. 'I can do those for you, Evie.'

'Not like I can,' Evie snapped. 'Please set the table for Mrs Moore's breakfast preparation. It's finnan haddock today, braised kidneys yet again, scrambled egg and bacon, and for some reason his Lordship wants kedgeree with it again, so kedgeree he will have. He leaves for Leeds immediately after, so we've no need to bother with such overblown guzzles for a while. Now, familiarise yourself with lunch when you're done with setting the table. You'll find the menu in the front of Mrs Moore's book.' Her tone was crisp because irritation and worry had begun to nag at her. Had she been joyous too soon? What had happened with the house? What if news of Mrs Moore's drinking was blabbed by Millie to others? By, there was never any bloody end to the ifs, buts and maybes of life.

She slipped from the basement to the henhouse, collected the warm eggs into the straw-lined basket and then headed for the vegetable storeroom, hoping that Simon had news for her, hoping that Simon was there anyway, because she just needed to be with him. He was waiting inside, in the shadows. 'Jack brought this to me at the bothy. I haven't read it.' She smiled as he took the egg basket in exchange for the note.

> *Evie pet,*
> *We have it. Just the paperwork to finish now. Grace is going to talk to her solicitor. Mr Auberon is not pleased. He came as we were leaving, so there might be some anger at the Hall. Remember to keep your mouth shut if the Forbes family are mentioned. We are too big and bad to need defending! Grace wants us all to call her by her first name. She declares herself a friend. I know it sounds dramatic, but destroy this note.*
> *Your brother.*

She grinned at Simon. 'We've got it,' she whispered, tucking the note into her apron pocket, and taking the proffered egg basket. 'I have to rush, it's the Bastard's last morning for a while and I haven't seen how Mrs Moore is yet. I don't know about that Millie, you know, Simon. One minute she's a pathetic little thing, the next she's spiteful, or maybe just silly.'

Simon was grinning. 'Forget about everything but the house, she'll settle. I'm right pleased for you, Evie,' but there was a sadness in his voice that Evie recognised, and knew it was because his da and mam were still in a colliery house, but when she had the hotel . . .

She reminded him of her plans and that there'd be a place for his parents, and he just shook his head. 'A living wonder you are, Evie Anston. You'd bend the cedar tree if you whooshed past it with all your energy, now get back and get those eggs on before you end up out on your neck.'

He made no attempt to kiss her hand as she left, but she could feel him watching as she strode up the path and heard his soft call. 'I'm so glad I know you, bonny lass.' She turned, walked backwards and said, 'I need to know that to get through the day, bonny lad.' He laughed and hurried into the walled garden, his jerkin flapping in the wind.

She half ran up the path and almost bumped into Roger as he stepped from the top corner store, the one nearest the backyard. He was smiling, but it was a strange hard smile. She stepped to the right, on to the verge, but he stepped with her. She was sick of his games. Behind him she could see the tools in the store. He said, 'Come and have a look, Evie Anston.'

She pointed to her basket. 'I need to get these to Mrs Moore.'

Roger reached for her, she stepped back, but he was too quick and grabbed her arm. 'It wasn't an invitation, it was an order.' He came so close that she could smell the alcohol on his breath and it wasn't even eight o'clock. What was going on, was drinking catching? She knew she was thinking nonsense, but what *was* going on? His hand was tight on her arm and suddenly he was behind her, twisting her arm up her back. The pain took her breath from her. She was still clutching the egg basket in her other hand, but what else could she do? Shout, you bloody idiot, she thought. Simon would come. She started to, but then Roger's hand was over her mouth and he was pushing her from behind, into the darkness of the store.

He said against her ear, 'You heard what I said to Len that day, didn't you? You were the only one near enough, and he was the only one I told, him and his bloody oily rags. You came round that corner too sharpish after our row, and before you did I heard a noise. You were there, listening. You told someone about the house-buying. How dare you? I'm on a warning now, and I'm banned from here, back to valeting for his Lordship who is in a foul mood, and just who do you think will get the brunt of that? He's going to make my life hell and I can't leave, for he's said I'll get no character.' He removed his hand from her mouth. What could she say? He knew it was her, but he mustn't know why. She said, 'It's what you wanted, isn't it, to go back to his Lordship as his valet? It's promotion.'

He jerked her arm higher up her back. She gasped with the pain and leaned back to ease the tension. 'You stupid bitch. It's punishment. He'll run me ragged and then I'll be back when he's finished his fun and it's all your fault. You lost them the houses, didn't you? I want to know who you told about them, and I want to know why.'

Evie shook her head. 'I don't know what you're talking about. I didn't tell anyone, why would I? It's nothing to do with me.' She felt his grip weaken and prepared herself, taking her weight on her right leg and then stamping down hard on his foot with the heel of her left boot. 'Ouch.'

His grip loosened, she spun away but he was faster, blocking the doorway. He shook his head, his face red, his mouth set in a grim smile. 'You really, really, shouldn't have done that.' He advanced and she kept the egg basket between them, wanting to cry out but not daring to. What if someone came and he said she'd passed on the gossip? No matter how many times she denied it, questions might be asked, and answers discovered. No, she was Evie Anston and she must stay that way.

He reached for her. She stepped back. He lunged again. She dodged to the side, but caught her foot on a hoe. She held up her hand, saying, 'You'll be late for his Lordship, or Mr Auberon or whoever you are looking after.'

He shook his head, lunged again and found her throat, fingers one side, thumb the other. It hurt. 'It's early yet. I've seen his Lordship and Mr Auberon, who felt it his pleasure to give me another tongue-lashing.'

He was squeezing her throat. 'So, one more chance – who have you been blabbing to, because it's spread so quick it's reached the wrong ears.' He was enjoying this, she could tell from his face, but he had no idea she'd gone straight to the horse's mouth. Relief drenched her. She shook her head. 'Let me go.' Her voice was so faint that it reminded her of the cold of Fordington and Jack's rescue. Jack. She concentrated on all that he had ever told her.

Roger was close now, his suit immaculate, his lips pursed, and then his mouth was on hers, and his tongue forcing its way into her mouth. She gagged. His hand still held her throat; she could barely breathe. He lifted his head, licked her cheek. His hand was away from her throat and grabbing at her breast while his other was on her back, pressing her against him. The egg basket was in her hand, dangling at the side of her. She mustn't break them.

He was kissing her neck, and he had backed her to the wall. Her ankle caught the hoe again. It fell to the ground with a clang. Something jabbed into her back. She thrust against him, pushing. He laughed and threw her arm to the side. She twisted her head away from his probing mouth. There were gardening hand tools on the shelf which ran along the side of the store. He was clutching at her clothes, tearing at them. Dear God, he might find the letter. Jack. Jack, I'm waiting for an opportunity, like you said to do.

She stopped fighting, relaxed against him, and he laughed. 'That's what you are, eh, a whore that plays with men. I knew you'd want it but it won't be enough. You'll pay, Evie Anston, because of what you've done.' He was speaking against her throat.

She felt along the shelf, made contact with a bucket, found the handle, and while he was pulling at her bodice she swung it round and made contact. All she hit was his shoulder, but it shocked him. She stamped on his foot and lifted the other knee sharply into his groin, and that did hurt.

She pulled away, slapping at him, hissing. 'You bastard, lay a hand on me again and I'll hit you with more than a bloody bucket, d'you hear? I'll bloody well castrate you.'

He was moaning, bent over double. She ran out of the store, across the yard, down the steps to the kitchen, her eggs still intact though her sleeve was torn. Mrs Moore asked why. She said she'd caught it on the henhouse door.

'Oh yes, or perhaps, oh no,' Mrs Moore sniffed, pouring tea. She stirred the kedgeree. 'You've taken a long time about it, I have to say. Dress your hair, and what are those marks on your neck?'

Evie said nothing. The fewer questions the better and besides, she deserved her punishment. She had caused Roger grief by passing on the gossip but now they were even, and it was best no more questions were asked. She merely shrugged. 'It's this chill and the henhouse dust made me cough, I expect I put my hand to my throat.' They set about the breakfast but first Evie stoked up the furnace and threw in Jack's note. It wasn't until they began to prepare lunch that the shaking started.

It continued until Roger came in after luncheon

had been cleared. He found her in the big pantry, coming to stand next to her, bold as brass, whispering, 'If you don't have me, I'll take your friend Millie just as I took that Charlotte. Think on, Evie Anston, it's up to you.' He stepped back into the kitchen, bowed to Mrs Moore. 'Farewell, ladies. I'm not sure when I will be back for good, but back I will be.' He flicked another bow to Millie. 'You keep yourself as beautiful as you are this day, Miss Millie, and we'll maybe have a chance to get to know one another better when I return.'

Mrs Moore snorted, looking from a flushed and smiling Millie to Evie. Evie stared at her trembling hands. She couldn't allow that, Millie was too frightened of life, too silly. All that day and the rest of the night she wrestled with his words and as dawn broke all she could think was that she would warn Millie and look out for her, because there was no way she was selling herself for anyone's sake, ever.

Chapter Eleven

During that week and the next Mrs Moore and Mrs Green warned their staff against Roger in every way possible, because they were not going to have any girl of theirs getting to know 'that snake in a suit' any better on his return. Mrs Moore was concerned for Evie. 'I'm not a fool, I know perfectly well who the fox in the henhouse was,' she snapped at Evie, and her outrage seemed to energise her. Within days the swelling and pain subsided and there was no gin top-up in her tea. So, good things come out of hiccups, Evie told herself.

The atmosphere in the servants' hall was lighter without Roger, much as the weather now that they were into May. 'Can't believe it's just little more than a month since I arrived,' Evie said as she started on the salt-bake mix which she would wrap around the roasting veal, and ten days since Roger had attacked her. 'Aye, it seems to have galloped along,' Mrs Moore murmured as they worked together preparing dinner on Wednesday afternoon. 'It'll all calm down a bit now with Lord Brampton gone, and I daresay we won't have to fiddle about with tea for his young ones for a while. They won't need the succour, and it's grand he won't be laying hands on Mr Auberon for a while.'

Evie stopped in her mixing. The flour was up to her elbows. She grated in more salt. Mrs Moore looked through the windows into the passageway and whispered, 'I shouldn't have said that. We have to be careful. Just think, someone repeated to someone else, which set off a right to-do, that the Bramptons were to buy Froggett's houses, or so the gossip goes.'

Evie snatched a look at her and then concentrated fully on rolling out the salt bake. 'I can't imagine who that could be.'

Mrs Moore laughed quietly. 'Strange, isn't it, Miss Evie Anston? Now, it's your afternoon off, so away with the apron. I'll finish that.' She was studying her recipe book, running her finger down the page and tutting. 'They've requested ice cream. It's such a nuisance.'

Evie removed her apron and hung it on the peg, passing behind Mrs Moore who said quietly, 'I'll unlatch the pantry window, just in case, and you give my wishes to Miss Manton.'

Evie sped down the back paths to the bothy, intent on the time, and on her bicycle and the glory of the cowslips in the wild area, and the primroses. Soon the bluebells would be out and the air filled with their fragrance. Everything seemed good, and it was only in flashes that she felt Roger's mouth and tongue again, and his hands tearing at her.

As she approached the bothy she could see Simon inside whittling a long thin branch into a walking stick, waiting for her. She hesitated, knowing that she had avoided him for well over a week, since Roger's attack, to the point where Millie had said as they lay in bed one night, 'Gone off him, have you? Poor lad, he likes you. You don't know how lucky you are, Evie. You have so much more than I will ever have.' Her voice was harsh and angry. Evie had pretended sleep, wishing yet again that Annie hadn't asked to share with Sarah, leaving her with the dubious pleasure of Millie's company.

Simon looked up, his mouth pursed in a silent whistle. 'Hello there, Evie Anston. I wondered if I had grown two heads or something?' He smiled but his eyes were bruised beneath, as though he hadn't slept. She knew hers were the same.

She stopped for a moment, wanting to run away, but Miss Manton was waiting for her, and she wasn't another Millie, for heaven's sake. She pushed back her shoulders and laughed. Even to her own ears it sounded false. 'You have one head still, bonny lad, and a grand one it is too.' Yes, that struck the right note.

She entered the bothy but couldn't reach her bicycle because she'd have to go through Simon to get there, and he clearly wasn't about to move. He folded up his knife and put it in his pocket. He blew on the walking stick. Shreds of wood flew into the air, spiralling to the ground like sycamore seeds. He held up his handiwork, eyeing it up and down. 'I've been working on this as I've waited for you in the store-room, but it's been Millie. I don't want to see Millie.' His voice was firm. 'See how much I've done when I could have been snatching words with you instead.'

He dropped the walking stick and removed his cap, running his hand through his red hair. He did not move towards her but waited, and she knew that he'd wait all day if he had to. He was like Jack, solid, fierce, strong, kind, understanding.

She approached. Her handlebars were almost in reach. They were rusted and would need sanding with emery paper. She would buff them until they gleamed like the fender. He crossed his arms. 'Don't you like me any more, Evie?' She couldn't bear the pain in his voice.

She shook her head and he straightened, reaching for the walking stick, slapping on his cap and striding to the door, but she called out, 'No, I didn't mean that. Stop, please Simon.'

He did, turning in the doorway. She couldn't see his face against the brightness of the day, in which the last remaining petals of blossom clung to the branches, and the clouds scudded towards the Stunted Tree. 'What did you mean then, Evie? If things have changed, then they have and that's all there is to it, but I need to know.'

She told him then, of Roger and how she couldn't quite get her head straight enough to be with him, Simon. It came in fits and starts and throughout it he said nothing. Finally he swung round to face the sun and as she watched he raised his walking stick and broke it across his leg, throwing away the two halves. He stayed there. So, that was how it was. Like everyone else he thought the woman was to blame. Why had she said anything? Why?

She gripped the handlebars and pulled her bicycle out from amongst the others. It would be all right. She would be fine. She would paint placards and listen to the speaker and worry about the wisdom of votes before taxes and none of this would matter at all, none of it. She would cook, and one day she'd have her hotel, and her family would be out of the pit, that was what was important. She wheeled her bicycle towards the entrance but still he stood there with his back towards her. She said, 'Please excuse me.'

He shook his head, then stood aside, half in and out of the bothy. She pushed past but suddenly his arm came up, creating a barrier. His voice was hoarse as he shouted, 'You never ask me to excuse you, Evie Anston, do you hear me? You never have to ask anyone to excuse you. You ask for help, that's what you do. You could have called, I would have come. How dare anyone hurt you? How dare he lay his hands on you?' Then his arms were round her, at last they were round her, and he was speaking into her hair. 'I'll kill him, I'll bloody well kill him if he ever comes near you again.'

Her bicycle fell against her and slid to the ground

as she lifted her arms and held him, feeling safe for the first time since Roger. Simon kissed her then, on her forehead and cheek but not her mouth, and she was glad because even though it was Simon, all she saw was Roger.

The meeting was under way by the time Evie and Grace Manton arrived, and by then they were on first-name terms. The doors were unlocked to their coded knock. Rat-a-tat. Rat-a-tat. It was locked after them, 'To repel boarders,' the doorkeeper whispered, grinning. They tiptoed to the back row. A young woman was onstage talking of the strength of the female sex, the need for their vote in order to help shape the country, and annotating the price women had so far paid. They heard how the speaker had been arrested and imprisoned along with many others, after heckling and throwing bricks through shop windows. They heard how one of her friends had even put a burning rag into a post-office letter box. She paced the stage and told how though the Pankhursts' campaign of damage had created harsher sentences it had also driven Asquith to reconsider the question of votes for women.

Grace murmured, 'How pleasant to have such a smart hat. Ostrich feathers, eh? I suspect it cost more than a worker would pay to keep his family for a month.' The woman next to her swung round, surprise showing on her lined and weary face. 'More, I reckon. It's said that unlike her sister and mother

Sylvia Pankhurst is on the side of the workers. She's got her priorities right.'

The applause was polite, and their chairwoman took the stage and announced that a member of the Liberal Party would be talking in Newcastle to support the People's Budget. 'We must go, we must heckle and disrupt. We must insist on the vote before taxes. I have chalked on the board the time of the train we will take and we need as many of you as possible. I know all the excuses – you would lose your jobs, your husbands, your children, but think of the cause, think of the women coming after you.' Some women were stamping their feet, cheering, clapping.

Some of those towards the back were not, including Grace and Evie, and their new friend, Betty Clark. Grace muttered, 'I daresay she doesn't need to work, never has, never will. What's going wrong here, we're losing our way aren't we?'

Mrs Dale, the newly appointed chairwoman, waved the hall to silence. 'I invite comments from the audience.'

One by one, women stood and agreed with Mrs Dale. Grace whispered, 'Will you or I risk getting hung and stand up and say what we think?'

Evie smiled. 'I will. The parson might not like me taking you home with a rope round your neck.'

But then someone from the front of the audience stood, and Mrs Dale waved for silence again. It wasn't until she began to speak that they realised it was Lady Veronica. Evie gripped Grace's arm. 'She mustn't see me, I'll be dismissed.' Grace said, 'Shh.'

Lady Veronica was saying, 'It's irresponsible to take this attitude. How does it show that we are worthy of the vote? We need to give more to the poor, we should concentrate on that and support Lloyd George, not disrupt . . .' The hall erupted with boos and some cheers, all of which drowned out the rest of her words. Evie stood up to see better but Lady Veronica was being pulled down by someone sitting next to her. Who? They peered but couldn't see.

Grace pulled Evie down too, saying, 'I saw her here once but thought she was on a fishing trip, something to tell her friends, something to laugh about. We were polite and neither of us 'recognised' the other. We need to get you out before she sees you, but isn't she magnificent?' She resumed clapping and cheering, and Evie too. In fact, all the back row were clamouring their support. Evie shouted above the melee, 'Shouldn't she have a chaperone? What on earth would her family say?'

Mrs Dale and the committee, ranged on chairs at the rear of the stage, were appealing for calm, hushing with their hands as though the suffragettes were a pack of rampaging hounds, and perhaps we are, Evie thought, starting to laugh at the absurdity of it all.

Grace was still clapping, her eyes alight, her face flushed. She said, 'Perhaps she does have one, but not the sort of which Lady B would approve. A friend perhaps? I am just so surprised at her, but why, when Miss Wainton was such a supporter of women's votes? I should have realised.'

Evie wished she'd met Miss Wainton. Easterleigh Hall must have been a happier place in her time. It was then the first brick came through a window, with a burst of sound and crashing of glass. It silenced the women. The brick had hit a woman sitting two seats away from Evie. There was a great pounding at the door, and the yelling of men. For a moment Evie couldn't think or react, and it seemed it was the same for everyone. Then chairs scraped. Women moved. Jeers were heard. Another brick crashed through a window, this time nearer to the front. More glass, more screams. Now the women were rushing, but not to any one point. They were milling, panicking.

Mrs Dale called, 'Back exit. Make for the back exit.'

It wasn't the first time a meeting had been invaded, which was why the doors were always locked and no hall would be booked unless it had a rear exit. It was the first time for Evie, though, and for a moment she could do nothing but stare helplessly as the bricks came thick and fast. 'To the rear,' Grace shouted, then the doors cracked open and men roared in, red-faced from the booze, their scarves tied at their necks, their caps cockeyed on their heads, racing for the women who scattered, shouting now, not screaming, throwing chairs in the way of the men, and then stampeding in a body to the exit, those that could. Groups were cut off, surrounded.

Evie and Grace raced through a gap with Betty Clark but Evie saw Lady Veronica over to the left, near the stage in the path of a mob whose fists were flying. 'Mucky buggers,' Evie shouted above the noise. 'We need to get her out, we need to keep her anonymous. Think if the Bastard got to hear of it.'

Grace took a moment to take in the situation while Betty kept on towards the rear, then Evie was forcing her way back against the tide. Grace joined her and together they stepped over fallen chairs, discarded bags, all the while being pushed, shoved and knocked by fleeing women and jeering men. The sound seemed almost to drown out thought and they acted by instinct. Bricks were still flying through the windows, and they dodged them as glass showered down and was crunched underfoot.

Lady Veronica was moving forward now, pulling the speaker along. Their hats were lopsided, their feathers flapping uselessly. Evie and Grace stared at one another, unable to accept that Brampton's daughter was with this girl who'd just spoken about being imprisoned for her views. 'If her father knew, he'd strangle her with his bare hands,' Grace shouted against the noise.

'Aye, but she spoke against her.' Evie's reply was lost as a man grabbed her coat, throwing her off balance, wielding a pick in his other hand. Evie felt herself being wrenched to the ground. His breath was foul in her face and heavy with beer. He was no pitman for there were no blue scars, no staining of the skin. Grace was beating his back. He loosened his grip. Evie scrambled to her feet, stamping on his boots, but they were steel-capped. He kicked at her, catching her shin. The pain took her breath away, but only for a moment, for then she went for his eyes with her nails and he swore, swinging the pick at her, but Grace grabbed his arm. Evie wrenched the pick from him. It was too heavy and whacked into the floor. She wrenched it up by the head, jabbing at his belly, taking the wind out of him. He groaned and dropped.

Grace laughed, wild and high. 'I should offer the other cheek but instead I want to slap his.' She gestured Evie onwards, pointing towards Lady Veronica, who had been separated from her friend by a stream of women powering towards the front entrance now; all the men were within the hall, it seemed, and heading towards the rear exit. Some women had picked up chairs and were attacking the men, who were backing towards the stage, their arms up, shielding themselves.

Lady Veronica was hatless, her fair hair awry. Evie clung to her pick, holding the head and wielding the handle, jabbing a way clear towards her. Grace had grabbed a chair and was stabbing like a lion-tamer. They seized Lady Veronica, who was now swinging a chair at the men. Grace shouted, 'Leave it now. Come out. You mustn't be recognised.'

Lady Veronica's eyes were wild and she pulled free of Grace, who grabbed and shook her. 'It's me, Grace Manton. Come, now.'

At last the wildness cleared and the young woman nodded. 'You're here?' 'Not for long,' Grace yelled as they were jostled by two women who were beating at the brawny hands that had captured them by their skirts. Grace led as they fought their way to the front exit, Evie keeping her face turned away. Lady Veronica was unlikely to recognise her anyway, hidden in the pantry as she'd been while the siblings scoffed cakes. One of the women in front called, 'The journalists are here, and the police. Cover your faces.'

Lady Veronica looked half mad with excitement and fear. Evie saw her reach up to find her hat gone, and now fear won out. She hesitated. Evie snatched off her own and pulled her shawl over her head, half hiding her face. She took her hat to Lady Veronica and pulled it low over her brow. Her friend had caught up with them, also hatless, and placed herself at the front. 'Walk behind me. I don't mind the publicity, it helps the cause.'

Together they pushed and shoved out into the early evening air. Evie and Grace flanked Lady Veronica, jostling through the jeering crowd. Evie called out to the police, 'You should be in there, arresting the slecky heggins, not outside where it's canny and safe, man. It could be your mam in there.'

One laughed, and struck her with his baton. 'My mam's got more sense.' Evie braced, Grace tugged her on. 'No, we need to get away from here.'

There was a blur as a woman hurled herself at the policeman on Evie's right. It was Lady Veronica's friend, and she left Lady Veronica exposed. Cameras were flashing. Evie pulled the girl's hat down harder and dragged her through the melee. An egg burst on her cheek, some man stuck out his foot. She jumped. Grace took over, charging the men, catching up with a group of women and staying in their wake. Finally they were through and out into the dark street. It seemed that silence fell. Utter silence. Evie stepped back out of sight.

Grace was asking the whereabouts of her Ladyship's carriage. 'The groom is waiting at the Red Lion stables. He thinks Lady Margaret and I are visiting with friends of Lady Esther.' Lady Veronica's voice was shaking.

Grace took her into the stables, but Evie remained on the road to avoid the groom. She wiped the egg from her face. 'By, I could have had that for my breakfast,' she said aloud but couldn't smile.

The trip home was quiet except when, soft-voiced, they talked of how women were hated. How, even within the group, they disagreed.

Evie's shin was hurting badly by the time Grace dropped her at the crossroads. She rode her bicycle back to the bothy and slowly dragged her way up the path, reaching the vegetable-garden wall, and then felt an arm around her. 'Busy day, bonny lass.' It was Simon and he kissed her hair as she described what had happened, but did not mention Lady Veronica. It was best that no one else knew.

Chapter Twelve

It was November at Easterleigh Hall and though Evie had thought the first month had flown, that was as nothing to the summer months when the sun had baked the earth hard and dry. Undaunted, the gardeners had taken water from the butts and then the lake to ensure that vegetables and fruit had continued to grow. Evie's visits to Simon had continued, and so had the sea-coaling, and with each week she felt more love for the bonny lad, and more delight in the home that the Forbes now owned; so some things had changed, but only some. Here she was, yet again hiding in the pantry just because Auberon and Veronica wanted a piece of cake in the warmth of the range.

She almost tore the paper as she ticked off the sacks of flour, currants, and blocks of salt, making a list of goods needing replenishment. Mrs Moore had decided that she must learn the restocking procedure, the stocktaking procedure and all places in between until they became second nature, because if Evie intended to run her own kitchen, not to mention a hotel, this would be necessary.

As she worked she thought of the fields which the

Forbes' house overlooked. Though it was more than a half-mile walk to the pithead for her father and brothers, they gloried in their sense of freedom and empowerment. Grace outlined the progress of the work on the other two houses on their way to the meetings, which had become a picture of calm after the storm.

The assault had unified the group, for now, a situation helped by the passing of Lloyd George's so-called People's Budget in the House of Commons, so the pressure for votes could be brought to bear by them all. But the whole shenanigans had revealed schisms within the women's movement that Evie had not dreamt could be there.

She examined the shelves and bit back her irritation. Millie was told constantly that she must refill the shelves methodically. It went in one ear and out of the other, for the girl could reduce even the most efficient system to a shambles in no more time than it took to scream, and one day Evie would. The trouble was that the moment anyone took Millie to task she folded up into a gibbering mess with shaking hands and pale face, which Evie had begun to think she rehearsed. So, for the sake of the timetable, either Evie or Mrs Moore ended up feeding her cups of tea and sympathy, and putting her on to a canny little beggar of a task that required little diligence.

Soon that old fat Father Christmas would be thudding down the chimney giving the maids more debris to sweep up, so it might be an idea to write a request for the foisty lass to work as she should. Surely by 1910 she'd have sorted herself out?

Evie took a moment to go through the upcoming catering as she totted up the boxes of tea. There was still one shooting party, with guests arriving on Friday, but it was the last, which was a grand relief all round. Archie and James were tired of hoying out with the hampers, James in particular as he was not only valet for Mr Auberon, but for Lord Brampton when he returned for the shooting parties, as Roger remained in Leeds.

Mr Harvey would be especially delighted when November was finished and with it the shooting, for serving out on the moor was like living in a barn full of holes, he said. He'd taken to wearing two pairs of long johns beneath his trousers, or so Mrs Moore had confided this morning, though how she knew Evie preferred not to imagine. Her thoughts must have shown because Mrs Moore said, 'That face is not a pretty sight, Evie Anston, now get cracking with the toast.'

Evie replied, 'I expect my face is no worse a sight than Mr Harvey in two pairs of long johns.' Mrs Moore laughed until her chins wobbled. Her rheumatics had been much better all summer, though it was not a good idea for her to miss her rest in the afternoon when sitting with the Brampton whelps, as Jack still called them.

As always, Evie left the door ajar and heard and

saw the two whelps discussing the blocking of the People's Budget by the House of Lords, dropping in and out of French as they discussed their father's determination that the peers should stop this budget that pandered to the working classes. Would they be pleased at how they'd brought on Evie's French? Perhaps not, daft beggars, Evie thought. Lady Veronica said, 'I do hope that he doesn't make a fool of himself and us this weekend in front of the guns by going on and on.' Auberon took the last fancy after Lady Veronica had shaken her head. 'No, you have it, you need it. How's it going at the mine?'

Mr Auberon spoke in French with his mouth full. Damn, Evie thought, the tablecloth would be flecked with crumbs. 'I'm learning from Davies, you know, Ver, and I can think much more clearly when Father's away. It's just awful that we have to economise. I hate it but I can't take another beating. Not yet. I have to let my ribs recover. Every accident down that god-forsaken pit makes me wonder if it's my fault. Well, it probably is, but I have my targets, and I am trying to find a way to allow some new props.' He shrugged. 'At least this weekend I can show that production's up and costs are down.'

He changed into English. 'It's remarkable when you think of it, Ver. Coal is just essential for every-thing. It's the most magical of material, it underpins the Empire, it underpins Father's steelworks. It's like a living thing.'

She replied in French, 'Yes, but it kills, and more

so when we don't consider safety. There's a world of difference between trying and doing, Aub.'

Evie saw Mr Auberon stand, his face flushed. 'Thank you Mrs Moore. Veronica, I have work to do.' He strutted to the door, his head held high, but as he left the kitchen and hurried down the passageway Evie felt a surge of pity, pity which had been emerging throughout the summer as she had listened to so many of these discussions.

What must it be like to have a father like his, and it was all very well for Lady Veronica to be so righteous but who the hell hoyed out to rescue Auberon when he needed it?

She stopped, her pencil hovering above her list, wondering where all that had come from. Let's just get you a soapbox, shall we, Miss Evie Forbes? But she was coming to realise that nothing was black and white. Most people did the best they could, and there did not seem to be the same black heart in Mr Auberon as there was in his father.

She'd told Jack of Auberon's reluctance to make the economies, but her brother had not wanted to hear such claggy dottle. When she had spoken about it to Simon he had merely laughed and kissed her, and told her not to worry about things, they'd all work out. With his kisses all else faded. She smiled now and longed to be with him.

When Lady Veronica had also left Evie emerged. Mrs Moore sat at the table, sighing. 'I'm going to have to pass this teatime business over to you, Evie.

I'm too tired. I need my rest especially with Christmas looming. Can you manage? Does Lady Veronica ever see you at the meetings? Will it be safe for you? Otherwise it must be Millie and I don't think the world is ready for that.'

Lady Veronica always sat at the front at the meetings, but nowadays with Lady Esther. They were trusted to be visiting Lady Esther's aunt, who was also a suffragette, unknown to the family. Lady Margaret Mounsey, who had launched herself at the police, was in prison, though her parents, friends of Lady Brampton, had moved swiftly to keep it out of the newspapers and away from their society friends. Lady Brampton thought Margaret was on tour with an aunt in Italy, or so Veronica told Auberon over tea. Was she hunger-striking? Evie baulked at the thought.

Lady Veronica had sent a note of deepest gratitude to Grace, thanking her and her friend for their help. That was all. She never looked in their direction when they were seated in the meeting hall. A new hat had cost Evie five shillings.

Evie gave Mrs Moore the list of provisions needed and hugged her. 'She won't recognise me, we're invisible, aren't we? Let's not give them the chance of objecting, we'll just do it and I'll say that you're too busy preparing the menus for the Servants' Ball, and by the time that's over it will have become a pattern.'

In fact, Lady Veronica sent a message to Mrs

Moore the next day that they would not be resuming their teatime treat until the new year, as the demands upon their time were too onerous. Mrs Moore screwed up the paper and put it into the coal bucket. 'They've fallen out, more like, after that little spat yesterday. They'll get over it, brothers and sisters usually do. Now come on, girls, we have a lot of work to do.'

'When haven't we?' Millie moaned.

By December the frosts were hard in the morning and at night, and Evie huddled under her blanket which was reinforced with her shawls and coat, but still the ice coated the inside of the windows. In the Forbes' house there were fireplaces which actually held fires, she had told Mrs Moore as they warmed themselves at the range. The traditional Servants' Ball was to take place on 4th December in the servants' hall and the family would attend, hopefully just for a few moments. Tension was rising above stairs now Asquith had announced that the forthcoming general election meant that he would be going to the country to get a mandate which would force the Lords to submit and approve the budget. It was causing the Bastard to huff and puff and almost blow the bloody place down.

Evie had lain in bed last night wondering whether the women's vote, if it had been granted, would help to produce a clear victory. Or would the majority vote with the Tories? Again she felt confused and was glad that work was so hectic that to worry about anything else was pointless.

In the two days before the ball they cooked as though there was no tomorrow, creating meals for upstairs as well as economical ones for the ball, funded with reluctance by Lady Brampton. It was something that employers were supposed to do, and some smiled and were gracious and gave over the use of the upstairs ballroom. The Bramptons didn't, and the funds provided were minimal, so the kitchen was grateful for the gifts of cream, eggs and steak from the surrounding farms, and half a pig from Home Farm.

This time it was Mrs Moore who whined, not Millie, as she and Evie rolled out pastry for the pies that would provide some of the sustenance. 'Fine for everyone else but who's cooking the food as usual, and those gardeners will eat more than the rest of us put together.'

Evie poked her in the ribs which were well hidden beneath the rolls of fat. 'Come on, you're looking forward to dancing the Gay Gordons with Mr Harvey, you know you are.' Mrs Moore shrieked with laughter. 'That'll be the day. Now, what are you wearing?'

'I've bribed Lil to alter the dresses Grace gave me for the four of us. Mam's given us ribbon to thread through my bun and enough left for Sarah, Annie and Millie.'

Lady Veronica was lending them her phonograph,

Mr Harvey told them over lunch the day before the ball, which was more than they'd thought they would have from the Bramptons. 'They have also mentioned that Lord Brampton will be in attendance with the rest of the family, and I have been informed that we must prepare for the return of Roger.' Evie laid down her knife and fork, feeling sick. Mrs Moore looked down the table at her and stood up. 'Come along, girls, time we were getting on. Sarah, Millie, Annie, bring out the dishes.'

As the girls busied themselves she hustled Evie out into the kitchen, tightening her apron as she did so, pointing to the kettle. 'Put that on for us, there's a bonny lass, and you're not the first and you won't be the last to get into a fisticuffs with that particular snake, so don't take it to heart. Let young Simon help you.'

Mrs Moore heaved herself on to her stool, drawing her recipe book towards her. It had translucent splashes of old fat on each page, just as Evie's had now. She thought of them as medals. Mrs Moore rolled her shoulders. 'Now come along, we have so much to do, and I want to remind the girls yet again that Roger is not a man to join around the gooseberry bush.'

The servants' hall was glowing with soft light, cast by the candles on the tables. Orange and yellow chrysanthemums decorated the corners of the room, and their scent mingled with the melted wax. Mr

Harvey and Mrs Green led the servants into their own hall. There were no gasps of delight because they had created it themselves, but there was a general sigh of satisfaction. Lord and Lady Brampton were waiting one side of the furnace along the right-hand wall, and on the other side stood Lady Veronica and Mr Auberon. Evie slunk in behind Mrs Moore, not wanting to see Lord Brampton close up, let alone actually speak to the Bastard, but he was walking towards the servants, his usual frown deeply in place, his lips so thin that she wondered how, or if, Lady Brampton could bring herself to kiss him.

Lady Brampton, Mr Auberon and Lady Veronica were approaching also, each taking on a section of the staff as though they were advancing on the enemy. Perhaps they were.

Evie curtsied as Lady Brampton came to Mrs Moore. 'I am delighted that the standard of cooking is rising each month, Mrs Moore. You are indeed a treasure.' Lady Brampton's smile was kind, her eyes were cool.

'I have an excellent team, especially Evie Anston, Your Ladyship.' Mrs Moore gestured to Evie, who wished she wouldn't. She didn't want to be exposed in any way, and neither did she trust this family. They were quite capable of dismissing Mrs Moore and employing Evie in her place because she would be cheaper. She said, 'Forgive me interrupting, Your Ladyship, but Mrs Moore is too kind. Her advice is crucial to me. I just do as she says and would be lost without her.'

As she spoke she noticed Lady Veronica swing round and could have cut out her tongue, but Lady Brampton was speaking. 'Yes, I can see that you are too young to be so skilled.' She passed along. Evie flushed with anger but also relief. Mrs Moore was safe, but was she? She glanced at Lady Veronica, who was passing along the line as though she was Queen Alexandra. She came abreast of Evie, and there was no recognition. Mr Auberon followed her, nodding and smiling at everyone, saying how nice it was to see them, though all the servants knew that the family were wondering how long they had to stay with the appalling unwashed who should remain invisible, and who they most sincerely wished were not traditionally entitled to a party once a year.

Mr Harvey called for silence and thanked Lord and Lady Brampton for their generosity, and as he did so Evie felt the touch of Simon's hand on hers. He was panting as he stood beside her, whispering, 'We're all late, we couldn't do up our collars, and then the ties.' She didn't mind how late he was as long as he came. She squeezed his hand, wanting to wrench off her silly little organza gloves and feel skin on skin. 'You look wonderful,' he murmured.

She was wearing a deep green taffeta dress. She and all the other girls had pulled in their corsets just that little bit more, and though they could hardly breathe it was worth the pain. Simon was wearing a suit, with rounded stiff collar and dark blue tie. He looked different, but it was a good difference.

At last the formalities were over, but still the family stayed. Archie and James were in charge of the phonograph but with all the chatter the music couldn't be heard, so no one danced. Simon and Evie circulated, careful not to seem glued together, but always within reach of one another. Millie stayed hot on their heels. Simon whispered, 'She doesn't seem any less fretful.'

Evie liked him leaning so close, and the feel of his breath on her cheek and neck. 'I can't make her out,' she murmured as they sidestepped Mrs Green in close conversation with Mrs Moore. 'She's timid one minute and then spiteful the next, and totally idle. It might come of having no father, or having to live with relatives. I don't know, I try to be patient but by, lad, I don't do a very good job.'

His hand was running up and down her arm while they were hidden amongst the throng and she hoped he would talk of them, their future, their present. He said, 'This music is hopeless, I'm going to ask Bernie and Thomas to come with me and collect our fiddles, we can do better.' She felt disappointment so sharp that she couldn't respond. He continued, 'Then I can take time out to dance with you, because I haven't done that yet, Evie Anston.' Everything was all right again.

In his absence she stood with Lil, whose hair was piled on top of her head with a bone comb just off to one side, watching the stilted groups. They nudged one another as Lady Veronica struggled to make conversation with the head gardener, who was taciturn enough on his own territory and impossible in this situation.

They watched Mr Harvey discussing with his Lordship the possibility of replacing the phonograph with the fiddlers. Lord Brampton shrugged, his frown deeper still. His reply was curt. Mr Harvey bowed slightly as Lord Brampton moved away, and nodded to Mrs Green.

The boys were back and the two footmen drifted from the phonograph with relief written large on their faces as the fiddlers began, and soon the room was given over to dancing. The candles wafted in the breeze created by the Gay Gordons, and reels of all types, and a few waltzes, some of which Evie danced with Simon. She was in heaven, and never wanted the evening to end, loving his smile, his red hair which glinted in the light, his hands which gripped hers, and then clasped her to him for the waltzes. Their bodies were close then, perhaps too close, but she didn't care.

At length Mr Harvey called a pause for the food, and Evie dragged herself from Simon and hurried off with the other kitchen staff and the footmen and under-footmen. By the time the food was placed upon the table an orderly queue had formed, and tables had been set up around the room. Mr Harvey declared that the musicians should be served first, at which Lord Brampton's frown grew ever deeper. The servants longed to laugh as the family sat at their table to await their turn.

After the Bramptons had been served by Archie and James, the queue moved quickly. Evie sat with Simon, Bernie and Millie, who glowed as she listened to Bernie talking of his Irish uncle who had been a fiddler too. Simon reached for Evie's hand below the table and she didn't notice the food she was eating, the food she and the kitchen staff had slaved over, but somehow her plate was soon empty, and so was Simon's. Bernie leaned across to Simon. 'What do you say, Si, to us entertaining this mob while they finish? Have you the puff?'

Simon stood. 'If Evie has. She used to sing in school, if I remember rightly.'

Evie leaned back, laughing. 'You go and make a fool of yourself, if you want, pet, but leave me out of it.'

Simon shook his head. 'Never knew you to step back from a challenge, Evie.'

She went then, and together they sang. 'If you were the only girl in the world, and I was the only boy.' Simon had a wonderful voice, and hers sounded good enough here, with him. They sang requests, they sang while the others danced, they sang until their throats were dry and then they sang some more, and all the time she wished she could loosen her corset. It was when they were crooning to some Ragtime that she saw Roger enter, and her voice faltered for a moment.

Simon turned to her, puzzled, but she had picked up on the beat again, looking only at him. His eyes were focused on her, his hand gripping her fingers. The song ended, he bent to her, saying, 'I'm here. You know I'll always be here, right by your side.'

'I know,' she replied.

Roger was weaving his way through to them, clapping along with the rest, but before he reached them Lady Veronica and Mr Auberon had moved to stand in front of the fiddlers and singers. Lady Veronica said, 'I thought that delightful. You are all so very talented.'

Mr Auberon pressed a coin into each of their hands. 'Excellent, truly truly excellent.'

Roger was examining his nails. The Bramptons moved away, and before Evie could check how much she'd been given Simon said, 'Wait here, I'll talk to Roger.'

She held him back. 'We'll both go.'

They went together and Roger looked from one to the other, his collar immaculate, his suit freshly pressed and a small rose in his buttonhole. Evie said, 'It's a shame you returned. It's been so delightful in your absence, which gives you your answer to the proposition you made before you left, and Millie has far too much sense than to listen to any of your nonsense. She has quite agreed with the advice of the upper servants about any liaison with you.'

She walked on, side by side with Simon, accepting the plaudits for their performance, seeing Mrs Moore having a firm word with Millie, Sarah and Annie and all of them nodding fearfully, and she knew it would be about Roger. This had been the best evening of her life, especially with the Brampton family now taking their leave so the party could really begin. Mr Auberon had given them all a guinea. 'It's generous,' she said. 'He's got more than enough, pet,' Simon replied.

It was cavil day the following Sunday and Jack sipped his beer in the club Reading Room, waiting for his turn to draw, though this time he would let his marra pull out the placement. There'd already been several abnormal placements called, but a man just had to accept his luck. So far Alec, Si's da, had pulled a placement in the top seam, which was good coal and easy to hew, but Ben, his father's old marra, had pulled an abnormal one, which he accepted with a philosophical nod of his head. He was probably thinking of his next painting, not the shallow, low-roofed danger of his shale placement. Jack wasn't thinking of the draw, but of the negotiations surrounding the Eight-Hour Act, the results of which were to be announced in about a month. Jeb had heard nothing of any interest from the union agents. He felt his stomach twist. The men should be kept informed, it was only right.

Jack was called up with Martin, who hummed and kissed his lucky rabbit's paw before drawing his ticket. Thomas, the checkweighman, read out, 'No. 13.' Jack slapped Martin's shoulder. 'You've a lucky touch, lad. Always had, always will.'

Timmie was waiting near him, but as a trapper he wouldn't need a dip. His da came to him. 'Good news travels fast, Jack. That's a pure seam.' It didn't matter quite so much now they had the house, but the balance still had to be paid to Grace and Edward, and money put to one side in case of a strike or a downturn in piecework rates.

Jack stared into the distance, feeling anxiety clawing at him, for they'd not win any strike unless it was national, and then only if there was no coal stockpiled. There was plenty now at Hawton and Easton. He'd tried to argue the case against coming out with Jeb, saying they had to wait until the National Federation of Miners agreed to back them and call out all the pits.

He grinned at Timmie as he came up, a beer in his hand. Jack rumpled his hair. 'How's the beer?'

'Right grand, Jack.' There was a dark blue scar on the lad's forehead, and several on his hands, and it was as though Timmie felt blooded. Well, he'd learn. 'You stay careful, you hear me,' Jack said, gripping his brother's shoulder.

Behind him his da was coughing. He needed to be out of the pit before too long, so thank God Evie had the plan for the hotel and was growing in experience, thank God they would keep their house if his da had to retire.

Timmie was watching as his da shouldered his way towards the bar, and he said, 'Are we helping Grace again next Sunday? She'll need someone to run the houses, won't she, when they're finished, if she is to start a retirement place? D'you think . . . ?' He pointed towards his da.

Jack wanted to hug the lad. 'By, you've been giving it some thought, haven't you? I expected those would fly past your two brain cells, but you must have grown another. Aye, he'd be right grand as boss of the houses.'

Timmie punched his arm and Jack rousted him in return before pulling him close. 'You're canny, you are. I'll get Mam to bring it up when Grace is at the houses.'

Timmie shook his head. 'You know she won't mention it, she'll see it as charity. Ask Grace yourself, you're round at the houses often enough.'

Jack moved away, uncertain suddenly. 'We owe them, that's why, and she needs help,' he snapped and moved to the bar, barely hearing Timmie say, 'I didn't mean anything by it. You *are* there a lot, that's all. She needs the place set to rights, so why don't I help as well as you, then it will be fixed quicker.'

Waiting for a beer, Jack realised then that he didn't want it fixed quicker. He didn't want anyone helping but himself. She was nice, quiet and gentle, she smoked Woodbines, her green eyes were beautiful. She listened when he talked.

Ben came up and slapped his back. 'I'll get that beer in for you, man. Might rub a bit of your luck off on meself.'

'No, you're all right, Ben, I need to clear my head. I'm getting on home. See you at the allotment tomorrow, man.' He walked out, the frost creating a layer of crystals on everything. There'd be a hoar frost in the morning. He went by way of the parsonage. The lights were on and he thought he saw her drift across the window. He paused for a moment, imagining her chaotic hair as it fell so often from her bun, her freckles. How could someone years older seem like his age?

The strike began on 1st January 1910 because the agents hadn't had the bloody sense to involve the men in the decision, and there was little to do until it ended in April except gather up coal from the slag heaps or beaches, sell what they could, and eke out the days. By that time one general election had taken place but had not given Asquith the majority that would mean he had a mandate from the public to push through the budget to fund the reforms. There would need to be another election, and still the Lords held firm in their blockade. It seemed distant to Jack, and nothing to do with the humiliation of defeat and empty pockets, as he stood with the committee in Davies' office, their caps in their hands, while Davies and Mr Auberon sat at their desks.

Jack saw the whelp's eyes on him, and him alone, and heard his laugh as Jeb admitted defeat. 'So, Jack Forbes,' Auberon said. 'You're just an agitator, always were, always will be, and a grasping one at that, one who snatches things when they're destined for your betters, so what can we do to bring you to heel?' Jack felt the shock as though it was a blow. Of course, the house. What price was he to pay? For the first time above ground he felt fearful.

Auberon continued, 'So, Jack, who's the daft beggar now? I don't feel it's me.' Jeb turned to Jack, a question in his eyes. Jack shook his head. Daft beggar? What was the bastard talking about? Jeb raised his eyebrows and said to Mr Auberon, 'The committee is in this together, and no one thinks you're a daft beggar. Why would you think that? Mr Davies, what's this about?'

Mr Davies stared over their heads as though wishing he was elsewhere. Mr Auberon just laughed again. 'Well, why would I, Jack?' Jack didn't understand but in that instant he knew that he was going to be dismissed, for whatever reason this fool could drum up. Was this going to spill over to the men, to Evie?

Auberon lounged back, knowing now what it was like to have someone at his mercy, and for the first time he understood his father.

255

'I am not going to dismiss any of you, because you are experienced men and we need you.' He picked up a pencil from the desk and rolled it between his fingers, seeing their surprise and relief. He continued, 'I am not in the business of cutting off my nose to spite my face, so you will start work in the shifts Mr Davies and I have designated and in accordance with the Eight-Hour Act. As recompense for the upheaval this foolish strike has caused I will be taking over the designation of placements. There will be no cavil any longer in this pit, is that understood?'

Relief was superseded by shock, and then anger. Jeb spoke. 'You can't do that. It's our right to decide where we work. It always has been, it's a democratic process.'

Jack had clenched his hands into fists and was balancing on his toes. Auberon's reply was immediate. 'You are mistaken. I most certainly can and will do it. There is no legislation regarding the cavil, there is only tradition, and what's more I am most conscious of the importance of democracy to you all and therefore I give you a choice. You, the committee, resign and the men continue with the cavil, or you stay and they lose it. In the interest of democracy I insist you put it to the general vote.'

The silence was profound. Jack said, 'I resign.' The others followed, though more hesitantly.

Auberon placed the pencil carefully on the blotter which lay on his desk. 'And I refuse your resignations.

It's easy for you, Jack Forbes, with your house. If these men resign they will be evicted. They can't all cram into the parson's clever little idea, can they? So, I repeat, you must put it to the vote.'

They did, catching men as they came on each shift over the next two days. The vote was carried out in the club. They voted to lose the cavil. Every member of the committee received abnormal placements and Timmie was moved from trapper to putter, but in Jack's abnormal placement. Their income would be reduced, their safety at risk. His da, who had remained as deputy on the wishes of the men, had the kist nearest to the worst abnormal placements, including Jack's.

Auberon rode home on Tuesday, ran up the stairs to change, was about to call into the sitting room to tell Veronica of his achievement but midway he noticed the time. His father was waiting for him in the library. Auberon entered. 'Well,' his father ground out between clenched teeth. 'You dismissed them as I suggested?'

Auberon shook his head, his legs like water, his voice too high. 'No, I didn't.' His father stepped forward. Auberon stood his ground, moving on to his toes as Forbes had done, and found it gave him courage. He explained his actions. There was a silence and his father paced to the window, staring out at the cedar tree. Did it give him peace, as it gave Auberon? Did this man ever desire anything as pale as peace?

257

Auberon found his voice again. 'You see, they have been hoisted on their own petard. They wanted democracy, they've got it, and they are there as an example of our power. If they had been dismissed we would have replaced them and they would have been forgotten. It's called rubbing salt in the wound.'

His father's shoulders were shaking and a strange noise was building. Auberon realised he was laughing. 'Chip off the old block, you are, my boy. Damn it, we're turning you into a Brampton at last. A brandy is in order.'

He pointed to the sofas either side of the fireplace. Auberon had never been permitted to sit in the library. It felt strange. He did so, and his father came to loom over him, handing him brandy, and then sat opposite, raising his glass. 'To you, my boy.' His smile was ghastly and unseen by Auberon until this day.

Auberon sipped and the brandy seared his throat. He had drunk too much in the last two years and it hadn't helped with Wainey's loss, with his loneliness. Would anything ever? He allowed himself to sit back as his father did, crossing one leg over the other as he also did. The fire was lit, the flames flickered and soothed. It was strange to be in his father's presence without pain. It was good, it was bloody good.

'Drink down the brandy, boy.' He did as instructed and accepted another. Again his father loomed over him and before he could stop he shrank, but then straightened. When he left ten minutes later, light-headed, he mounted the stairs to his room. Once there he leaned back against the door. He had been clever, he had been unforgivably clever but it was the only way he could think of to keep the committee in their houses and their families fed.

But had it really been necessary to put all the Forbes into the same area of the mine, where they would all suffer if there was an explosion or flood? He knew the answer to that and the worst thing was that he knew he'd do it all over again, because Jack Forbes had laughed at him, told that Manton woman he was a daft beggar and been at the forefront of the strike, whatever Davies said about him being the only calm voice speaking against it. He was known as an agitator and agitators got their comeuppance.

Ver knocked and he moved from the door to his sofa. The fire was unlit, and it was cold. She entered. He waved her to sit. She stood instead, just inside the door.

She said, 'Well done, Wainey and Mother would be proud of the way you've outwitted Father and kept the committee in work, but I simply don't understand why you've taken against the Forbes family in this way, especially as Jack Forbes was the one who warned against the strike. Dr Nicholls told us all about it at dinner during the strike, you know he did. Be businesslike, Aub, and rotate the abnormal placements in the interests of fairness, then you can reinstitute the cavil after a year or so. By then Father will be too involved in the dreadnought contracts he's almost got in his pocket. Once the extended steelworks is in full production he'll barely think about the pits.'

He drew out his cigarette case, took one. Lit it and stared at her through the smoke. 'Forbes laughed at me in Froggett's yard, he called me a daft beggar, so let's not talk about it any more. Come and sit down.'

She joined him, looking tired. 'You can't let that make you behave badly. I expect he regrets it if he even remembers.'

Auberon drew on his cigarette again and said nothing for a moment. Then, 'How are your women getting on?'

Veronica sighed, her lips pursed as they were when she was angry, but her feelings weren't his problem. She said, 'The Pankhursts are supporting Asquith's proposed Conciliation Bill which offers votes to married women of property and wealth only. They call it a foot in the door, I call it wrong, really wrong. We need all ranks to have the vote. Meanwhile I have the damnable "coming out" conversation morning, noon and night while our stepmother is here.'

She leaned forward, staring at the Indian rug. 'Nothing stays still, does it? There's so much division, so much wealth, so much poverty. Sometimes

I wonder if there's going to be a revolution. I'd revolt, wouldn't you, if I was them?' She pointed in the direction of Auld Maud.

'But we're not.' What more could he say?

Chapter Thirteen

Two years had passed and still Evie's menfolk were in their abnormal placements, still the cavil was suspended and still she was here, serving tea to the nobs in the kitchen. It was March 1912 and the strikes which seemed to hit every area of the British workforce during 1911 had spread to the mines. A national strike had been called to force owners and government to agree on a sensible minimum wage within the Coal Miners Bill.

Evie eased her back and wished Mr Auberon and Lady Veronica would hurry with their tea and go.

They'd avoided the kitchen like the plague during the extraordinary heat of the long summer last year. Mr Harvey said that according to the *Daily Sketch* it was going to go down in the record books as the hottest summer ever. Well, they should have brought those record books into the kitchen and she would have shown them what heat really was.

She sat at the far end of the kitchen table cutting up vegetables for the upstairs dinner, double-checking the menu while the Bramptons chatted away in French. Mr Auberon said to Lady Veronica,

'We'll win this strike if our stocks last, but it's a big if. A national strike's such a different kettle of fish. I'm scared, Father is, all the owners are. Ships are stranded in port for lack of fuel, even the *Titanic* is going to have to go slow on its maiden voyage or not at all, if it's not over soon.'

'I know all about this, Aub,' Lady Veronica sighed, but he clearly wasn't listening, just tapping the table and then dragging his hand through his hair. Lady Veronica was pushing her pink iced fancy around her plate.

Mr Auberon shook his head. 'I'm going to have a hell of a job when this one's over, trying to keep the committee in work. I should have returned the cavil a year ago but there was so much else to think of. At least then I could just take it away again. What the hell do the miners want, blood?'

Evie had to bite hard on her lip not to shout that what they wanted was a minimum wage of 5s a day for men and 2s a day for boys, but Lady Veronica pushed her plate away, saying in a harsh whisper exactly Evie's words.

Mr Auberon replied, 'Of course I know that, I wasn't asking for facts. They won't get those rates, Asquith's told them, but they will get something and they will have shown us their combined muscle. I think what they want is for the govern ment to decide the guaranteed wage, but they'll have to accept that the actual amount is to be decided by arbitration between the owners and the union executive, district by district. I damn well wish it could be a government decision, because can you imagine the rows when it comes to arbitration here?' He dragged his hand through his hair again.

The furnace needed replenishing, but how could Evie do that with them still blathering?

'Ver, now that the Germans and French are interfering in Agadir the country'll need even more ships to cope with the naval race, so let's hope Father gets busy with that and stays out of my hair, then there'll be some hope for the men.' His laugh was high-pitched. 'At the moment all he can think of is that we're feeding the Galloways, who've been taken out of the pit for the second time in two years to gallop in the fields. The pumps are running but we're not producing coal. It's money that can't be recovered.'

Lady Veronica held up her hand. 'For goodness sake, Aub, his steelworks is thriving, the price of coal is high and he's selling off the stocks, bricks are piling out of the Brampton brickworks. It's a nonsense. He can pay a decent rate. He should.'

Mr Auberon seemed to deflate suddenly. 'Of course he should, but he won't, none of the owners will. The only thing is to bring the mines under the ownership of the government and then the men might stand a chance. Sorry, heresy, I know, but I'm just letting off steam, I'm feeling bruised with Father on my back all the time.'

Lady Veronica looked anxious. 'Has he . . . ?'

Mr Auberon shook his head. 'No, I just meant it as a figure of speech. Whatever happens, I need to keep the committee in work or the heart will go out of the men and we'll never get it back.' He put his hand up. 'Yes, I know I'm repeating myself.'

He was speaking quickly and fiercely but Evie understood every word, and for that she was grateful to the Bramptons, but only for that.

Veronica started to speak again. 'It's a bad business, Aub. No matter how busy you've been, the cavil should have been remembered, it's a poor excuse, and as for the Forbes family . . . Have you yet moved the youngest boy, at least?'

Auberon shook his head. 'Not yet. I know, I'm a bloody fool. I just let personal . . . Oh well, never mind.'

Evie continued scraping the carrots that Simon had dug out from the barrel of sawdust in which they were stored. He had wanted a kiss for every one, and she had been happy to oblige. She hoped . . . Well, what did she hope? She hoped for marriage, but she hoped also for independence. She hoped the strike would end, she hoped the workers' demands would be met. Most of all she hoped for safe placements for her family. She hoped she could hate Mr Auberon and Lady Veronica, but he didn't want to dismiss the committee, and at the Suffrage meetings she spoke out for universal suffrage, which was now the internal bone of contention. Yes, she should loathe them, but somehow . . .

She slipped the carrot into the pan and picked up another, shaking herself free of the confusion. Part of her task here was to report on the Bramptons, so Evie had told Jack last Wednesday that Bastard Brampton had scorched off to London for an appointment with Asquith and tomorrow, Sunday, she would tell him that Auberon didn't want to dismiss the committee. He'd say words were cheap. He'd say as usual that it was his fault that the family were still in the bad placements and question himself again about the 'daft beggar' business, which he still couldn't understand. He'd end up cursing all Bramptons to the ends of the earth, as he had done last Wednesday when they'd been checking the rabbit snares on the Stunted Tree.

She placed the carrot in the pan – so many, for just Mr Auberon, Lady Veronica and the chaperone, Mrs Benson. Five courses had been ordered for lunch and dinner every day since the strike began. 'What a waste,' Mrs Moore had said, on the first day.

By the second they had looked at one another and nodded. 'No, it's not a waste at all,' Mrs Moore had said.

The meals came down almost untouched, leaving a huge table of leftovers, far too much for the servants' meals the next day, but more than enough to take to the bothy to be collected by one of the strike committee for distribution. 'Lady Veronica has been taught well by Miss Wainton after all,' Mrs Moore had said. Evie felt that Mr Auberon must have known, too.

Yes, she wanted to hate them, but . . .

Behind her the range was rumbling, reminding her again that it needed feeding. The clock on the wall was ticking, time was getting on. Mr Auberon had reverted to English and was discussing the continuing naval race between England and Germany and the problem of Home Rule in Ireland. His hands had become a man's and were tanned and hard against his white cuffs. As she glanced towards him he dragged at his hair again. He'd not have any locks left at this rate. He caught her glance and smiled. She nodded as a good servant should, with eyes lowered. His were as blue as the sky had been this morning. He spoke. 'Perhaps we are holding you up, Evie?'

She shook her head. 'No, we have time.'

He no longer looked through her any more. He would ask after her well-being, he would talk of the lateness of the spring, or the harshness of the winter. He would discuss her love of cooking, but only when Lady Veronica was absent. When she had been recovering from a recent chill he had brought her local honey. 'It has healing properties,' he had said. 'It's something to do with the pollen.' He had placed it in her hand. Their fingers had touched, and he hadn't flinched from contact with a servant.

The dachshunds were with them today, yelping in their sleep. They often came into the kitchen from the yard and Mrs Moore tutted, then fed them treats, after which they curled up on Evie's mam's proggy mat in front of the range. Things had changed over the last two years, but stayed the same as well. It was confusing. She looked at the carrots in the pan, remembering her family's abnormal placements.

She pushed the pan away, along with the thoughts.

Perhaps the country was like this, not knowing how it felt. The workers had their own Labour Party now, and the Liberals were still in power in spite of another election. The People's Budget had been passed through the Lords and legislation was in place to prevent them blocking a financial bill ever again. Women were rebelling. Revolution had been so close throughout last year's long hot summer of strikes, and was it coming again with the miners' strike? Jack spoke of it often. There was and had been so much violence. Roger in the garden store, the Lea End lot, the men who raged at the women's meetings, the police and strikers in Wales . . .

She picked up the knife and the last carrot, scraped it, then lobbed it in the pan. She wiped her hands on the damp dishcloth and began on the potato chips, cutting them so fine as to be translucent, dropping them into a pan of slightly salted water. They'd go well with the guinea fowl. Cooking was grand, it was calm, it made her happy.

Lady Veronica's voice cut through her concentration. 'These cakes are quite delicious, Evie. Would you convey our thanks to Mrs Green? Every day she produces a miracle.' Evie smiled. 'Yes, of course, Your Ladyship.'

Mr Auberon asked, 'And Mrs Moore, she is quite well? I miss her, please tell her that.'

Evie grew more alert. 'Yes, I will, Mr Auberon, but she needs her rest period, just as Mrs Green and Mr Harvey do, not to mention the other servants.'

She watched them exchange an uncertain look. He flushed and said, 'Yes, of course and I'm glad she is being sensible, but perhaps we're being unduly inconvenient by joining you down here. I'm so sorry, it's just that we enjoy it very much but then you don't have your rest?'

In spite of herself Evie felt sorry that she had spoken the words she had longed to say for so long. She shook her head. 'I don't need a rest. This is your house, and everyone needs a place where they can feel comfortable.'

She had wanted to say, yes, I reckon I do need a rest, we all do, a proper rest, you silly beggars, but for some reason she wanted to see the uncertainty gone from their faces. She looked across at the servants' hall, where the servants were sitting on benches around the table or a lucky few lounging on the old settee from which horsehair bulged. No one was looking into the kitchen, of course. 'They never came, they never stayed, they were never here,' Mr Harvey said at the start of every year.

What must it be like to be uncomfortable in your own home, to come down into the servants' kitchen for privacy, ease and comfort? Privacy? Evie stirred with guilt. She continued to slice the potatoes. But then she looked once more at the servants' hall, for there was someone missing, surely? She scanned the girls. Yes, Millie. Now she searched for Roger, who had been returned to Mr Auberon in January. She relaxed, he was there, reading the *Sketch*. Lil and Millie had become as thick as thieves over the last two years, but recently Lil had cast her friend aside after being elevated to Lady Veronica's lady's maid. Within two ticks there was Roger, comforting Millie, looking over her head at Evie, challenging her.

Now he was like a bad smell, lingering where the girl was, causing Mrs Moore to sit Silly Millie, as some called her, down yet again with Sarah and Annie to give them the same old malarky. They had all agreed that to be foolish was a bad mistake, but Evie wasn't convinced that Millie meant what she said. The girl was becoming more lazy, cocky and resentful by the day. It would be good to dismiss her, but with a reasonable character so she could find something else away from Roger, but Mrs Moore didn't like to give up on someone. 'Besides, we'd drown in tears day after day until she went.'

Evie looked up at the scrape of a chair on the flagstones. Mr Auberon and Lady Veronica were preparing to leave. Evie stood, as any good servant should. Mr Auberon held the door for Lady Veronica, who paused, looking back as though to speak, but then she half shook her head. 'Thank you, Evie.'

Mr Auberon waited a moment, then smiled and said quietly, 'Yes, thank you. The cakes were exceptional again, Evie. You are an accomplished cook. We won't be taking tea down here tomorrow, we have a visitor, so you will be relieved of our company.'

They left and seemed to have taken the air with them. He knew about the cakes. What if Mrs Green heard? How did he know? The kitchen clock chimed, and it was time to prepare tea for the upper servants. She called for Millie; there was no answer. She went to the back stairs. 'Millie, I need you to take tea trays to the upper servants.' No answer. Where was the girl? She ran up the steps to the yard and there she was, smoking a Woodbine in the shelter of the garage. Evie beckoned to her. 'Come along, time's ticking away and you know Len won't allow smoking near the cars.'

Millie drew long and hard; the cigarette glowed. She threw it to the ground and stubbed it out under her boot. She started to leave and Evie shouted, 'Don't leave the stubs. For goodness sake, how often must you be told?'

Millie shrugged and pulled her shawl tighter around her, and only then did she pick up the stub. 'Wash your hands before you take their trays,' Evie instructed. She scooted back down the stairs and took Mrs Moore's tea to her rooms, knocking. 'Come in, lass.'

Mrs Moore's cheeks were flushed and there was

a gin bottle stuck down the side of her armchair. Her feet, ankles and knees were now so swollen that on some days she could barely walk. The pain must have been intense. Evie placed her tea on the occasional table and Mrs Moore said, her eyes rheumy, 'Sit down, Evie. We've a few moments before the chaos begins.'

Evie sat opposite her. There was a fire in the grate but why not, when the master was the owner of a couple of collieries? She stared at the fire. It was Easter soon. Would the miners return to work? She felt absolutely drained with it all.

Mrs Moore sipped her tea. 'I can't go on, young Evie. It's my hands and my feet. What's to become of me?' She was rubbing one hand gently on the other, as though she was washing them.

Evie shook herself upright, reaching across and gently holding the cook's hands. 'You can go on. I've said again and again that I am happy to go on cooking, with you helping when you can. You simply cannot leave me alone with Millie.'

They both laughed. Evie continued, 'It's worked well and will continue doing so. You are my teacher, I need you, we all need you.'

Mrs Moore shook her head. 'Mrs Green will notice one day, or Mr Harvey. They will be duty bound to report it to her Ladyship, who will be only too eager to replace me with you. It will be so much cheaper. What is to become of me when that happens?' Her voice was breaking.

Evie was on her knees now, stroking Mrs Moore's hands. 'No, they won't notice, why should they? And you know your rheumatics come and go. Soon you will have improved again. Summer will be here before we know it.'

Mrs Moore interrupted. 'It's not fair. You are working while I'm getting the pay and you won't let me share. I can't return to Miss Grace, she has Sally now. It will be the workhouse.' Her voice broke completely.

Evie stood up and went to her. Millie knocked. 'Evie, time's getting on.'

'Start the soup, please, Millie. White soup, the recipe's in my book.'

'But I'm not sure I can do it.'

Evie whispered, 'One day I will put her in the stockpot and be done with it.' Mrs Moore's laugh was tearful. Evie raised her voice. 'We're discussing the engagement party for Lady Veronica. Just read the recipe and we'll be out shortly.'

To Mrs Moore she said, 'You see, you can't be so cruel as to leave me with her. You're still training me, I need you so much. Soon we'll have the hotel. We are all saving, my family and I, and though the strike will take some of the money we'll get there soon. I said 1914, but if it's 1915 it won't be the end of the world, and then everything will calm down, it's all become so tumultuous somehow. Either way, you'll be with us, so no more nonsense, if you please.' She shook her slightly. 'Come on, we have work to do.'

Mrs Moore said, looking up at Evie, curiosity lightening her eyes, 'Did Lady Veronica mention the Rt Hon. Captain Williams or the wedding at tea? Not quite the blushing bride, is she?' She tried to ease herself up from the chair and Evie helped, shaking her head. 'Nothing was said at all. I expect they'll marry in London, but I wonder if we'll be making the cake? We'll have to put cold compresses on your hands if we do, because you're the only one with the skill to decorate it. I'll be watching carefully, mind. It's something I need to learn.'

She walked with Mrs Moore to the door. 'I'll come back for the cup in a moment and where would you like me to hide the gin? And what if Millie had come in?'

Mrs Moore reached for the door, saying nothing until she was in the passageway, and then she muttered, 'Better to stop the habit altogether maybe, pet?'

Together they strolled to the kitchen, welcoming the warmth and light. Evie muttered when she saw that Millie had done absolutely nothing about preparing the soup, 'Aye, it would be better for you to stop, perhaps, and certainly better for someone else to actually start.' Both were laughing quietly as they went to the table and showed Millie, yet again, how to make white soup, wondering if this time she would listen.

After dinner Evie slipped out into the yard to meet Simon, round the corner from the store. He held her close, kissing her hair, neck, mouth, and she loved the feel of his body against hers and wanted more, but didn't know what. No one talked of what came next, not even her mother. The moon was huge and lit the path as they strolled along, his arm around her. They didn't speak, there was no need. They were as one and she loved him with all her heart. She wished it was the two of them marrying instead of Lady Veronica and if it was she'd not only talk about it, she'd leap into the air and keep going, right to the moon.

She stared up at the great white orb. 'It does look as though it has a face, doesn't it, Si? I wonder what's up there.'

He stared too. 'We'll never know, pet. No one will ever know, so we can just keep guessing and singing or writing about it. But one day, when we're married, it won't matter. It will be as though we're both up there, just being happy.'

Evie hugged him. One day, yes. They talked about it so often but it was only after they left service that they could marry, and they weren't ready yet. She said, 'By then we'll have Mrs Moore living with us, you doing the gardens, Jack doing something, I don't know what, Timmie too. Mam and Da and your parents will do something. We'll get a hotel nearer the sea, we'll have lots of guests. You can sing and Bernie can play the fiddle and I'll cook.' He was kissing her now, smothering her words, and she quite forgot what she was saying as the heat rose in her.

The next day Lady Veronica came down into the kitchen at teatime with another young woman. It was Lady Margaret Mounsey, the one who had hurled herself into the melee outside the meeting in Gosforn when they were trying to protect Lady Veronica. Evie bobbed, her head down. Would she be recognised? Surely not, it was so long ago. Lady Margaret's face was thin and drawn and she trembled as she sat at the table.

Lady Veronica was apologetic. 'Would it be too much trouble to take tea down here? Lady Margaret will be visiting for a few days, perhaps until the engagement party, and expressed a wish to join me here. She has been unwell and I wanted to discuss invalid food for her, if you and Mrs Moore would be so kind. But please continue with the five courses for me. No doubt Lady Brampton will give us the benefit of her company at some stage, perhaps at Easter, when we might have to reconsider the number of courses.'

Evie had already made tea and fancies for Archie to take upstairs, and she sent Millie scuttling to inform the servants' hall that the kitchen had unexpected visitors and Archie need only take tea for the chaperone, Mrs Benson. Millie took a tray to the butler's pantry for Archie and then the heavy tray with the servants' tea, and knew to remain there until Lady Veronica had left. Evie placed a tablecloth on the top end of the table, and hastily laid up for the two women. Lady Margaret's hair was dragged back in a bun. It was a sad sort of dull brown, and her skin tone was pasty, her chin was strong, her nose rather long and thin. By, she was just like a horse.

'I can make an egg custard, Lady Veronica,' Evie suggested.

Lady Veronica shook her head. 'No, I don't mean you to do it now, Evie. I know you're busy. Perhaps at dinner there could be something light – fish and then the egg custard.'

Lady Margaret stared around the kitchen. The copper glowed but this young woman seemed to absorb light and give back nothing; her eyes were dull and somehow she wasn't here. Where was she? In the cells? On hunger strike and being force-fed like the others? Lady Margaret lifted her skeletal hand to her hair with such effort that it might have weighed as much as a coal tub. Evie knew from the January meeting that she had been arrested yet again for public damage to a letter box; in other words, she had burned the mail. She had then hurled a brick through a local councillor's window, frightening the family. Did Lady Brampton know? Obviously not; no suffragette would be allowed to sully her home, and God knew what would happen if she discovered she harboured one in her own family.

Evie insisted. 'I will make an egg custard now if you would pour the tea.'

Lady Veronica did, without a murmur. The egg

custard took little time, but it would have to be eaten without setting. Evie explained this, providing a spoon, putting it in Lady Margaret's hand as though she was a child, then guiding it to her mouth, slowly and firmly and again and again.

No one spoke until the bowl was empty. Evie took it through to the scullery and on her return was pleased to see Lady Margaret sipping tea with a vestige of colour in her cheeks. Evie smiled at Lady Veronica. 'I suggest that we start with simple foods and build up slowly. I also suggest that small portions are less off-putting. Beef tea and a few spoonfuls of jelly and perhaps some oat biscuits should be readily available for her Ladyship to nibble during the day.' She stopped. Did that make it sound as though Lady Margaret was a horse? Well, the apple didn't fall far from the tree.

She hurried on. 'Some days the appetite may fade but it will return. There is a habit to overcook vegetables for those unwell, which destroys all goodness, so I suggest we prepare them al dente. I would also like to keep the skin on potatoes, which is where the goodness is contained. I will confer with Mrs Moore, and with her advice Lady Margaret will improve quickly.'

Lady Veronica smiled. 'I knew I could rely on you, Evie, you and Mrs Moore. Wainey would have liked you as much as I and my brother like you.'

Evie could think of no reply. Servants weren't liked, they were just there. She bobbed a curtsy.

Lady Margaret spoke then. 'You remind me of someone, Evie. Yes, you do but I can't think who.'

There was no thank you for the egg custard, there was just this, and Evie felt exposed. Lady Veronica cut in. 'I am looking forward to you meeting Captain Williams, Margaret. I'm sure you'll like him, everyone does.' Her tone was crisp.

The conversation then roamed around the marriage and Lady Brampton's delight but clearly Lady Margaret was tired and ill, and soon became monosyllabic. As they left she looked again at Evie. 'It is strange, I'm sure that somewhere in this muddled head of mine is the memory that we have met.'

They did not return to the kitchen but instead took tea in the drawing room, and Evie felt more secure. She and Mrs Moore sent up lightly boiled eggs for Lady Margaret's breakfast, broiled chicken for lunch with a simple pudding. Dinner might be a carefully cooked piece of cod, removed by an egg custard.

As the days went by they provided beef tea at all hours of the day, since the appetite was a strange thing and came and went according to its own clock, Mrs Moore reiterated. She showed Evie how to make the drink without the slightest trace of fat on the surface, using piece after piece of greaseproof paper. Evie didn't mind the extra work, because she was learning, always she was learning. They might well have convalescents to stay at their hotel.

*

The engagement party took place two weeks later, at the beginning of April, the week all the Durham miners returned to work. The strike had failed. They had to accept the owners' decision over a minimum wage. The Rt Hon. Captain Williams' parents resided near Cumbria, in a home that resembled a castle, so Mrs Green told Mrs Moore, and she doubted they knew one end of the coalfield from the other. 'Lord Williams is a viscount, old stock, not new like Lord Brampton. Not as rich as the Bramptons, but then who is? Old money is small money these days. New money is big but grubby money. He's the eldest son so will inherit what there is, and Lady Veronica will inherit an old lineage. Lady Brampton is cock-a-hoop.'

In the kitchen no one was cock-a-hoop, they were all too busy and had been all week, what with the invalid food on top of everything else. Mrs Moore had concentrated on the engagement cake, decorating it painstakingly with her swollen hands, and it was ready the day before, nestling in the pantry in all its glory. She sat on her stool on Saturday issuing instructions as all the staff flew from one chore to another. The kitchen was alive with the banging of pans and the delivery of provisions from the co-operative store and Home Farm, not to mention the passage of flowers from the garden.

They slaved from five in the morning to lunchtime, with Mrs Moore cracking the whip, though that was into empty air where Millie was concerned. The girl disappeared with monotonous regularity and was to be found smoking Woodbines in the yard. 'I need me breaks,' she complained after Evie had called her in yet again.

Mrs Moore said, 'You need a good kick up the backside, you silly lass. You *must* do your share. It's not fair on the others. Sometimes I think you are working well, but it doesn't last. What am I to do with you?' There was no answer, just a pout, but as Mrs Moore sighed and resumed her work Millie said, 'I've had a hard life, and you don't care.'

For one moment the kitchen fell silent. Everyone stared at her. Mrs Moore lifted the rolling pin but then replaced it slowly. 'I'll tan your backside with this one of these days, see if I don't, you silly little madam. There's many more with worse stories than yours and they work just grand. Now get on.'

At lunch they were allowed an hour to put up their feet. Evie was too hot to stay in the kitchen and slipped outside, fanning herself. It was cloudy and the breeze had become light, which worried her because the furnace needed a stiff breeze to perform to its utmost. She strolled down the path into the vegetable garden, hoping to see Simon, but there was no one working there. She walked on down to the bothy; perhaps he was here? Along the way were cowslips and soon there would be bluebells. She slipped inside, but no Simon, so she rested a moment, perching on an upturned barrel which had been moss-covered from the damp winter until she'd attacked it with some hessian on her last visit here.

Almost immediately she heard footsteps approaching but they weren't his, for Simon sounded like a shire horse crashing through bracken. Instead it was Millie and Roger who appeared in the doorway. Millie blushed but Roger just looked, then laughed. 'Well, what a nice little meeting place for us all. You fancy a bit of a smoke in private, do you? Well, Millie and I'll just take ourselves off somewhere else, shall we?' He swung the girl around and she giggled. Evie struggled to find words, but all she could come up with was, 'Don't be late, Millie. We have to be back soon.' What more could she say? She wasn't the girl's keeper.

She stayed firmly in the bothy, however, because if Roger saw her leaving he'd bring Millie back here to do heaven knows what in the darkness and privacy. She waited for fifteen minutes and only then did she go, searching for them in amongst the trees, not knowing what she'd do if she saw them up to something. It would likely be the murder of them both.

Millie was in the kitchen when she returned. Evie dragged her into the pantry. 'Look, you know what he's like. I've warned you that he said he'd target you to get back at me. Please, please don't play his game.'

Millie tore herself free. 'Mind your own business, Evie. If he takes me walking it's because he likes me and it's nothing to do with you. Not everything is, you know. Just because Mrs Moore teaches you all the time you think you're someone special, but you're not, you're just a servant like me.' Her face was twisted and she shouted, 'I like him, can't you see that? You're lucky, you've got a family, a home, and a boyfriend, what have I got?'

Evie pulled her back, shutting the pantry door behind them so that the whole world couldn't hear. 'I know I'm lucky, but choose someone else. What about Bernie, he likes you and he's a grand lad.'

Millie shook her head, crossing her arms. 'He's an under-gardener and Roger's a valet. You might like someone who grubs in the ground but I like clean fingernails and someone with prospects. I'm going to get out of here, just you wait.'

'But Roger won't . . .'

Mrs Moore opened the door. 'Come on girls, I won't have this shouting. Get out here now.' She shook her head slightly at Evie. 'Leave it,' she mouthed. 'We can only do so much.'

When they retired to bed at midnight Millie lay there silently. Evie said, 'I'm sorry I upset you, Millie. I just worry about you.'

There was no reply. Perhaps she was asleep.

Veronica and Auberon leaned on the balustrade of the terrace at the end of the party. There was a slight chill in the air. They had begun to come here again now the passing of time was lessening the distress.

Auberon ran his hands along the stone, feeling the lichen. Had Wainey felt . . . No, enough. Why was he thinking of death on the day of Ver's engagement? Perhaps because she seemed so unhappy?

She stood motionless at his side, staring down on to the formal gardens, the box hedges so neatly clipped, the daffodils and tulips visible in the bright moonlight. She said, 'Soon there'll be sweet william and roses and a myriad of others. The air will be overlaid with scent.'

He said, 'I like your Richard Williams. He's a good man. He was in the Officer Training Corps ahead of me at school. We admired him, really we did, Ver.'

Veronica stepped away, and stared up at the house. 'I know he's nice. I admire him too. I just don't love him, but as Stepmama says, what's love got to do with anything. It should have something to do with it, shouldn't it, Aub? Sometimes I wish I hadn't become involved with votes for women. It's made me think about my life. I don't want marriage yet, I really don't. I don't know if I want it at all. Look at Father, look at what he's like. Mother wouldn't have married him if she'd known, so he must have changed. Perhaps all men change once . . .'

Auberon put his arm around her shoulders, she was shivering despite her stole. 'Listen, I haven't a clue, Ver, about love. Yes, I suppose we must change if we marry because it *is* different, but men aren't all like Father.'

'But how do you know? What makes a man become a brute?'

'Father's not a brute to you, Ver.'

Veronica pressed her head into his shoulder. Thankfully, his father hadn't laid a serious hand on him for over a year. The strike had been universal, not peculiar to Easton, and Brampton had his own problems with a prolonged strike at the brickworks. 'He's not a brute to me because he's got you, poor Aub.'

Neither spoke, continuing to look out across the lawn. To the right, the rear stables were just a dark shape but Auberon could hear the huffing of the hunters, the sound of their hooves in the stalls. An owl hooted. 'Did he hurt Wainey, do you think?'

Veronica swung round. 'For God's sake, for the last time of course he didn't, that imagining is for books. Don't think of it, Aub.'

He shook himself free of memories. 'Be happy, Ver. Richard's a good man. Trust him. He might even let you continue with your interests, you never know.'

'He chose to be a soldier, to fight, to kill?' He felt her shivering again; a breeze had sprung up. She continued, 'But never mind, he'll be away a lot and anyway, the knot isn't tied just yet, so there's more time for me to be me.' He watched as she turned away from him. She traced shapes in the lichen, then beat it with her fists. She stopped suddenly. Behind them the staff were clearing the ballroom. Soon they would reach the terrace. She spoke again. 'I'm sorry, Aub, what about you?'

He laughed quietly. 'I'm almost enjoying life. There's a purpose to getting up in the morning now I'm getting the hang of the mine, and Father's been too busy to pass even a glance over my shoulder. I've had time to think: there was a dog in the yard at Froggett's, so I wonder if Forbes meant him when he said daft beggar? I thought of it as I was talking to Margaret. Not sure why but she does look rather like a dog, or is it a horse?'

Veronica laughed out loud, the only time he'd heard her do that this evening, and slapped his arm. He continued, 'I fear I've made a fool of myself, a bloody fool. But dear God, I still hate Forbes. I don't like being bested, Ver, but I just must return the cavil. Father's still saying no, but I'm working on it.'

Ver tucked her arm in his. The servants were clearing up the terrace now. It would have been good to walk beneath the moon with one of his dance partners this evening, but they'd all seemed to lose interest when it became clear that he had a job. It was not something they could understand. People of his class should go to their club, hunt, shoot, and fish. At the end of each dance his partners had no longer smiled, but examined their dance cards and darted on to the floor again with someone more suitably connected.

Ver had danced mainly with Richard, but so it

was expected. They made a fine couple. 'Perhaps love will come to you?' he suggested.

Ver's stole had slipped and he adjusted it for her, but still she shivered. He removed his jacket and placed it around her. 'Perhaps. Aub, I have so much I want to do but if I do it and say no to marriage, what happens? Out on the street with Society turning away? Will I become a punchball for Father? You and I have no money now he's taken control of Mother's inheritance, and I've no training. I'd perhaps be better off being Mrs Moore, or Evie.'

Auberon drew out a cigarette from its case, tapped it, lit it, and inhaled. Evie? Lately he'd been thinking a lot about her. The way she sat at the end of the kitchen table, the sweep of her eyelashes, her hands so deft and fingers so fine. Had she really thought they believed it was Mrs Green who had baked the cakes? Did she really believe that Wainey wouldn't have told them of Mrs Moore's increasing disability and chide them that they must protect their cook? But there was no need for them to do so, because Evie was there.

Veronica said, 'It's all such a muddle, isn't it, Aub?'

'A muddle is exactly what it all is.' He drew on his cigarette again. An owl hooted again, a fox called.

Did Evie not know that he would recognise her voice as belonging to the one who had berated a supposed stable boy, a girl who cared that the horses shouldn't die, and the boy shouldn't lose his job, and who had looked on him with such sympathy when she saw his face?

One day soon he would try and find out where the Anston family lived, because he wanted to know all there was to know about her. For a moment he toyed with the thought of . . . But no, his father would say that he was taking them back to the gutter in one generation, and he'd be right. It was hopeless, stupid and hopeless. He shook himself free of such nonsense.

'We both have things to sort out, Ver.' The servants were taking the chairs from the terrace and returning them to the ballroom. 'I think I'll return the cavil and let it be generally known, which will leave Father with no way of changing it without looking a complete fool. It's taken me too long to come up with a solution. I feel really bad about it.'

'He'll punish you,' she said. He peered over the balustrade, wondering what was rustling at the base of the rambling rose. He could see nothing but he'd had time to think and said, 'Don't worry about that. He's probably too busy to concern himself.' Auberon dropped his cigarette, grinding it out. 'Do one thing for me. Now the strike's over, please let the kitchen know that we are quite happy with three courses. I can't face the sight of any more feasts, dearest Ver, and Stepmama is complaining at the cost. Your ploy of saying that it was to prepare you for entertaining in your married life has worn thin.'

Neither slept well that night. Veronica tossed and

turned at the thought of a life she didn't want, with a man she didn't love. Auberon lay awake because he had a cavil to restore, and an assistant cook who intruded into his thoughts too often.

Chapter Fourteen

On Wednesday 12th May 1912 it was announced that the cavil would be reinstated very soon. 'But I expect we'll only get it if we are all good boys,' Timmie grumbled on the following Sunday. 'Not that Mr Auberon made the announcement. He got his monkey Davies to do it, the words dropping from his mouth as though they were bloody pearls before swine.'

His mam, busy on the proggy rug, clipped his ear as he passed. 'By, enough of that language from you, young man. You're sixteen, not a snotty lad any more, and you know your manners so use them, especially in front of your sister and her young man, and be glad the ruling can't be changed now it's been made public.'

Outside the early summer sun was bright but cool.

Timmie sneaked a cake from the plate on the table, which earned him another clip around the ear. His mam said, 'Pass those to the lovebirds.'

Timmie carried the plate to Evie and Simon, who were sitting on the sofa near the range holding hands and laughing at him. Evie loved being in this house, the family home, loved being in the heart of her family. The three years since she'd been at Easterleigh Hall had brought so many changes, so much improvement, so much happiness. She squeezed Simon's hand. 'Each time I pitch up, Mam, there's something new. That's a grand little mug on the dresser.' There were spring flowers from the verges in a jam jar, and yet another proggy mat in progress that some of the retired women neighbours were helping with. Her heart swelled.

Timmie made his way to Da's chair, put his feet up on the fender, and read *The Times*. Evie sank back against Simon, relaxed and joyous, though it had been a difficult morning with Millie flouncing about the kitchen, and sneaking out into the yard presumably to meet Roger. 'Leave it all behind, pet,' Mrs Moore had said, packing up some ham for her to take home for Simon's family and her own. 'The girl will come to her senses, and believe me she's not the first to have fallen slobbering at his feet – can't see why, never have been able to, but there you are.'

'Was there never anyone for you?' Evie had asked.

'The Boer War has a lot to answer for,' Mrs Moore replied, placing the ham in Evie's basket and covering it with old rags so no nosy parker could see. Who had Mrs Moore lost? Evie knew better than to ask, because the cook's face had closed. As she and Simon cycled to her mam's they had talked of that war but it was difficult to think what it could be like, out there in the sun fighting people who disappeared into the veld. 'Exciting, I should think,'

Simon said. 'But war can't happen now we've got all these alliances in place.'

They soared down the hill and she shouted, 'Then why are we building so many warships? It's been going on for almost six years and what's it all for? They say we're in a race with Germany, so what happens when someone wins?'

Simon laughed. 'Howay, it's not about that, you daft beggar, it's about putting money in the pockets of the steel men like Brampton, so come on, it's not our problem.'

'And why has Christabel Pankhurst rushed off to Paris to live in safety, leaving her mother, sister and others to carry out her orders and get imprisoned? I heard Lady Margaret say it's so she can lead the campaign undisturbed, like any good general. How very nice for the woman.'

Now, here in the kitchen she wondered again, about the warships and about Christabel and about when exactly the cavil would be brought back, but Simon was squeezing her hand, then kissing it as he heaved himself to his feet, stretching his arms and rolling his shoulders. 'I'm going to check on your da and the pigeons,' he said, reaching across and stroking her cheek before heading for the back door.

Timmie leapt to his feet, thrusting the newspaper down the side of the chair. 'I'm coming with you and then we'll go down to the club. Jack said he'd meet us there.' The door slammed behind them.

Evie moved over to sit opposite her mother at the kitchen table, taking one of the proggy tools, and starting to force strips of fabric through the hessian to create yet another rug to sell at the market. They were popular because Mam took care with the pattern, mapping it out on the hessian, rather than doing it just as the colours came. 'Your Simon's a bonny lad. They're a nice family, so they are,' her mam said, discarding a brown strip in favour of a bright green. 'Grace is popping in to see you before you head back, she wants an update on Mrs Moore. She's with the old 'uns next door, tinkering in the garden I expect.'

'I want to talk to her too, Mam. I need to see if there is any way she could take in Mrs Moore if the family find out about her rheumatics. She's getting herself in a grand old do about it again. I think Veronica and Auberon would be all right, but I know Her Supreme High and Mighty won't.'

Her mam forced another green strip through the hessian and pointed to a spot on the rug which should also be green. Evie obeyed, knowing better than to ignore. Her mam said, 'We can bump Timmie in with Jack and take her in ourselves if it comes to it, so just enjoy the day. Now, tell me more about Millie and this beggar Roger. It's hardly her fault she's a bit dippy, you know, pet. Her father was smashed up so bad in the pit accident that there was nothing they could see that reminded them of him, and then she had to live hand to mouth with her aunt. She's never felt safe, that's the problem.'

Evie nodded. 'I know, Mam, it's just that she's a slow worker and won't listen. By, not to mention we've tried again and again to tell her about Roger.'

Her mam grinned, her hair so much glossier than it was when Evie first went to work at the Hall, and her lines seemed fewer. Life was good for her in the cottage and she loved having the garden, rather than a yard, tending the vegetables while Da concentrated on the leeks for the annual show. She also had chickens and a pig down the end, and had passed their allotment on to someone else. 'You're a fast worker, Evie, you mustn't measure everyone by your standards because it'll make a bad teacher of you. And, bonny lass, would you listen if we said Simon was not the man you thought he was?'

Evie retorted, staring at her mother in shock, 'But he is.'

Mam laughed now. 'Aye, and you're surprised when Millie responds in just that way?'

Evie put down the strips and the tool, defeated suddenly. Was she a bad teacher? She dragged herself back to the moment and to the kindness in her mam's eyes, and smiled. 'Yes, and of course Roger might have changed, though pigs might fly. Anyway, it's none of my business.'

'Yes, I think that about says it as it is and I've had more than enough of this rug, I fancy another cup of tea.' Her mother gathered up the strips, tools and hessian, folding up the rug with the bits inside. She put it in the basket in the corner and tested the kettle on the range. 'Pop next door, pet, don't wait for Grace to come. Bring her back for a cuppa if she'd like one. Do you think she's different these days? Do you think she has a Simon in her life? There just seems to be a bloom about her.'

Evie stopped at the door, startled. 'I never thought of her in that way. She's a bit old for that.'

'By, give the woman a chance. She's only thirty. I reckon it's her choice she's not married, because she told me she needs to make something of her life and fears she'd have to give it up when a man and children came along. Now why d'you think she'd feel that way?' Her mother's smile was wry as she cast around the room, full of drying pitmen's clothes.

Evie had struggled with the thought of marriage herself, because there was nothing more she would want in life than to be Simon's wife and have his children, but she wanted to be a person too, with her own hotel. It was all so difficult.

'Away with you,' her mam said. 'You've got the look that tells me you've the worries of the world back on your shoulders. Go and get Grace and let's have a laugh.'

'How's Da's cough?' she asked her mother over her shoulder just before she left the room.

Her mother smiled. 'You know how it is, now off you go.'

Evie said quietly, 'We can start looking for a hotel in a couple of years. I reckon I don't need to work in Newcastle, I've learned enough about house-keeping by watching Mrs Green, and I know about budgeting from her and Mrs Moore. We can start small, Mam, just a few rooms, probably in Gosforn and we'll do the best food ever. We'll get Da out of the pit, we'll get them all out, never you worry. We'll make them safe.'

Her mother nodded. 'Aye, pet, happen we will.' It was what she always said. She hung the tea towel over the fender to dry.

Evie left the house through the front door, walking along the path with leeks planted, spring greens almost over, peas coming along nicely. Today they weren't gathering sea coal, because they gave them-selves a Sunday off a month. They wouldn't have to do it for much longer, they really wouldn't. The house loan had been paid off within the first six months, with Jack and Timmie working twice as hard to make up the low coal grade. Evie had added her wages, her mam had sold her vegetables and proggies, Da had bred his homing pigeons for sale, Timmie had sold the rabbits he'd poached, Jack had fought and was still fist-fighting with ever more aggression. Evie had asked why. He'd just said why not, when you've been given dirty placements.

'No,' she'd said, 'there's something more.'

'Leave it, hinny.' He had sounded tired and jaded.

His nose was beginning to flatten under the blows and his right ear was thickening.

She walked down the track along which the cottages ranged. The retirement cottage had proved to be a blessing, a complete miracle as they kept people from the workhouse. Grace was in the front garden now, the brim of her hat being pulled and pushed by the wind that was tugging at Evie's skirt and plucking at her blouse and shawl. Evie looked at Grace very carefully, and saw the beauty of her face now. There was, well, not youth, but something soft, calm, and lovely.

Grace came to the gate, a trowel in her hand, a wide smile lighting her face. 'Evie, how lovely.'

The front garden had been given over to vegetables, just like Mam's.

In the house next door there was a family whose father had lost a leg in the pit at the close of the year. 'I've got him out of his bed at last. All he needed was to feel he could be useful,' Grace declared, kissing Evie on the cheek, and then rubbing the dirt off. 'Sorry, I've made you grubby so I must be earth-smeared.' She rubbed at her own cheek, but Evie laughed and took over. 'Let me, you're making it worse.'

Over to the right, way above and to the north of them the stunted tree on the hill was visible, bending over as the wind began to assert itself. She stood back. 'There, spotless, almost.'

Grace grinned. 'Come in and survey my estate.' She led the way to a swathe of newly dug earth.

'Rather late to sow, perhaps, but the beans might have a chance.' She knelt on an old sack. 'Mr and Mrs Joyce are in the back sorting out the compost.'

'Talking of Mr and Mrs Joyce, Mrs Moore is fretting about her own retirement.' Evie crouched and handed the first of the broad bean plants to Grace, who dug a hole, planted and firmed it up. Grace's voice was thoughtful. 'Fretting, whatever for? There will always be room for her, but you'll have your hotel sooner rather than later and she could be useful, bless her. Your da left it to me to tell you that Edward and I will buy your house when you find your hotel.'

They heard the front gate opening and the sound of boots on the path. Evie recognised her brother's stride. 'Jack.'

She flew down the path and into his arms, and his hug was as tight as it had always been. 'Jack, I've missed you, man, but I've no news, or no more than you know. I didn't know when the cavil was coming off or I would have told you.' He kissed her cheek and set her down and she saw that he was not looking at her, but over her shoulder. 'Good afternoon, Grace.' Jack snatched his cap from his head.

Grace started to rise from her knees. He slipped past Evie and held out his hand to help. She dusted off her hands and took his. 'You're always so kind.' She sounded different.

'No, it's nothing.' He sounded strange too. Evie

looked from one to the other wondering. There was a silence. Grace examined the trowel in her hand and he perused the garden. 'It's looking good,' he said in the end, waving his hand towards the newly planted leeks. 'Good to get the broadies in too, and the potatoes will need earthing up soon.' Evie listened and watched. Jack added, 'I can earth them . . .'

Timmie came running along the lane then, calling across him, 'Jack, why are you here? You said you'd be at the club. You're always here. Grace must be tired of you, man, gawking at her garden.'

Jack blushed and walked back down the path. 'How could I not be here, with Evie home?'

'Well, don't mess about. Da's already gone and Si too. You can see Evie another time, man. Da said I could have two pints today, so hoy away with you.'

Jack put his hand on the gate and turned to Evie. 'Another time then, Evie, or Timmie'll have my guts for garters. Grace, it's been grand to see you. Let me know if you need help with more digging, or earthing up.' He slipped his cap back on, turned, cuffed Timmie, got him in a headlock and dragged him down the road.

Evie stared after him. Grace came up behind her and put an arm around her waist. 'You have two wonderful brothers, they are both so helpful, and your father too. But at the moment what I'd really like is one of your mother's cakes and a cup of tea.'

She smelt of lavender and the earth but her voice was just a little bit different.

Evie cycled back alone. Simon had gone with the others to the club, where women were not welcome, and she missed him. Although sitting with her mother and Grace eating too much cake had its attractions, it didn't compare to his company. Her mother had tutted, 'It's men, they need their lives.' Evie had muttered, 'And we don't?'

There was little light with the moon behind racing clouds, but her eyes adjusted and she could see well enough as she reached the bothy, quietly propping up her bicycle and padlocking it. Grace had sent a note for Mrs Moore and she checked it was still in her basket. It was. She hurried down the back path alongside the walled garden, past the vegetable stores and then the corner store where Roger had grabbed her. Instinctively she moved to the right here. She had almost turned the corner when she heard a giggle from the store and 'Shh, be quiet.' It was Roger. Was it Millie too? She stopped, about to turn, and then her mother's words echoed. She should mind her own business, and she'd done all she could.

She moved on, hearing the dachshunds barking and skittering in the stable yard. She looked to the left and there was Mr Auberon by Tinker's stall. He was often there, but never smoked now. She hurried down the steps and into the kitchen. The servants' hall was busy with laughing housemaids and footmen, dancing to the fiddles of Bernie and Thomas. She slipped along the passageway and pushed Grace's note beneath Mrs Moore's door before joining the dancers, and singing for them. Millie was absent all evening.

Chapter Fifteen

Summer faded into September and Da's leeks were ready to be pulled for the village show. Grace's retirement gardens were grand too. Some produce was sold at the market, some would be entered for the show, which was to be judged by Mr Auberon.

On the day of the show the meeting room at the club reeked of onions and leeks, and when the judging was finished and the villagers were allowed in there was a yellow rosette placed by Evie's da's leeks and it was Grace who had First Place. Bob Forbes smiled and shook her hand. 'It's all in the digging,' he said.

'And the muck,' Grace replied.

Evie looked closely at the leeks. Were Grace's really best, or was Mr Auberon biased as always? She couldn't tell.

The following week Lord and Lady Brampton returned from the London season with Lady Veronica, and within a week the shooting parties were under way and the kitchens were busy providing hampers and outdoor picnics, Mr Harvey was in two pairs of long johns, and the evening meals were gargantuan. Fresh air and the slaughter of birds must do that for one, Evie grumbled.

At the end of September, she and Simon sat on the barrels in the bothy. His arm was tight around her and he was kissing her neck but all she could think about was the Bastard's whelp, for that was how she had started thinking of Mr Auberon again. She said, 'At least I don't have to look at him or stick under the same roof now he's out on his ridiculous Territorial exercises. He's running away from the miners, that's what he's doing, because he can't face them. How can he not yet lift the cavil after the announcement was made? He promised Si.'

He squeezed her so tightly that she could hardly breathe and said into her hair, 'Try not to worry, pet. It doesn't help, just think of your hotel and the success it will be, then you'll all be happy, and that's all that matters.'

She shook her head. 'No, you have to be happy too.'

'I have you, how can I not be happy as long I can entertain the guests with my songs.' He mimicked her usual words, 'It'll be the best thing in the world.' She slapped him lightly but it was the first time he had mentioned the importance of his singing, and she was surprised. She had thought it was the gardens he loved, and knew that she must not forget what he'd just said.

In October she and Grace continued to go to the suffrage meetings when the shooting parties allowed, feeling more relaxed there because of Lady Veronica's absence. Mrs Moore commented, 'I gather Lady Brampton is dragging her round the county when there's a lag in the shooting.'

At the meetings they did not hesitate to stand and let their voices be heard. Evie had argued at the last one that the present campaign of violence was damaging to the reputation of women. A member of the committee had leapt to her feet. 'You ridiculous girl, we must perform these acts to create an impossible state of affairs in the country to prove that it is impossible to govern without the consent of the governed.' Grace had whispered, 'Perhaps she's swallowed a dictionary?'

Still the louts continued to pelt them with eggs or tomatoes as they left, or as they heckled politicians. 'It could have been bricks not eggs, let's be thankful,' Grace always said as they wiped their clothes clean on the return journeys, for they had agreed they would protest but not destroy.

By the end of October Mr Auberon had returned from playing soldiers and was back at the mine. Would the cavil be returned now? 'I won't hold my breath or you'll be burying me by evening,' she'd told Simon as she fetched herbs.

The cavil was not returned. On Thursday Mr Auberon resumed his downstairs tea, smiling as he took up his fork and tried a small piece of Battenberg. 'Perfection,' he said.

The range was damped down low preparatory to baking meringues for dessert, the servants were in the hall and Millie was heaven knew where. What was the point in asking any more?

'Your dreams, Evie?' Mr Aubcron said, eating more cake and patting his mouth with his napkin. 'What are your dreams?'

She was busy beating egg whites with the range oven door slightly ajar to further cool it down. She felt like saying, 'I'll have the cavil returned, please sir, and then you can have your meringue. After that, I'll have a cool breeze up my skirts, thank you very much.' Instead she admitted only to hoping for a senior cook's role.

She knew that she must not address a question to him but she did, into the silence that had fallen as he patted his mouth with the napkin again. 'And yours, sir?'

'Fly fishing,' he replied, cutting another slice of cake. She laid aside the whisk and replenished his cup of tea. He smiled. 'Sit here for a moment, Evie.' He pointed to the stool near him. She hesitated. He said, 'Please, I get a crick in my neck if I have to look up, or a strained voice if I have to shout down the table.'

She felt it an order and sat, feeling uncomfortable. 'Fly fishing,' he repeated, pouring in his milk. 'I renewed my acquaintance with the sport while on manoeuvres.' How reassuring, she thought, to know our country's safety is in the hands of soldiers whose manoeuvres include fly fishing.

He loved it, he told her – the tranquillity, the skill,

required, the silence except for the whir of the rod wheel and the birds. 'One day I am going to France, I will take my horse and I will ride along the length of a particular river and I will fish where the spirit takes me.'

Well, no doubt he would, as he wouldn't be staying in the pit for ever, and would then have all the leisure in the world to do exactly as he wanted, whereas . . . He smiled, and his face lit up, his eyes crinkled. What a shame such lovely eyes and beautiful smile hid a heart of stone. She suggested a scone but he shook his head, and took a slice of chocolate cake.

'Might as well be hung for a sheep as a lamb,' he laughed, and again his face lit up, and for a moment she found herself smiling in return. He sat straight these days, his shoulders back, no longer bowed. They only became so when Bastard Brampton returned and was displeased, as had happened after it had been announced that the cavil would be reinstated. It was then Mr Auberon had sat carefully, and moved judiciously, and she longed to say, 'Wallop him. In the chops. That would show him. And be a man, give us the cavil anyway. My brothers Jack and Timmie would in your position, and me da would never have taken it away from the miners in the first place.'

Would she stand up against the Bastard? Well, she'd never know, but this whelp had reneged on his promise, so he was as much of a bastard as his father and the memory of his bruises left her unmoved.

In mid December Evie and Mrs Moore decided to tackle the Nesselrode pudding recipe Lady Brampton had requested for the pre-Christmas dinner she had planned. As they worked they talked about Millie, who had ground almost to a halt and could only be termed a dawdler of the first order. Evie and Mrs Moore had tried to teach her with care and kindness, they tried to prod her with anger but nothing worked.

'She's making a fool of herself with this Roger, that's the problem. She's got no thought of anything else,' Mrs Green said, popping her head around the door as they lined up the ingredients, and then left.

Evie looked at Mrs Moore, who shrugged, checking the utensils which Evie had laid out in Millie's absence. 'Of course Mrs Green and I have discussed it. Where is the girl, anyway? She'll have to go. We can't carry her any longer. I don't like to dismiss someone but there's too much work and it's unfair on you lasses.'

Mrs Moore settled herself on her stool in front of the ranges and started to check off the ingredients that Evie had brought from the big pantry, pointing at them with a wooden spoon handle. Evie said, 'I sent her to lie down now she's finished preparing the servants' lunch. She has a bad headache.'

Mrs Moore tutted. 'You're too soft. Forty chestnuts, Evie?'

'In the bowl. She didn't look well.' Evie stood at her side.

Mrs Moore said, 'She'll be in trouble soon, anyway, and have to go with no character and more tears than she ever dreamed. He won't be dismissed, the man never goes. If we send her away now we could save her because I'll give her a character, of sorts, and there'll be distance between them. You mind my words, he won't be bothered with someone he has to make an effort over. He likes his plums daft enough to drop off the trees into his hands.'

Evie looked over Mrs Moore's shoulder at the recipe, and weighed the candied citron. 'One ounce, does it say? I suppose you're right, looking at it like that.'

'Yes, one ounce. You and Simon don't . . . ?'

'Two ounces of currants? Of course we don't.' Evie wanted to, of course and so did he, but they had plans and those came first, they told one another to damp the longing.

Annie was clattering in the scullery. Evie said quietly, 'Someone could leak Simon and me to Mrs Green and Mr Harvey, then we'd have to go, too,' she said, weighing up two ounces of stoned raisins.

'You're discreet,' Mrs Moore snapped, 'unlike that young lady. And no one wants either of you to leave.' Roger opened the kitchen door and passed through on his way to the bell corridor, smiling the same old smile that made both women long to slap him.

'That looks tasty, ladies, a little something to keep a good man going.'

Neither woman even looked at him, and where was the good man he was talking about? Not here, that's for sure. They blanched the chestnuts in boiling water, removed the husks, and pounded them in a mortar until they were smooth. 'Enough, do you think?' Evie asked Mrs Moore. She nodded.

Evie rubbed the pounded chestnuts through a fine sieve and mixed them in a basin with a pint of syrup, a pint of cream and the yolks of twelve eggs, which Annie had to collect in Millie's absence. 'Put it over the low hotplate now, lass, and don't stop stirring,' Mrs Moore instructed.

Evie did so, stirring, until she thought her arm would drop off.

'Now don't let it boil,' Mrs Moore warned.

They put the mixture to set in the icebox and tomorrow they'd move it into the freezing-pot. They put maraschino cherries, currants and raisins to soak, and Evie pounded sugar with vanilla. 'Such a shame really about Millie,' she said. 'She could have learned much more than she has. I've tried, I really have.'

Mrs Moore grunted, 'You have, lass. She was set on her course, it seems to me. It's nothing to do with you, or me, or anyone else.'

Evie's guilt was almost gone. But it was only 'almost' for hadn't Roger targeted the girl originally because of her?

That afternoon Mr Auberon and Lady Veronica came for tea, but explained that they would be unable to inconvenience Evie again until after Christmas, and apologised, yet again, for being in the way.

Over tea, with the suckling pig hissing on the spit, they slipped into French and Mr Auberon explained to Veronica that he was going to be extraordinarily busy for the next few months, and so were Hawden and Auld Maud pits because they needed to provide more energy for the steelworks. 'Father's signed a big steel contract, and it might be due to me, in part. The middleman's a military admirer and he classes the Territorials in that, and my involvement might have helped firm the contract. Father will have to keep to his word now and not oppose the return of the cavil. So that's a new year present for the pits, and at last I can get some sleep. It's been preying on my mind so.'

Lady Veronica looked up. 'That's wonderful, but it's so late and it appears as though *you* reneged. He's such a devil.'

Mr Auberon shook his head and drank his tea but Lady Veronica merely played with hers, her frown deep. Evie saw Mr Auberon push his cup and saucer away and drag his hand through his hair so savagely that she longed to slap his hand and tell him to break the habit, or he'd tear it out by the roots. 'He's like a damned spider, spinning a web. I think he's going to be trying for a contract with Germany next. I saw a letter on his desk with a Berlin address.' There was disgust in his voice.

'But is that patriotic, with the naval race in progress? What is the matter with you, Aub, why didn't you speak out?'

'The matter is the bloody cavil, isn't it? I can't oppose him or he'll close the pit. That's what he said. "Keep your place or watch your men take to the road." The fact that he needs the coal wouldn't matter. He'd buy up another pit.'

Evie was listening hard as she drew up menus for tomorrow, and didn't know how she felt except that her hatred for the Bastard knew no bounds. So, the cavil would be reinstated in the new year. So, she worked for a monster who had a son who could not fight his father. But who the hell could? Behind her the smell of young pork was sweet. There would be cold meat and pickle for the servants' supper tomorrow.

Evie continued flicking through her bible, not reading the words. Last week Mrs Moore had iced the Christmas cake. She was in a good phase at the moment, and not drinking. The Christmas puddings were already made and so too were a million mince pies. She began mentally to tick off the other treats – such as sugared almonds which they would try to make tomorrow – because it was easier than thinking of the life this young man was forced to live.

Today Mrs Green and the housemaids and footmen

had been decorating the Christmas tree which Simon, Thomas, Alf and Bernie had set up in the great hall this morning, before coming down for tea and scones. They were covered in pine needles and gathered around the range, laughing and talking about the gifts Father Christmas would not be bringing them.

Tomorrow the house servants would complete the tree and then prepare the rooms for the intended guests, to include Lord and Lady Williams and Captain Richard Williams, of course. The captain's younger brother was away with his regiment, his sister was married and in her own home with her own set of in-laws to bother about, according to Mr Harvey. Evie looked for further recipes, though today they would prepare a plain dinner for upstairs of soles à la crème removed by roast suckling pig and pheasant, removed by vol-au-vent of pears and compote of Normandy pippins.

Lady Veronica was rising and Mr Auberon leapt to his feet, pulling out her chair. 'It's good to have her back, isn't it, Evie?'

Evie stood as she should, knowing no one would pull out her stool. She smiled. 'We're all pleased, Lady Veronica, for it's not quite right without you.'

To her surprise she realised she meant it. Lady Veronica flushed and moved to the door, which Mr Auberon held open for her. 'Thank you, I agree, it isn't right anywhere else.' She switched to French. 'Auberon, it is no better, there is still no love.' They left and Evie watched them walk along the passageway. Poor rich bairns, she thought, grateful for her life and half able to hope that the bad placements were over for her family. But she had been here before and dared not trust.

Millie returned to the kitchen from yet another rest on her bed, or had she slipped out? Who knew? Whatever the cause, her nose was bright red with cold. Or was it more tears? Evie's heart lifted. Had Roger seen her off? Millie stood by the end range and pulled her shawl tightly around her, as though she was defending herself against the world. Well, she would be soon if she didn't get the wake-up tea for the upper servants. Immediately it was all rush and eventually Mrs Moore arrived, restored by rest and tea. 'I have to say you make a nice pot of tea, young Millie,' she said, settling herself on the stool. 'Now fetch the puff pastry from the ice room, pet.' Clearly she had not told the girl of the plans for her dismissal.

Millie did so, and Mrs Moore winced as she rolled out puff pastry on the marble slab. Evie and she had worked out which tasks she could perform without too much effort. 'Did Lady Veronica seem well?' Mrs Moore asked, leaning down on the rolling pin. 'I expect she's ready for a rest after her gallivanting.'

Millie said, as she rolled out the pastry for the servants' game pie which was a particular favourite of Mr Harvey's, 'Lucky for that lot. What about us, we're rushed off our feet.'

'Well, some of us are,' shouted Annie from the scullery before coming into the kitchen with her sleeves rolled up and her hands like raw steak. 'Where were you, Millie? You left before luncheon's tidying up was finished and Sarah and I had to do it. It's not fair. Mrs Moore, you need to do something.'

Millie didn't look up as she whimpered, 'I was getting the vegetables from the store.' Annie came closer, arms akimbo. 'You know Simon had already brought them in, so don't lie. Why did you nip out? But why am I asking that? We all know why. Where he goes, you go.'

Evie felt a headache begin. Mrs Moore was pressing down on the pastry cutters. 'Enough now, Annie. It's not your place to ask where your betters have been.'

Annie strutted back to the scullery. 'Betters, that's a good one. She's no better than she ought to be, and if you're making buns, Mrs Moore, you should ask what she's got in her own oven.'

There was a total silence in the kitchen. Mrs Moore stopped in mid cut, Millie in mid roll, Evie in mid baste. The only sounds were of the scullery maids banging and crashing the kitchen pans, plates, sieves and whatever else had just been used for dinner preparations.

Millie began to weep on to her pastry. Mrs Moore stared at Evie, then nodded. She didn't look at Millie, but her anger was only too plain as she shouted, 'Now is not the time for snivelling, Millie. Stop dripping on to the pastry, make the pie, do just as you would normally do, then you and Evie will have a little talk.'

Millie was still crying. She dropped the rolling pin, and dragged her arm across her eyes. Her nose was running. Please, not on to the pastry, Evie urged silently. She thrust her own handkerchief at the girl. 'Wipe your nose, go and wash your hands, and let's finish and then we'll sort everything out.' She sounded so confident, though she knew there was nothing to be done if Annie had been correct.

Somehow they staggered through food preparations and no one asked the question that was in all their minds. Over dinner in the servants' hall Evie made it her business to sit next to Millie, gripping her thigh when it seemed as though she would dissolve yet again, ignoring Roger's look of triumph which she understood too well. Yes, Millie was a bloody fool who had thrown herself at him when he lifted his little finger, but he had lifted it in the first place because of Evie. Damn them both. Poor stupid lass. She stared at him, hoping her contempt was withering. He just nodded, satisfied.

Once dinner was served she dragged Millie up to their room, sitting on the girl's bed, pulling her down beside her and holding her, rocking her, their feet on the proggy mat she had sneaked in to make the floor kinder on their feet. It was the one she and her mother had been working on in the spring. There were paper chains around the room too, and holly with bright red berries in a vase. How absurd they seemed now. If Mrs Green did one of her bedroom rounds it would be a relief to remove them.

Evie asked, 'How far gone are you, pet?' Her headache was pounding. She was tired and out of her depth and wanted Mrs Moore to handle everything. But then she sat up straight. No, she was this girl's teacher, it was up to her.

'Not quite three months. He won't have anything to do with me, Evie. He just won't.' She was crying now as she had never cried before, and that was saying something.

'What have you tried so far?' Evie asked.

'I said I'd do anything he wanted, anything, if he'd just marry me.'

Evie felt her irritation build. 'No, what have you tried to sort out the problem? Have you been to your aunt, will she have you?'

'She can't. Mam sleeps on a chair in their kitchen because there's no room. I can't ask her.'

Well, at least she has some consideration for others, Evie thought, her opinion of the girl rising slightly.

Millie was wailing now. Evie soothed her. Millie's cries grew less and Evie said, 'You have a decision to make, do you want the child, or not? But first, do you understand what will happen to you if you have it?'

Millie pushed herself away. 'You've got to help me. If I get rid of it, then he'll marry me, I know he will.'

Dear God, what was the matter with the girl? 'And if he doesn't?'

'Then at least I'll be free of it and I'll have a job, otherwise I'm going to be dismissed and I'll be in the workhouse and the bairn will be taken away to live in hell with the other bairns. They die there, don't they, Evie? I won't have a character even if I can get out of the workhouse, so I won't get back into work and I'll be on the streets. I have to get rid of it or I might as well top myself.'

'No, that's not going to happen. You will never go to the workhouse. I'll find you somewhere rather than that.'

Millie grabbed Evie's arm and shook her. 'Just help me get rid of it, please. I must. I simply must get rid of it.'

Evie had been waiting for her to say this but it still shocked her, and she realised she was gripping her hands together so hard that her fingers hurt. But she must help, of course she must. She stared up at the high window. It was dusk and there was no moon. She looked around the room. Millie's outdoor clothes were draped across the back of the only chair, one from the storehouse. Wasn't there something about jumping off chairs? She didn't know. And she just wanted to shake the silly stupid girl, but how would that help? Though perhaps it might?

They heard footsteps now, in the passageway. Evie put her finger to her lips and both girls sat silent as ghosts waiting for them to pass, but they didn't. The handle turned. Please don't let it be Mrs Green. The door opened. It was Mrs Moore, her face creased from the effort of climbing the stairs. She was panting.

'Annie and Sarah are boiling water. They are bringing it up in jugs to top up the bathwater. You will use the bathroom one floor down, you will not bring the tin bath up here. But that is assuming you want to try and solve this problem?' She waited, shivering. Only now did Evie realise it was freezing in the bedroom. Millie nodded. Mrs Moore handed her some pills. 'They're pennyroyal, and Beecham's Pills and quinine.' Millie took the pills and sat with her hands on her lap. Mrs Moore handed Evie a bag of mustard powder and from her pocket came a bottle of gin.

'It's all I can do,' she said. 'Now hurry to the bath. I have had a word with Mrs Green and no one will interrupt you. I will continue with the upstairs dinner preparations and Annie will help until you are free, Evie. Remember that whatever the outcome, girls, you must never mention this again. If it works I will call in a friend to help at the end if necessary. We can't have the doctor, or you will be instantly dismissed. Evie, if something happens tonight, come and get me. I'll have to send you to my friend by bicycle.'

'Yes, I'll take a lamp and hang it on the handlebars. You know, none of this is fair,' Evie said. 'Roger gets away scot-free even if we tell on him, because it's always the woman's fault.'

Mrs Moore was leaving the room, but stopped to say, 'Isn't this what I've been telling this silly lass since you all came? Millie, it's the way of the world. But you keep on fighting, Evie. You keep on fighting with your ladies and keep your legs together, and you too, from now on, Millie. Remember that you're not without blame.' Mrs Moore shook her head at Evie, her message clear. Say nothing about the decision to dismiss the girl. First things first.

The bathwater became bright yellow when the mustard was added. Sarah and Annie didn't speak but their faces said it all. They were torn between pity, anger, and relief – relief because it wasn't them, and after this, it wasn't likely to be. As Evie helped her into the bath Millie clutched at her. 'It's so hot.'

'It has to be.'

Millie eased herself in, the steam rising, her clasp on Evie's apron lessening until she let go entirely and sat in the five inches of water. 'Sweep it over your belly,' Evie advised, though she didn't know if this was the right thing to do. Millie did so, her skin reddening with the heat. 'My pills,' she gasped.

Evie handed them to her, and the gin, and while the girl took them she swept the hot water on to her belly again and again.

Once the water cooled Millie dried herself and dressed while Evie cleaned the bath with salt. 'There.' It was spick and span. They returned to the bedroom and Millie jumped from the only chair. Again and again, then Evie shook her until her teeth rattled.

They returned to the kitchen in time to dish up the soles à la crème, the suckling pig, and pheasant which Evie had plucked in the game room, the maggots falling to the floor, the smell obnoxious. It should have been Millie's job, but she had felt sick the moment they had entered. 'I should have known then,' Evie whispered. Mrs Moore shook her head. 'If anyone should, it was me. It's not as though it's for the first time. It's getting to be a habit with that creepy-crawly.'

They dished up the vol-au-vents and compote.

Evie and Millie barely slept that night, but nothing happened. Or the next day. Finally Christmas was with them, and on Christmas morning Evie opened the present from her family, a bracelet which she tucked into her drawer, together with a photograph frame from Si. Later the servants lined up in the hall to receive their presents from the Bramptons. Their packets of uniform material were wrapped and presented as though they were the Crown jewels. They each curtsied or bowed as they took their gifts, and all wanted to throw them straight back at Lady Bountiful. Why couldn't the woman find it in her heart, or from her pocket, to buy them something nice?

They trooped back down and their kitchen duties continued until two in the morning, and still nothing had happened with Millie.

On New Year's Day 1913 Millie was given notice after lunch, because Lady Brampton had recognised her swelling belly for what it was as she collected her Christmas present. She required the return of the material. As Millie packed and the servants went about their tasks quietly, Roger was seen in the yard smoking. Evie could not bear it, any of it. She talked to Mrs Moore about Grace's houses, and was given permission to take time off to accompany Millie. 'I will mention this to Mrs Green. Return when you can,' Mrs Moore told her.

Evie walked home with Millie pushing her bicycle, balancing Millie's wicker box with her possessions on the saddle. They skirted the mud on the rutted tracks once they were off the Bramptons' tarmac road. Leaving Millie ensconced in her mam's kitchen, Evie called on Grace in the parsonage. Time was short so they spoke on the doorstep, their breath cloudy in the chill air. 'I'm so sorry, Evie, but it isn't suitable to have a pregnant girl in with the rehabilitating miners in the second house, or the retirement house, really. I will try and find something, somewhere, if you can wait. I myself have a full house of ailing parishioners.' Grace clutched her shawl up to her chin.

Evie knew they couldn't wait, or could they, if her mam let Millie stay for a while? 'Thank you, Grace, I'll see what else I can sort out.'

On her return, she found Da sitting in his chair, smoking his pipe and scanning his pigeon magazine. Timmie was at the kitchen table, his sleeves rolled up and his blue scars visible, painting a lead soldier that Evie had given him for Christmas. They were his passion, and when finished, this one would take its place with the others on the shelf in his bedroom. Jack was sitting opposite Timmie reading *The Times*.

'Not sure about these suffragettes of yours, Evie,' he said, looking up. 'Doing a lot of damage with this arson and losing a bit of support, I reckon.' He rattled the paper and returned to it, then said, 'It's New Year and we've been given a day off, but can you find out exactly when the cavil returns?' Evie shook her head in warning, nodding towards Millie. Jack understood immediately. They didn't want anyone to know that Evie reported back from the Hall.

Millie sat on the sofa with Mam, who was knitting a scarf for Timmie's walk to the pithead of a morning. Evie came to the range, warming her hands. She shook her head at her mam and Millie. Millie's eyes filled again. The men continued with what they were doing.

'She says it's not appropriate and I can see what she means,' Evie explained. Her mam nodded. 'I thought that would be the case.' Her needles were clicking, the scarf was growing, the range was crackling and spitting with the poor-grade coal. Nothing changed, everything changed. Millie looked terrified. Evie squeezed on to the sofa. No one spoke.

Evie said quietly, for the women's ears only, 'She'll try but we'd have to wait, and where can she go until somewhere is found?' The silence continued and Evie felt as though her breathing had stopped.

Her father looked up at the clock on the mantel. She followed his gaze. It was time she left. He cleared his throat, leaned forward and tapped out the ash from his pipe on to the fire. Millie was completely still, the tears sliding down on to her shawl. Her da said, 'Well, the minute you lower your voice you know you've got us all listening, so is anyone going to say anything? What about you, Mam?'

Her mam chuckled. 'You're the man of the house.'

Jack laid down his newspaper and called across, 'Grace would help if she could, so for heaven's sake, the pair of you, Millie's going to be staying here at least until the bairn is born and you knew that the moment you brought her here, Evie. Tell the girl to stop the waterworks and relax. Timmie and I will bunk together and he'd better not snore.'

'It's not me who snores, it's me mam.' They all

laughed, her mother dropping a stitch, then wagging a finger at her youngest. 'You're not too old to have your backside walloped.'

Timmie pulled a face and grinned at Millie. 'You can decide what's to be done once the bairn is born.' His hand was steady as he painted the dark green jacket of the fusilier.

'Aye, that'll be right, lad. Now, you get back, pet. We'll take care of the lass.' Her mother patted Millie's leg. 'Hush now, pet. It's sorted.'

Millie was wiping her face with the edge of her shawl. She said, in a voice faint with relief, 'I'll do all I can to help, honestly I will. Thank you, from the bottom of my heart.'

As Evie prepared to ride away she turned and waved to her mam and Millie standing in the doorway, and she blessed the family she had been born into, and then laughed aloud at the thought of wringing help from Millie. Perhaps though, pregnancy might bring about changes, and at least she and the baby would be safe, and cared for.

Just as she pushed away, Millie called. 'Evie, Evie, I have to tell you something.'

Evie stopped and waited, the wind icy, cutting through her coat and two shawls. The smoke was being swept from the chimneys the moment it appeared. Millie ran to her, more tears streaming down her face. 'I said something, I thought it would make him marry me.'

Evie held on to her handlebars, eager to be off.

'Well, whatever you said you should have known he'd do a runner anyway. Think of the others he's got into trouble, like Charlotte.'

She started to push down on the pedal, but Millie held her back, gripping her arm with surprising strength. 'No, listen to me, Evie. I told Roger you were a Forbes and must have passed on the news of the houses. I told him before I left today. I'm sorry, really sorry.'

Evie stared at her. What? What? 'You what?'

Millie was weeping and Evie was sick of the sound of it. 'I told him. It was the one secret I had that might help me. I'm sorry. I'm right sorry. You'll lose your jobs, you'll need to find work, move. All of you. What about me?'

Evie wasn't listening any more, she was powering away, head down, forcing the pedals faster and faster. She had to get back. She had to stop him telling Mr Auberon. They weren't ready for the hotel yet. Damn Millie, damn her to hell, but even as she chanted this she wondered if in her position she might have done the same.

By the time she reached the bothy her legs were shaking with exhaustion and sweat was running down her back. She flung the bicycle in with the others and tore up the back paths. The sky was full of snow, she could smell it on the wind. She pounded past the vegetable store. Her mind had been working furiously: she must find Lady Veronica, she was her only hope. If she left it would be without a character or further training and alongside her would be Mrs Moore, who could no longer be protected. As for the menfolk in her family? Well, she knew the answer to that.

Sometimes Lady Veronica walked the dogs in the formal gardens, sometimes in the arboretum. Evie rushed through the yard, and then to the stables where she stopped, listening for the barks of the dachshunds – nothing, just the stamping of hoofs in the stalls, and the whistling of the stable lads who were stirring the bran. Her heart was pounding, her thoughts in chaos. Think, think. Calm down. She started back towards the rear stables, heading for the formal gardens, but then heard faint barks. They *were* in the arboretum. She ran back down the yew path alongside the front lawn and the cedar. Her hat slipped – fearing to lose it, she snatched it from her head. She had decided on her lever, and was ashamed but determined.

She ran along the haha, crossed the grid and hurtled between the acers, chasing the sound of the dogs. 'Please let her be alone,' she panted. 'Please, please.' There were the dogs, skittering around Lady Veronica's feet, barking as she held out a biscuit. They were getting too fat. How trivial. Why did the mind come up with nonsense?

The breath was heaving in her chest and a stitch was slicing into her side. The dogs must have heard for they left Lady Veronica and tore towards her, then back to their mistress, then towards her again, nipping at her boots. Evie slowed to a walk and approached. Lady Veronica stood watching her, puzzled. 'Evie,' she said, 'am I needed? Is there an emergency?'

Now she was here Evie couldn't think how to start. She blurted out, 'You owe me a hat. I don't need it, I have another.' She waved hers. 'I was there, you see, at the meeting. It wasn't just Grace who saved you, it was me, too.'

Lady Veronica held up her hand as though she was stopping a runaway horse. 'I know, of course I know. I'm not stupid. Lady Margaret also recognised you when she heard you speak. I've often wanted to share my thoughts with you about the route the Pankhursts are taking, but it's just so difficult, isn't it? You're not supposed to be there, and neither am I. Heaven knows what Captain Williams would think. Hush, Currant.' Lady Veronica gave the dog another biscuit. Evie started to speak, but Lady Veronica sailed on. 'I have your hat, it reminds me all the time of what's important. We simply must have the vote, mustn't we?'

Bugger the vote, Evie wanted to shout. Instead she said, 'I simply must keep my job and you are the only one who can help me. I'm a Forbes, you see. My name isn't Anston. Roger has discovered this and I know he will tell your brother, and I will be dismissed. I will tell your father of your suffragette activities if you don't help me, and Lady Brampton, and Captain Williams.' The shame of those words would remain with her wherever she went. The wind was bending the branches and the temperature had dropped further. She realised she was shivering. She looked at the hat which hung limp in her hand.

The dogs were jumping at Lady Veronica, and then at Evie. Her nose was running; she found her handkerchief and blew. Still nothing was said. She forced herself to meet the eyes of her mistress at last. Lady Veronica had paled, her hands were clasped in front of her. She said, 'I would have helped anyway, Evie. You didn't have to blackmail me.'

For the first time for a long while, Evie cried. It was all just too much, and the tears wouldn't stop coming and neither would the apology which she repeated and repeated, shame making her want to sink into the ground and never emerge. Lady Veronica reached forward and wiped Evie's face with her gloved hand. 'My dear, we all do what we have to do, and now I want to know what's happened to bring this about.'

Evie knew she would never forget that this woman had reached out and touched her, comforted her, when normally *they* would only receive a letter if it was on a salver, not given by hand. She had to pull herself together, she had to, because time was running out. She told Lady Veronica then, about the attack by Roger, about Millie's pregnancy and the revealing of Evie's secret. 'She kept it for so long.

She could have told him before but she didn't,' Evie concluded.

Lady Veronica nodded. 'Well, Evie Anston, because it's best that we know you as that, I will be speaking to Roger the minute I return to the house. Do we have any ammunition, do you think? Does he take wine from the cellar, or steal in any other way? A pregnancy won't be a threat, he knows that. It's always the woman's fault.' The glance they shared was bitter.

Evie shook her head. 'I don't know.' It was hopeless.

Lady Veronica called the dogs to her. 'Go back and help Mrs Moore. We can't have you leaving because Mr Auberon and I know that she can't manage without you, though it's best that we keep this between us, don't you think?'

Lady Veronica put on the dogs' leads, and hurried away. 'Thank you,' Evie called.

Lady Veronica waved a hand but didn't turn. 'This will now be forgotten, Evie, and I lay claim to the hat for ever. Is that acceptable?'

It was, indeed.

Lady Veronica found Roger in Auberon's dressing room, brushing down his dinner jacket. She slipped through the door quietly and closed it behind her, leaning back against it. She disliked this odious man intensely. He was like a snake and used his position to overawe silly girls who then faced a life of ruin.

Everyone knew but nothing was done, and it was time that changed.

She said, with no preamble whatsoever, 'Roger, it has been brought to my attention that you have been stealing from Lord Brampton's cellar.' She had no proof of this, it could be quite untrue, but what did that matter when it came to an accusation by a mistress to a servant?

Roger turned, his thin face stunned, and the brush dropped from his hand. 'That's a lie.'

She stood straight, recognising the incipient violence in the man, for, after all, she had spent much time with her father. She kept her expression as disdainful as anything her stepmother could drum up and knew she must speak with no hesitation or uncertainty. 'I will do nothing about it but will expect absolute discretion concerning the name of our assistant cook. I will not be without her and it is I who will be lady of this house on my marriage, for this will be our home. We cannot afford to be without someone of her skill, but we can afford to be without a valet. You would be easy to replace. Remember that my father has already had occasion to be displeased with you over the loss of the Froggett houses. One word, Roger, just one word and you will never work in this or any house again.'

The rapid passage of emotions across his thin full lipped face was fascinating. Fear, anger, fury and fear again. Finally there was acceptance and hatred. Well, that was mutual.

She left the room without another word. Power was addictive and dangerous, and must not be abused. With one word she could ruin a person's life. Whether she told Aub about Evie was debatable. He *should* know, but did he *need* to know?

Chapter Sixteen

Timmie's bait tin clattered against his belt as he and
Jack walked ahead of their father on their way to
their Saturday shift at Auld Maud. It was 5 a.m.
and dark. It was a bit of a leg but he liked the
walk, and Mam's scarf kept out the worst of
the wind. It was 2nd January 1913, and he swore
he'd heard a cuckoo yesterday on a walk, but Jack
said it was a pigeon if it was anything. 'It's bloody
winter, you daft beggar.'

'Is it colder this winter, do you think?' Timmie
pulled his muffler over his nose.

'A bit, maybe.' Jack sank a hand into his jacket
pocket, his bait tin clattering as loudly as Timmie's,
his tools hitched over his shoulder.

Timmie told him that he had just one more lead
soldier to paint and then he'd have the whole regiment. There was no reply. 'Did you hear that, Jack?
Just one more to go.'

'Aye, I heard you, but it's like walking next to an
empty vessel, with all the chat from you. It's before
dawn for pity's sake, man.' Jack was quieter these
days, he had been for months now, but perhaps Millie
might make a difference. Timmie had grumbled that

she was a bit of a feeble lass really, and cried a lot. Jack said that you did when you loved someone and you couldn't have them. Timmie thought his brother was trying to take Millie out of herself.

He nudged Jack. 'Let's go to the club tonight, shall we? I fancy a beer.'

His da called out, 'Not too many for you, Timmie. You're still only sixteen and haven't the head for it, or have you forgotten the last time? Your mam won't have that mess on her proggy rug again. You'll be seventeen by spring, so celebrate then.'

'Howay, Da, I'm doing a man's job and no, I haven't forgotten, how can I with you lot reminding me every Saturday. I'll never have as many as that again but it'll never be your fiftieth birthday again, will it?' They were entering Easton and Martin, Jack's marra, came out of his backyard and fell in next to Jack. Tony, Timmie's marra, came from his yard and fell in next to him. 'We're like the whelp's Territorials, marching in step,' Timmie called back to his da.

Jack tipped his cap at him. 'Platoons don't talk, they march.'

Tony said, 'Or they're lead and sit on a shelf and do nothing, while the rest of us work.' They laughed.

Steadily they were gathering men including Ben, his da's old marra, and Sam. Ben walked with Bob, talking of his painting. He'd offered to paint Timmie's collection in action, when the final soldier was finished.

'Not long now, Ben,' Timmie threw over his shoulder.

Jack called out, 'That's what he said a week ago.'

'Well, it takes time. No need to rush it. Now we have Millie it's been harder to concentrate with all her caterwauling.'

His da called, 'Ah, she's getting sorted, aye, she is. She'll move on when there's somewhere for her. Grace is on to it, isn't she Jack?'

Jack grunted. 'How should I know? I only dig for her from time to time.'

All the men grew quieter as they trudged up to the pithead. It was the first day back. Had the whelp kept his word at last and reinstated the cavil? Davies was waiting for them, holding up a piece of paper. He was grinning. 'It's here, lads. Cavil's reinstated. You can draw any time you like now, so have an extra beer tonight.' There was no cheer. They should have had it months or a year ago, or two, but quietly they looked at one another and smiled. Timmie slapped Jack on the shoulder.

'You'll be sorting the drawing then, Jack?' Martin asked. 'Aye, it'll be the committee who'll do that,' he replied.

Timmie saw his smile and knew that Jack was relieved. He'd have the chance of drawing a better placement at long last and what was more, Da had just heard from Davies that an extra beer was in order. He grinned across and his da shook his head in mock exasperation. 'Aye, I heard, but remember the rug.'

Discarding their jackets and picking up their tokens and lamps, the men shuffled into the cage, their spirits lighter. Timmie was on the tub today, though sometimes he was with the wagons and Galloways. He preferred the ponies, and his mam had given him a carrot for them. He closed his eyes as the cage plummeted into the darkness. He couldn't bear it, but he'd never tell his da or Jack. They seemed to take it in their stride but Jack always stood with him as he did today, his arm touching his, and the pressure comforted him.

At the bottom they trudged to their placements, the heat and the smell, and the dust sinking into his lungs before he'd gone more than a few yards. Their lamps lit the way, a dull glow. Tony came with him to the stables which had been carved out of the rock and coal, and they each fed a carrot to their favourite, Twilight.

Timmie said, 'They know us, Tony.' He loved the snuffling of the muzzle against his palm, but not the slobbering bits of carrot that fell from Twilight's mouth. He shook his hand free of them, and then pulled the pony's ears. He left Tony to harness up and trudged the mile to the placement he would be serving today.

Jack scuffed along. He was tired, always tired now. Sleep was slow to come, because all he could think of was Grace. It was pathetic and he kicked out at the dust. Martin elbowed him. 'Watch your step, I don't want any more muck in me than's there already, you silly beggar.'

'Sorry, man.' He'd hoped the longing for her would fade in the face of her indifference. After all, she just needed someone to dig. He'd tried other women, of course he had, but she was there, in between, and it made for this anger that gnawed at him. No wonder he won his fights every time. It was a way for it to come out.

His da was walking behind him, but not for long. He stopped at his kist and called out as Jack and Martin plodded on, 'I'll check the roof and the props at Ben's seam, then I'll be along.'

'Aye, Da.' His father had survived two strikes as deputy, at the request of the men. They wanted him checking their placements – he was thorough and painstaking. The economies were still in place and the recycling of the props had increased. But the cavil was reinstated so Jack's coal grade could be better, and Timmie's run of tubs stood the chance of improving once out of Brampton's control. He made himself listen to Martin talking about the football. Always it was the footie, and he smiled now. He liked routine, he liked what was normal.

Martin took the lead, humming as the roof dropped lower and lower, taking the scabs off their backs, and half a mile in Martin knocked his head on an outcrop. The hum became an oath. The roof sighed, the pine props creaked and hissed, coal dust fell into their eyes as their lamps shone a yard or so in front. They stopped, waited. It was nothing. Jack fell back a few more paces, trying not to breathe in or swallow more dust than he had to. 'Nearly at the face, lad,' Martin called, trudging on.

Within ten minutes they were there, crouching even lower as the roof sloped to two foot six or thereabouts. 'It's a bugger of a face, and it's going to be grand to have the chance of better,' Martin shouted to him. He always shouted at the face. Jack had asked why but the lad didn't know. He just did. So he kept on doing it and it had kept him safe so far. 'Hang on,' Jack called. 'Wait for Da. He's coming, I can hear him swearing, he'll have caught his head, so it's not just you, lad.' They both laughed as his da appeared, crouching and dragging two short props and a stool.

Jack said to Martin, 'I'm sorry, lad, for the poor . . .'

'I don't want to hear that again. I told you last time, and the time before that. It's not your fault the whelp's the bastard who put us here again.'

'I've brought you a cracket,' Da said. 'I reckon you could cut in and make more headroom.' He handed the short stool to Martin and peered in the gloom at the roof, wedging a prop under a miniature fault. He held his lamp higher, checking again. 'Keep your eye on that, lads, and I'll be round in a few hours.'

He patted Jack as he passed. 'Keep careful, lad.'

'Always, Da.' His da's face was already black with dust, his teeth white even in the low light from the lamp. Jack's would be the same. How the hell could a pitman offer someone like Grace anything, and why would she look at a lad, for that was what he was alongside her. She was around thirty and he coming up to twenty-three, but he never thought of age when he was with her.

His da's footsteps were receding. He took the pick and worked with Martin until his da came again, bringing two more props, examining the roof and eating his bait with them where the roof was a bit higher, crunching coal dust as well as bread and dripping.

Down by the cage Timmie and Tony stopped work and sank on to their haunches. They had stripped off their shirts and were sweating in the heat, gulping down water from their tin bottles. It was warm but wet. They ate their bread and dripping and kept enough to feed Twilight, who was standing patiently a few yards from them. Mam had given Timmie four cakes, two each. He divvied them up.

'Millie made them after our Evie went back to work yesterday. Our Evie taught her.' Tony nodded as Twilight shifted his weight from foot to foot. Timmie scooped the last of the cake crumbs into his mouth, nodding towards the Galloway. 'What d'you reckon he thought about being dragged away from the fields after the strike?'

Tony wiped his mouth, took a drink, leaned back his head and sighed. 'A load of bollocks is what he thought.'

Timmie knew that he and Tony would be marras for ever. There was no one else he'd rather be working with. By, but he was a heathen all the same, since he'd not cross the road for a lead soldier. He jammed the stopper in his water bottle. 'Up and at 'em, man,' he said. 'The tubs'll be piling up.'

Bob eased himself up. 'I'm away, lads. Take care now.' He stooped very low, stumbling along the seam, listening, always listening to the roof, to the sides, and cursing as an outcrop caught his back. Another scab torn away. He groaned quietly, feeling the soreness of his knees, the stiffness in his thighs and back. Sometimes he thought he'd not be able to get up for a shift, but it wasn't an option. Young Evie was getting so close now to being able to manage a hotel, so she said, and to hear Millie talk she was a right canny cook, his lass was. He felt the grin crease the dust on his face. She was right, they should start small. There was a sound. A crash, a whoosh of air. He turned, and stumbled back to the face.

There was a heap of coal between Jack and Martin. 'It's all right, Da, I was taking the last of the top coal and the wedge stuck fast. I took the pick to ease it and the whole bloody lot came down, right between the two of us. It's our lucky day. It just got our bloody ankles, nothing too bad. Just a graze.'

Bob felt his heart beating too fast and too loud.

'Then don't take a bloody pick to it. Worm it out, use a bit of nous, for God's sake.'

Jack grinned at his da. 'Calm yourself, man. You're not getting rid of us that easy, is he Mart?' Bob could hear the shake in his son's voice, and in Martin's too as he replied, 'Not unless he's placed a charge and is waiting to blow it just as we pass.'

'Clear that lot,' Bob ordered, 'and call in the putter. I'm off to see Timmie, at least he's got a grain of sense about him.'

The other two laughed as he set off again, his nerves jangling. He stopped on the way to check the props at the other faces, and all along the seams. He had to draw out some props from a seam that was defunct, hauling them back quickly, gathering them as the roof sagged but held.

Timmie checked that his token was still strung inside the tub, because he didn't want to work like this and find the weighman didn't know it was his piece. He pushed the tub down the dark hot low seam towards the face, black sweat pouring from him. The cakes had been grand and he wondered again what it would be like living in a hotel, away from the village, from his marras, and a bit of him wanted to go, but most of him wanted to stay. Here was his life. Here, in this bastard of a pit with the dark, and the sounds of cursing, singing, tubs, picks, boots, and the charges his da set.

He slowed, wiped his forehead and spat into the

dark at any rats lurking, then shoved hard again, his shoulders straining, his head lowered. Bastard seam, just too damn low for Twilight and Tony. There were other deputies, but his da was the best. He was the best at everything, well, next to Jack. 'And by, I wouldn't want to be anywhere but near Jack,' he said. He liked to hear his own voice, otherwise it was too dark, too creaky, too hot.

He was on the uphill now, and he got his back to the tub, shoving it, forcing his legs to brace against the weight. It was so damn dark but somehow your eyes learned to see. Sid and his marra were working this seam. Timmie liked Sid, he'd buy Timmie a beer at the club without a lecture, and let Timmie buy him one back.

The seam was levelling out and the roof was lifting. He stood straighter, then totally upright. The relief was immense but he knew it would drop down again soon, which it did. The rails ran right up to this face but you couldn't get a pony along here, not in a million years. He'd hitch up with Tony on the way back but he'd be down the Fenton seam now, picking up some other tubs. The roof was bloody low again, but Sid was working the face in a high-roofed cavern and he'd be there soon. He shoved again and heard Sid calling, 'Got a tortoise as a putter, have we lad? Hope you paint your toy soldiers quicker than this?'

Timmie shouted, 'They're not toys, they're lead soldiers. Accurate, they are.' The men laughed.

He helped Sid's marra, Dave, to shovel in the coal as Sid continued to hew, his back bare in the heat, and bleeding. He'd knocked scabs off and had a cut. Well, who hadn't?

'Watch the descent, lad,' Sid called as Timmie shoved the heavily laden tub away from the face. 'Can't have that last soldier we've all heard about being left unpainted.'

They all laughed, again.

He shoved the tub along, his back and shoulders aching even more under the strain, ducking down as the roof lowered, his arms spreadeagled and gripping the edge as he breathed in and tried to remember where the descent started. It wasn't steep, but you could get a bit of a lick going if you didn't pull back in time. He felt it then, the easing of weight, and it seemed too soon. He leaned back, pulling, but it wasn't braking as it should, but then it caught. His thighs and arms were tight and felt as though they'd snap, daft beggar that he was. He breathed out hard with relief.

Then he heard his da calling, 'Timmie lad, just coming to see all's well.' He was coming along the track. Timmie lifted his head, relaxed just a fraction and that was a mistake because the tub seemed to pull away. God, it had a life of its own. It was going down the slope and he threw himself backwards, digging in his heels, gripping the tub, harder and harder but it felt as though his hands were slipping and his father was there, somewhere in the dark ahead of him. The tub was gathering speed, quicker, quicker. His heels were skidding along within the tracks. He tried to hammer in his heels but he was moving too fast.

Timmie called, 'Get off the track, Da. Get off the bloody track.' He couldn't hold the tub. His mind was racing. He let go, running alongside, racing it, beating it. He threw himself in front, digging in his legs, slowing it. 'Get off the track, Da!' he screamed but it was pushing him, shoving, it was too strong, he couldn't hold it. Just couldn't hold the bloody thing and now he could see his da, flattened against the wall as the tub was pushing him faster than his legs, pushing, pushing. He tried to shove back but he was going over. For God's sake, he was going, his legs weren't working, they were lagging. He must get away from the front, he must leap for the side, but it was pushing him, shoving him, down. Down. He just couldn't stop it, and he saw his da leap out and on to the track, his hands outstretched.

'Timmie!' he heard him screaming, 'Timmie, my lad.'

'Da,' he called but he knew it hadn't left his throat because it was too late, his face was in the dust and there was no light. Just a thundering noise and a huge and massive pain which never seemed to stop.

Bob had reached his son after the tub had passed over him. He held him as the tub jolted off the rails and into the side, tumbling the coal over his legs while some fell down to the track, the tub crashing after it. 'I need to check the props.' He could hear his voice. 'I should check the props, Timmie lad.' He was howling, but he should check the props. He should listen to the roof, for the creaks and the groans and the hisses. He should, but all he could hear was his own howling and then there were hands on him, holding him, easing him to the side. Sid was shouting, 'Get Jack, for God's sake get Jack.'

Jack and Martin squirmed and writhed back from the face more quickly than they had ever moved in their lives, following Dave who had hollered, 'Jack, you're needed, now. It's Timmie. It's your da.'

Once they were able they crouched and ran and it didn't matter that the outcrops tore at their backs and heads. They ducked and weaved past other hewers and putters, who dropped their tools and followed. They were out to the narrow tracks and the buzzer was going. Someone was dead. Not his someone. No, not his someone. 'No, not my someone, not my someone,' he was shouting, and Martin was shouting back, 'Nay way, lad. They're too canny.'

The men were gathering, but parted like the Red bloody Sea and it *was* his someone. It was his lovely someone lying there crushed between the rails, crushed like a bloody fly. He knelt, knowing that Timmie was dead, but he couldn't be, he had his soldier to paint. He turned him over and there he was, his young, lovely Timmie who wasn't lovely any more, who didn't look like Timmie any more, whose mother must never ever see him like this.

Someone handed him some sacking. 'Here lad, put this over him. We'll bring up a tub and take him back.' The man was shouting over this awful howling that Jack couldn't understand. What was that noise? What was that awful awful noise? 'Shut up, just shut up.' He tried to stand but his legs gave way. Sid and Martin held him up. 'Steady lad, it's your da,' Martin said.

Jack saw him now, by the side of the rails, sitting slumped against the wall. His mouth was open and he was howling, like a dog. Another deputy was there and Jack somehow found strength and ran to him. 'Da, where're you hurt?' He gathered him in his arms, and he was wet with blood, sticky blood and Ted the deputy shook his head. 'A broken leg, lad, that's all. But he's just seen his son killed and that's your Timmie's blood and he can't stop the noise. You need to be strong for them all. For them all, you understand.'

Jack did, and he rocked his da until the wagon came along pulled by Twilight, driven by Tony who didn't know. No one had told the lad. Why didn't they tell him? Why? It was filling his head and that was what he said to his da. 'Why didn't they tell the lad? Why, Da, he was Timmie's marra?'

It was then the howling ceased. Completely. He felt Da straighten his shoulders, and pull away. 'Take care of the lad,' Da told Sid, who had hold of Tony and wouldn't let him go to Timmie. 'The rest of you, get me to the cage. Get Timmie there too. It's time we went home.'

But his da was taken to the infirmary, while Timmie was carried on the stretcher to the colliery cart. The manager stood next to it, his hat removed. Mr Auberon did not join them. Was he even at the pit? If he had come, Jack would have killed him. He had reinstated the cavil too late. Too damn late. Far, far too late. Timmie was wrapped in sacking but Jack removed it and laid his jacket over him, and his father's jacket. The bonny lad deserved better than hessian.

Tony went to tell Evie. He'd lose his money for the time he spent. 'What does that matter?' he said, his throat tight and hurting, loneliness already in him, because his marra was gone and he hadn't finished his soldiers. 'He hasn't finished them,' he kept on saying as he started running.

Jack called after him, 'Try and find Simon first. He should be with her.' But it didn't sound like Jack.

Evie was making pastry for the dessert flans, plum for one, apple for the other. Mrs Moore was resting. The servants were laughing around their table, some playing pontoon, some reading, some sleeping, some sewing. Most had waited up to let in the new year and they were still recovering. The new kitchenmaid, Dottie, was cleaning the fender. She was a worker and it was a welcome relief. She wasn't from Easton but near Gosforn, and her da was a hewer. Dottie said, 'By, you can get a good shine going on this, Evie.'

Lady Veronica had said she would be down for an early tea at three. Evie snatched a look at the clock. Heavens, in ten minutes. The cakes were ready, the end of the table prepared with a table-cloth. True to her word, Lady Veronica had not mentioned their discussion in any way and neither had Evie, but it was evident that after the initial awkwardness there was a more relaxed attitude between the two of them. Not a friendship, of course, but the occasional glance, especially after it was reported that though Emmeline Pankhurst had been imprisoned, Christabel had not returned to Britain to support her.

'Do that later, Dottie. Get yourself off to the servants' hall after you've put the stuff away, her Ladyship will be down any minute.' Evie snatched another look at the servants' hall and there was Roger, his head down over his newspaper. As though he could sense her he raised his head and stared, pure hatred in his face. Well, so be it, she didn't love him either. She would never know what had been said by Lady Veronica, but whatever it was it had been enough.

Evie felt the draught from the kitchen door and looked up. It was Simon. She rushed to check the kettle. 'Come on in, lad, but make it sharp. Lady Veronica will be taking tea here in a moment.' She hurried back to the flan pastry, concentrating on that for it must be cleared away within two minutes. She called, 'Were you born in a barn? Shut the door, then give yourself a quick warm in front of Dottie's gleaming fender. You're just in time with those apples, I was about to come searching for you. That store's worked well this year.'

She heard Simon say, 'Dottie, can you go and fetch Mrs Moore, quickly.' There was something in his voice that she had dreaded. She held the rolling pin absolutely still. If she kept it still nothing would have happened. Absolutely still. Nothing will have happened at all. He was beside her now, reaching forward, trying to take her hands from the rolling pin. He mustn't. Mustn't. She slapped him away. 'No,' she whispered. 'No.' She shouted.

He wasn't listening, but was taking the rolling pin from her because she was hitting at him. Hitting at her wonderful Simon, and his cheeks were wet, his eyes red, his lips trembling, and now Mrs Moore was here, pulling her down on to the stool. And Lady Veronica came then, looking from person to person. Mrs Moore was talking to her. 'No,' Evie said, and stood. 'No,' she repeated, beating Simon away.

It was a bloody circus and she still didn't know who was hurt because no one was speaking and she was reaching for the rolling pin, again and again.

Then there was a voice calling, quite gently, but firmly. 'Evie, I insist you sit down and sit still. Do you hear me? *Sit still.*' It was Lady Veronica. The authority was absolute. She sat still and watched as Lady Veronica took a cup of tea which Mrs Moore must have just made. So the kettle had boiled? Yes, it must have. Lady Veronica would need a plate for her fancies, but nothing worked. Her hands stayed still. She should find a plate.

Lady Veronica was handing Simon a cup of tea. 'You will drink this, Evie. You will drink this.' Simon held the cup to her lips. It was bone china, for upstairs. She couldn't drink from this. She shook her head. Mrs Moore said, 'Drink it now.' She drank. It was sweet. She hated sweet tea.

Lady Veronica said, 'Simon, when you have finished you will share your news with her. I will leave you now. Mrs Moore, I'm sure you can manage with Dottie today because Evie will need to be elsewhere.'

Calmly she awaited the answer. Evie watched them both, and their faces were sad, indescribably sad. Everyone was so sad. Simon said, 'Drink again.'

Mrs Moore said, 'Of course, my Lady.'

'Very well, I will come again in thirty minutes.' She left.

The tea was sweet. She gagged. 'Drink it.' There was firmness in his voice. When the cup was half empty she shook her head, her eyes fixed on his. He nodded and still his lips trembled. 'Da?' she asked.

'He's in the infirmary. Broken leg.'

She sagged with relief. Only a broken leg, that

was all, just a leg and so everything was all right, but it wasn't. She knew that really, because Si was so sad, so terribly sad. She knew it because so was everyone else. Simon held her face, held it and drew close. She said, 'Jack?'

'Jack's fine but Timmie's dead.' He said it quickly as though that would help. His arms were round her now, holding her tightly, stopping her from falling from the stool as though she had no bones in her body and everywhere was so dark, so quiet and dark.

Lady Veronica insisted that her trap should be used. Simon had been given leave to drive her and it was as though she was floating way up above the ground, just floating with bits of black overwhelming her now, then again, then again. Simon sang softly to her but she didn't know what, all she knew was that he was here and she clung to him and would never let him go.

They drew up at the house. He lifted her down and she still wouldn't let him go, but whispered, 'You will never be a pitman, will you? You must always be safe. I can never lose you. I can never lose Jack. How can I bear to lose Timmie?'

He kissed her forehead, her cheeks. 'You never will lose me. We'll never lose one another.' His arms were tight. He said nothing about Timmie.

In the house her mam was mashing tea, Grace was sitting with Millie, who was crying. When was she not? Jack was sitting at the kitchen table painting the remaining lead soldier. He didn't look up, or speak except to say, 'He didn't suffer, Evie. Don't you worry about that, pet. He didn't suffer.'

Evie sat with him at the table. Her mam brought more tea, sweet. Why? It didn't help. She drank it. Her mam said, 'I don't know why you're doing that, Jack lad. Leave it now. Rest.'

Evie knew why. She always knew with Jack. 'They need to be finished because Timmie will need them with him,' she said, and then she went to the front room to her lovely boy. But he was closed in his coffin because he shouldn't be seen, so how could he have felt nothing?

Jack watched Grace rise from his da's chair at eight in the evening. 'I'll leave you now. Millie, can I help you up to bed? Perhaps the family need to be alone?' she said.

Mam was sitting on the sofa with Millie. 'She can stay here, not just now but later, and be family. We'll need the laughter of a bairn.' Her voice was quite steady, her tears were done for now, but then she'd had a lifetime of waiting for this to happen, they all had. Jack had finished the last fusilier. It would be dry by morning. He followed Grace to the front door, opened it, and held it while she passed close to him, and out into the dark and cold. He was calm, he was dead. He seemed strong, but that was expected, and tomorrow he'd be back in the pit, because he was a pitman and they still needed food on the table and savings for the hotel.

He followed her to the gate. She smelt as she always smelt, of lavender. He held the gate as she passed through, and followed her. She had brought her bicycle; would she be safe? The moon was full and lit the track. She mounted and pedalled slowly away. What if she fell? What if she was hit by one of the few automobiles, or a cart galloping, what if . . .

The tears were coming now, and they couldn't be stopped and it didn't matter because the family couldn't hear and she was on her bike and neither could she, but then there was a clatter, and the sound of running, and then she was here with her arms around him. 'Cry all you like, Jack Forbes. Cry for your lovely brother.'

Her arms were strong, and she was stroking his back, his hair, and he sank his head against the top of her head, her glorious hair, and let the tears run and run and his breath come in gulps, and he knew his body shuddered but he couldn't stop, and all the time she stroked his head, his back, his hair. Slowly, slowly he quietened, his breath grew deep, and his tears finally ceased, but still they held one another and it was where he had wanted to be for so long, and where he wanted to stay for ever.

The retirement house door opened and a dog was called in. Jack withdrew, standing straight, looking deep into her eyes. 'Thank you,' he said, 'I'm sorry.'

'Never be sorry,' Grace replied, her voice fierce, her cheeks wet with her own tears. 'Never, bonny lad. I'm here whenever you need me.'

She was so close, so very close. He reached out and took her hand. He kissed the gloved palm. There was so much he wanted to say, but never could. Not to a woman like her.

He dropped her hand. She turned, then swung back and held her hand to his cheek. 'You remember, if you ever need me, I will always be here.'

Grace picked up her bicycle which she'd let crash on to the track and cycled away. If she had stayed she would have said too much and what sort of a fool was she, to love a young lad. How could she have taken advantage of his grief, she was an embarrassment to herself, to women, and it must stop, this minute.

At Easterleigh Hall Lady Veronica had paced in the drive while Raisin and Currant chased one another around the cedar tree, waiting for Auberon. She didn't have to wait long before he trotted up on Prancer, saluting her with his whip, calling, 'I'm late for tea, but not too late I hope?' He eased his boots from the stirrups and dismounted. She walked with him towards the stables, the gravel crunching beneath their feet. She said, 'There's no tea today.'

'What?' He turned, annoyed. 'But I left deliberately. Why not?'

'Evie has had to leave for a few hours, a death in the mine, and so the kitchen is short-staffed.'

They were in the stable yard and Auberon handed Prancer to a groom, but he himself slung the stirrups over the saddle, undid the girth and carried it to the tack room. Veronica followed and watched her brother's thought processes grind painfully slowly round and round. He walked towards the front steps. 'In Auld Maud? But there's only been one death today and that was a Forbes. Yes, a couple of injuries, but only one death which makes it pretty much par for the course.'

She stopped as the dogs ran ahead and up the steps and then hesitated, turning back and running to her. She held Auberon back, wanting to talk to him out here, away from the servants' ears and her stepmama. 'So, tell me again just who was it who died today, Aub?'

He shifted uncomfortably at her side. 'Timmie Forbes.'

'Yes,' she said. 'So work it out.'

She reached down to stroke the dogs. He said, 'You mean . . .'

'Indeed I do. Evie was too scared to admit to being a Forbes as she felt she would lose her job, if she was taken on in the first place, with a name like that, a brother like Jack. You kept that boy in a poor place out of spite, and why? Because you could, Aub, and now he's dead. I should have reminded you. That's my fault. The cavil was reinstated too late.' He was slapping his boots with his whip. She waited. He said, finally, 'What have I done?'

She walked ahead. 'Abused your power, and I have allowed it. We must learn from it and not let this boy's death be wasted.'

Chapter Seventeen

Millie's son was born early, four months after Timmie's death, on 2nd May 1913. She named him Tim and it brought comfort of a kind to the family. Roger stopped Evie a month later as she was walking in the arboretum during her rest period. 'He's mine, you know, that child your family's taken in. I have a right to him, and besides, the minute I crook my little finger she'll be back, so don't get too attached.'

Evie muttered grimly, 'Excellent, nothing would please me more. Then the child will have a father to provide for him.' It was clearly not the answer he expected because he strode off, or did he strut off? She watched him for a moment as he disappeared amongst the chestnuts, but nothing mattered anyway.

The months passed in a dark blur. The kitchen teas had long since ceased and she was glad, because she didn't want to see Mr Auberon, didn't want to bake cakes or fancies for the man who had killed her brother. Simon was in her life, there for her, always, and that began to matter again and they talked of marriage, but not yet, because she couldn't stop work when her family needed the hotel even more now her da's leg was healed, but stiff. He had been back at work within six weeks, but his mobility was restricted and she expected him to have been dismissed, but instead he had been given easier areas and didn't have to squeeze into low-roofed seams. Perhaps Mr Auberon was sorry. He should be.

In January 1914 Grace came for tea with Evie at her mam's house on her Wednesday afternoon off. She and Grace helped with the proggy rug, and as Grace pushed through a slip of red material she smiled at Evie. 'I'm going to the meeting of the suffrage group that has set up in a smaller hall in a poorer district of Gosforn. It's based on the policy of Christabel's sister, Sylvia Pankhurst's socialist East London Federation Suffrage. They're not in tune with the arson and the damage to property, and they want votes for everyone, not just for the financially established few, or those middle-class women who are married. Come with me, it's what you've argued for. It's time, Evie, it's been a year. You must start doing more than existing. I will meet you at the crossroads.'

Evie said, 'That sounds like a speech you've been preparing for a while.' She stroked the rug. 'It's going to be grand, Mam.'

Her mam nodded. 'Don't change the subject, our Evie. Take it up again, you need it and it needs you.'

Evie looked at Millie sitting on the sofa, her feet up on the footstool, with Tim suckling while she ate a cake. 'Would you vote if you had the chance, Millie?'

Millie shoved in the last of the cake and stroked Tim's head, or was she wiping her hands on his hair? You never knew with this young woman. She seemed to be reverting to type, if indeed she'd ever left it. 'What's any of it got to do with me, Evie?'

Evie looked at Grace. She'd felt no emotion for such a long time, but now irritation was niggling. How many felt like Millie when it had everything to do with them, and was she really wiping her hands on her child? Shut up, don't be absurd.

She had to go, had to breathe fresh air, now. She stood and hurried from the room, out of the front door, standing in the crisp cold, staring out at the snow-covered fields. The clouds were a grey-blue, with pink at the edges. They were beautiful but she was unmoved. 'What's the point?' she murmured, her breath visible. There was little wind. The smoke from Grace's houses went straight up and she watched until it dissipated. Had Timmie dissipated? No. He was still here. She felt him all around.

Grace called from the hall and joined her, bringing a shawl which she placed round Evie's shoulders, speaking low and firmly. 'We have work to do. We need to reach people like Millie. If they had a stake in how they are governed it would enthuse them, motivate them, surely. Come with me on Sunday.'

Evie really didn't care, one way or the other, so why not?

*

Grace collected her at the crossroads. Sally, the bay mare, was sweating lightly, and Evie gave her a carrot, courtesy of Mrs Moore. There had been further flurries of snow since Wednesday but today the sky was blue. Evie climbed into the trap and settled down opposite Grace, who clicked Sally on. Neither spoke as they trotted through Easton and out on to the Gosforn road. Evie didn't chat these days. It took too much effort. Grace didn't chat either. Evie looked at her. Grace smiled, but in a weary and sad way. They seemed to have no need for words, and gone was the gulf of older and younger, employer and employee. The bloom that had settled on Grace had gone. The joy inside Evie was gone.

The snow was banked up on either side of the track, but the advantage of having a Brampton looming over them all was that he paid to have his roads kept clear of snow, all the way to the railway station at Gosforn. Grace said, 'The weather will keep the men away from the meeting anyway. They're fair-weather bullies and will be in the pubs keeping warm over a beer.'

They talked about Tim, who was seven months old now, and smiling and laughing. 'Will Millie ever leave?' Evie wondered. 'Or just sit there with her feet up for ever?'

Grace shrugged. 'Tim is good for your mother and father, and Millie is quite helpful, Evie. You must be fair.' She clicked the reins. 'Besides, Jack seems to adore the child.' Evie stared ahead. She thought she heard pain in her friend's voice.

The trap rolled over a lump of snow that had tumbled from the bank. What had happened with Jack, or had anything? Perhaps she had imagined it. She gripped the sides of the trap, all the while picturing herself with Simon and their child. She could almost feel her in her arms, feel the grasp of a hand on her finger. She would be called Susie after Mam. It would cheer up both her parents to have their own grandchild. She might even have a look of Timmie about her. At the thought of her brother she felt the drenching pain, and knew that it would never go, but would eventually become more and more manageable.

'I have to make 1914 a good year. I'm looking for small hotels already. We just need one at the right price; my cooking and household management are now as good as they'll ever be,' she told Grace.

'It's essential to have a dream, Evie.' They were entering the outskirts of Gosforn and some of the pavements had been cleared of snow, some hadn't. Who else had talked to her of dreams? She couldn't remember.

'What's yours, Grace?'

There was silence. 'Dreams are for the young.'

Evie reached across and gripped her friend's hand. 'You're never too old for them. Never.'

They left Sally and the trap at the rear of the meeting hall along with several others, seeing the lights on, hearing the chairwoman talking. Grace grimaced. 'Late again.'

'As always we'll head to the back,' Evie smiled.

Grace laughed. 'We know our place.'

They tapped lightly at the back door, which was locked as it should have been. Betty Clarke, who had often sat with them at the previous meetings, held her finger to her lips and handed them each a copy of the agenda as she let them in. Evie and Grace tiptoed to the back row. Some of the audience turned, and smiled. As they settled themselves Grace nudged Evie and pointed towards the front with her copy of the agenda. There she was, in the front row, but without Lady Margaret. Grace and Evie exchanged a look and Evie's respect for Lady Veronica grew a little more.

February thawed unseasonably early and March came in with a blast of heat, and soon after snowdrops, then crocus and daffodils, bloomed in profusion. Mr Harvey announced in the servants' hall that Lady Veronica would at last be marrying, in the local church. The reception would take place at Easterleigh Hall, if that was convenient to Mrs Moore and Evie.

He waited. Mrs Moore nodded. What else could she do? They could hardly say, 'Well, actually, no. It's too much bloody work.' But in any event it would be a learning process for Evie, who would make sure that she bore the brunt of the workload, though the drink was now a distant memory as Mrs Moore's rheumatics remained at bay.

Later, Lil came into the kitchen bursting with the gossip her position as Lady Veronica's lady's maid made her privy to. For once the kitchen was eager to hear it, because they had thought that Captain Williams would remain posted in India for ever, with Lady Veronica an engaged but unmarried spinster.

'Well, what a barney there was,' Lil said, standing there with her hair as always escaping from her cap. 'There was Lady Brampton with steam coming out of her lugs and Lady Veronica as calm as you like saying that she wouldn't marry the wretched man, even though he had returned unless . . .' Lil paused. 'Yes, that's what she said, wretched man, unless they married here, in the village where Wainey was buried. What do you think of that, eh? Wretched man indeed, I don't know about you all but I think he cuts a fine figure of a bloke.'

Mrs Moore stopped her there, with a wave of her hand. 'You run along now. We've heard enough, it was nerves, that's all. Just nerves.' As Lil flounced off Evie asked Dottie to cast eggshells in the stock while she and Mrs Moore exchanged a look. 'Wretched man, indeed,' Mrs Moore mouthed. 'Poor girl, poor him, what will the future hold?'

The wedding was planned for the merry month of May. 'Well, that's a laugh,' said Annie.

Outside waiters and three extra kitchen staff had been set on for the day, and Mrs Moore had established her overall authority by 7 a.m. on 8th May, the day of the wedding, without ever raising her voice. There was, however, an uneasy sense that the bride would not appear at all. Mr Harvey would allow no chat, and insisted that preparations were approached as though it was to be the wedding of the century.

Household servants had started preparing the marquee and the ballroom several days in advance, the gardeners had readied urns of flowers, colour co-ordinated, pink and white, while the kitchen staff had spent the previous week cooking mountains of food.

It was to be a cold buffet, Lady Veronica had decided, in spite of Lady Brampton's protests, and Evie had written the menus, ten a day until eighty were ready on the evening of 7th May. By this time preparations were complete for an eve-of-wedding feast for the bride and her visiting relations and friends. On the day of the wedding Evie and Dottie rose at four and made tea for the upper servants, and amazingly Mrs Moore entered the kitchen just five minutes after them. Dottie made porridge for the servants, all of whom were up and busy by four thirty.

Before preparing upstairs breakfasts Mrs Moore and Evie rushed to the big cool room and ticked off: salmon à la Genevese, cold asparagus soup, red mullet, brill (with its sauce yet to be made), crimped salmon, ribs of lamb, veal and ham pies, roast saddle of mutton with asparagus (at Lord Brampton's insistence, though they were thankful it was not rabbit pie), stuffed shoulder of lamb, lark pies, fowl au béchamel, tendrons de veau with purée of tomatoes, jellies, all to be placed down the middle of the table. Dishes of small pastries, compotes of fruit, blancmanges, fruit tarts, cheesecakes and small dishes of forced summer fruits were also ready.

By five thirty the servants' breakfast was almost finished, and the servants' hall remained cluttered with the guests' valets, lady's maids and chauffeurs. The kitchen staff thrust spoonfuls of porridge into their mouths while they prepared the upstairs breakfast, cursing the need for so many dishes. The house servants had disappeared as there were rooms to prepare for additional post-wedding overnight guests, as well as the ballroom and marquee seating to be finished.

By eight Evie had chased and caught the lobsters who had escaped from the buckets in the cool room, as usual, loathing their screams as they were plunged into the boiling water. By eight thirty she had finished the sauces, the mayonnaise, the collared eel. The lobster was cut up and would be served in cut-glass bowls. Dottie was at her elbow, learning, always learning, and Evie thanked her lucky stars daily that she had her and not Millie. It made for such a smooth-running kitchen, and they all treasured the change. The imported kitchen staff arrived and were quick and willing, and Mrs Moore instructed them with gusto.

By eleven the food was complete and the house servants had finished, and they all clattered up the back stairs to change into clean aprons, for they had been invited to sit at the back of the church for the ceremony. Lil's voice could be heard rising above the hubbub. 'She looks so lovely, I just hope she doesn't lock her bedroom door and refuse to come out.'

In their room Evie checked Dottie's hair, and Dottie hers. Dottie muttered, 'What if she doesn't come? Oh my heavens. All that food.'

Evie shrugged. 'Can you imagine her parents if she doesn't?'

Dottie laughed. 'I'd rather not.'

Evie straightened her apron. Poor Lady Veronica, how lonely she must feel.

The carts were waiting in the stable yard to take the staff to the church, a church which some of them attended on a Sunday. Others went to chapel, or not at all, which was permissible due to the Bramptons unconcern about spiritual matters.

Edward was officiating at the wedding and the service had already begun by the time they all slipped in at the back, Mr Harvey leading. The church was decorated with greenery and pink and white forced roses to replicate the house decorations, and there, in a delicate long white gown, was Lady Veronica. Evie breathed a sigh of relief. She turned, trying to find Simon who had been down here already with Bernie and Thomas, putting the final touches to the flowers. He was on the right side of the church, and as always seemed to sense when she was seeking him. He smiled, mouthed, 'We'll likely be next, Evie, pet.'

She nodded and smiled too. Yes, soon, for a small guest house near Fordington was to be sold in December of 1914. They'd heard only last week. Da had registered their interest immediately, taking an afternoon to drive the cart to Fordington, but she had yet to tell Mrs Moore. She glanced at her as she sang at her side, knowing that the sea air would invigorate her, and that she'd probably want to help a little in the kitchens. Evie's heart was full as the hymn soared, overwhelming the organ which was played by Grace. Poor Grace, she wanted to ask Jack if anything had happened between them, but from his demeanour she knew she must not.

Her thoughts turned to Simon. Lady Veronica had asked him to entertain her guests and sing with the professional band that had come from Newcastle and were setting up in the ballroom. Apart from Lady Veronica paying him five guineas, the experience would help him when he sought work. Why, perhaps he'd set up his own band with Bernie and Thomas, and of course he was right to want to keep the guineas for himself. It had just been a surprise, that was all.

Lady Veronica was saying, 'I do.' Mrs Moore looked at her and sighed. 'All that food, I couldn't have borne it to go to waste.'

Mr Harvey was waving them out of the church. Evie bit her lip to prevent the laughter spilling out.

Once James and Archie had led the team of waiters to the marquee, Evie and Mrs Moore fanned themselves in front of the ranges. It was done. Evie brewed tea, relishing the silence because everyone was up in the stable yard, or by the yew walk watching the excitement, and soon they'd be dancing to Simon and the band, hidden from the family.

'Was Simon nervous?' Mrs Moore asked, dunking a ginger biscuit, her glasses perched on her head.

'A little, but looking forward to it. He has such confidence in himself.' Evie leaned over and helped herself to a biscuit, dunking too, and sucking the tea from it before thrusting it into her mouth.

'Lady Veronica will remain here definitely, Lil told us,' Mrs Moore said, easing her back as she sat on the stool.

'I suppose it's a good idea. He's posted down in Folkestone, isn't he, so at least she'll feel comfortable here. I thought she might go with him, but . . .'

Mrs Moore nodded. 'Exactly. But. I don't know, I really don't. It does make you wonder if they'll ever live here together, but then this class is different to us.'

Was this the time to tell her about Fordington? Probably not. What if someone else bought the guest house? Evie reached for another biscuit. 'With this Home Rule thing in Ireland he could be sent over there, I suppose. Or even the Continent. Germany wants colonies, Jack said, and might try and take ours. Why don't they go and find their own, or perhaps we could share. Or perhaps we shouldn't have colonies?'

Mrs Moore slapped her gently. 'For goodness sake, lass, stop worrying about the world, will you? If it isn't votes for the masses, it's world peace. We're cooks in a kitchen, one of whom will have a hotel and a husband as soon as she can manage it, if I'm any judge of what's what.' She held her cup with both hands, unable to bend her swollen fingers.

'What do we call our blushing bride?' Evie asked.

'She wishes to be known as Lady Veronica, as always, and he will be Captain Williams, and I'll tell you what, pet, it will be a blessed relief to see less of Lord and Lady Brampton, who prefer London and Leeds anyway.' Mrs Moore eased herself from the stool and placed her cup on the table. 'You go and listen to your young man while I go and rest like the virtuous soul I am.'

Evie laughed, helping her to the door and watching her limp along the passageway. 'I'll make tea in a couple of hours.'

'Yes, and then later we'll enjoy the champagne with a little bit of lobster, there should be plenty left. Enjoy yourself.' Mr Harvey had said that there would champagne for supper, by order of Lady Veronica.

'I will.' Evie ran up the stairs towards the yard. The weather was still set fair, with a blue sky and sunshine. In the stable yard the servants would be speaking in whispers and watching the proceedings, and some would have gone to the yew hedge where they could peer through in places. She stopped on the top step to listen to Simon, whose voice soared true and beautiful, enhanced by the backing of the professional band.

As she moved into the yard she heard a sound behind her, and turned, but too late. She felt hands on her arms, grabbing her from behind, pulling at her, dragging her backwards down the steps. She lost balance, almost crashed to the ground, but was hauled upright and dragged to the back door.

'What?' she gasped. 'What?' The grip was so tight that fingernails cut into her arms. Suddenly those hands swung her round. A man loomed over her. The smell of drink made her gag. It was Roger, of course, who thrust her away, but did not let go. 'So, you bitch, my son won't want me? We'll see about that, and you? You'll have me, whether you want me or not. A Forbes, eh? It *was* you who spread the word about the houses.' He backed her to the wall, rammed his arm across her throat. She could hardly breathe. His hand gripped her chin, his mouth closed on hers.

She pushed at him, hit out, but he was feeling her breasts, panting in her face. She could still hear

Simon's voice soaring over everything and she should call out, but how could she with this bastard's mouth over hers? Then his hand was moving down, lifting her skirt. He had rammed his knee between her legs and she still couldn't breathe. And still Simon's song soared, still Roger's mouth was on hers and she was tight against the wall and couldn't lever back to punch, or kick because his knee was pushing her legs apart and her skirt was to her waist.

She used her head then, as Jack had always said to do. She butted him, hard across the nose. Blood spurted. His arm on her throat sagged. She pushed, he stepped back, his balance gone. There was a roaring anger now as she pummelled his chest, kicking, scratching, stamping, and finally driving her fist into his solar plexus. He fell on the stairs, his arms up. She followed up, hitting, kicking, and the anger drove her on because Timmie had died, louts had thrown tomatoes and bricks and there had to be an end to it all. She kicked again as he lay at her feet, huddled, his arms protecting his head.

At last she was done, the breath heaving in her chest, her hair loose, her cap God knew where. She stood over him, shaking now. She hissed, 'When will you learn? Never touch me again. Never come near me or my family and leave your son alone. Now get out of here.'

She put her hands on her hips so that he wouldn't see them shaking. It wasn't fear, she didn't know what it was, didn't care. She waited while he scrambled to his feet, a scratch down the side of his face, his clothes smeared with grime. He didn't look at her as he lurched up the steps and stumbled across the yard towards the garage. The chauffeur would be with the servants, but in Len's sleeping quarters he'd find a brush and sort himself out. She watched him all the way and only when he had entered did she turn and hurry up the back stairs, the shaking now taking over her whole body, the pain in her back and hips from jolting down the stairs catching with each step.

In her bedroom she stripped off her uniform, poured water from the jug into the bowl and washed, dressed in her second uniform, fumbling as she tied her apron, then repaired her hair, her arms aching as she lifted them above her head.

She started towards the door, and then her legs failed. She staggered, made herself hold firm, and managed to reach her bed. A wave of sickness caught her, the shaking grew worse. She sank her head into her hands, heaving. But no. She thrust her hands into her lap, fisting them. They hurt. She smiled. Jack would be proud.

She sat straight and waited for the shaking to stop, because it would. She remembered Jack saying that he shook after a fight. Tears threatened and she tightened her fists. She wouldn't cry. Not over Roger. She sat like that until the shaking had quite stopped. It could come again, but not as badly. She heard the clock chime, and stood. She felt a deep satisfaction. No one, ever again, would touch her when she did not want to be touched. No one.

She eased her way down the stairs and up the steps into the yard, refusing to allow herself to look around in fear. She strode into the stable yard, where the servants were not just listening, but dancing. It was then she realised that Simon was still singing. She moved to stand next to Dottie. 'Shall we dance?' she suggested. Dottie curtsied. 'Do let's, your highness.'

They whirled to a waltz and she ignored her aching limbs, and she ignored Roger as he entered the stable yard. He had a scratch down his cheek and was pale, and he rubbed his abdomen. She was glad, but knew that it would never be over until one of them left.

A dance floor had been set up on the terrace to extend the ballroom, and the bride and groom were dancing. He looking ecstatic, Lady Veronica as calm and collected as always. What must it be like to marry without love? She hummed along to the music, so glad that she was Evie Forbes.

In June when they were sea-coaling at Fordington one Sunday afternoon Jack took Evie to one side, staring at the oily sea as the sun baked down and the breeze was gentle. 'I've asked Millie to marry me, bonny lass.'

She dropped her shovel. 'You've what? Why? I

thought . . . Well, never mind what I thought.' Because what had she thought? She wasn't sure. 'Why, Jack?'

He was still looking at the sea. His face had been drawn ever since Timmie died, and the light and energy that had always bounced from him was absent. He said nothing, just rammed his hands into his pockets and shrugged. She swung him round to face her, but he pulled away and continued watching the sea. She stood in front of him. 'But you don't love her?'

He squatted and threw bits of coal into the sea. 'I love the bairn, he's a little belter and he needs a father. I can't have him growing up a bastard, and I like Millie. It's good enough, Evie. We can't all be like you and Simon.'

The air of sadness which cloaked her brother was almost tangible. 'Is it really enough for a lifetime, Jack?'

'At least I have a life. Just listen, Evie. We can't change what happened to Timmie, but the bairn didn't ask to be born. I can't do anything about Timmie but I can do something about the bairn.' He rose and she hugged him. 'Jack, please think about this. You have a right to be happy.'

He eased her from him and walked away. She watched, and wanted to run after him, but instead she picked up the shovel again and saw that Simon was near. Of course, when wasn't he? He came to her, putting his arm around her shoulders. 'Millie's just let it out. If it's what he wants, let it go, Evie.'

'I don't understand him. He doesn't love her.'

'It's his decision, and he loves the boy, that's all that can be said.' They heard her da calling, 'We've coal to collect, or are you on strike?'

Simon waved. 'On our way, boss.' They started up the beach.

Da called again, 'Come on you two, there's work to do and have you heard about Jack joining the Territorials, Simon? He's just told me he took up the whelp on his offer. Davies says that Lord Brampton has decided that it would be a good thing to encourage the men to join, God knows why. He's offered them a shilling a day on top of their wages. Sounds like an excuse for a holiday to me, and why not?' Her da was standing up on the cart, looking from them to Jack, who was now working with Martin further along the beach.

'What?' Evie exclaimed. 'The Territorials? Is he mad?' They approached the cart and Da threw them a sack, his voice harsh as he said, 'You can't blame the lads for getting out of the pits for a while.' Simon asked her to hold the sack, saying, 'Let me shovel in this lot.'

Evie shook her head. 'What's Jack thinking of?'

Simon grinned. 'I said, hold the sack.' He waited until she did so, then told her, 'The whelp asked the gardeners to join after the wedding. Everyone who does is getting one Saturday off a month with pay plus the bob a day while they train, and a paid week under canvas.' He was shovelling the heap of coal into the sack and the sun glinted on the sea behind them. 'He said it would be good for him to get to know us better. I don't want to know *him* any better, so turned him down.'

She tested the weight of the sack. 'I wouldn't have thought Jack wanted to know him better, either. It doesn't make sense.'

Jack was approaching with an empty sack, which he gave to her. 'Let me help, Evie.' He took the full load and swung it up on to his back, calling as he returned to the cart, 'Accidents happen, Evie, they can happen anywhere, especially in the Territorials.'

Evie let the sack fall and whispered, 'Jack, don't be foolish.' She made to follow him, but Simon raised his eyebrows. 'He's not a fool, he won't do anything silly. Don't worry, just hold the sack.' She did so, and the breeze was stronger now.

On Saturday 6th June 1914 there was another wedding to cater for. Again it was at the village church, and again there was a grave to consider. Timmie's, though, lay far from Miss Wainton's. Again Edward officiated. Mam held Tim, who shrieked and giggled all the way through the service, and when the couple left the church there was a Territorial guard of honour led by Martin, who took over the sergeant's position while Jack was otherwise engaged. Her da shook his head. 'Boys and their playtime. I reckon they just like a uniform, daft beggars.'

The wedding breakfast was held in the village hall and had been cooked by Evie and her mother, with Millie's help. Millie seemed happy, Jack held Tim and put his arm around his wife. They kissed as they cut the cake. Grace and Evie clapped, but there was a deadness in Grace. Evie said, 'There's someone for you, somewhere.'

'I know there is, I've met him.' Grace's voice was flat as Jack took Millie in his arms, swirling away to the strains of 'If you were the only girl in the world' sung by Simon, with Bernie and Thomas accompanying him. Lady Veronica had given them leave. She had returned from her honeymoon two days before, and Captain Williams had returned to his posting in Folkestone immediately, Lil informed them.

As Jack danced, he saw Evie and nodded, his colour high. He'd been drinking, she could see that, but why not, at his own wedding? He saw Grace, who was talking to their mam, and there was everything in his face. Then he whirled past Evie with Millie. His smile was tired as his bride talked and laughed.

The friends and family danced and sang until midnight, and then she and Simon walked back to Easterleigh Hall. His arm was tight around her, and he pulled her to him, kissed her and against her mouth he said, 'Can we please get married the moment we have the hotel? It could be a Christmas wedding.' He laughed as she clasped him tightly.

'Most certainly, bonny lad.' Her mouth was as eager as his, but then they walked on and he said, 'I've been thinking, you know, I'd like to join the Territorials after all. I felt out of it today, wishing I could have been one of the guard of honour. Besides, it sounds good fun and someone has to keep an eye on Jack. Just think, Evie, we'll get paid for playing silly buggers in a field somewhere every Saturday.'

The night was warm, the moon so bright she thought she could have read by it. Sheep baaed as they passed, and an owl flew across their path. She could see the Stunted Tree in the distance. 'Why not? You'll be one of the gang again, and not have to fight your way in this time, you'll just have to play about with guns. What could be more fun? You daft beggars, you.'

Just three weeks later, on June 28 Evie read in the newspaper that the heir to the Austro-Hungarian Empire had been assassinated by a Serb-sponsored terrorist and that Emmeline Pankhurst was still in prison. That same week Lady Margaret arrived, having been released from prison by virtue of the Cat and Mouse Act. She needed feeding up and then they would arrest her again, and she would go on hunger strike again and so it would go on. Evie and Mrs Moore shook their heads at one another when they heard. Mrs Moore said, 'I thought Lady Esther had taken the place of Lady Margaret as a friend?'

Evie told Dottie to have a rest in the servants' hall

while the ladies were down for tea, then continued setting out the cakes. 'I suppose old friends can surmount a division of ideals.'

'That sounds too complicated for me,' Mrs Moore sniffed, tucking the *Sketch* under her arm and taking a cup of tea to her room.

Lady Margaret and Lady Veronica arrived within five minutes and sat in the kitchen sipping tea, though Evie thought they'd have been much better advised to take advantage of the sunshine. Lady Margaret looked almost translucent, but still much like a horse.

'There, you see, you two,' Lady Margaret said, including Evie. 'We're suffering for you, we'll get you the vote and what do you do, eat cakes while we starve?'

It was the fear of further imprisonment talking, no doubt, but Evie still wanted to remove the cakes. Lady Veronica winked and Evie stifled a smile.

Lady Veronica said, passing one of the wicked cakes, 'Dearest Margaret, do treat yourself, and why not let someone else create mayhem while you just stand on the sidelines for a while? People could so easily be hurt or killed. There are other ways, and we should be insisting on votes for all classes, not just the higher echelons. But this is old ground, and none of us will change our minds.'

Lady Margaret pushed away the plate. 'Your branch is just so smug. You just don't understand. If you thought about it you'd know that if we get the vote for us it will be a foot in the door, and people like Evie will be given it in due course when we have made sure they know how to handle the power.'

Lady Veronica was rising now, her napkin crumpled at the side of her plate. 'Thank you so much for tea, Evie, but it's time we left you to your work.'

She put a hand under Lady Margaret's elbow and helped her to rise. Lady Margaret shook her head. 'I'm not going until I hear what Evie has to say.'

A lot, thought Evie, but merely replied, 'People like me would prefer to have it now, if you don't mind, Your Ladyship, along with the rest of you. We do have minds and we do feel we should take a hand in the governance of the country just as much as you.'

Lady Margaret flushed. 'Well, you would say that, how could you do otherwise? You wouldn't want to jeopardise your position here, would you, by disagreeing with Lady Veronica? I gather your employers have no love for the Forbes, so you must feel rather insecure.' Her face was thin and sallow, despite the flush that was rising up her neck. Her hands were trembling. There were deep rings around her eyes, which were full of fear. She was hitting out like a small child.

Evie said gently, 'You're not well. Best go and lie down.'

Lady Veronica led her friend from the kitchen, calling back, 'Thank you, Evie, for the tea, of course.'

*

That evening, after dinner was cleared, a dinner which had included calf's-foot broth and stewed rabbit in milk, and the kitchen was on the way to being spotless under Dottie, Sarah and Annie's strong hands, Evie slipped out for some air, as usual. She and Simon strolled along the paths, breathing in the roses which were planted to the right of the walled garden specifically for picking. He snipped off one and trimmed off its thorns. They didn't need to speak any more, just *be*. He held her hand lightly while they discussed how many hotel rooms they could manage, and which would bring in sufficient income to keep them all. Simon wanted them to be able to hold wedding receptions, and she thought that if they had the correct costings it would be an excellent idea. 'But we'd need gardens for the guests to stroll in,' she said. He laughed. 'I rather thought you'd say that.'

Darkness had not fallen yet, and as they wandered towards the east wing she thought she saw someone moving about near the rear stables that housed the carriage horses and the hunters, including Prancer. No, not near, behind. Simon had seen something too, and they started forward, then stopped. 'It'll be Norman checking Prancer, he took a bit of a tumble on the cobbles,' Simon said, pulling her to him and kissing her. 'I need to go in soon,' he murmured. 'The old man's on the warpath because his under-gardeners have all been out after hours. He thinks the summer sun's gone to our heads.'

She reached up and drew his head down, and kissed him long and hard, releasing him only when she felt him begin to laugh. 'I'm so in love with you and so excited. We're on our way, Evie. We're really on our way.'

The horses seemed to be joining in, neighing and stamping over in the rear stables. Evie grinned, and pointed. 'You see, they agree.'

Simon moved forward. 'What's that?' He pointed and at first she could see nothing, but then she saw smoke, or was it? Though it was still vaguely light, it was difficult to make it out. They moved closer, and could smell it now, and there it was, seeping out of the hayloft above the stables. 'Dear God,' Simon gasped.

'Not the horses,' she whispered. They were running and now the smoke was billowing, and they heard the neighing, and thuds as the horses kicked out in the stalls. 'Come on.' Simon grabbed her and together they ran along the path, the roses snagging her skirt. She tore free. 'You go on, you're faster,' she shouted.

He reached the stable yard ahead of her, heading for the double doors. She saw him pull, then curse. 'They've been padlocked.'

Smoke was coming out under the huge doors, neighs had turned to high-pitched shrieks.

Evie rushed for the alarm bell, clanging it, shouting, 'Fire, fire!' Simon hunted for a steel bar, a brick, anything, and found a shovel leaning up against the wall. He bashed again and again at the padlock. The banging and the bell were causing even more panic. The thuds of hooves and the cries of the horses could be heard above everything, and now there was the crackle of fire. 'God, Evie, it won't break, the bloody thing won't break.' Evie rang the bell harder and harder, almost screaming, 'Fire!'

Stable lads were coming now, with Norman in the lead, and at last the padlock burst. Evie and Simon rushed in with the lads but the air gave the fire fresh impetus, and the straw flashed into flames. They were thrown back but were unhurt. All around was the crackle of burning hay and straw and the high pitched whinnying of the horses. They were joined by Archie and James under the command of Mr Harvey, but he was elbowed aside by Norman, who issued orders. They all began to open the stalls, leading the horses out, the hunters rearing and bucking through the smoke and flames.

Under-gardeners arrived too and the head gardener, Stan, ordered them back out to pump water from the pond. Evie returned, heading for a back stall, grabbing the halter of a bucking mare, feeling no fear as she led her out, seeing Simon doing the same, avoiding the flames, coughing in the smoke, ducking as burning straw floated down from the loft.

Roger rushed in and tore the reins of a hunter

from a stable lad. 'You go back for another.' He led it out into the open, leaning back against the huge shoulder, slowing the horse to a walk. Evie was just behind him and took the mare to the side, stroking her, whispering, 'It's fine, girl. It's fine.' The mare was skittering, snorting, and then she reared. Evie kept hold of the rope, searching for Simon. Was he safe?

There he was, with Prancer, handing him to a stable lad who instantly calmed the beast. Another lad took Evie's mare. The under-gardeners were bringing up the pumps and spraying the building with hoses. Steam rose. She saw Mr Auberon and Lady Veronica, she with a shawl around her, he in his shirt and trousers. He shouted, 'Not you, Ver. Stay out.' Evie watched as he ran into the stable and there was a crash of falling timber. 'Aub,' Lady Veronica screamed.

A stable lad was leading out a hunter which reared in panic, his blanket singed. Evie held Simon back as flames burst through the hayloft windows, and then the final horse bucked and reared out of the stables, led by Mr Auberon. It was Big Boy, who had a stitched thigh from a hunting accident two weeks before. Mr Auberon was smoke-covered, his shirt black with soot. He passed close by. Evie said quietly, 'You could be taken for a pitman '

He looked at her. 'That'd make me proud, Evie Forbes.'

There was a burn on his arm which was blistering.

'You'd best get that tended,' she murmured. He replied, 'It's little enough after Timmie.'

'Yes,' she said. 'But it's something.' There was no anger in her any more. There had not been since she had fought against Roger. In many ways Mr Auberon was a good man, but he'd made mistakes, though who hadn't?

Lady Veronica rushed up and dragged him away, while a stable lad took Big Boy. Evie remembered that other night in the front stables, what seemed like years ago. Who knew how anyone would react when beaten by their own father? For the first time for a long while she felt a renewal of sympathy for him.

Out in the yard Roger was telling of his exploits but Simon said, 'Howay, you daft beggar, you took the horse from a lad and sent him back into the inferno.' That was all; it was enough.

Over there, in the background, was Lady Margaret. Lady Veronica was dragging Mr Auberon past her. Something was said and by morning Lady Margaret had gone. The stables were a soaked and smoking wreck. Everyone was told it was a freak accident, perhaps a lightning strike, perhaps a hoof against stone causing a spark.

Lady Margaret never came into the conversation and she mustn't, because otherwise she might one day shout out Lady Veronica's involvement in the suffrage movement. Everyone knew, however, that it was the policy of the Pankhursts to carry out arson attacks on private property. Did the stupid girl always do everything she was told, Evie wondered.

Within the week the rebuilding of the stables had begun, and Captain Williams had returned to check that Lady Veronica was safe and sound.

Chapter Eighteen

On Sunday 1st August 1914, the start of the bank holiday, Jack and Martin had crawled up the eastern slope of the Stunted Tree, their red armbands appearing more like brown after they had scuffled along the ground. They rested in the lee of a scattering of gorse bushes which grew two-thirds of the way up. Jack had insisted his team traverse the ground full-length and on their elbows until they reached the highest of the bushes. 'Take a breather now, lads,' he whispered. They rested easy in the narrow strip of shade which gave some relief from the baking summer sun, relishing the sips they took from their canteens. Jack wiped his mouth and grinned across at Martin. 'Beats sweating at the coalface, eh lad?'

'Aye, let's just sweat on a hillside instead, up to our arms in sheep shit.' There was low laughter. Jack joined in. Over on the left was Lieutenant Brampton, whose platoon had been designated the red team and who was easing out around the gorse. If he wasn't careful Lieutenant Swansdale's green platoon defending the crest would let go a load of blanks and they'd have lost the exercise and the free beer, the daft bugger. Jack checked his rifle. He liked the stock of this one, it fitted his shoulder just fine. He turned and held it to his shoulder, getting Brampton in his sight. Bang. He could almost hear the non-existent shot rifling out of the barrel and into that self-satisfied skull. Now, that would be an August Bank Holiday to remember. 'Steady, lad,' Martin murmured.

Jack shook his head, lying back, staring up at the sky through half-closed eyes. 'When I get him no one will know, don't you worry.'

Colin, the lance corporal, crawled up and rolled on to his back next to him. 'Sarge, I've just crawled through a load of sheep shit, I need a smoke and a pee, and I'm wet through with sweat. I might as well have stayed in the damned pit.'

Jack held up his hand. 'You'll be back down there if I hear you above a whisper again, Col, and before you ask, no, you can't stand to do a pee, and no you can't have a Woodbine. Swansdale'll have scouts out, or lookouts at least. You send up just a flicker of smoke and I'll have you.'

Simon was up with them now, bringing the periscope that Jack had devised the night they arrived on exercise. He'd just known the gorse would be good cover from which to observe.

Brampton was crawling over, his face burned from the sun, but not as badly as the pitmen. They weren't used to it.

Jack eased up just a fraction, his uniform coarse

round his neck, reaching for the periscope, raising it. He could hear Brampton panting as he nestled in next to him. 'Any movement, Sergeant?'

Jack slid the periscope over. 'Check for yourself,' he paused. 'Sir.'

'Good idea of yours, Sergeant,' Brampton whispered, raising the periscope.

'Aye, my brother Timmie, you know, the one who was killed in your pit, made one of these when planning a battle with his lead soldiers.'

Lieutenant Brampton lowered the periscope and the colour rose up his neck. There was an uneasy silence. Simon raised his eyebrows at Jack. Colin studied an ant climbing a blade of grass, Bernie whistled silently. Martin was signalling to those who had just reached them to stay down, stay quiet.

Brampton whispered, 'I caught the glint of binoculars. They're on the alert. Not long now. Get the men ready please, Sergeant. I'm so sorry about Timmie. It was totally my fault.' He was checking his hunter watch. The diversionary attack by a third of their platoon led by Corporal James Smith, the footman, would take place at two thirteen. It was Brampton's idea to make it an odd time. It was Jack's to create a diversion.

Brampton crawled back to his group. Martin gripped Jack's shoulder. 'Might be time to give him a break, man. I'm sorry to say you make a good team and he's made you up to Sergeant, he's given your da a good kist. He's just apologised.'

'He killed Timmie.'

'But not deliberately. He's a lad, like us.'

'Bugger off, Mart.' Jack felt as cold as he had done since Timmie's death and it was time something warmed him. He knew the only thing that could do that now was to see the whelp six foot under. 'Keep your head down, Corporal,' he grinned. He knew it didn't meet his eyes. He glanced across at Brampton, who was snatching a look at his watch. They were all waiting, but there were worse places to do that. He turned on to his back again. On Friday his father had handed him *The Times* which was going on about how many treaties Germany had broken, how it had been pushing its military ambitions and how, if the government didn't help France and Belgium, Britain would be guilty of the grossest treachery.

He shielded his eyes from the worst of the glare and tried to make shapes out of the white clouds that ambled across the sky. But if there was to be fighting surely it would be in Ireland, where private Catholic and Protestant armies were already creating havoc? Would he go to war? He wouldn't need to, they had armies for that. But by, it would give him a chance with Brampton and then he could clear his head and be back for Christmas, with everything sorted. Maybe he'd settle better with Millie, even get Tom into her hotel. The lass had waited and worked for so long and she was ready, really ready, and the solicitor had said they'd have first refusal on the guest house.

Martin punched his shoulder. 'Can you hear them?'

Jack turned to his front, raised himself into a crawl. A third of the platoon under Ben's boy, Steve, were letting rip with their blanks on the other side of the hill and he could almost see them charging as the shots rang out. Brampton was crouched as though he was on the starting line of a race, counting off the seconds with his hand. He and Jack had decided on thirty seconds for the lookouts on this side to be drawn across in support.

'Remember, silence on the approach, silence until they see us. Pass it on,' Jack hissed. He saw the men nod as they each received the reminder. Behind Brampton they were receiving the same order and he saw Roger nodding, his face a picture of misery, and now Jack's grin did reach his eyes. On the exercise and drill Saturdays the valet was seconded as batman to Brampton and had to train too. It delighted the whole platoon. He barely knew his left foot from his right, and 'About turns' were a bloody disaster.

Jack kept his eyes on Brampton and at the signal he surged forward, forcing his way through the gorse via the badger run he'd spied earlier, which made the going easier. He had ordered the men to find similar spots and do likewise and soon they were doubled up and powering up the hill, their rifles held across their chests. He could hear heavy breathing behind him. Martin was at his shoulder as he always was. To Jack's left Brampton was keeping pace, and so were the men except for Roger, but no one considered him a man, so that didn't count. He'd be rambling, staying out of danger, Jack knew he would.

So far, they had not been spotted. There was just the distant sound of orders shouted and blanks fired towards Steve's group to the east. It could work, it could bloody work. The blood was pumping, his weight was forward, they were cresting the hill and there was hand-to-hand fighting on the other side and a small group huddled together to the left with blue armbands, the designated injured. The referees stood in a small group to the rear of these, one of whom was Captain Williams of the North Tyne Fusiliers, back from his foray to Folkestone. The water butt, the holy grail, was in the centre with a guard of eight, who were oblivious to the red team's approach.

On the far side Swansdale turned, saw them, and rallied half his platoon before charging towards them. Jack flanked to the right, Brampton to the left as they had planned. Swansdale had to divide his charge but didn't beef up the holy grail guard. 'Cut 'em off, cut 'em off,' Swansdale and his sergeant were yelling.

Brampton screamed, 'Corporal, take the left flank, I'll take the right. We've got your flanks, Jack.'

Jack snatched a look at Martin. 'No stopping, come on Si, come on the rest of you.' He hadn't altered pace and now Brampton's men charged into the melee, clashing with both flanks of the green team, who stalled momentarily, only to rally. Jack tore ahead, closing in on the water butt, hearing his men behind him. By, it was like chasing down the parson all over again. There were just the two guards now, bringing down their rifles, aiming. Jack swerved, Simon tight behind him, Colin too. Bang. The referees called. 'No. 14 down.' It was Martin. Damn it, but Colin knew to take over, knew to run at a swerve.

'On your left, Forbes. On your left.' It was Brampton shouting a warning. Jack saw the raised rifle butt and swung his arm, deflecting the blow, then making contact with the man's jaw; he sagged and dropped. The water butt wasn't far now, but Swansdale's men had broken through and were roaring towards Jack's platoon. He shouted, 'Si, take two men and secure the butt. The rest, with me. Colin too.' He swung into the attack, charging the green team, clashing rifles, face to screaming face with Colin beside him, kicking out, head-butting. Brampton joined them, forcing back the opposition, creating a straight run through for Simon. Jack saw him reach the butt with James and Andy. The referees' whistles blew but Swansdale's team didn't stop, fury etched on every face, and so no one stopped.

Beside Jack, Brampton's pistol was discarded in favour of a rifle that he snatched from one of the green platoon and with it he was fielding them back, just as Jack and the others were doing. The whistles blew again and this time Brampton seemed to come to himself and stopped, shouting, 'Enough, men. Enough. We've won.'

Swansdale's sergeant had other ideas and crashed his rifle butt into Brampton's face. Brampton sagged against Jack, blood spurting from his nose and mouth. Jack heard the whistles blowing frantically. Beside him Colin said, 'Well, I'm not having that, man.' He raised his rifle stock but Jack blocked him, and blocked the sergeant's rifle which was crashing down towards Brampton for a second time. 'Leave it to me,' he yelled, dropping his rifle as Brampton sank to the ground, and jabbed at the sergeant's ribs again and again, before taking his feet out from under him with a sideways kick. 'That'll teach you, you daft bugger.'

The fighting ceased, and soon all the men were bending over, resting their hands on their knees, panting. After he had regained his breath Jack looked around and signalled Roger over to Brampton. Around him the red team were jubilant, slapping one another's backs while Swansdale's men, from Hawton Pit, sulked, gathering in groups. The referees stood together making notes on a clipboard. The sun was still hot, the breeze gentle.

Roger was still on the periphery, examining his nails. Brampton was still on the ground, spitting out blood. He rolled over on to his side now and tried to scramble to his feet. He needed help. Jack turned away and it was Colin and Simon who hauled him up. Jack's uniform was splattered with Brampton's blood, and why the hell hadn't he let the sergeant's rifle fall on the little shit just once more?

The referees were gesturing to them all to start back to camp. Martin pretended to limp back to Jack as they headed down the hill, digging in their heels to stop their momentum. 'Just call me Lazarus,' he said. Jack laughed. 'Aye, I will, lad. So, what's it like coming back from the dead?'

'Not bad at all, especially when we've bully beef for tea. Can they come up with anything else, d'you reckon? Maybe some of your Evie's chicken pie?' Martin slung his arm round Jack's shoulder, nodding towards Brampton who was walking back with Captain Williams. 'Not you, was it, who mashed his face?' His voice was low and serious.

Colin broke away from his group and eased up beside Jack. 'By, that was some lesson you taught the sarge. Teach him not to mess with one of us, even if it is the bastard.'

Jack said, 'But he's our bastard.' He was astonished at himself.

'Well, I reckon you're right there. He's not all bad, is he, not like his bloody da.' Colin slid on down the hill, racing with the other boys and men. Jack and Martin looked at one another, checked with Simon who was cutting across towards them. They all nodded and joined the race back to camp, which was set up half a mile from the Stunted Tree. Even that turned into a competition between the red and green teams, and Jack held his men back and let the greens win. But the greens still sulked, because it was a win that had been handed to them. When they went back to the pit after the bank holiday they'd have to face their marras, and failure was never a good move.

Jack heard Brampton saying to Swansdale as they shook hands in front of the mess tent, 'Not a good day for you, Thomas.' His speech was clumsy but whose wouldn't be, talking through lips as swollen as his.

'Nor for you, Aub. I saw what happened and I'll deal with Sergeant Harris,' Swansdale was ripping off his green armband which he handed to Brampton, who did the same. Blood was still running from the cut on Brampton's cheek, and from his nose which was surely broken. 'No, it was the heat of battle, let it go, Tom. For God's sake, who knows better than I that mistakes are made.'

Captain Williams was over to the right of the tent. A messenger had come beating up on a grey, and handed the referees a note. Jack saw their faces, saw the note drop to the ground. Williams picked it up again and hurried to the Territorial officers in front of the tent, his face grim. Martin nudged Jack. 'What's amiss, man? Let's get the beer down us unless they take it back because they haven't paid the bill. I've a throat like the bottom of the canary's cage.'

Jack looked once more towards the officers, and then joined his platoon at their mess. They'd been promised beer, and they got it in tin mugs. It tasted wonderful. They stripped off their jackets and in shirtsleeves they lolled on the ground. Jack loved August, the fields of corn, the smell of heat-soaked grass, the long evenings, the longer shadows. It was the final fling of summer.

They lit up Woodbines, and some had pipes. All the men, red and green, were here now, swapping bands and stories now that tempers had cooled. Winners and losers were friends again. 'Amazing what a beer can do,' Jack murmured to Martin.

'Aye, that it is. Maybe it's what that lot need?' Martin nodded towards the officers who were listening to Captain Williams.

'It's not a welcome speech from the set of their faces,' Martin said, picking some grass and throwing it up in the air to see the strength of the wind, which was a waste of time because you could feel it well enough, Jack thought.

He said nothing, but he thought of the news of the past week and for a moment he wondered. But no. But what if . . . But how? On a day like this? And would it be Ireland or Europe? It would be neither.

Simon said, as he stuffed tobacco into the pipe he had taken to smoking, 'They'll have made a mess-up somewhere. Probably because the whistles blew and we kept on doing what we were doing. Bet he's calling us a rabble. That's it. We're a rabble, you lot.'

They were laughing now, and Martin checked his watch. 'I could kill for some food but it's only three.

Never thought I'd be longing for that damned bully-beef muck.'

Jack was still watching Captain Williams. The officers, some of whom had acted as referees, saluted, stepped back and walked behind Williams as he strode towards the men. Jack stood. 'Squad, attention,' he shouted. The men scrambled to their feet, stubbing out their Woodbines, or holding their pipes by their sides.

When he reached them, Williams' subaltern used the whistle to cut through the remaining chatter. Williams said, 'At ease, men.'

They moved as one, standing with legs apart. Captain Williams raised his voice. 'Our plans are altered. We are to dismantle the camp immediately and head for home. Why? The equipment is needed elsewhere as the military are in a precautionary state of emergency in view of the situation in Europe. Thank you for an excellent exercise. Quite excellent.' He spun on his heel. The men stared after him. Jack shouted, 'Dismiss.'

The men faltered, looking from one to another. Several grabbed up their beer and downed it in one. All followed. Simon cursed. 'So, it's back to work for us.'

Martin shook his head. 'Just our bloody luck. We'll be down Auld Maud come Monday, bank holiday or not, what's the betting on it.'

Brampton came to Jack. 'Please call them to order, Sergeant.'

Jack did so. Brampton said, 'No, you'll have your holiday. If there's really to be a war, God knows when you'll get another if they need us. We might not be back before Christmas. So, tomorrow you are with your families. You will be paid as though you were on your usual rate. Stand them down, Sergeant.'

Jack did so and the questions began. 'War?' 'Where the hell did that come from?' 'But we've an army for God's sake, they won't need us.'

They dismantled the camp in near-silence and the day seemed darker to Jack. Much much darker. There might be an army, but they were the Terries and could be needed. It wasn't just a game after all.

Lady Veronica heard the sound of horses on the gravel drive shortly before six on Sunday evening. She was walking Raisin and Currant in the formal gardens and hurried back towards the front lawn, not expecting either Richard or Auberon until tomorrow. Neither was she expecting their bank holiday guests today, for heaven's sake. The staff had only just finished preparing the bedrooms, not forgetting the suite for Lord and Lady Brampton. Their arrival was the only blot on the landscape. Stepmother would raise her eyebrows, wondering if Veronica had news to tell of a son and heir. Well, she hadn't. Was it because she lay there wondering when it would be over?

As she reached the cedar tree she saw Richard and Aub. What on earth? They should still be at camp playing soldiers. Damn it again. That meant another evening with Richard, and worse, another night. She set her shoulders and approached the men, who had halted, their horses pawing the ground. She called, forcing a smile, 'What's happened, have the men revolted?' Richard looked rather splendid in his uniform, it had to be said, but he was still her husband, still someone who had curtailed her life into a morass of visiting and entertaining and a dark nothingness. He raised his stick to his cap. 'No, it all went very well, but give me a moment, Veronica. I'll tell you in just a moment.'

Aub's face did not look splendid. She called after him, 'Spoils of war, Aub?'

She waited for them in the Blue Drawing Room, standing at the window looking over the balustrade to the distant hills. Some of the harvest had been taken in, and the sun on the stubble seemed almost rosy. They had looked so sombre. Was it because the Foreign Secretary had proposed a meeting of the major powers to try to stop Austria and Serbia squabbling over the assassination? But surely no country would be stupid enough to go to war. It was more likely that their exercise had come adrift somehow. Men took their games so seriously.

The door opened. She turned and Richard entered, his face drawn and weary, and she experienced the same pang of guilt she felt whenever he returned on leave. She should be warmer towards him, but she couldn't or perhaps wouldn't. She breathed in deeply. She must try harder and perhaps tonight she would, if she possibly could. She said, 'You look tired, my dear. Everything is ready for the party but perhaps we'll have to settle for lobster vol-au-vents after all. I know your favourite is crab . . .'

He shook his head. 'Please, Veronica.' He joined her at the window, standing at her side and staring at the view as though he was soaking in every curve, every shadow, every birdsong, for now there were blue tits on the balcony. Without turning he said, 'It really doesn't matter to me about crab, my dearest. You see, I'm so sorry to leave you with it but I won't be here. I've been recalled. Well, we've all been recalled. This is still the precautionary period officially, but you need to prepare yourself for my absence. Prolonged, perhaps. Not that this will be a hardship for you.' His smile was wry, his eyes held their usual hurt. 'So, continue with your party. I have asked Roger to pack me and I will come to you here before I leave. I have asked Stuart to drive me, if you can spare the Rolls-Royce for a few hours.'

Then he was gone. His words registered at last. She ran after him. 'What do you mean, recalled?'

He was pounding up the stairs. 'The Navy has been ordered to sail north to take up position at Scapa Flow. God knows what's going to happen. The German troops are gathering.'

He was gone, into his bedroom. He shut the door, firmly.

She did not see him again until he presented

himself in the drawing room at eight. She said, 'I've held dinner for you and Aub.' She should have gone to him while Roger packed, but what would she have said?

He sighed. 'I have no time for that, my dear. I leave now. James is bringing my valises.'

She walked from the room with him. 'You should eat. I'll ask the kitchen to pack something for you.'

'I'll eat on the way.' He was almost leaping down the stairs, and she ran to keep up with him. At the front door he shook Mr Harvey's hand. 'Thank you for your kindness. Look after Lady Veronica, Mr Harvey. She will explain.'

Behind them she heard Auberon calling at the top of the stairs, 'No, I'll take the valises, thank you James.'

He also ran down the stairs, washed, looking marginally better. He carried the valises to the car and Stuart stowed them. Richard stood with Veronica beneath the porticoed entrance, staring at the cedar tree. 'It looks as though it will withstand anything.' His voice was quiet.

'Will it have to?' Veronica asked.

He took her hand, and kissed it. 'I think we'll all have to. If it's war I doubt it will be over soon, no matter what the newspapers say. Look at our industry, our machinery. Think of the size of the artillery, the submarines. Think factories, think armaments. It will be a different sort of a war, Ver. A damned slog, and that's what my general thinks too.

I will try and get word to you, of course.' He dropped her hand but made no effort to kiss her. He just walked away, in uniform, perhaps to war.

Veronica wanted to run after him, but to say what? She did nothing except watch as he and Auberon shook hands, and talked, intensively, but only for a few moments. Then he turned and waved before entering the car. Stuart rolled away along the drive.

By morning she had received phone calls from most of her guests to explain that they could not attend because all the trains had been commandeered by the government. She knew it was for troops. It was all happening too quickly, far too quickly and she couldn't really think. Was Richard based locally, or embarking, and if so, to where?

Aub told her over breakfast that Richard had arranged to have him gazetted into the North Tyne Fusiliers along with any of his Territorials who wished, as they had excelled at exercise and their warfare training almost equalled that of the regulars. 'He was reluctant, but I insisted. I don't want to miss it. I gather Father had already had a word with the general, who was a sobersides and said it would not be quick, but that's not what everyone else is saying. I'll be talking to the men later today at their fete day, because they won't want to miss it either.'

'It won't be over soon,' she snapped. 'Take Richard seriously, if he says it's going to be a slog, then it is. I forbid it. Stay here. It's not a damned game and

402

what am I to do with all this food? I've no one coming, not even Father.'

Auberon laughed through his swollen lips. 'Well, there's a silver lining to every cloud.' Within a second they were both laughing but it was high-pitched and strange, and Mr Harvey was standing by the sideboard looking as though his world was steadily crashing around him.

Veronica stopped laughing quite suddenly, feeling cold and frightened. 'Mr Harvey, let's not worry the staff with any of this until we know for sure. Would you mind?'

It sounded like a question, but it was an order.

Veronica and Auberon visited the kitchen after breakfast and informed them that there was a problem with trains and most of the guests would be unable to attend, so they had cancelled the party altogether. 'Captain Williams is unable to be here either,' Lady Veronica said.

There was a long silence and Evie wondered if upstairs had overlooked the fact that those downstairs had eyes and ears and read newspapers, and had the brainpower to put two and two together and make four. Did they really think they hadn't noticed that Simon, Bernie and James were back early from exercises, the captain had disappeared quick as a wink and that they of course knew the trains had been cancelled, for James had overheard Mr Harvey telling Mrs Green.

'We would like you to take the food down to the fete, if that is all right with Mrs Moore. You must all go, have a good time. One never knows . . .' Veronica tailed off.

The next day, 4th August, the Germans marched into Belgium. Britain as guarantor of Belgian neutrality handed an ultimatum to the German ambassador in London and by eleven o'clock that evening Russia, France and Great Britain were at war with Germany and Austria.

Chapter Nineteen

Those who wished had been accepted immediately and unusually into the North Tyne Fusiliers and had left yesterday, within days of the declaration of war, just like that. The house seemed half empty. Evie prepared Lady Veronica's breakfast which she had thought to restrict to a few dishes – a decision that had been vetoed by Mr Harvey, who insisted that standards were to be maintained, at least until further notice.

Archie delivered the food to the dining room. Evie had to prepare the porridge and take it to the servants' hall, because Dottie had left three days ago for Newcastle. She would be looking for work in one of the new war industries that were already setting up, as though they had known for a while they would be needed. Kev the bootboy had gone too, to the recruitment office. Evie and Annie cleared the table, feeling the loss of Sarah, who had followed Dottie yesterday.

Mr Harvey entered the kitchen with Mrs Green. Mrs Moore was stocktaking in the big pantry. He called her out and explained that Lord Brampton had telephoned late last night, requesting that he raise Lady Veronica from her bed as he wished to speak to her. Mr Harvey had done so, and this morning Lady Veronica had conveyed to him his Lordship's request that they use Easterleigh Hall as a convalescent home for the troops. Mr Harvey's mouth was so pursed it must have hurt.

Evie smothered a smile. The telephone had only been installed a few months ago, and Mr Harvey felt it was a machine liable to explode at any moment and held the receiver with trembling hands. But a convalescent home? Perhaps that was the only good idea the Bastard had ever had in his life.

Mr Harvey asked Mrs Moore and Mrs Green to accompany him to his parlour where they would discuss the viability of such an undertaking, as Lady Veronica had requested. He ended, 'We should consider whether to lay in extra supplies anyway for our day-to-day needs, as others are doing, or to lead by example and not panic buy; patriotism versus pragmatism, to buy or not to buy?'

Evie watched the house servants hurry to their tasks. Lil had left for London. James and Arthur and three of the other male indoor servants had left with the platoon. Bernie, Thomas and Simon had gone too, and several more of the other under-gardeners, and over half the grooms.

Evie sat suddenly at the kitchen table. Simon.
She'd said, gripping his suit lapel, 'You can't go.'
'I must,' he'd replied, his hands covering hers.

She could remember the feel of those hands, warm and strong. 'But Si, not you.' She mouthed those words again now. 'You're safe here. Someone must live. Jack's going, Timmie's gone. I need someone to be safe, can't you understand?' She'd been shouting by the end. He'd pressed his mouth on to hers, saying, 'I'll live, I know I will and it will be over soon. The gang are going, so I must. It'll be exciting.'

She looked down at her white knuckles, which were gripping the table so hard that her fingers had gone numb. The oven cloth lay in a heap and she picked it up and threw it across the room. 'Exciting? What about *our* gang, you stupid, lovely lad? Damn the war. Damn it to hell, and damn Auberon for taking you.'

She reached for the photograph she carried in her apron pocket. They had gone to Gosforn, he in uniform, she in her best dress, and found the studio. There they were, with an aspidistra poking up behind, as though they were frozen in black and white. Soon she must put it in a frame, but not yet. She replaced it, patted it. Not yet.

Annie called from the scullery, 'Fat lot of good that little tantrum will do, Evie. They're marching round some square near Newcastle with Roger buggering up the about turns, so what's all the fuss about? It will all be over before they're needed, the daft beggars, and if they do go they'll be as much use as that oven cloth and be sent home. They're not soldiers, so they'll just get in the way.'

Mrs Moore was opening the door into the kitchen. 'The generals would differ. They'll say they're needed, pinch their cheeks and take them away.' Suddenly everyone was laughing. What else could they do, really?

Mrs Green came into the kitchen and sat at the table. How strange. 'We can't manage on the staff we have left if this is to become a convalescent home for the soldiers, so what do you suggest, Evie?'

Mrs Moore settled herself beside the housekeeper. 'I told her you'd have some ideas, Evie. You always do.' Both women looked at her as though she had the answers to the problems of the world, but she had none. Mrs Moore called through to the scullery, 'Stop lurking over those pots and have a cuppa with us, Annie. We need to put our heads together if we are to convert this place as Lord Brampton wants. It's just nonsense. It won't be needed.'

Evie poured tea. Perhaps it wasn't nonsense, and if any of the North Tynes were injured she wanted to be one of those that helped. As she passed around the tea she wondered if Lady Veronica would want Captain Williams here, poor devil, taking with him the merest kiss on the hand, or so James had reported. And why no baby on the way? They'd only been married in May, sure enough, but even so.

Annie joined them, her hands as red and raw as

always. Evie insisted, 'We need experienced staff in the kitchen, because this is the powerhouse. Food is vital, for staff and patients. Annie, you must take the position of kitchenmaid now that Dottie's deserted us.' She held up her hand at Annie's shaking head. 'I know you like your little empire in the scullery and think it will be too difficult out here in the kitchen, but it won't. You've seen we have a method that works.'

She had to be careful because nothing must be said about Mrs Moore's limited involvement in front of Mrs Green and she merely looked hard at Annie, who finally changed the shake to a nod, and a grin. Mrs Moore was looking into space. Evie continued, 'We must get at least one more, if not two, for the kitchen as well, and perhaps two in the scullery, then there's the laundry. By, it will be heavy on that, but that's your pigeon, Mrs Green.'

Mrs Green pulled out the notebook that she attached to her belt with string, and wrote furiously. Mrs Moore sat with her swollen hands around her cup, and set her lips. Evie stared; she'd never seen the cook look so serious and felt a tension build. Mrs Moore spoke. 'Yes, indeed we must have Annie promoted, and others to help because, Mrs Green, I confess I barely manage and haven't been able to for a long while now.'

There was a long silence with just the range crackling and the stockpot bubbling, and Evie's heart sank. Why now? When she was needed like never before.

Mrs Green said quietly at last, 'We all understand that, Mrs Moore, and are, and have been, cognizant of the situation.' What long words you use, Evie thought. But what do you really mean, because if you cause Mrs Moore to be dismissed then I go too. As the sale of the guest house has been cancelled, I will find war work. But she said nothing yet because Mrs Green was smiling slightly, with a kindness that was not often evident.

Annie said, 'I don't understand the words, but I'll go if Mrs Moore goes.' Mrs Green shook her head. 'I don't think anyone is thinking of any more of the staff leaving. Mrs Moore might not have the hands any more but she has the wisdom, don't you agree, Evie? I think everything should remain as it is and I'm sure, as is Mr Harvey, that you have already come to an amicable financial arrangement?'

Evie and Mrs Moore looked at one another. All this subterfuge, and the upper staff knew all the time. Mrs Moore reached out and touched Evie's hand. 'Yes, indeed. I persuaded Evie just a few months ago, at last, to share my income and since Lady Veronica was kind enough to increase my wages at about the same time, it has made it more equitable for us both.'

So there, Evie grinned to herself, Mrs Moore can use long words too but any further discussion was interrupted by shouting from the yard, and the sound of horses, hooves, many of them. Dear God, not fire again?

Evie and Annie ran out of the kitchen and up the steps. In the stable yard several khaki-clad soldiers were struggling with roped horses who were shying and baulking as Raisin and Currant barked and snapped at their heels. At the entrance to the stables the head groom barred the soldiers' entrance with a pitchfork.

He yelled to Evie, 'Fetch help.'

A sergeant was bearing down on him, shouting, 'Stand aside. This is necessary for the war effort.'

Mrs Green puffed up the steps. 'You've got young legs, Evie, so run upstairs and fetch her Ladyship from the dining room.'

Evie rushed back down the steps, up the back stairs, her heart hammering, turning off for the first floor. She slammed back the green baize door into the dining room and tore in.

Lady Veronica was reading *The Times*. Mr Harvey swung round, moving from his position as guardian of the kedgeree at the sideboard, his hand up, his face appalled.

'Excuse me, my lady, but they've come for the horses, the army that is. The dogs are down there too. It's bloody chaos, begging your pardon.' Evie was panting. 'They're taking the lot, or I think they are. They've already got some roped from somewhere else.'

Lady Veronica threw down the newspaper. 'Come with me, Evie, I'll need you.' She ran round the table towards the landing. Mr Harvey stuttered, 'This is most unusual, Your Ladyship. Staff should use the baize door.'

Lady Veronica didn't slow but shouted from the landing as she headed for the stairs, 'Oh be quiet, Harvey. Come on Evie, I won't have them just barging in. It will be stones through the window next. Remember the hat, Evie. I need you. Mr Harvey, get Stan, the head gardener, and what men you can summon.'

Evie joined her, rushing down the main stairs and across the hallowed ground of the front hall. She opened the huge door for Lady Veronica, then they were both through, running and crunching along the drive towards the stable yard. Evie's ankle twisted, the pain stabbed. She ignored it and ran on, catching up and keeping pace with Lady Veronica, then into the stable yard. Here, three soldiers were holding back the grooms, whose numbers had been depleted as half went to war. Other troops led start-led horses, rearing and bucking, out into the yard. Some already had their halters threaded through with ropes.

The horses had spilled into the kitchen yard as well. Raisin and Currant were still barking and milling and Mrs Moore and Mrs Green had corralled the sergeant at one side of the huge stable doors, blocking his way. Annie was there too, with a saucepan which she brought down, trying to hit his head. The sergeant parried the blow, twisting the saucepan from her hand, and brushing aside the elderly women as though they were nothing.

Evie was charging now and hurtled into him, knocking him off balance. He stepped backwards and she charged again, pursuing her advantage, pushing at him and now Annie was with her. They jammed him against the stable wall. 'Don't you touch them,' Evie was shouting. 'Don't you dare touch these women.'

Annie yelled, 'I'll clobber you if you move.'

Rough hands were on them, dragging them back, but now Lady Veronica stood beside them, so that the sergeant would have to push against her if he moved. He put up his swagger stick as though to strike. 'Put that down this instant and instruct your men to unhand Miss Forbes and Miss Fisher. And before you take any horses from this establishment you will talk to me, do you understand, or has common courtesy deserted you in this rush to abscond with our possessions?' Lady Veronica snapped.

In her voice was all the fury and frustration of years of . . . well, what. Bastard Brampton, perhaps, Evie thought. Currant was jumping up at the sergeant now, and only stopped when Lady Veronica roared at him, 'Enough, for God's sake, you ridiculous dog.'

The soldiers holding Evie and Annie let their

hands drop at a look from their sergeant, who groped in his breast pocket and handed Lady Veronica a requisition form. 'You are required to hand over all horses at this establishment, and I believe there is a stable behind the house in which there are the hunters and field horses.'

Lady Veronica read the form and handed it back. 'Carry on, Sergeant, but if you touch Tinker I will shoot you.' She pointed to Tinker's stable. 'She's fifteen years old and not an asset to the military in any way.'

The sergeant straightened, tucked his swagger stick beneath his arm and ground his heels into the cobbles as he marched from her. 'I think that's a fair point, Your Ladyship.' He was flushed, and rattled. Evie felt the excitement roaring inside her as she watched him leave and at last understood why her menfolk had gone to war. It was, after all, just a game, a damned game.

By lunchtime the horses had gone and the remaining grooms too, because without their animals what was the point? Together they trooped off to the recruitment office in Gosforn. Lady Veronica would attend to Tinker herself, she insisted.

After lunch Lord and Lady Brampton arrived, to the surprise, and disappointment, of them all. Len their chauffeur appeared in the servants' hall in his uniform, with his boots glistening as usual. At teatime, Lady Veronica crept into the kitchen unexpectedly just as Evie was about to enjoy a mug of tea. She held her finger to her lips, her eyes red from crying. Raisin and Currant skittered at her feet before settling under the table. She sat and stared at nothing, and then lifted her head. 'I need your help, Evie. Father says they have to be shot. They're German dogs. He's insane as well as a bastard.'

Annie had come to the doorway of the scullery and now she faded back into her burrow. Evie knew from the newspapers that this ridiculous panic was affecting the whole of the country like a plague. She sat down and poured tea into the enamel mugs she had set out for Annie and her. She needed some, even if Lady Veronica did not. It had been a hell of a day. 'Well, *I'm* not going to do it, my lady,' she said.

Lady Veronica threw back her head and laughed. 'God, I wish you lived upstairs, Evie.'

'Aye, well you'd get no objection from me,' Evie muttered taking Annie's tea through to her, and whispering that she should slip out through the rear door of the scullery and into the servants' hall that way.

Lady Veronica was absent-mindedly drinking Evie's tea when she returned. Evie collected another enamel mug from the dresser. Lady Veronica watched, then blushed, and put down the mug. 'I'm so sorry, Evie, I wasn't thinking, I didn't realise. Oh, damnation and bugger. Evie, can you find someone who would have my babies? I will pay for their keep, of course, but this war won't last long and then I can take them back. I will not have them shot and that's that.'

Evie smiled. 'I'll need a few hours off to go into the village and ask around.'

'I rather hoped you'd say that, and thank you for being my right hand this morning. Please thank Annie for me.'

Evie said, 'I'd have done it without mention of the hat.'

The women smiled at one another. 'The slate's wiped quite clean, I believe,' Lady Veronica murmured.

Mam had the dogs, of course. 'Why not, pet,' she said as Millie and Evie helped with the proggy mat, while Tim built bricks on the floor. He was crawling fit to burst, and attempting to pull himself up. He'd be walking soon. He was a grand lad at sixteen months. 'Tim will love them and it won't be for long. Christmas they say it'll be over. You know they came for your da's pigeons? Someone told them that he had some good homers. I believe it was Mr Auberon's batman. Your da's right upset, he is, Evie, but he'll have the shift to take his mind off it.'

Millie was concentrating harder than usual on the proggy mat, shoving through a blue length, her head down. Tim knocked his bricks over with a clatter. 'How could Roger have known about the homers?' Evie mused, her eyes fixed on Millie, remembering Roger accosting her on the bank holiday. Surely she wouldn't have told him? But what was the point of even asking? By a huge stretch of the imagination it could simply be put down to common knowledge.

Tiredness had carved deep lines on her mam's face, but she smiled as she checked the clock. 'Grace is at the retirement house today. Why not pop in before you leave, she's still not herself, you know.'

Evie did so, strolling along the path to the front door which Grace opened before she could knock. 'I saw you arrive at your mam's and hoped you'd come.'

Her face was similarly tired. She stepped on to the path. Evie said, 'Mam's taking the Brampton dachshunds, so if she finds them too much, would your families have them for a bit? It won't be for long, will it.' She sounded more cheerful than she felt.

Grace linked her arm in Evie's and they studied the marrows. 'I'll ask them, dearest Evie, but I was coming across to tell you that I'm joining the Voluntary Aid Detachment, you know, the VADs.' Evie wasn't surprised, somehow.

'Well, a sight more exciting than cooking.' She nudged her friend, and then nudged her again. Grace laughed gently and nudged her back. 'Nothing's more important than *your* food. When will the convalescents come, has it been decided yet?'

They stood at the gate. Above them the Stunted Tree was as unchanging as ever and now Evie's mind seemed to stutter and stop, then circle round again and again. Yes, it hadn't changed in centuries. The pits had come and the valleys had changed, but not the Stunted Tree. It had always been there, just quietly there. But what if the Germans came, what if their guns blasted their homes, their country? What if they destroyed their houses, these houses?

She gazed at her family's home, and the retirement and emergency homes behind her, and down towards the village, and the pit gantry, the slag heap. What if they tore into their houses like the soldiers had charged into the stable yard, but with rifles blazing?

Evie turned to Grace. 'It's really here, isn't it? War is really here and nothing will ever be the same again because they're taking our own men, not just the soldiers, so it really is going to be a long job, isn't it?'

Grace had her arm around her. 'Some say so. But think, Evie, they'll need the women because the men are going, so we can prove ourselves. We can show them that we're just as good as them, and when it's all over they'll have to take us seriously. You know there are no more meetings for the duration, and that Christabel has declared a truce. We're to be good girls and support the men.' She stopped, then shook her head. 'But though it will help us, we're at war and everything else, including votes, is trivial and like ashes in our mouths.'

Neither spoke, just looked around. How could it be such a glorious day? The sheep were in the meadows, the cows in the corn, but dear God, no horses. They were gone to war.

Evie said at last, 'Will you come to see the men off when they finally go? If you're still here, of course? They'll train down to Southampton.' She opened the gate, wrapping her shawl more tightly around her, feeling chilled though the weather was balmy.

Grace moved to the gate and opened it. 'Why would I? I have no one who is leaving.'

Evie just looked at her. 'You must come. Who knows if you will see him again.'

Veronica dined with her parents and listened to her father as he ranted at the loss of his hunters. 'Why that idiot husband of yours couldn't pull strings I do not know.'

'He was too busy going to war, Father,' Veronica said, wondering how Evie could produce such magnificent quenelles when she had had barely an hour, or had Mrs Moore managed to squash them through the hair sieve? She knew the answer to that. She needed to learn to cook, it was disgraceful that she knew the terms but couldn't have done it to save her life. She stopped. Why did everything come back to life and death?

'Of course he was, and I spoke to him about gazetting Auberon. I can't have Richard shining and Auberon shirking.'

'Auberon doesn't shirk, Father.' She hated the way he used his knife to peel his apple. It was as though it was a weapon; slicing and slicing. Why didn't he use a dessert knife and fork?

419

'Don't contradict your father,' her stepmother said sharply. 'You are in his home and should show proper deference, especially as he has allowed you and your husband houseroom.'

'Yes, Stepmama.' Veronica was damned if she'd call her Mama after that little homily.

Archie was at the sideboard. What did the staff think about when the interminable pettiness of upstairs life was played out in front of them? Why had Archie not enlisted? Ah, Auberon had said some must stay. What about the pitmen, they could have stayed safely in the pit? But what a nonsense that was with one dead every few weeks, more injured and the same throughout the coalfields. Veronica laid her napkin on the table. When could she go to her room?

Lady Brampton was looking at Lord Brampton. 'My dear, weren't you going to discuss with Veronica setting up a hospital here, rather than a convalescent home? You thought the latter smacked of malingering, I seem to remember?'

Once he had dismissed Archie, Lord Brampton described his plan; discussion was an extravagance unknown to him. He listed the steps that he had taken, the provisional order for beds, dependent on final details, the employment of the nurses and VADs, the gazetting of Dr Nicholls as Medical Officer in Chief. 'I have obtained funding from various sources.'

'I'm sure you have, Father.' Veronica's tone was

dry. 'Will you both be on hand to assist?' She could barely keep the contempt from her voice.

He flung his napkin on to the table, pushing back his chair. The simmering violence of the man frightened her. It was ever thus. One moment she stood up to him, the next she feared him.

'Do you think I have time to spend on the housekeeping of a hospital? It will be your task to decide the details of how and where everything will be set up. You were bleating to your stepmother about preferring work to the prospect of marriage, so perhaps you'll make more of a success of this than you have of the pathetic disaster of the other. Still no grandchild, I gather?'

There it was, the mental blow between the eyes. He should be sent in against the Germans to use every one of his dirty tricks to wreak havoc. She sat quite still. Outside, the sky was darkening. Soon it would be September and with the relentlessness of nature, autumn would come. It was unchanging, while everything else went to hell. The worst thing was that her father was right. She had made a pathetic marriage and it was solely due to her. It wasn't Richard's fault. He was just a man, but she didn't want a man, not yet, and besides, he had chosen to kill as a career. Who knew what he might turn into?

Her father said, 'You will arrange to send down produce to London from the Home Farm and gardens. I will be in Leeds frequently, but London more often. I will not be here above and beyond the bare necessity.'

'Well, we must endure the loss as best we can.' She wished she was able to keep her mouth shut. It was then that he reached back in a lazy circular movement. She watched it happen, saw the flash of his arm as it struck, felt the shock throughout her body and wanted to groan with the pain of it. Her stepmother delicately touched her napkin to the corners of her mouth. 'Perhaps you'd like to retire to your room for the evening. We will be leaving after an early breakfast and your father will make a list for you of his requirements.'

Veronica stood, her legs trembling. She fisted her hands, turned on her heel and left the room, but not before she'd noticed that her stepmother's hands were trembling, and in her eyes was a mirror of her own fear. For the first time she wondered if the price the woman had paid for the riches her father had accumulated was proving too high.

She climbed the stairs, her head swimming. She vomited in the bathroom, and was pleased that Lil had left her employment. She wanted no one to see her like this. She struggled to her bed and lay down, looking out at the last of the August afternoon. If Auberon had been here he would have taken the blow in her place. Richard, though, would have parried it like the sergeant had Annie's saucepan, and would then have killed him.

'But would he really have done that for me?'

She whispered the words. She could see him so vividly for a moment, feel the kiss he had laid so gently upon her hand before he left, and something stirred.

Chapter Twenty

It was 15th August, a week after the men had left, and a beautiful day. The Forbes relatives were quiet as they clambered into the train that would take them from Gosforn to Newcastle to say goodbye to their men. Lady Veronica travelled in First Class, of course. Evie nudged her mam. 'There are advantages to being downstairs staff, at least we're all in this together.' Her mam raised a smile, and clutched Tim to her. He reached for the balls Millie was juggling. Evie had never been able to juggle, no matter how many times Jack had shown her, and she felt a shaft of jealousy that he had done the same for Millie.

Millie snapped, 'Leave it, Tim.' She dropped a ball. 'Bugger it.'

'Not before the bairn,' Mam urged.

Millie sighed and passed one of the balls to her son, who tried to throw it across the carriage. Grace who was sitting opposite, caught it one-handed before it fell to the floor, and threw it to Evie, who threw it in turn to Alec, Simon's father, who tossed it to Da. A laughing Tim received it from Da and gave it to his mother, who smiled and threw it to Alec and so it went on, and soon they were all laughing, and booing those who dropped it. It was as though they were on an outing.

Outside the countryside flashed by. Wives, brothers, sisters and parents got on at the next station where the engine shrieked, blew off steam, and the wheels ground on the tracks as doors banged shut until finally they were moving again. The men gave up their seats to some new arrivals and moved to the corridors, leaving the women in possession of the carriage. Evie and Grace looked at the ball. Should they, shouldn't they?

'Here, give it to me, for Pete's sake,' Millie said, taking the ball and tossing it to one of the new arrivals who blinked, came alert, caught it and on it went. Anything was better than thinking that their men were embarking.

Men were embarking.

Men were embarking.

The wheels drummed it again and again, and not even the ball-throwing stopped it going round and round in Evie's head. She could tell from every face in the carriage that their feelings were the same. It was too hot. Surely it was? She pulled on the leather window strap and lowered the window two holes. The wheels thumped over the points, the train shrieked as it went under bridges, the smuts blew in. Grace waved them away but they'd already landed on her face.

'Evie, shall we put the window up?' she suggested.

Evie grinned. 'Sorry about that.' She did so, and

the noise abated. 'Here, lick this.' She held out her handkerchief. Grace grimaced. Millie called, 'You're not in your kitchen now, Evie Forbes, keeping everyone spick and span for the bosses.' Evie looked at her. What had a kitchen to do with handkerchiefs? She supposed it was Millie's way of keeping her in her place in front of strangers. They were looking at her now, realising she was in service.

Grace was dragging out her own handkerchief. She licked it and handed it to Evie. 'Do the honours please, Evie, I can't look like a grubby schoolchild. And don't forget, Millie, Evie is doing a training for much greater things, sensible girl.' So stick that in your pipe and smoke it, Evie thought as she rubbed at the greasy smuts ineffectually.

Her mam said, 'Away with you pet, give it to me.' She handed Tim to Evie. 'I brought soapy flannels for the bairn, and they'll do faces better than lick and scrub.'

By the time they drew into Newcastle Central station Grace was restored to her former glory, or so Evie said as they exited their train to be greeted by a cacophony of shrieking whistles, gasps of steam, shouts, clangs, chaos. Their little group was borne along by a crowd that was rushing to the platform which held what seemed like hundreds of khaki-clad soldiers, and on the way they passed Lady Veronica standing to one side, looking lost. Evie and Grace struggled against the tide back towards her. Grace gasped. 'What's happened to her face?'

Evie shouted into her ear, 'She bumped into a door a week ago, or in other words Bastard Brampton hit her, just like he hits Auberon. It's the same bruising, the same split lip. She hasn't said, of course, but I'm sure. It looks a damn sight better than it did.'

They were being knocked by the passengers rushing towards the troops. 'Your Ladyship,' Evie shouted, 'come with us if you wish, you'll get trampled in the rush on your own.' She saw Lady Veronica smile carefully. 'How kind, I was momentarily confused and Grace, you're here. I heard that Edward was indisposed and was hoping you could come in his place. I'm sure it's a great comfort to everyone.'

Evie urged her forward. 'We need to keep up with the flow, and we don't want to be late. It's our last chance to see them until . . . Well, until.' Grace tucked a hand in each of their arms. 'Until they arrive home safely,' she said, drawing them into the constant stream of tense relatives.

They made their way over to the far platform, which was the longest at the station. Above the melee they spotted a placard waving aloft, painted with the words 4th Battalion North Tyne Fusiliers, C Company. Lady Veronica whispered to Evie, 'They could learn a bit from our placard-painting, couldn't they, Evie?'

'Aye pet, that they could.'

Lady Veronica smiled. 'It's so good to be called pet.'

They were forcing their way through the crowds in the direction of C Company. The embarkation train was already huffing and puffing, but it couldn't leave, not yet. 'Not yet,' Evie said aloud.

Lady Veronica said, 'It wouldn't dare, Evie, it would have you to reckon with.'

The three women grinned at one another. 'Us,' Evie said. 'Us to reckon with, the monstrous regiment of women.' Grace squeezed their arms and together they marched abreast and it was as though the sea parted, because suddenly they were there with the placard propped up on one of the Victorian pillars and the men searching for their loved ones. Where was Mr Auberon's platoon? Where?

She saw Jack with Tim in his arms, and Millie, her face flushed, looking around while hanging on Jack's arm. Martin was with them, and his mother too. Millie smiled at someone as he called to her. It was Roger. Evie watched as he came towards Millie and Tim, his son. Her brother stared at Mr Auberon's batman, daring him to lay claim to the child he, Jack Forbes, held in his arms. There was no way the child should grow up being influenced by such a person, or so Jack had told Evie the last time she had seen him.

Her da was just behind him, but moved to place himself between the two men. Her mam was off to one side, listening gravely to something Captain Williams was saying.

'I must go, Jack might need me.' Evie darted

forward, but Simon emerged from the milling crowd. Grace held her back. 'I'll do it, you go to Simon.'

Everything else was forgotten as she ran and stumbled in between everyone else to reach him, just as he was trying to reach her, and then she was in his arms and he held her, burying his face against her hair. Where was her hat? What was it about hats? What did it matter?

His khaki was rough. It felt so strange. Everything was so terribly strange. All these men leaving, going to fight, but they'd be safe, because they were strong, brave pitmen. But no, Simon wasn't a pitman, he was a singer and a gardener, and he was gentle. He said, 'I love you, I love you.' Again and again, and she was saying it too. His lips were on hers, their eyes fixed on to one another, her arms locked around him, and his around her.

Jack was here now. 'Let her go for just a moment, Si. A brother has some rights and the lass has to breathe.'

It was Jack who held her now, so big and strong. 'I'll take care of him, bonny lass,' he said. 'Never fear, I'll take good care of him.' Her mam came up, tapping her shoulder. 'Let your mam give Jack a cuddle now, Evie.'

Evie stepped back and saw Grace on the other side of her mother. She saw the love shining from her. Over her mam's head Jack was looking at Grace, and his love matched hers. Evie ached for them, but now there was someone by her side.

'May I speak to you, just for a moment?' It was Mr Auberon, or rather, the Rt Hon. Lieutenant Brampton. Evie was impatient. She wanted to be with Simon. She looked for him but he was with his father and mother, so she swung back to her employer. 'Yes, Mr Auberon, just for a minute though.'

He looked older, stronger. The sun had tanned his face. His eyes were a deeper blue. How sad that he had no one to wish him goodbye except for a sister. She softened. 'I wish you well, Mr Auberon. I truly do.' And she did.

Everything was in the past and though Timmie had died, he'd died with his family around him, whereas if . . . She swallowed. His smile was strained. He bent a little closer, saying quietly, 'Please, I ask you to be my sister's support. You attended the same meetings, you both sided with the socialists. If you can bear to do it for a Brampton, please be her support, or even her friend.' He touched his cheek, then his lip. 'Teach her to protect herself. Forgive me asking. I have no right, but you're a wonderful woman, Evie Forbes.'

He straightened now, his colour heightened. He reached for her hand, held it, bent over it, kissed it. He straightened, gave her a half-salute and then he was gone into the melee and the whistles were blowing, the steam was gushing from the boilers and the men were dragging themselves from all they had known. Where was Si? Here, here. He held her, kissed her, but Jack was pulling him away, his sergeant's stripes coming into play. Martin, too, was playing his corporal's role to the full. They were going, piling into the train, hanging from windows. Evie, her family, Simon's family and Grace stood together looking for their men, but then Evie glanced around. Where was Lady Veronica?

She saw her standing back near the placard, quite alone, and hurried to her, taking hold of her arm because she looked so frozen, so pale. 'Come with me. You're not alone, we've all got one another.'

Lady Veronica turned then. 'I couldn't let my husband kiss me. I couldn't.' She touched her bruises. 'The poor beggar,' Evie said. 'You can do better than that, he's not the one who clobbered you, for God's sake. Pull yourself together, he's a good man.' She walked Veronica over to their group. 'You can blow him a kiss,' she said. 'He's there, on the carriage step.'

Captain Williams was looking along the train, checking that all the doors were shut. The guard was waving his flag. Suddenly Lady Veronica called, 'Richard, Richard. Be careful, please.' He couldn't hear. Evie joined in, then Mam, then Grace. 'Richard, Richard, this way.' He looked towards them at last and Lady Veronica blew a kiss. 'Be safe,' she called. 'Just be safe and come home.'

He was scrambling into the carriage as the guard slammed the door but he leaned from the window, waving. He returned the kiss and his face was alight with love. Evie put her arm around Lady Veronica, whose face contained something, but what? Simon was leaning out as the train shunted forward, screeching and grinding, and then he was gone, pulled back because another man leaned out, waving, and then he was gone, and another took his place.

Veronica felt the pressure of Evie's arm and made no attempt to move away from this group, from their friendliness, their warmth. Everything was different now; nothing that was 'proper' seemed to matter. Britain was at war, her brother was gone, Richard too.

She watched the train leave, smelt the coal, heard the steam, and the crying around her. 'You need a friend,' Aub had said.

'Esther is living in London. Margaret used to be a friend but she came to us only to burn us down. How could she?' she'd replied.

'You have Evie. You think the same, you go to the same meetings, so make her a friend, Ver, at least for the duration of the war, and never be alone with him again. Never.'

On 18th August, after laying over at Folkestone for several days, Jack herded the platoon on to the cross-Channel ferry which was to take them across to France. Their packs were a damned nuisance and all sixty pounds of them dragged at their shoulders and banged into the bloke behind, or swung into the bloke beside them if they turned. 'Down packs,' he ordered. They did so, Martin digging him in the ribs and saying, 'I'd rather be in the pit than slopping about on the top of this great bloody sea. Makes you feel right queer, man.'

Jack squatted down, dragging out cigarette paper and tobacco from his pocket. 'Get down, out of the wind, and there's a bucket over there if things get bad.'

Simon was leaning on the rail, enjoying a last look at Blighty. The blokes were singing, 'Who's your lady friend?' and he joined in. Jack strung the tobacco along the paper, rolled it, licked it, smoked it. Who was his lady friend? And did she love him? He knew she did. After the station, she knew he did. He had withdrawn after Timmie's death, because she had told him she no longer needed his help to dig, his help for anything. Why? If only he'd not listened, gone with his gut. One day he would ask her to be his love, somehow. But what about Millie?

He exhaled, the wind snatching at his breath. He owed Tim the chance of a decent life, and if Roger ever approached the boy again he'd kill him. He took a drag at the cigarette, the tobacco burning red. He'd made that threat before about Brampton and had done nothing, but there was still time and Roger was different, anyway. He wasn't a fool or a bastard, he was just evil, a snake.

Martin was hanging over the bucket now, poor beggar, but it wouldn't be long.

Lieutenant Brampton was moving between his men, returning their salutes, saying, 'How are you? No one too sick?' Doing his duty, Jack grinned, but he looked right poorly himself. He got to his feet as Brampton reached him. 'Everything all right, Sergeant?'

Jack saluted, pinching out the remains of his cigarette. 'All present and correct, sir. We've a few not so well but a bit of solid ground beneath their feet will work a treat, either that or a good slab of fatty pork in between some bread.'

He kept his face still as Brampton's face paled even further and he rushed away. Bernie called across, 'You're a heartless beggar, Jack Forbes, with a cast-iron stomach.' Jack watched Brampton proceed, keeping in contact with the men, smiling, joking when all he must have wanted to do was vomit. He hated himself for admiring the bastard.

Above them the gulls were wheeling. Would Da still go sea-coaling? Yes, of course he would. Would he grow his leeks? Probably even more seriously than ever, with the war on. Would the pigeon fledglings he'd bought off Alec survive? Of course, if his da had anything to do with it.

By, his homing birds would do well for the army, and those that survived would be home by Christmas, along with everyone else, or so his da said. Jack squeezed his way along the ferry, listening to the singing, seeing some men playing cards, some writing letters home already, some just talking, sitting on the deck propped up against their packs. At the prow the officers were assembled, clustering around the colonel.

Jack stood quietly watching them, rolling another cigarette, lighting it behind his cupped hand. Such fancy clothes these professional soldiers wore, like those who had already gone to fight, and die. What the hell was going to happen to make it stop by Christmas? He looked back again at his own platoon, all previously Territorials. They were considered trained. Bollocks. They knew nothing of war, any more than he did. He smoked his cigarette down as far as he could, before pinching it dead. Dead. Words could take on different meanings, he thought.

As they approached the French coast at Boulogne the men crammed the rails, peering through the Channel mists at the marquees on the clifftop. They stretched along the cliffs and straggled up the slopes of the hills.

'That's where we're headed, is it?' Bernie was pointing to the encampments.

'Ours is not to know, or to reason why, lad,' Martin said, his colour on the verge of coming back now that the end of the torture was in sight. Behind them Jack wondered if this was where Grace would end up, because some marquees bore the sign of the Red Cross. It gave him comfort to think that she'd be there, safe but near.

'Ours is just to do or die,' Bernie finished for Martin.

*

They left port immediately, heading they knew not where, knowing that they just had to put one foot in front of the other and march along the slippery smooth cobbles out of the port and through one village after another, twisting their ankles and suffering huge blisters, feeling the sun beating down, stepping aside to let pass the London buses, London taxis, lorries and carts which were travelling back towards the coast with the injured.

They passed roadside cafes but didn't enter, and on the second day they entrained into a cattle truck and the old steam engine clunked them along for thirty miles, and they all slept. Jack dreamed of forming fours, right wheels, left wheels, and excavating trenches, and marching, marching until they thought as one. With one exception: Roger still wheeled right when everyone wheeled left, with a pigeon in each pocket. Jack woke with a start as the train pulled into a siding, glad to be awake, glad that Roger stayed near Brampton, as a valet should. What a world, that a servant came to war with his master.

They slept in a barn that night, ignoring the rats and shovelling down bully beef. Towards the end of the next day they slogged through Frameries, and the townsfolk cheered them. They were to sleep in another barn and Jack watched as Captain Williams gathered the officers together, and they all handed over cash. They bought a barrel of beer for the men, and for a moment Jack felt he would follow the beggars to the ends of the earth and through whatever was thrown at them.

The field kitchen made soup and on top of that they had bully beef again. Their blisters tended, they were on the road again the next day and could hear the guns, and the firing. Not long now, then. Jack and Martin exchanged a look. Around them stood slag heaps with the sun turning them to gold. 'Just like home,' Jack murmured. Simon called, keeping in step as he looked back, 'Where're we going, Jack?' Jack increased his pace and caught up with the front ranks. 'Not sure the officers know, so why should I?'

They stopped at another village that night, and the officers were treated to smacking kisses on either cheek, courtesy of the hairy mayor. In return they stepped back a pace and shook hands firmly, well out of reach of such foreign behaviour. The men laughed, though they did it quietly.

In response to an order from Captain Williams Jack told the men to dig trenches on the far side of some unused rail tracks, though exhaustion was dragging at them. 'Come on, we're getting closer to wherever it is we're going. You can hear the big guns, so who knows what's going to happen? Get digging.'

Some villagers came to help as Brampton inspected the work so far. Jack said politely, '*Merci, mais non.*' He explained to them in French that they must not assist the men, for if the Germans came they could be shot as *francs-tireurs*.

Brampton listened closely, and when the villagers returned to their houses he said, 'Your French is very good, Forbes.'

'Aye, me sister taught me. She needs it for menus, and recipes, doesn't she, and her . . . Well, she just needs it. Grace Manton taught her. She's almost fluent.'

As the men settled down for the night Auberon sat outside the officers' billet in the local chateau having a last cigarette and watching the flashes from the guns, and listening to the distant thumps. He thought of all the secrets he and Ver had discussed in the kitchen at Easterleigh, and ran his hand over his face. It had never occurred to him that kitchen staff would understand French. Presumably Mrs Moore had knowledge of the language too, as she had also been inherited from Miss Manton.

He leaned forward, his elbows on his knees, looking out at the trees in the distance. What colossal arrogance to assume that those downstairs, and miners and soldiers, knew nothing. He ran his hand through his hair. Had Evie fed Jack news of Auberon's response to potential strikes? Had she told of their father's behaviour? Was it she who had learned from Roger about the intended purchase of the Froggett houses? He started laughing now, softly. What a bloody amazing girl.

They marched a further five miles the next day into Belgium, towards the sound of artillery fire, leaving the trenches unused. It was 23rd August and they stopped in a village for a break. The villagers brought out bread and oil, with tomatoes. The town ahead was Mons, the mayor told Jack. It meant nothing to him. The men thanked the villagers and Jack sprinkled salt on the oil, squinting against the sun. Had there ever been such a wonderful summer? The fields were full of butterflies and heavy with wild flowers, scabious, cow parsley and poppies, such a profusion of poppies. Whatever was to come, it didn't half knock working at the coalface into a cocked hat.

He dug in his battledress pocket for the stub of a pencil he carried and wrote a quick note to Evie, telling her that he'd dobbed her in: Auberon knew that she spoke French. He told her that he loved her and to give his love to Tim, Mam and Da, and Millie, of course. He crammed it back into his pocket as Brampton approached. 'Tell the men to prepare for action, Sergeant.'

There it was, straight out of the blue. Jack stared again at the butterflies flitting from flower to flower, weaving in between the long sun-baked grass, at the new green growth showing amongst the stubble of the more distant cornfields. He sprang to his feet. 'Yes sir.' His salute was smart.

They deployed immediately, marching from the village towards the heavy guns which were firing rapidly now. German shells were landing half a mile in front and they kept moving towards them.

'Steady,' called Lieutenant Brampton, taking the lead. Ahead Captain Williams led the 4th Battalion, sitting astride his horse as though he was taking a stroll in Hyde Park. Lieutenant Brampton walked. He wouldn't bring Prancer, Jack had heard, in case he was hurt, but he'd been taken anyway. The talk was the daft beggar was trying to find him.

They passed a private leading a pack mule laden with ammunition. Two minutes later a shell landed. The mule and the man were gone. The blast caused them to stagger and duck. Shrapnel spattered. 'Steady,' roared Jack and Brampton together. Martin, marching at Simon's shoulder, called, 'By, lad, we could do with more than this beggar of a cap. A saucepan would be a grand idea.' He was humming, just like he used to in the cage.

Jack grunted. 'One day they'll think of something better, probably when the whole bloody thing is over.'

The incoming shells were slower than those of the British artillery, which was equipped for rapid firing. They were trotting now, their packs banging against their backs, until they flung themselves into the shallow trenches that fed into those of the 5th Battalion's. 'Took your bleedin' time,' a private said, ducking as more shells went over. Somewhere a church bell was ringing.

Jack and his platoon prepared to fire, lying across the front of their trench, elbows propping them up, rifle butts on shoulders. 'Hold your fire,' came the order. They held as the first patrol of German cavalry they had ever seen charged out of the wood to the left of them towards the line. For a moment it seemed like a storybook come to life, unreal, but then fear drenched Jack like nothing he had ever known, his mouth dried, his fingers froze. Closer they came. Closer. 'Fire,' Brampton screamed and now Jack was pressing the trigger.

These were men he was firing at. Living breathing men, and horses, but they were charging him and his marras. He pulled the trigger again, felt the recoil. Again and again he fired and wondered how he could live with the guilt of killing, but by the end of an hour that guilt was gone. It was survival that mattered. All day they fought, their barrels red-hot, as the Germans came across in waves only to be repulsed.

The battalion had been trained in rapid rifle fire and the rifles sounded more like machine guns. There was smoke, the sound of trains roaring through the air which were in reality shells. There were the screams, the neighs of horses. A British shell landed on a charging line of Hun cavalry. Carnage ensued. The cavalry gave way now to infantry who were approaching across the open ground only to be mown down, but there were so many, far too many.

Brampton came along the trench, panic writ large

on his face, his hands shaking. He ran crouching towards Jack. 'Hold the line, I'm going for help, Sergeant,' he yelled.

Jack turned from his firing position to block his path. 'No you're not, sir. You can send someone else, but you mustn't leave the line.' He could smell the terror of the man, almost taste it. It was contagious. If he ran, some of the men would run. Brampton hesitated, a shell crashed to the rear, a rifle shot zipped past their heads. 'Get down, you silly beggars,' shouted Martin, lying on his side, reloading before flinging himself back on to his belly again, and firing, firing, firing, and humming.

Brampton still hesitated, as pale as a ghost. He tried to sidestep Jack. 'Please sir. No,' Jack said firmly. For a moment neither man moved, and then Brampton nodded, his eyes on Jack. 'Thank you, Sergeant, you're quite right.' He ran back, crouching low, calling encouragement to the men. 'Hold firm. C Company will hold until we are told otherwise.'

They waited for orders and still the firing continued, still the mules arrived with ammunition, still the shelling continued, and the screaming of the injured, men and beasts. 'All well, Sergeant?' Brampton asked as he doubled over checking the line, slowly this time. He turned at a cry. 'Stretcher-bearer here,' he called. Charlie, Bernie's cousin, was hit.

'Everything's bloody marvellous, sir,' Martin panted, grinning at Jack, his face smudged with sweat and dirt.

All day the call went out for stretcher-bearers. All day they held the line and those that were pitmen stayed calm because they were used to living with injury and death, and this in turn helped others. With the evening the order came, at last, for them to retire. 'Overwhelming forces but we've diverted some attention from the French, which was the aim,' Brampton murmured to Jack as they slipped out of the trench after dusk had fallen, their legs like shaking dead weights.

Jack led one faction while Martin held the Germans in a rearguard action. In their turn, Jack's men set up their position and gave covering fire while Martin's unit leapfrogged it, running at a crouch, their faces dirty and exhausted. Again and again they did it, leapfrogging, running and then holding the Germans. They stumbled over the dead, and dragged along a wounded private until they reached the road and heaved him into a London taxi that raced off. At last the Germans faded as the British artillery roared and smashed and held them. Jack's platoon rallied in the village where they had eaten bread and oil and tomatoes a lifetime ago, shaking themselves down as though they were dogs, and now there were refugees passing them, streaming west, mingling with the soldiers while Jack hunted for Martin.

He couldn't see him. He chased from man to man. 'Where's your corporal? Where the hell is your corporal?' He gripped one man. It was Bernie. 'Where's the daft beggar?'

Bernie looked at the ground, his shoulders slumped. 'Shell took his head, Jack. There were two others killed. It was bedlam. Nothing we could do.'

'Don't be so bloody daft, now's not the time. Where's the bugger?' Jack looked around, searching for Martin. Bernie grabbed his tunic. 'He's dead, man. He's bloody dead.'

He wouldn't be dead. He couldn't be. They were marras. He ran from group to group, until Simon found him near the barn going from man to man. He held him while he struggled. 'He's gone, Jack.'

Jack wrenched free and started to run back to the crashing guns, to the frontline, skirting around the barn, heading off down the cobbled street alongside which men were sitting, hunched over Woodbines, or asleep, just for a moment, as total exhaustion took hold. Simon was hot on his heels, so close but he couldn't stop because Martin was out there. He swerved to get to the field, tucking in behind a broken cart, but then he was brought down by a thump on his back. He'd been charged, damn well charged by someone, but he had to get to Martin.

It was Simon who had charged and now he grabbed Jack's legs as he tried to scramble to his feet. The spokes of the cartwheel were broken. Some bugger should mend them. He lifted his fist to beat Simon from him, but Brampton's voice ground out from behind him. 'Enough, Sergeant. Get back to the men, Simon.' Brampton grabbed Jack, who was

444

pulling away. 'Stand,' he hissed. 'Stand, man. You have to leave your corporal, we have witnesses to his death. He'll be buried.'

'But not by me and I'm his marra,' Jack shouted, struggling free, only to be grabbed again. 'I gave him the order. I could have given it to someone else.'

Brampton had his shoulders now in a hard grip, forcing Jack to face him. Brampton was saying, his voice almost drowned by the rushing in Jack's head, 'You did your duty. He did his. You must come with me now.' Jack hit him then, on the jaw, so hard that the shock shuddered up his arm and into his shoulder.

Still Brampton did not alter his grip, though his lip split and his eye almost instantly swelled. 'You must come with me now, Sergeant.'

'Yes, so you can have me shot.' His knuckles ached, the wind was blowing and Martin was out there, on his own.

'No, not to have you shot, but so that you can rest like your men. No one saw you strike me. You made a mistake just as I did earlier. It's what we do until we learn, and then we make some more. Now we're going to move on, we have to.' It seemed as though everything had gone silent. There was no gunfire, no birds, no clatter of horses. 'Now, Jack. Now we move on.'

Jack knew he was talking of more than soldiering, knew from the intensity of his eyes, from the way he brought his head so close. But he was right. It had to be over, because he couldn't have the hell of this hate towards Brampton inside him as well as the hell of war all around, but the hate was such a part of him and he didn't know if he could let it go.

Around them shells were thumping, men were marching, scuffing their feet as they retreated. In the distance slag heaps reminded him of home, but his marra was dead. Quite dead. He nodded at Brampton. 'Yes, sir. Thank you, sir, but who'll watch me back? You see, I didn't watch his. I'm his marra and I didn't.'

He shrugged free and struggled towards his men, feeling as though each step required too much effort. Brampton walked a pace behind. 'We'll all watch one another's backs for that's what soldiers do, and sometimes even that's not enough. It's not your fault and it won't be the last time, damn it to hell.'

That evening there was a scratch roll call held in the village. So this was war, Jack thought, as he called out the names of the men in his platoon and too few answered. He could almost hear Martin saying, 'Like the bloody pit, eh. It's a home from home, lad.' He could hear his laugh, here in his head, where it would always stay. Aye, man, just like the bloody pit. Blood on the coal, eh?

He reported the figures to Lieutenant Brampton. 'Very good, Sergeant. Lead the men off. We have a long way to go.'

*

446

Auberon stepped back and watched the company march away. He stood straighter. He moved his jaw. He had been hit by a better man than his father would ever be, and he had stood his ground.

Chapter Twenty-One

The Easterleigh Home Farm harvest was finished as August became September, the plums picked and the greengages bottled and in the preserve pantry. It had been a matter of joining forces with Mrs Green to complete the task, but it had been enjoyable. As September advanced the fateful letters in buff envelopes began to arrive from the Front, because only dead officers were deserving of telegrams. The postmen took to pushing the letters through letter boxes, if available, as the constant tears of the recipients took their toll. Evie dragged her bicycle from the bothy and set out for Martin's uncle and mother.

She arrived, leaning her bike against the cottage wall, and knocked on the front door, not going through the backyard as normal. Martin's uncle answered and Evie stayed outside to talk to him. She didn't want to go in and make the family feel they had to gather their strength, exhausted as they were. 'I have a meeting about the hospital with Lady Veronica at the Hall, but I needed to come.'

Martin's uncle said, 'Well, pet, if the Germans hadn't got him, the pit probably would have. Poor Jack though, he's lost his marra but perhaps we pit people are better placed than most to bear it, we're so used to . . .' His voice broke, he wiped his hand over his face, and his smile was weary as he closed the door.

What an appalling epitaph, she thought, as she pedalled back, making herself concentrate on the meeting ahead. She'd learned within days of their return from Newcastle that work and concentration were the answer, as Mrs Moore had said long ago. After the retreat from Mons, Liège and Namur had fallen. Jack's platoon had been further depleted but he, Simon, Bernie and James still lived.

Evie watched as the grouse flew free across the fields. No shooting parties this year, not here anyway. She pedalled hard, sliding in and out of the ruts. The honeysuckle crawled over the walls. Were they crawling towards the Germans now? Was Simon safe? She took a hand from the handlebars and patted the photo in her pocket. It had never reached its frame because she needed it with her, night and day.

She made herself see the pigeons pecking at the wheat that had fallen from the stalks, and then the sheep still as statues on the low slopes of the Stunted Tree. She turned into the Hall drive. The leaves in the arboretum had not yet begun to turn, though some were falling. Perhaps because of the hot dry summer? She'd ask . . . No, she wouldn't, Simon had gone.

She padlocked her bicycle and ran along the back path, round the storeroom and alongside the walled garden, into the yard. Len and Stuart, the chauffeurs, were in London or Leeds with Bastard Brampton who was busy with his steel and brickworks, leaving Mr Davies to run the pits, all of which were working to full capacity. So the greedy grubber and others like him were doing very well, thank you. But it didn't matter where the man was, as long as he wasn't here.

She tore down the steps, snatching off her hat and shawl, throwing them on to the bootbox in the bell corridor. Only Lady Veronica's bell rang now, and that seldom. She more often came down and spoke to them.

Evie spun into the kitchen. Mrs Moore had prepared tea and Mrs Green, Mr Harvey and Annie were already tucking into a sponge cake, though the choice wasn't as numerous as it had been because prices were already rising.

'We can't have waste,' Lady Veronica had said. 'We simply can't in times like these. There's a war on.' Her own food had become simple and differed little from downstairs. Good grief, soon she'd be taking her meals with them, and would probably be happier. What must it be like to be so alone? If it weren't for the hospital plans would she have hoyed off to London to help the war effort, or to dance at the Ritz like Lady Esther? Evie and Mrs Moore felt not.

The clock read four and here was Lady Veronica, hurrying down the passage, her bruises gone. 'She's coming,' Evie warned, pouring tea for herself and Lady Veronica, carrying her own to a free stool next to Mrs Moore. They had put out the china cups, but enamel mugs would have been quicker. There were pencils on the table for note-taking. Each had their own notebook.

Lady Veronica knocked as she always did, and should. Mrs Moore invited her in. She took her place at the head of the table, a notepad and pen in her hand. 'I have heard today that Easterleigh Hall has been approved as an auxiliary hospital and I have the recommendations from the board. I want to outline some thoughts, and discuss with you how we are going to apply their recommendations,' she told them.

She described the plans for an officers' hospital and convalescent home. Dr Nicholls had been transformed into a military doctor. Evie wondered if there had been a magic wand involved, because Nicholls was a portly gentleman with not a militaristic bone in his body. She kept the query to herself. She began to make notes as the others debated using the ballroom as the main ward. Lady Veronica chewed her pen. 'How many beds will it take?'

Mrs Green thought thirty. Should they or shouldn't they keep the billiard room as it was, Mr Harvey wondered, a recreation for convalescent patients? Mrs Green wondered if the bedrooms could be utilised, leaving just three – one for Lady Veronica, one for her husband during his leave, and one for

Mr Auberon. It was agreed. Mr Harvey asked how many beds Lord Brampton had ordered. Lady Veronica said, 'He put in a general request, it's up to us to come up with the final figures.'

Only Evie remained silent, listening intently, waiting, waiting.

At last it had been decided that the billiard room should remain as it would be good for the officers' morale, the dining room should remain as the dining room, and the two drawing rooms would become the Officers' Mess, the Orangery a rehabilitation and games room. The smoking room would convert into Lady Veronica's drawing room, the library would be the drawing room for the nurses, doctors, and VADs, though they could overflow into the servants' hall and storerooms in the basement which would be made homely. More bathrooms were to be added, and sink rooms for the bedpans and assorted nursing procedures.

How delicately put, Evie thought.

Lady Veronica continued, 'The kitchen remains the kitchen. All the houses on the estate should be utilised as staff accommodation. Now that brings me to staff.' She looked expectantly at Evie, who was doodling in her notebook.

Carefully Evie placed her pencil down, looking around the kitchen, gaining strength from its familiarity. She knew most of what there was to know about managing a kitchen and she could work anywhere now, and in a few moments, she might have to.

Collecting her thoughts she spoke firmly, her eyes on Lady Veronica only. 'I am not prepared to recruit any of the villagers to work at a hospital that caters only for officers.'

She saw the shock, but didn't falter. 'If we must segregate the ranks, then so be it, but I'm sure that Sylvia Pankhurst, if she was here, would stipulate that we catered for all injured. I know that you are repeating the recommendations of the board, Your Ladyship, but I suggest that we have the right to make our own decisions.'

Mr Harvey looked fit to explode, Mrs Green was almost crying with mortification, Mrs Moore was smiling slightly and Annie just looked from one to another.

Lady Veronica broke away from Evie's stare and made notes on her pad, then looked up. 'Absolutely right.' Her smile was magnificent. 'So, let's rearrange the rooms, shall we, but perhaps we'll need more tea, Evie, and next time, let's have it in enamel mugs, shall we?'

Yet again Mr Harvey looked dangerously close to explosion, and Mrs Green as though she needed to lie in a darkened room.

The next morning Evie cycled back to Easton, knocking on doors, explaining the problem, reassuring the villagers that Lord and Lady Brampton were busy with their other concerns and had left the running of the hospital completely in their daughter's hands, at which point the volunteers came thick and fast. She collected names of wives and daughters, and retired fathers and uncles, both for work around the estate and in a nursing or housekeeping capacity, as there would be a mountain of cleaning and laundry. She explained that rotas would be drawn up and Lady Veronica's trap would be brought into use for those who didn't have bicycles. 'Tinker's contribution to the war effort,' she smiled.

She ended up at the vicarage, where Grace and Edward were heaving two valises into the trap. 'Thank you for the message, Grace. I'm sorry you're going, but glad too, if you know what I mean. It's what you want.'

'Yes, it is. I have my Home Nursing and Red Cross Certificates and am now a VAD. I need to be doing something to help, but I'm scared to death.'

Edward had his arm around his sister. 'The men will be lucky to have her. I'll fetch your shawl, Grace.' He hurried inside. Grace came to Evie and hugged her, saying quietly, 'I need to be near him. I need to know I can reach him if he is hurt and that I can bring him home safely to his family, and Simon to you, if need be. Poor Martin, poor all of them, Jack will be suffering at the loss of his marra. It's not going to be a quick war, though we will probably win. But in the doing it will break all our hearts.'

Evie's last call was to her mam. She helped her and Millie to hang out washing, while Mam agreed to help inasmuch as her duties as a wife and grand-mother allowed. It was the same answer that Evie had received from many of the women. 'We need a nursery for the children, someone to look after them while you all work. I'll sort it out,' Evie said, pegging up a sheet Millie handed her. There was a decent breeze. Millie was reluctant to join the growing bank of helpers. 'The Hall has bad memories for me,' she complained, crossing her arms and looking petulant.

Evie ignored her longing to slap Millie, so normal was it. 'Perhaps you'd like to help in the nursery, then you could have Tim with you.'

Tim was playing with a small wooden train that her da had made him, sitting on the path and making choo-choo noises. Her mother was pegging up Da's trousers. Millie snapped, 'I'm a trained cook, so the kitchen's where I'll be if I'm anywhere.'

Evie sighed, trained my Aunt Fanny, it was the extra food she was after, and the thought of having Millie back gave her a headache. But of course she could be shifted elsewhere once she arrived, if she arrived.

That afternoon the Home Nursing course and Red Cross First Aid course began, and Evie smothered a grin as Dr Nicholls brought the newly arrived Matron to visit the group, which included two aristocratic neighbours of Lady Veronica's as well as a bevy of servants and villagers. Matron said, her bosom as large as a shelf, 'I only want people who will work, not people to turn up at the end of the day to soothe a few brows and hold a few hands. You will be dealing with disgusting dressings, bedpans full of urine and excrement, men who swear and groan and smell and perhaps have maggots in their wounds. If you are not prepared for that, do not remain, do not return.'

Lady Wendover returned for the next session, along with all the servants and villagers. The beds began to arrive, and workmen banged from morning to night. Phone calls came from Lady Brampton with a long list of produce requirements for their London home which Stan, the ancient head gardener, flung into hampers and delivered to the station, cursing at the extravagance.

By the end of September all those who had taken the courses had received their certificates. They now knew that of the 90,000 men who landed in France, one in every six had become casualties and the army ranks were dreadfully depleted, and the hospitals dreadfully full. According to a letter received from Grace it was becoming clear to the soldiers, and the nurses and doctors, that the technical development of modern weaponry had rendered the old methods of war obsolete, but had that knowledge reached the generals? At Easterleigh Hall the pace of preparation increased and sleep became a luxury. The staff also received leaflets with instructions for cooking invalid food.

'Pap, just pap, bonny lass,' Mrs Moore said, slamming about with pans and sieves. 'They need fresh fruit and vegetables.'

Evie agreed, adding, 'We're not overcooking things either, because as you said we might just as well fling the goodness down the drain. We'll just cook lightly. Keep the skin on potatoes, that sort of thing, as we did with Lady Margaret. We'll need two stockpots, we're going to be a factory down here and we need to feed them when they want feeding, not when the army says they must eat.'

'You're right, Evie lass, they're our soldiers, that they are, and they will have the best. We just need someone to tell her Ladyship and for her to tell Matron.'

Mrs Moore had a renewed vigour, and though her rheumatics were sliding into a bad phase there was a sparkle about her that had been gone for too long.

'You can run up those stairs now and do just that, then,' Evie said, preparing a game pie. The grouse and pheasant had been bred and the gamekeeper had insisted they must be shot and he would breed more for next year. They'd need them. There were a great many birds hanging in the game pantry, of which a few had been sent to the Bramptons, but not as many as ordered. Lord Brampton was too busy to shoot, too busy setting up an armaments factory, according to Lady Veronica.

'You cheeky young madam, as if I'm going to run up those stairs indeed.' Mrs Moore was laughing as she disappeared into the pantry, then tutting at the stock-taking that needed to be done. 'We need our staff replenishing yesterday, along with the produce, my girl. You can tell her that too.'

'Shouldn't Mr Harvey?' Evie had rolled her sleeves up to her elbows and was sprinkling flour on to the pastry. She hadn't time to go upstairs and besides, the kitchen staff stayed below stairs, as Mr Harvey had said, insisting that the rules continued to be obeyed.

'He's with Mrs Green sorting out the bedrooms, or trying to get the workmen to sort them out anyway. Stop shilly-shallying, silly lass.'

'I could say the same for you, hiding in the big pantry, for heaven's sake, bossing me around as though it was what you were born to do.' Evie rolled out the pastry and carried it on the marble board to the cold cupboard just down the passageway. She dusted off her hands and pulled a face at Mrs Moore as she entered the kitchen. Mrs Moore only laughed, slapping her bum, before Evie hurried past the bootbox, which was empty. Everyone now cleaned their own footwear, even Lady Veronica.

Evie took the back stairs two at a time. Lady Veronica would be in the ballroom with Dr Nicholls, or so she had told them yesterday over tea in the kitchen, at which all the upper servants gathered regularly now since there was so much to discuss, even Mr Harvey. Quite what he felt about relinquishing his head-of-the-table role to a mere slip of a girl, even if she was a lady, was something Evie longed to know.

As she entered the ballroom she was struck by the change. It was to be the other ranks' quarters: bed after bed were waiting in rows, with small bedside tables on the left of each, and screens which would ensure privacy when it was needed. There were central tables for recreation. A wooden partition had been erected halfway along to divide those who were extremely ill from those who were in recovery.

Gone was the glory in more ways than one – the chandeliers had been taken down because of the danger of dust falling into wounds. Men hurried everywhere. Hammering made it necessary to shout. Did Simon shout over the shells? Evie shut her mind. Concentrate.

The bedrooms and dressing rooms and whatever other space could be found were being refashioned into individual officers' accommodation. The nurses and VADs would double up in the servants' quarters – which were emptier by the day as they left for towns, or the war – and wherever else room could be found.

In the ballroom Lady Veronica and Dr Nicholls were poring over a large sheet of paper on which four chunks of builders' wood stood, holding it down at the corners. Lady Veronica looked up at Evie's approach, startled, then alarmed. 'Is all well, Evie?' Then she turned to Dr Nicholls. 'This is Evie Forbes, my . . .' She paused. 'My friend who creates miracles in the kitchen with Mrs Moore, and will be the power-house of our patients' recovery.'

Dr Mason Nicholls smiled at Evie, his uniform stretched across his belly, his buttons looking for all the world as though they were about to fire off in all directions. A sight too many pies in the beggar's gut, Evie thought; he'd be a useful weapon on the front line. 'Hello Evie, how is your mother, and what about your father now?'

'Grand, Dr Nicholls. You look a picture in the uniform. You be careful or all the ladies in the village will be after you.'

He roared with laughter. They were all shouting above the builders' noise. There was dust in the air, and sawdust on the dust sheets, and motes danced in the sun as it streamed through the windows which would need drapes, surely? 'Mrs Nicholls would certainly have something to say about that. I was just explaining to Lady Veronica that we won't be receiving cases straight from the battlefield, but we will be having men suffering from the after-effects of gas gangrene as well as other wounds. It's new to us. There is anaerobic bacteria in the Belgian soil, it's mainly agricultural after all, and we're seeing it infect the simplest of wounds, and all that can be done is amputate. Sometimes it works, sometimes it doesn't.'

Evie wouldn't think of anything other than the men hammering, and the man behind Lady Veronica carrying in some two-by-four planks of wood. Lady Veronica was checking her lists. 'So we will be receiving amputees, lots of 'em,' the doctor said.

'We'll win but it will break our hearts in the doing of it,' Evie murmured, thinking of Grace. The other two just looked at her. 'Indeed,' said Dr Nicholls, all laughter gone and his face a picture of sadness.

Lady Veronica swallowed, looked out of the windows and after a moment turned back to Evie. 'You needed to speak to me?'

'Mrs Moore wants you to know that the kitchen will be supplying anything and everything, but never the pap described in the leaflets we were sent. Instead the food will be lightly cooked, the vegetables al dente, the fruit as plentiful as possible and as the goodness is in the skin no peeling will be done, even of carrots. We will be on call twenty-four hours a day, because the sickest of men will know when they want to eat, the army will not. In fact, much as we did with Lady Margaret, if you remember.'

Dr Nicholls was grinning. 'I rather think I can detect an Evie Forbes directive in there somewhere. But yes, I agree completely. I will instruct Matron.'

Evie left them, wanting very much to be a fly on the wall when anyone tried to instruct Matron in anything.

By November the opposing armies had ground to a halt, each in entrenched positions. Edward received a letter from a friend and told Evie's da, who told her, that it was felt this situation would vary very little with each subsequent month that passed. Indeed, all that altered were the soldiers because each day young men queued outside recruitment offices to replenish the dying platoons. 'These in their turn will die, won't they,' Mrs Moore said to Evie.

In late November the first of the wounded arrived at Easterleigh Hall. Millie had decided to take the Red Cross course and help upstairs, to the kitchen's utter relief. Judging from the regular nurses who sat in the servants' hall or cluttered up the kitchen on that first day, her decision was not received with total joy, for she was worse than useless. Lady Veronica did not achieve a much better report because she didn't know how to sweep the floor properly or boil up the facecloths, or wash the sick bowls before sterilising them, she explained in the kitchen after her shift.

'I'm a complete fool, though I manage to produce sparkling bedpans,' she sighed. 'They taught that on the course. How absurd, and appalling that I know so little.'

The next day Evie led Lady Veronica into the scullery and tied a hessian apron around her waist. Lady Veronica looked over her shoulder and laughed. 'A charming bow would be nice.'

Evie grinned. 'You get what you're given in our neck of the woods, Cinderella.'

She handed Lady Veronica a broom, took one herself and demonstrated how to brush without drenching the world in dust. She then led her to the zinc-lined sinks, filled them, placed cloths and scourers into her hands and soda crystals in the water, and insisted she wash pots properly. Annie and Mrs Moore stood by the range, their hands over their mouths until their laughter became too loud, at which point Evie ejected them, while Lady Veronica stared at the ruin of her hands, then plunged them yet again into the hot water, shouting over the clatter at Evie.

'I must learn to cook as well. They are setting up little kitchens so that the men can make themselves coddled eggs if they feel the need, and things like that. Or if they can't then the nurses will.'

She came down again the next morning, and while Millie was upstairs reading to a sergeant in the Fusiliers who had been shot in the face and whose eyes were in jeopardy, Evie taught her how to make cocoa, and then a roux.

'I'm a complete fool,' Lady Veronica repeated. She poured in milk, stirring continuously.

'No, you're a high-born woman with a social conscience. I don't see anything foolish in that.' Evie looked at the clock. 'But I need you out of the way now, because we have a million lunches to prepare. Go and find someone to inflict your new-found skills upon.' Mrs Moore was studying the lunch plan, running her finger down the page. Annie was preparing the table. The new scullery maids were managing very well with no old hands; they had come up from the village, fresh from school. The servants' hall was filling with staff, nurses and orderlies, with Mr Harvey back in his place at the head of the table.

Out in the corridor a bell rang, the front hall bell. A visitor? Normally the orderly on the desk handled these. Archie left to answer it. 'I want to finish this,' Lady Veronica protested. Evie took over. 'You'd better go. What would the neighbours think?' The two of them laughed. Lady Veronica hurried to the kitchen door.

'Apron,' Mrs Moore called. Lady Veronica pulled it off and threw it on to a stool. 'Good shot,' Evie called. They fell silent. Shot? No. Lady Veronica rushed out, pinning up strands of hair that had escaped.

She was only gone ten minutes before she reappeared but this time with Lady Margaret, looking thin, worn and old.

There was utter silence. Evie, Annie, and Maud, Barbara and Sheila, the three new scullery maids, exchanged looks. Mrs Moore just stared at the young woman, then at Lady Veronica.

'Lady Margaret is here to help,' Lady Veronica said, carefully looking at no one, her voice strained. 'I thought I'd make a cup of tea for her, if that's all right with you?' She directed her question at Mrs Moore and then Evie. Both nodded.

Lady Margaret was settling herself on a stool where she had sat all those months ago, before she had burned the stables. Had everyone forgotten that, Evie wondered. For pity's sake, she could have killed people, let alone the horses. Lady Margaret was staring at Lady Veronica as she put the simmering kettle on to the hotter range plate. '*You're* doing that?' She sounded outraged.

Lady Veronica had moved to the dresser and was collecting enamel mugs. As she returned, she gave Evie and Mrs Moore a quick grin. 'Yes, I am. There's a war on and I need to increase my skills so Evie and Mrs Moore are teaching me. Aren't they wonderful? There's so much I don't know, it's absurd. I think we could all do with some tea, don't you?' If Evie lived to be a hundred she would never forget the amazement on Lady Margaret's horse-face, swiftly followed by further outrage.

Lady Veronica mashed the tea in the pot and poured for them all. She pushed a mug to Lady Margaret, who picked it up as though it was something she had found under her shoe, and then replaced it. 'Perhaps you'd like some milk in your tea, Margaret?' Lady Veronica said firmly. 'We don't always have time for the niceties, so we use what is to hand. If you wish to stay here and help you must accommodate the changes.'

There, it was said. Everyone else in the kitchen found something fascinating to look at, staring at it as though they had found the mystery of the universe. Lady Veronica added milk to her tea. 'Come on everyone, let's sit down and catch up on the day.'

Yet again Lady Margaret's outrage rose a notch

as they did so, each taking a stool. Evie said, 'I will take over the roux, Lady Veronica. We're having mullet with a fairly bland sauce.'

Mrs Moore read out the menu, and Annie and Maud talked quietly together. Lady Margaret finally poured a little milk into her mug and drank it, examining the lip carefully before she did so. Clearly the interloper would welcome a steriliser in the kitchen, as well as those provided for the nursing staff.

At the end of each day Evie, in lieu of Mrs Moore who was resting her eyes in her room, had been joining Matron, Lady Veronica, Mr Harvey, Mrs Green and Dr Nicholls in the front hall, sitting around a small table while they discussed the patients' progress and needs. Evie would bring them up to date on availability of food and proposed menus. Special diets were also discussed, and this evening, a few days after Lady Margaret had arrived, she suggested that they make a nominal charge for the cakes they supplied for the patients' visitors, who congregated in the newly designated tea room, formerly an anteroom leading off the hall. 'The money could be put to good use buying books and games for the patients, and even the staff,' Evie finished.

Dr Nicholls smiled at her. 'Why not?'

Matron shrugged. 'Nothing to do with me. What about Mr Harvey, Mrs Green and Lady Veronica?'

Evie checked with them, but they were already

nodding, and making a note in their little books. Maud had wonderful handwriting and she could write the notices of charges that could be pinned on the tea-room door and placed on the table. Evie then asked if Lady Margaret could manage the money on top of pouring tea, for it was she who had volunteered to run the tea room. 'If she can then it will permanently release Lady Wendover to help in the wards, which is where she'd like to stay. After all, she did do the course with us.' Everyone agreed.

'What an asset she is,' Matron declared. 'A woman who is not afraid of rolling up her sleeves, just like you, my dear.' She smiled at Lady Veronica.

'I roll up my sleeves and have for years,' Evie muttered.

'And you have lovely arms, too, my dear,' Matron said, laughing.

They discussed the new intake of men. There were nine amputees who had arrived in ambulances. There were several patients wounded by shells and progressing well. Three had gone home on leave. 'In order to become fit enough to return to the charnel house in due course,' Dr Nicholls said, which was his usual response. Christmas was coming and there was no festive cheer in their hearts but always cheer on their faces.

Archie appeared then, from the tea room, stooping to whisper in Lady Veronica's ear. She looked startled and then furious. 'Excuse me, I'm needed. Evie, perhaps you'd come too? Archie, would you hurry and find the two visiting relatives who have received white feathers while I discuss the matter with Lady Margaret. Try and find them before they reach the patient and urge discretion on them. We can't have any loss of trust or confidence.'

Lady Veronica rose, and Evie too. The others stared from one to another, and then at the tea room. 'Please,' Lady Veronica said, 'carry on. I don't want this to become obvious.'

To Evie, as they walked steadily but unhurriedly, she said, her voice cold and grim, 'Perhaps you would take Lady Margaret downstairs, by the ears if you like, and I'll talk to the visitors.'

In the tea room several families were standing at the refreshment table, as though struck by lightning. Three young men stared at white feathers they had clearly just been handed by Lady Margaret. Evie marched round the back of the table and firmly took her by the elbow. Lady Margaret resisted. Lady Veronica addressed the young men, who had dropped the feathers on to the table as though they were red-hot. 'I am so very sorry.'

Evie said quietly into Lady Margaret's ear, 'If you don't come with me, I will hit you, very hard.'

The woman strode with Evie through the hall to the green baize door at the back, every inch of her defiant. In the kitchen Evie shoved her on to a stool, hissing, 'How bloody dare you?' Maud came to the entrance of the scullery, a cloth in her hand, her mouth open.

'We've been told to by Christabel. She said white feathers are to be given to all men of military age out of uniform. This is our new cause. We will show that we are fit for the vote with our war work, and this.' Lady Margaret's face was pale but determined.

Annie had been knitting khaki head-warmers for the troops at the table while a white soup simmered for a young soldier. He had been unable to eat for the last two days but had suddenly fancied soup, like his mother made. Annie dropped several stitches.

Evie snapped, 'So, you want all the miners out of the pit, all the essential workers to be slaughtered on the front line, all those men convalescing and on leave to strut about in uniform. Do you intend to do everything you are told for the rest of your life, you silly lass? How on earth do you think you'll be fit to have a view on the government of this country if you follow rubbish like this? So just how do you propose that we run the country with no men?'

Lady Margaret stood up then, her face fierce, her voice savage. 'The women will run it, of course.'

'Wonderful, just wonderful. You get down the pit then because you know what to do, do you?' Evie was raging, hammering on the table with her fist. 'You don't even know how to boil a bloody kettle. God save us from vicious women like you. Look around you at people who run hospitals like this. They, and we, are the ones showing that we deserve the vote, and that we don't bully our way to it by dishing out bird feathers, you silly bloody woman.'

The door opened. Lady Veronica slipped in. 'The father and son were stopped before they reached the ward, and they'd rammed the feathers in their pockets anyway to dispose of later. The father is a pitman, the son works in armaments. You will never set foot here again, do you hear me, Margaret? How many chances do you need? You may sleep here tonight, and then I will take you in the trap to the station. Now, you will come with me to my room and stay there.'

Annie had been sitting as though frozen all this time, but now picked up the dropped stitches and continued knitting as though nothing had happened. 'Knit one, purl one,' she said as Lady Margaret left with Lady Veronica.

Bedtime came late in the hospital, and shifts were taken by the kitchen staff to provide twenty-four-hour cover for the men. It was Evie's shift this night and she was already weary, but Annie was on duty with her so that would help. The dining-room bell had rung twice already and an egg custard requested, and then bacon for a young lad who was dying. It was Tony, Timmie's marra, who had arrived three days ago with gas gangrene.

'Tony wants to smell it again. Not taste it, but smell it,' Nurse Brown told them as she collected his tray, the bacon crispy. 'He'll die tonight.'

As the evening progressed there were also the

usual nightmares from the patients, some screams, after which the lads needed tea. Until the small kitchens could be set up the kettle was always simmering in the kitchen. The VADs acted as waiters, thank the Lord.

Evie and Annie took the opportunity to drag out their knitting as the last VAD left, bearing a tray of tea for the nurses on duty upstairs. They settled themselves on stools and continued with the khaki head-warmers which were in demand. 'My brother says it's right cold in the trenches,' Annie sighed.

'I can't imagine what it's like to be that cold and damp, and to be shot at.' Evie knitted one, purled one. She wasn't a natural, but if it helped . . . Was young Tony dead yet? Was he with Timmie, were they galloping together on the Galloways?

Knit one, purl one.

Was Simon alive? Don't think.

Knit one, purl one.

Was Jack alive? Knit one, purl one.

Of course they were. She'd know if they weren't, surely. Knit one, purl one. Were they injured? Was there a new battle? Don't think. End of the row, turn. Were they in trenches? Were they cold? Wet? They never said in their letters, their precious letters which she kept beneath her pillow.

Were they alive? Knit one, purl one

The ball of wool fell to the floor and rolled under the table. She poked with her feet to bring it towards her. A bell rang. Annie ran out to see who could be summoning them before it stopped clanging. She returned, puzzled. 'It's Lady Veronica's bedroom. She usually comes down.'

Evie was off the stool, her knitting forgotten, and she took the back stairs two at a time.

What had happened? Lady Margaret was in the room. What had she done now? She tore along the landing, past the officers' rooms. It was amazing how many decently sized cubicles you could create out of one guest bedroom, and still they felt spacious.

She heard screams as she approached Lady Veronica's suite. They were high-pitched and female. An amputee officer on crutches appeared in his doorway, Lieutenant Harold Travers, who loved salmon. 'Is everything all right, Evie?'

'It's just a nightmare, don't worry, Harry. Back into bed with you. If you can't sleep let me know what you need. I'll produce a miracle when I've sorted out this little problem.'

He waited. 'Call me if you need me.'

A nurse was outside Lady Veronica's door, about to enter. Evie waved her away. 'Let me, I'll call if needed. Lady Veronica has already rung.'

She opened the door and went in. The curtains were undrawn and the moon was bright. She saw Lady Margaret crouching over Lady Veronica on the bed, screaming. They were struggling. Evie hurled herself across the room.

'Margaret. Margaret. Stop now.'

She reached for the woman, who swung round.

Something thumped into Evie's arm, then her hip. Margaret was like the patients in the midst of nightmares that took them somewhere no one could follow, fighting demons no one else could see, or hear.

Evie caught her arm, wrenched it up behind her back, up and up. 'Stop it, I said. Stop it.' Without releasing her arm she grabbed the woman's hair and forced her head back. Lady Margaret struggled for just a little longer and then stopped and so, too, did the noise.

After a moment Evie let her go and she slumped, half on to Lady Veronica who was crawling to the edge of the bed. Evie blessed the fact, yet again, that she had a fighter for a brother.

Lady Veronica half fell on to the floor, then recovered. She was in her nightgown, her hair in a plait, and she was panting as she reached for Lady Margaret, gathering her up in her arms. 'She's not in her right mind. Oh God, Evie, she seems demented. She woke thinking she was in prison, thinking they were coming to feed her. I went to her bed but it made it worse. She ran at me.' Veronica gestured from the spare bed to hers.

Evie sat on the bed, suddenly weak, suddenly feeling sick. Her arm was wet. She touched it. Yes, it was wet. Her hip hurt. That was wet. Her clothes were wet. She stared at her hand. Yes, wet. Lady Veronica put on the light. They both saw the blood, then the scissors where Margaret had dropped them, red-stained.

Lady Veronica fetched the nurse, who inspected the wounds. 'They'll need a stitch or two. What about her?' She checked Lady Margaret, who was now lying on her bed. Evie heard Harry call. 'Is there a problem? Do you need me?'

Evie called back, 'It's fine, Harry. But thank you. It's good knowing you're there.'

Lady Veronica carried a bowl from her bathroom, and bathed her cuts with a white towel. 'Mrs Green will have my guts for garters, Evie Forbes, using a towel like this,' she whispered, keeping half an eye on Lady Margaret as the nurse left to fetch Sister. She came, quietly, and efficiently administered a pain-killer, and stitched Evie's arm and hip carefully, because, she said, she still wanted the standard of cooking to be maintained. The women laughed softly, though Evie could still feel the pain. Lady Margaret was silent, as though at last asleep. 'I'll have to wash my clothes and I need a clean apron. I really object to that,' Evie said, her teeth chattering.

Lady Veronica smiled, but she was shaking too. 'I'm so sorry, Evie, it should have been me.'

'What? I don't think so. Matron would be even less impressed if you swept one-armed.'

Evie's mind was running at two levels. She was knitting khaki, knit one, purl one. She was talking to Lady Veronica. There was no space to worry about Simon, about Jack, about poor little Tony, and for these few moments she was at peace.

Sister checked and sedated Lady Margaret and

they agreed that she should be left to sleep, and then she made for the door. Lady Veronica said, 'Sister, would you ask Harry to keep himself available? All he could do is bash her over the head with his crutches, but he needs to feel useful.'

How they were all learning, Evie thought, as she shrugged off their concern and found her way to her room, smiling at Harry as she passed, explaining that Lady Margaret, who had been force-fed many times, had had a nightmare and had no knowledge of what she'd done. 'Just a few stitches,' she reassured him.

'Poor woman. I understand her.' His face was pale, his eyes too dark. He was the son of Sir Anthony Travers and had joined up from school. He had led a privileged existence, he had told her a few weeks ago as she checked that each man was happy with their luncheon. 'War came as a bit of a shock, not quite what I expected,' he had joked, but the laugh hadn't reached his eyes. He should have been asleep, but like many that was a distant memory for him.

She changed her uniform and was back on duty within ten minutes. There was a war on, this was nothing. The pain really struck in the early hours, and Annie insisted on dragging in an armchair from the servants' hall and pushing Evie into it. 'I'll wake you if I need you.'

'The chair's a good idea. We'll keep it here because there's no need for two on shift to stay awake.'

Lady Margaret would be nursed in Lady Veronica's

room, because she had fought her war for too long. It had broken her, but not for ever. Here, at Easterleigh Hall, she would recover. 'We'll keep the scissors in the sewing basket where they belong, shall we?' Dr Nicholls said as he met them outside the bedroom in the morning, his bag in his hand, his white coat on preparatory to entering to treat his patient.

Lady Veronica smiled but insisted, 'Please remove your coat. They wore white coats to force-feed.'

He did so immediately. 'Good point. Let's make notes on this. There must be many women suffering in the same way.'

Lunch was as busy as usual, but Mrs Moore, Annie and Evie had things down to a fine art, and now they had at least two other kitchen assistants from the village every day, so it was never frantic. Young Bert and Joseph from Hawton went rabbiting daily and there were still the grouse and pheasant, so they were becoming more self-sufficient. Stan the head gardener had agreed to pigs rooting around in *his* orchard, so that boded well for the spring, with all the piglets that had been born.

The clatter of pots and pans being washed after lunch was as loud as it always was, and Evie's stitches were pulling, so Mrs Moore shooed her out of the kitchen at two in the afternoon. 'We can't put up with martyrs down here, lass. Move yourself up those steps and get some fresh air. Be thinking about the Christmas menu while you're about it. We're going to need to produce a feast out of our reserves, I think. Stock is getting scarcer at the co-op with the panic buying, even though they're doing their best to order in for us.'

Evie walked out into the stable yard with its empty stalls. These would soon take more pigs as Lady Veronica felt that it was wasted space, and indeed it was. Perhaps they could have more in the rear stables? She strolled out to the drive, saw Harry using his crutches to manoeuvre himself down the front steps and joined him.

'Harry, how are you today? Did you enjoy the rabbit pie?'

'Great grub, Evie.' He was such a lovely lad, and at least he would not be returning to the Front. His parents were so relieved that they had brought flowers on their last visit for all the staff. These had lasted for many days in the front hall and gave it an air of elegance which was at odds with the hustle and bustle, somewhat calmed by the arrival of the orderlies who manned the front desk. 'You should have your muffler on,' Evie said, drawing her shawl tighter. 'Annie will be cross. She spent many hours and many swear words making it.'

Harry laughed, and then they turned at the sound of a bicycle crunching on the gravel. It was Arthur, the young telegraph boy whose family lived in Easton. Evie and Harry watched him. Crunch, crunch. Her heart seemed to beat in time with every turn of the bicycle wheels. Harry eased a hand from his crutch and gripped her arm. He said, 'Try not to worry until you have to.'

The boy skidded to a halt. 'Can you take this, missus?' The lads hated these telegrams, because they all had fathers or brothers or friends out at the Front. Evie said, 'Of course.' But she wanted to insist he took it away again. She read the name of the addressee. Harry saw it, sighed, and almost whispered, 'Would you like me to take it to her?'

'What, and carry it in your teeth?' They almost laughed. She looked at the cedar tree – so still, so strong. She entered the hallway, leaving Harry in the fresh air, which he would ruin by lighting his pipe, balancing on his crutches. Lucky boy, lucky mother and father, for there would be no such telegram for them now.

There was snow on the wind. Would it be a snowy Christmas? Think of that. The orderly saw the telegram and smiled sympathetically. Evie walked to the green baize door, opened it, and went down to the kitchen. Lady Veronica wasn't there. Evie checked the kettle. Yes, simmering as usual. She saw her knitting on the chair. Knit one, purl one. She made tea, poured it into a cup, not an enamel mug and added sugar, lots. She walked slowly to the door, and called down to the game pantry where she'd remembered Annie was teaching Lady Veronica to pluck disgustingly ripe grouse.

'Veronica, will you come here?' She'd never called her just Veronica before, but now the woman needed to know that she had a friend, a proper friend, and she needed to be warned in advance.

Veronica came into the kitchen, her face pale. She saw the cup and saucer. She knew, Evie could tell. She knew. 'Who, Auberon or Richard?' Evie made her sit. 'Let's see, shall we?'

It was Captain Williams, wounded in action. One leg and one arm amputated to avoid gas gangrene. He was in hospital in Le Touquet. 'You must go and fetch him back yourself,' Evie said. 'You really must. He needs you.'

Lady Veronica was rereading and rereading the telegram, her fingers shaking, her lips forming the words. She murmured, 'Of course I must.'

She packed immediately, and Evie's da, who was working in the gardens on his off shift, drove her in the trap to the station. As they disappeared down the drive Evie, standing by the front steps, thought of those words again. 'Yes, it will break our hearts,' she sighed, and gestured to Harry. 'If you don't come in we'll be treating you for pneumonia and Matron will put me on bedpan duty, and that might mean she cooks.'

He smiled, emptying his pipe on the grass while he rested on the crutches. 'A fate worse than death, for us,' he said. He tucked his pipe into his hospital blues and swung his way over. She told him of Captain Williams. 'That's his war over then,' he said with a satisfied smile.

Evie nodded. 'Indeed it is.'

She thought of Lady Veronica. As well as breaking hearts war could begin to heal them too, and this might be a case in point. She accompanied Harry inside and then arranged with the orderly for Captain Williams to be assigned the main bed in Lady Veronica's room. She had insisted on that before she left, tears in her eyes. 'He's my husband, where else should he go? Please free his room up for more patients, Evie.'

A letter arrived from Grace the next day. It was the second Evie had received from her.

Dearest Evie,

I can get no further than Le Touquet at the moment. The convoys come in and we rush to attend to them, and take down their particulars on slips of paper. My feet are swollen from rushing about. My dreams are full of maggots in wounds, of bedpans that I am emptying, of instruments I am sterilising in operating theatres. I hold kidney trays of instruments as the surgeons operate, or the triage nurses investigate. You know, Evie, these brave souls poke at wounds so terrible that no one would believe such horrors. I think I dream because I'm too busy to sort out the images while working. We VADs are called Very Artful Darlings by some, and Victim Always Dies by others. I have a friend, Lady Witherspoon. She had never washed a cup till she came here and is absolutely marvellous and flinches at nothing.

I have Captain Williams here. A telegram has gone and I have sent this with a friend so that it follows, hotfoot. He has lost an arm, and a leg; this bloody gas gangrene, but at least it's halted the beast and he'll live. He needs to come home, his sole thought is of Veronica. He talks of bruises, to her, not him. He talks in his sleep of her, and his recovery will be so much better at home. She must come for him. Tell her.

I send my love to you, dearest Evie. Write to me again. And no, before you ask, I have heard nothing of our friends, except that it's stalemate after the Marne battle. We know the casualty lists and so far they have not been amongst them. I miss Easton. I miss you, but I love my work. It makes me feel a valuable human being. We can never go back to being appendages, can we?

Your friend, Grace.

Evie folded the letter and placed it beneath her pillow, where she kept the letters from those she loved. Besides, Grace and Jack should lie together. She reread all her letters every night by the light of the oil lamp. She knew every one by heart. Simon's last one had told of his love for her.

'*The trees, Evie, were proper trees when we came. Now they are stumps, and the birds have gone. Such is war.*'

She peered through the window out to Fordington. Would they ever fetch sea coal again, all of them? Well, no, not all of them, for Martin, Tony and two

481

others of the marra group had gone, and Bernie. The pitmen's families had been allowed to keep on the cottages until they had found alternatives, at Mr Auberon's decree. Families whose pitmen had enlisted kept their houses, with his father's surprising agreement.

Things were changing, a few for the better. Yes, such is war.

Chapter Twenty-Two

Jack, Simon, James and another private staggered into the casualty clearing station carrying a youngster. 'Only sixteen, he is,' Jack told the VAD. She looked so young herself, so tired, and so blood-spattered. He surveyed his men with their muddied puttees, muddied boots, muddied hair and knew he looked the same, but at least the mud hid the boy's blood.

Tommy was dead, Jack had known that the moment after the shell hit the road, but they couldn't leave him there, by the side of the road, alone, especially not so close to Christmas, poor little bugger. He checked the other VADs quickly, but none were Grace. Where was she? Safe? God, he hoped so, but he knew many nurses were losing their lives.

The four men turned to leave, stepping over the walking wounded who were sitting or half lying on the ground, some smoking. There were grunts, groans, screams. There was the steady shouting of triage nurses and orderlies, and the barked orders from the doctors up to their elbows in blood. There was the stench. None of it was new. It was just how things were. Martin would have said, 'A home from bloody home, bonny lad.'

They rejoined Brampton's platoon and Jack marched the men in fours back to the line which had been their destination when the whiz-bangs came over; they were still coming. Jack skidded on the frosted cobbles. Tommy's parents would be told he suffered no pain, but what else could Brampton tell them? The truth? He screamed his life away while the lice crawled all over him? Perhaps not.

They were reinforcing the line at Givenchy, casualties were streaming back along the road towards the aid station and Newton, the new captain, was ahead with Brampton.

'Williams was a good bloke,' Jack said to Simon, who had grown quieter by the day and merely nodded. It was hard for the lad, he wasn't used to death like the pitmen, he wasn't used as they were to the darkness of the trenches, which were now being dug deeper and had the look of permanence. What a way to fight a bloody war. It was supposed to be cut and thrust by a proper army and get the hell out of it. Now it was cut and thrust and then entrench, attack, counter-attack, count your dead, bring in more lads who were more at home with a plough . . .

It was shift more sandbags overnight, stand up to your knees in mud, slip on your dead mates, freeze your ruddy bollocks off, itch with lice, the latrine a bucket rammed into a trench wall, food that might be, sometimes, brought up from the rear. Static it was, this war, and lucky if you moved forward or back even a few yards. Lucky if you lived. Lucky if the few yards didn't cost hundreds of lives, and thousands of limbs.

Jack looked at Simon. Aye, the lad was a gardener, used to creating life, to planting seeds, cutting vegetables and flowers, used to being in daylight, to loving Evie. Jack was marching alongside him now. He liked to do that with the weaker ones, but everyone was weak sometimes and he had to get Simon back home. He must. Evie. Lovely Evie and her friend Veronica. Would it have to be Lady Veronica now Williams was back?

The pace was lifting. They were closer, the noise was greater, the frost had been drowned by the mud and if he couldn't feel them twisting his ankles he'd not know the cobbles were there. Beside him Simon was laughing, just laughing and laughing, his unshaven face drawn and exhausted like everyone else's. 'What's up, Si?'

'It's just such a bloody joke, Jack. We plug up the lines. We hide in the trenches, we shoot them, they shoot us. What's it all about?'

The laughter stopped. Johnny from Derbyshire flung over his shoulder, 'Didn't you know, Si, We're here, because we're here, because we're here. Ours is not to reason why.' He waited, and then sang, with the whole platoon joining in, 'Ours is just to do or die.'

Jack grinned at Simon, who was laughing a proper laugh now. 'Answer enough for you, lad?'

'Aye, but I'd rather be like the captain, at home tucked up with the wife.' Simon hitched his rifle. 'On the other hand, it'd be a mite better to be home with all your bits attached. Evie said in her last letter that Lady Veronica came out for him, said Grace saw him at Le Touquet.' He patted his tunic pocket. Jack drew a deep breath. Grace. Lovely Grace, but then they heard the sound of more incoming shells and the platoon slid into the roadside ditch. Jack tasted mud, foul, evil-tasting, germ-laden mud. The water was icy.

'Damn it to hell,' Doug ground out. He was a recent recruit, a pitman who'd joined with his marra, Chris. He was a steady lad who'd helped them shift Tommy without being told. 'You get on to the front of the column, find Chris when this silly beggar's stopped wasting his ruddy shells,' Jack ordered him. 'A man needs to be with his marras.'

The shelling was subsiding. Men scrambled up the muddy sides and out of the ditch, the memory of the hot showers from last night washed away by the brackish icy water. They formed up and headed towards the crashing and screaming guns and the flashing lights, and towards the stench of blood, guts and mud.

Jack slid on the cobbles again. His rifle clanged against his water bottle. Ahead he saw Brampton doubling towards him, shouting, 'Sergeant, take over this ammunition.' He pointed to where it had been discarded in the road. The two ammunition carriers were being stretchered back, their mules dead. 'Yes, sir,' Jack yelled.

Doug and Simon lugged 1,000 rounds of machine-gun ammunition between them, while Jack, Johnny and the rest of the platoon carried their rifles for them, and distributed the remaining ammunition. 'Nice evening's walk, lads,' panted Corporal Steven Mace, his rifle slung round his neck.

They slid and scrambled through the mud, passed the support trench and headed without stopping for the front line. The flashes lighting up the sky were brighter, the screams and explosions pounding around them louder, and ahead was the outline of the trench. 'Well, about bloody time,' Jack thought, gesturing his men in and then slipping into it himself. Now the icy mud was up above their knees, and there were no duckboards. They struggled along, the mud dragging at their feet, threatening to suck off their boots. The parapet had been rebuilt with sandbags full of clay. They passed a lookout.

'Huns are counter-attacking with a bit more punch,' the lookout yelled as Jack passed. 'Happy times, eh Sarge?' They slid into the enfilade, the long corridor trench, and tried to hurry towards those they were reinforcing.

Enfilades made Jack feel exposed. If the enemy surged and broke into the trench there was no zigzag o help defend against their advance.

Captain Newton was doubling along the trench towards them, with Brampton at the rear, and behind him Roger whose face was as white as the moon. So far no bullet had found the batman, but to do that one would have had to wind its way into one of his numerous hidey-holes. Jack watched the man with hatred. Hatred seemed to be his constant companion now. If he stopped hating one person he moved it on to someone else, just couldn't do without it.

Newton shouted, 'Sergeant Forbes, the hand bombs are useless, nothing to set off the safety fuses. Lieutenant Brampton says you're a pitman. Know anything about setting charges?' Jack nodded, shouting back over the barrage, 'I was a hewer, sir. Me da's a deputy. I learned from him, sir.'

'Excellent. Override them then. Carry on.' He continued down the trench.

Bang. They ducked, earth and burst sandbags showering over them all. Jack yelled to Brampton, 'Where are they?'

Brampton led him along to Doug. Simon followed but Jack shouted, 'Not you Si, you won't understand.' They were slipping and sliding through the stinking mud in Brampton's wake to the bombers' trench. It was empty. All gone. Dead or wounded? Who the hell knew?

Brampton yelled, 'We're in a bit of a salient here, much like Froggett's houses, eh Jack.' Perhaps he was smiling, but his face was so drawn and filthy that it was hard to tell. 'Germans are within throwing range. I was a good bowler in my day but I need a bloody ball. Can you strike the fuse?'

Once Jack would have shouted, 'It's not a bloody game.' He knew better now, it was one way of staying sane. He and Doug hunted through their pockets for matches. He had some, he knew he had. He patted his tunic pocket again. Yes, here.

Bang. They ducked. Doug had matches too. Brampton was crouching on the fire step, holding a hand bomb. He said, 'A corporal has fashioned these. I think they're reliable and we need to get it right, Jack. Newton's just told me we're on leave for five days over Christmas. We can get out of this for a few days. We can . . .'

Bang. Crash. Earth showered, Doug grunted, shrapnel slicing his arm. He dropped his matches and stooped to save them as they sank in the mud. 'No,' Brampton and Jack roared together. Doug stopped dead. Jack said as he propped his rifle against the wall of the trench and took a match from his box, 'Don't get mud in it, lad. Whatever you do, don't get mud in a wound. You don't want gas gangrene. Where're your field dressings?' His fingers were so damn muddy. He wiped them dry on his tunic.

Doug shook his head, dragging out a white hand-kerchief. 'I gave them to that other poor bugger we took to the aid station, Sarge.'

'Get rid of that handkerchief too unless you're

about to surrender, or you'll get yourself shot. Get yourself a khaki one when you're next shopping in bloody Paris. I'm out of dressings too, what about you, sir?' Lieutenant Brampton was already shaking his head. 'Used them up earlier.'

Jack shouted above the racket, 'Get a clean bandage from Si. He carries extra. I've none left. Go now.'

Jack didn't watch as Doug doubled back, but stooped over the bomb fuse. Brampton said, 'You light 'em, I'll throw them.'

'Hold one for me, sir.' Jack held a match head on the end of the fuse and struck the matchbox across it, shielding the flash with his body. It lit. Brampton stood on the fire step and lobbed the bomb towards the trench. Machine guns rattled as he ducked back, his hand out for the next. 'Too slow. He'd never bowl me out.' His face was set and pale.

Jack said, 'You're right there, sir. He'll never get us, we're going home. I know we are, we all are.' He lit another fuse. Brampton threw the bomb, ducked down, machine guns rattled, kicking up mud, spattering it over them.

The barrage was thickening overhead and in front, and to the sides. Jack cursed salients, they were too bloody vulnerable to flanking attacks.

They moved along a few yards to another fire step. The machine-gunners would be targeting the former. 'Quick as you can, Jack,' Brampton yelled over the barrage. They were panting as though they had run a thousand miles. Bang. Another shell. Hot shrapnel tore through Jack's water bottle and mud showered.

Jack lit another fuse, Brampton lobbed the bomb. More machine guns rattled. Shells exploded. Had he ever had a different life, Jack wondered as the ground shuddered. Would they ever really get out of it?

'Sergeant, another please.' They were moving back fifteen yards to another fire step, varying the pattern. Suddenly there was a break in the shelling, just like that. As Jack bent over the fuse he heard Simon's clear beautiful tenor sing 'Oh for the wings, for the wings of a dove. Far away would I rove. In the wilderness build me a nest, and remain there for ever at rest.'

Neither Jack nor Brampton moved, then shells pounded again. Jack looked up. Brampton had tears in his eyes. 'We're a long way from home, and I'm glad I'm with people who know it. I've dreamed of coming to France, I seem to keep repeating myself but I want to travel to the tranquillity of the Somme.'

Jack swallowed, unable to speak for a moment. 'We might get there yet, sir. After the war, we can go before we head back. Do a bit of fishing. Take home a catch to Evie.'

Brampton smiled. 'Why not? I'd like that, Jack. Now, another ball please. We haven't quite finished this over, and we need to win the match.'

Evie and Veronica sat in the hall in front of the Christmas tree after dinner, running over the requirements that had been decided at the daily meeting this afternoon. 'On top of all that, Richard would like an egg custard,' Veronica said.

Evie grinned, knitting another row of the khaki scarf. Knit one, purl one. 'Then he will have one and you can make it. Yours are a great success.' The huge tree had been decorated by the servants, nurses and walking wounded, and parcels were heaping up beneath it, sent by relatives or bought with the proceeds of the tea room. Knit one, purl one.

Veronica sighed, writing something on her notepad. 'I must sort out some gifts for the servants.'

'Not material, please.' It just came out.

Veronica stared. 'I beg your pardon?' There was an edge to her voice.

'We don't want material for uniforms, we want something nice, like any sensible person would, because we are people.' Evie could hear the edge in her own voice. Veronica looked so tired, but so was she. Since Captain Williams had been home Veronica had been working round the clock, during the day at the hospital and at night with her husband. His recovery was proving to be rapid. Knit one purl one, start a new row.

Veronica half rose, then slumped back into the spacious armchair. 'Of course you are, you all are, *we* all are. Leave it to me. I wonder what time they'll be here on Christmas Eve? Is Margaret behaving all right?'

The moment was over, feathers were smoothed

and all was well. Evie had thought that Captain Williams might alter things between them, but he had merely smiled and accepted their friendship. The poor man was barely alive when he arrived, so why would he care?

'Yes, Lady Margaret is recovering and the nurses are keeping an eye on her.'

Veronica said, 'I'm so sorry, Evie, that the servants' bedrooms were without coal, and always have been. It's unforgivable and will not happen again.'

Evie said, 'That's in the past, and I need to think more deeply about Lady Margaret, because you have enough to concern yourself with Captain Williams. I think she'd benefit from having a purpose, it might help her find a way out of this darkness that's overcome her. She doesn't want to return to her family for whatever reason, though I feel it's because they disapprove of her activities.' They laughed. 'And we don't?' they said in unison.

Evie waved her knitting at Veronica to bring her to order, grinning. 'Anyway I thought I'd put her to work. Do I have your agreement?'

Veronica opened her eyes and laughed so heartily that the orderly swung round from his desk, smiling. 'My full permission and good luck.'

Evie was still grinning as she laid down her needles and made a note

'Anything else?' Lady Veronica asked.

Evie felt the orderly's eyes upon her, and nodded to him. They'd been chatting as they hung some of the baubles on the tree and had noticed how the patients were cheerful and focused as they helped. She took up her knitting again. Knit one, purl one.

Veronica shook her head. 'Come on, my girl, spit it out. I always know when you're on a crusade.'

'It's the men. They have nothing to do as they start to improve. They need something, something useful just as Lady Margaret does. There will be the gardens in the summer but there are the glasshouses now, and we're so short-staffed. The walking wounded could help there. We need artificial limbs too, and they can be made in the workshops. We need crutches. Da and the pit blacksmith said they'd come up and sort that out. It's much quicker than waiting for some quartermaster to send them.'

Veronica was sucking her pencil, looking doubtful. 'A wonderful idea, but I don't like taking advantage. Should we pay them? I mean, I'm sure the officers are all right for money, but the men . . . ?'

Evie looked at the young woman and could have hugged her. She hadn't thought of that. 'Perhaps we should discuss it with Dr Nicholls and we could make it unofficial, so that we give them the money and no one is any the wiser. Now, let's get the egg-custard maker down into the depths.' She pushed her needles through the ball of wool.

They both walked to the green baize door and down the steps. Mrs Moore was in the kitchen, putting the finishing touches to chicken broth for the new arrivals who had been brought up from Southampton, the dirt still on them.

The laundry was going full blast, with women from the village operating it. Millie swanned into the kitchen, her hair soaked from the steam. 'We are being sent more sheets tomorrow. We'll have to work through the night. Did you know Jeb, the union rep, is off to war now?'

Somehow Millie had created a minor supervisory role for herself in the laundry, but nothing surprised Evie any more about anything, because she tried not to think outside the moment. Simon and Jack were coming home for Christmas, just for a few days, but they *were* coming home, if nothing happened. No, she had insisted to herself that she did not think of it. She concentrated on Millie. 'I didn't know but it's inevitable, isn't it? It could take a while yet to finish the whole damn thing.'

Veronica was making egg custard. Annie was in the servants' hall writing to her parents. Evie settled in the armchair, pulling a blanket around her. She had two hours to get some sleep before the late suppers, which were important to the men. Cocoa or tea, and cake. Prices were rising but panic buying had calmed down and supplies were adequate. Perhaps the war would be over in the new year and normality would return. What would Bastard Brampton think of that? He'd have to shut the armaments factories before he could make more money. She slept, to be woken by Mrs

Moore who was untying her own apron, and yawning.

'I'm off for some sleep now, Evie. Call me if there's a rush.' It seemed that Mrs Moore's rheumatics were continuing to behave reasonably well but even so, Evie would not call on her. She, Annie and two new women who gave up their evenings when their bairns were in bed would prepare tonight's cocoa and tea. The cakes had been made earlier. They would take up the trays and leave them in the care of the VADs in the hall.

Before the rush began Evie slipped up the attic stairs to check on Lady Margaret. The attic felt warmer than it had ever felt before, and the bedrooms were toasty, just toasty. Lady Margaret was sitting in the chair that had been imported from Mr Auberon's bedroom, now given over to a Lieutenant Colonel who had dreadful head and face wounds. The tin mask that had been suggested was appalling. Perhaps her father and the blacksmith could come up with something better?

Lady Margaret was struggling with khaki wool, producing something that could not, by any stretch of the imagination, be called a scarf. Her hair was unbrushed, as usual.

As Evie stood there she flung the knitting down, tears starting yet again. 'I thought I'd help you, but I've made a terrible mess. I'm good for nothing except keeping everyone awake. I'm tired but too scared of the dreams to go to sleep.' Her voice was limp, as limp as everything about her. Evie felt the heat from the fire. So, if it took a war to bring coal up the mountain just listen to what she was about to say to this woman. She walked across and picked up the knitting, tossing it on to the bed, and sitting down next to it. She started to pull it out, looking at that, not at Lady Margaret.

She said, digging out from somewhere a gentleness which she felt really too tired to produce, 'Lady Margaret, you're too good to be fiddling about with bits of wool, just look at how hard you worked for the cause. You thrived under it, didn't you, and now you have no direction. We need you. We need every woman we can find to help out, and I don't mean just to read to the men but to work.' She lifted her head and looked directly at Lady Margaret.

'Work? What would my mother say, not to mention my father?'

Evie looked around the room. 'Your mother and father? I don't see them here, and what did they say when you were in prison, what did they say when you arrived here? I didn't see them rushing to help you. Where are the letters that they've written? I haven't noticed any.' The gentleness had faded.

When she had disentangled all the wool and wound it into a ball, she left to continue her shift which would last until two in the morning, saying, 'Think about it, Lady Margaret. Choose your area, but choose one. Bank up the fire before you leave, if you feel you can start tonight. I'll be in the kitchen, so come and tell me what you'd like to do.'

Within an hour Lady Margaret appeared, with her hair brushed and in a bun for the first time since she became unwell. 'I don't know what I want to do but perhaps I can start here, while I find out. At least I can learn how to make a cup of tea, if nothing else.'

She stood at Evie's elbow as they answered the calls for broth for yet another fresh intake that had arrived, this time from Folkestone. It was as the two of them, pausing for a moment, climbed up the back steps into the yard for some crisp fresh midnight air that Evie thought she saw Millie disappear round the corner and down the path running along the walled vegetable garden. What on earth was she playing at, she should be in the laundry room? Evie hurried to the corner, memories of Millie's meetings with Roger surfacing, but there was no sign of her on the path. Well, it was probably a trick of the light and she would be in the laundry room. She was too tired to think straight, let alone see straight.

Lady Margaret was smoking at the top of the steps, watching her. 'Is everything all right, Evie?' she called.

Evie replied, 'Yes, I just thought I saw someone I knew.'

Lady Margaret stubbed out her cigarette. 'It's too cold for me, come and let me help you pour the broth into the tureen.' They went back into the kitchen and it was half an hour before Evie had time to walk along to the laundry. There was Millie, chattering to her staff, her sleeves rolled up, and steam soaking her hair.

By the morning of Christmas Eve there was an inch of snow, with more threatening. Veronica and Evie worked hard, anything to make the seconds, minutes, hours pass. 'They're coming,' they said, every time they passed one another. Evie's mam and da were smiling all the while too, as her mam looked after the villagers' children in the garage and her da helped Stanhope, the blacksmith, in the workshop with the men.

They would be here for lunch.

Evie thought she'd die with the tension. They were coming. There'd been no telegram bearing dreadful news about Mr Auberon, and he would have let them know if the men were hurt rather than let them wait for a letter, so they were coming and she allowed herself to think of something other than the present. They were coming, and soon she'd feel Si's arms around her, his lips on hers. She'd stroke his hair and hear his voice, and Jack would be here too, lovely lovely Jack.

Millie sang in the laundry and nipped out to the garage to see Tim. 'Your da's coming,' she cooed as she brought him into the kitchen for a biscuit. 'Go to your Auntie Evie, she'll sing to you.' Evie couldn't because she was up to her eyes preparing lunch, but she said she'd sing later, round the Christmas tree with Tim's da and everybody else, as the darkness fell.

Lunchtime came and went and they had not come. Now Evie and her da, who was not on his shift at Auld Maud until 2 a.m., walked up and down the drive in the bitter chill. The train was delayed, that was all. It was just delayed. Over tea her mam said the same. 'They are delayed, that's all. Just delayed.'

Lady Veronica joined them in the kitchen and prepared vegetables for dinner, with Lady Margaret's help. Veronica said to Evie, 'The train will have been delayed, Richard says that we would have heard otherwise.' Her voice was soft when she talked of her husband, and there was a light in her eyes that had been increasing since his return. Mrs Moore had said that sometimes two people needed to be thrown together to really get to know one another.

Simon's da, Alec, arrived from his shift at the pit and together he and Evie's da smoked cigarettes and patrolled the drive, the snow glinting under the hunter's moon. There'd be some rabbits snared tonight. Evie and Lady Veronica joined them after dinner had gone up. Lieutenant Jameson and Captain Neave loitered on the steps smoking their pipes, and over by the cedar others were swinging their arms to keep the circulation going. Harry was with them. He had a greatcoat on, and his head-warmer knitted by Annie, and was puffing on his pipe in spite of Dr Nicholls thundering, 'And what's the point of getting you better if you're taking that rubbish into your lungs?' But for men who'd faced far worse it was water off a duck's back.

'You would have heard if there was anything amiss,' Captain Neave told Evie as she stopped next to him, slapping her hands together. Veronica joined them, her shawl wrapped tightly around her. The lights were flooding from the house, and somewhere on the ground floor a few voices were singing 'Silent Night'.

An owl was hooting. No, more than one. The moon cast long shadows over the lawn and in the hedges creatures rustled. From the house came a silence, then a scream and a groan, nothing out of the ordinary here. The choir began again. The owls hooted, again. A door slammed shut. Millie joined them. A fox barked, and then there it was, the sound of crunching, carried on the light cold breeze.

The officers lifted their heads, their faces tense, their pipes glowing. Over by the cedar tree the men stood motionless, listening. Footsteps, or was it the telegraph boy's bicycle? Evie and Veronica held hands, so tightly.

No one moved, or breathed, but everyone looked, straining to hear, and see.

They saw pinpricks of light from cigarettes. Then they came, walking abreast in a line. Their three men, Simon, Jack and Auberon, shoulders hunched, feet dragging, greatcoats flapping, caps at an angle, and then another figure. Roger. Veronica and Evie ran towards them, and after a moment, Millie too.

They ran and ran and at last they were in their arms, and it didn't matter that the stench of mud and death clung to their men's clothes and skin, and filled the women's lungs, for they were here. It didn't matter that their faces were drawn, pale and exhausted. They had not really believed that they would ever see them again.

'We came straight here,' Simon murmured. 'We stink but we wanted to come straight here. We have to leave in two days because it took so long to get to you.'

His lips were on Evie's, and nothing else mattered. She wouldn't think of anything, not the lice she could feel moving beneath her hands, not the smell of war. She was used to that. What mattered was that he was home, they were all home, and for two days they'd be safe. 'I love you with all my heart,' she said against his mouth, and allowed joy to overwhelm her.

Also available in Arrow

After the Storm

Margaret Graham

**War can end more than one life, and break
more than one heart.**

*'I am in despair too, but I want to go on living,
fighting, getting out of here to something better.'*

Born into hardship in a Northumbrian mining village, it takes all
Annie Manon's spirit to survive the bleak years following the First
World War. As her family fractures around her, she longs to make
something of her life.

Through hard work and determination she eventually leaves
the poverty and despair of her childhood behind her. But then
war breaks out once more, taking her further away from her
dreams and those she loves most. And it is all she can do to
keep hope alive.

Previously published as *Only the Wind is Free*

arrow books

Also available in Arrow

Annie's Promise

Margaret Graham

**It was a time when family values meant more
than empty words.**

In the mid-1950s, Britain looks forward to a prosperous
future. And Annie Manon has come home to the North-east to
keep a promise.

With husband George and her brother Tom, Annie is eager to
start a new life for her family. And with her fledgling fashion
business she looks forward to providing work for the women
of Wassingham.

But not everything is rosy with the prospect of renewed hope. As
well as her painful wartime memories, Annie must cope with an
accident that cripples her husband, and she must deal with the
increasingly unreasonable behaviour of their daughter Sarah.

When Sarah leaves home for London, Annie is torn between
love for her only child and the need to keep her promise to
Wassingham's womenfolk.

arrow books

Also available in Arrow

Somewhere Over England

Margaret Graham

War will not break her spirit...

In England in the 1930s, eighteen-year-old Helen Carstairs braves the prejudice of friends and family to marry Heine, a young German photographer who had fled the growing horror of the Nazis.

But the storm clouds are gathering in Europe. When fighting breaks out, Heine is interned, their small son is evacuated and Helen is left to face the Blitz alone.

And the agony of war threatens to divide a family already tormented by conflicting passions of loyalty, shame, betrayal – and love.

Previously published as *A Fragment of Time*

arrow books

THE POWER OF READING

Visit the Random House website and get connected with information on all our books and authors

EXTRACTS from our recently published books and selected backlist titles

COMPETITIONS AND PRIZE DRAWS Win signed books, audiobooks and more

AUTHOR EVENTS Find out which of our authors are on tour and where you can meet them

LATEST NEWS on bestsellers, awards and new publications

MINISITES with exclusive special features dedicated to our authors and their titles

READING GROUPS Reading guides, special features and all the information you need for your reading group

LISTEN to extracts from the latest audiobook publications

WATCH video clips of interviews and readings with our authors

RANDOM HOUSE INFORMATION including advice for writers, job vacancies and all your general queries answered

Come home to Random House

www.randomhouse.co.uk